IT WAS NOT THEIR FIRST ENCOUNTER . . . NOR WOULD IT BE THEIR LAST!

Dazed, Cara looked up to discover the black eyes of the Earl of Malton looking mockingly down into her own. *"You!"* she exclaimed, forgetting any pretense at not knowing him. "And I should have thought you had enough sense to keep your horse out of the paths of other riders!" she snapped back, her green eyes beginning to flash as the dazed feeling left her. "What the deuce's wrong with y—?"

But she got no further. Lord Wrothby, steadying her, was assailed by the subtle jasmine scent that clung to her and by a sudden, overwhelming desire to kiss the glowing, pink-cheeked face lifted to his. Unable to think of any reason why he should not, he pulled her into his arms, enfolding her, and, bending his head, kissed her soft lips thoroughly. His hands drew delicious circles over her back and began to slip down her sides.

Stunned for a moment by his audacity, Cara came to life, exclaiming against his mouth and ineffectually struggling to fight herself free of him . . .

The Scandalous Masquerade

Marissa Edwards

ZEBRA BOOKS
KENSINGTON PUBLISHING CORP.

*For Tom Carmine
and Lewis H. Curd, Sr.*

ZEBRA BOOKS are published by

Kensington Publishing Corp.
475 Park Avenue South
New York, NY 10016

First Printing: August, 1993

Printed in the United States of America

One

"I think, *Maman,* if you don't mind, I shall retire early tonight."

"Cara? Don't you feel well?" asked Lady Brentwood, a delicate-looking blonde in her early forties. She looked up from the handkerchief she was embroidering to gaze at her daughter with a worried expression in her blue eyes. Her daughter was almost never ill.

Cara, feeling a twinge of guilt, rose gracefully from a divan which might have been said to sag in the middle and came to give her mother a kiss. "A slight headache," she said. "Please don't worry! I am certain I shall be right as rain by morning."

Her mother looked doubtful. "All right, my dear. I shall just set a few more stitches before I go myself. Good night."

Cara lit a taper and passed from the sitting room into a large hall barren of the usual *objects d'art* one might have expected to adorn its walls and recesses, and climbed its long staircase.

She entered her bedchamber and closed the door softly behind her, turning the key in the lock. Lighting the candle on her dressing table, she went to the cedar chest at the foot of her bed to take out a dark bundle

5

of clothes. With an efficiency that would have surprised many a lady's maid, she changed swiftly from her becoming, if outmoded, yellow gown into an old pair of her father's pants and a shirt and cloak he no longer had any need of. She drew on the boots that Cook's son had outgrown, piled her copper curls high on her head and secured them with pins, and pulled her father's worn hat down low on her forehead. *Maman,* she thought to herself, if you could see me now you would think there was more wrong with me than just a headache!

She put her thoughts firmly away from exactly what her mother *would* think of her and returned to her dressing table. She lifted her father's ring out of her jewel box. As she drew the heavy gold ring onto her middle finger, for luck as she always told herself, she whispered fiercely, "This is the last time, Father!" and strode purposely to her open window and climbed through.

Galloping across the fields instead of following the roads, Cara reveled in the cool night breeze and listened to the muffled thuds of her horse's hooves as they struck the grassy earth. Excitement and nervousness began to mount in her as they always did during her ride to rendezvous with Harry and young Jeb at the spot she had appointed for "Gentleman Jack" next to strike. She smiled to herself. How mortified the frivolous, preening dandies she'd held up would be if they knew that it was a woman masquerading as "Gentleman Jack" who had robbed them and not "Gentleman Jack" himself! She smiled again scornfully and thought, I don't doubt those spineless coxcombs would give up their valuables — and anyone else's too! — to *anything* wearing pants! Such a sight

6

as their own blood staining those ridiculous costumes should very likely give them the apoplexy! She chuckled in derision. "Why, I make a more convincing man than any one of them," she said to the back of her horse's ears.

She was, indeed, uncommonly tall for a woman, having inherited her father's height rather than her mother's diminutive stature. Her red hair and green eyes, quick temper, and imaginative nature had also come from her father, which was why, she supposed, she was now engaged in one of the most foolhardy and desperate ventures of her life. Poor Mama! she thought grinning. Two of us!

"Who goes there?" growled a low voice, interrupting her thoughts.

"Cara. How long have you been here, Jeb? Where's your father?" Cara answered softly, jumping down from her horse to lead him through the thick foliage bordering the wood from which they planned to launch their ambush.

Jeb appeared next to her, his stocky form hardly visible in the dark, and whispered, "Not long, miss. All's clear. Me dad's down a' the road settin' up th' logs."

As they spoke, old Harry, who had been groom to her family for as long as she could remember and himself taught her to ride, came quietly through the trees. "It's as good as can be. The roadblock's in place—now ye wait quiet and listen hard. If wha' ye've heared be true an' there be a party over Malton Park way, we've a quarter of a' hour leeway t'catch th' late-Johns on their way in to 'ave a fancy time—an' no' expectin' us'n ta remove 'em of ther baubles till on th' way back, b'Gad! Let's us'n git in position, an', Jeb!—no fidgetin'! Ye know wha' ye're t'do . . ."

"Please God you're right," agreed Cara as she

mounted her horse, pulled her mask up over her face, and started toward her position at the edge of the wood.

". . . ye've dun it enuf times a'ready," grumbled old Harry.

Cara smiled as he grumbled off to his own position. He didn't think any more of her masquerades as "Gentleman Jack" than her mother would have, provided her mother could have been brought to believe that her daughter was involved in such a masquerade. But the old groom had known Cara well enough to know that, wild or not, she would execute her scheme with or without him. Because he loved her as if she were one of his own, he had decided to help her to provide whatever measure of safety he could. She had promised him tonight would be their last ride. Only two more carriages—one, if the owner or his mistress were wearing enough jewelry—and she would have the funds to finance her purpose in risking their lives so recklessly.

She thought she heard the sound of a carriage in the distance. Butterflies fluttered in her stomach as she strained to listen. On the breeze came old Harry's call so softly she thought she imagined it. "Yer gun all primed an' ready?" She checked her pistol, cocked it, and edged as close to the border of the wood as she dared, keeping her horse on a tight rein.

Pacing the carriage by its sound, she let it round the bend and, as she glimpsed its lanterns, took aim and fired a shot across the road. Following the first shot with two more in quick succession, she galloped down the hillside to meet the carriage, now lurching to an abrupt halt before the logs, its horses plunging and rearing in fright.

Jeb dashed from the wood on the other side of the road, and old Harry rode up behind the carriage—

both their guns plainly visible in the lantern light to the shocked driver, trying to manage his horses and count his assailants at the same time.

"Stand and deliver!" growled Cara, in her best imitation of a man's voice.

The door of the carriage was flung open, and an angry female voice was heard complaining, ". . . were *my* driver, I'd sack him immediately!"

"And then how would you get home, my dear Countess?" drawled a deep voice in return. "Thomas!" it continued rudely, "Have you a cog loose, man?"

A tall dark-haired gentleman in evening dress, which appeared to be in some disarray, jumped easily down from the swaying carriage onto the road. "What the devil's — !

"Ah. I perceive. My apologies, Thomas," he said to the back of his driver, who was still endeavoring with some difficulty to get his horses back under control. Taking stock of the two pistols leveled at his heart and the third pistol aimed at his driver, the gentleman turned and spoke calmly over his shoulder, "I think, Marion, you had better give me your jewels."

"Are you mad?" asked the speaker inside the carriage, giving an uncertain trill of laughter. "Julius?"

A woman's face appeared at the door of the carriage. In the flickering lantern light, the curiosity on the classically beautiful features changed ludicrously to one of horror. "Oh! Julius, no!" she wailed. "Not my emeralds! I have not had them above two hours!"

Cara, possessing an ever-lively sense of humor, could not help a smile behind her mask.

"Your concern for me, my dear, is overwhelming," he remarked drily, removing the diamond pin from his cravat. "This, *gentlemen,*" he said ironically, "is all I wear."

9

Cara brought her horse nearer and threw down a sack. "We'll have your money then, too. Get her jewels. Put it all in that, and be quick about it!"

A loud, "Ohhh," issued from the carriage, and the woman fell back onto the cushions, in what seemed to Cara an artificial faint. She heard old Harry cock his pistol.

He saw no humor in the situation in general, and he didn't like the look of this buck in particular. He was a deal too tall, had not a pound of spare baggage on 'im anywhere, and hadn't whined once. Though he had taken his fleecing and what looked to be an interruption of dallying with his light o' love thus far with a calm, almost bored indifference, there was that about him that old Harry didn't trust. Into the bargain, the woman made him nervous with all the distractions she was about.

Apparently the gentleman heard old Harry cock his pistol as well, for he turned back to enter the carriage and collect the woman's jewelry.

Positively enjoying her role, Cara snarled, "Fainting won't save her. Be sure you get the rings her gloves are hiding." An indignant gasp met her ears, and Cara grinned beneath her mask. Served her right for wearing so many!

Several moments later, the gentleman jumped from the carriage with the sack. Unhurriedly, he walked toward her taking in, she felt nonsensically, every detail of her appearance and staring at her face as if he would see through her mask.

She shifted uncomfortably in her saddle and put out her hand to take the sack.

Obligingly he lifted it to meet her grasp. But even as she leaned forward slightly and her fingers closed, he let the sack drop and clamped his hand about her wrist, jerking her from the saddle! She heard the woman shout, "Bravo, Julius!" heard a shot fired and her horse whinny, and felt the beast begin to rear as she left the saddle to land sprawled before the gentleman's boots on the hard ground.

Old Harry's voice grated ominously, "Th' next one goes through ye heart, me brave buck."

And as Cara struggled to get her breath back, she looked up to receive full force the shock of the gentleman's dark eyes blazing furiously down at her. She became acutely concious that she would be no match against the unbridled rage of the tall, muscular body looming menacingly over her. Realizing what he might well do to her were old Harry's gun not trained on him, she shivered imperceptibly and scrambled to her feet.

Absurdly she noticed one of his arms holding the other where old Harry's bullet had struck him, and her eyes widened. She could see a dark liquid begin to ooze through his fingers.

"Oh dear!" muttered the woman in the carriage.

Jeb, Cara could see thankfully, held her horse. She bent to retrieve the sack and the pistol from the ground and walked hastily to her horse and remounted.

Swiftly, the three moved off into the darkness, old Harry and Jeb keeping their pistols trained behind them on the gentleman and his driver. As soon as they were out of sight around the bend, they split up and rode in three separate directions, taking care to keep to the dry grassy fields where their horses' hooves would leave no mark.

"Are you hurt, m'lord?" Thomas called anxiously as he got down from his driver's perch.

"No, Thomas. I shall need a few weeks to heal, that is all," said His Lordship, taking out his handkerchief and calmly beginning to tie up his wound with his

11

good arm. "Damn!" he cursed as he fumbled with it and dropped the handkerchief. Stooping to pick it up, he noticed something glint in the grass before him and bent down again.

"Let me help you with that, m'lord."

"I am fine, Thomas. Go and see about Her Ladyship." When his driver's back was turned, he brought what he had found into the light of the carriage lanterns: a heavy gold ring. He turned it over in his palm and saw the seal. A signet ring! You will pay for this holdup, my man, he thought grimly, and slipped the ring into his pocket.

"Her ladyship is recovered, m'lord."

As if to verify this, the countess called plaintively, "Julius! You are hurt. What are we waiting for? Let us get to Malton Park as quickly as possible. I swear I fear I shall swoon again!"

"By all means. Let us go home, Thomas. My guests will be waiting," answered His Lordship, getting a trifle awkwardly into the carriage.

Climbing back through the window into her bedchamber, Cara did not immediately miss the loose weight of her father's heavy ring on her finger. She was smiling as she began to change out of her father's old clothes, thinking about the amount of money her share of these last jewels would be. The woman had been wearing a small fortune: strings of pearls with a lovely gold-set emerald necklace, matching earrings, and bracelet as well as other bracelets and rings. She had saved the band from having to hold up a second carriage that night in order to reach the sum Cara had thought necessary to make it appear in London that she and her mother were living comfortably as well as stylishly.

12

What a great piece of luck for us that the woman had on so much jewelry! she thought. The gentleman's cash and diamond pin alone would not have been enough. Another holdup would have been needed. And she didn't like to admit even to herself how much her courage had been shaken by her encounter with the owner of that last carriage.

He had not been at all like the foppish carriage owners she had met with heretofore. He hadn't been content to just hand over their money and their jewelry and scuttle off intent on saving his own skin. She had to admire his bravery in spite of herself—and remembered the shock of his dark angry eyes blazing down at her. She remembered, too, that when she had picked herself up off the ground he had been a good head taller than she—a fact that was rare in her acquaintance. She was of the same height as most men she knew, or taller, either looking them equally in the eyes or, worse, looking down at them.

She hoped the gentleman's wound wasn't a serious one. Ironically she felt it was a great shame that the only man who'd had the courage to stand up to her had had to be the one to get hurt.

Old Harry had said he didn't think the wound was dangerous. A clean shot, he had said—dressed properly and cared for, it should heal in a matter of weeks.

If I hadn't let myself be distracted, no one would have got hurt, she chastised herself. How could I have thought the situation *funny!* she wondered, appalled at the way things might have ended. She shuddered and decided to put the entire matter out of her mind forever. We shall have all the money we require now, and, indeed, I need never even think of highwaymen again!

She scooped her nightgown up off her bed and drew it wearily over her head. Carefully she rolled her

13

highwayman guise into a bundle and dropped it back in the chest at the foot of her bed. Only then, as she locked the chest, did she miss with a sharp intake of breath, the heavy gold weight of her father's ring upon her middle finger.

Unable to credit that the ring could be gone, she checked her finger with the other hand. It *was* gone! Her mind flew back over the night's events, searching for a time when the ring might have fallen off without her knowledge. And she felt again the tall gentleman's viselike grip upon her wrist as he pulled her from the saddle. During the scuffle the ring might easily have fallen off.

A cold fear washed over her. She did not like to think of the consequences should the gentleman or his driver have found the ring. It would be a simple matter to identify the seal as that of the Brentwood family. What a fool she had been to wear it!

But it did bring us luck, she thought defiantly. We had not one mishap in all our masquerades until tonight. That, surely, can only be attributed to good luck. And very likely it is still there, lying in the grass where I fell. For who would think to look about for a ring?

But it is no use going back now to look for it in the dark. There is nothing for it—that shall have to wait until tomorrow. Let it be there, Lord, let it be there, please, she prayed, slipping between the bedsheets to lie staring into the darkness until her tired body overcame her anxious mind and delivered her to sleep.

She rose the next morning somewhat later than usual, donned her old dark green riding habit, and went downstairs to find her mother just finishing her breakfast in the dining room.

"Good morning, my dear. How is your headache today?" asked her mother. There was a small line of worry between her brows.

"Oh, 'tis quite gone. I am feeling much more the thing," replied Cara, pouring herself a steaming cup of coffee and feeling her conscience prick her again.

"Well, that is a relief then." Lady Brentwood sighed, and the wrinkle of worry vanished. "I felt certain you were coming down with the consumption from the wetting you received the day before yesterday out in that shower."

"*Maman*," Cara reproved, "you know I am not so frail as all that!"

"Yes, but you are not indomitable either, my love." Her mother continued to sit with her making small talk and drinking a last cup of coffee while Cara ate a quick breakfast of biscuits and honey.

"Well, I am off to see what the post has brought us, if anything," she said as she finished her last morsel of Cook's light biscuits. She rose and gave her mother a kiss on the cheek.

"All right, my dear. I shall be in the sitting room, I think."

Looking up at the bright blue sky and feeling her spirits soar as she breathed in the morning air, Cara walked the short distance from the house to the stable. Certainly no one had found it, and the ring was still there.

She saddled the one horse in the stable, saying, "Well, you might not be the best horseflesh I've ever ridden, but you keep your wits about you under pressure. And you are certainly cared for like a king," she added, noticing appreciatively the feed in his stall where old Harry had already been there. She rubbed the horse's velvet nose and mounted him, starting off across the fields for the road that approached Malton Park.

She loved old Harry as much as if he were an uncle

15

of her own. He had bought this horse for her out of his own savings at the beginning of their masquerades after she had spent the last of the money from the sale of her father's horse. With the money from the first holdup, she had paid him back. She had told her mother old Harry was just being kind, allowing her one of his horses to ride. And though she had told the groom not to worry with the care of the horse, he, like Cook, was too old and loyal a family servant not to continue in his duties just as he had always done them.

As she rode, Cara thought back to the days when her father was alive, and Brentwood Crest had been fully staffed with servants. Those had been pleasant days. But they were also the days of her childhood. For the last ten years she and her mother had begun doing without one thing after another as Charles Brentwood began making regular solitary trips to London to gamble, inevitably losing the money he had set out with. One by one he had let the servants go — except for old Harry and Cook, who refused to leave — sold the furniture of note in the house and all but one of the horses in his stable, and begun borrowing on the estate.

As she grew older, Cara, strong-willed, would lead her mother in attempts to try to reason with her father and make him see that he was throwing his savings away and ruining the value of Brentwood Crest. But it had seemed that every time she had almost convinced him that this was so he would win one or two games and a little money, and the cycle would begin all over again.

She had really thought she had finally convinced him before he went up to London the last time. He had promised her so earnestly, and she had believed him. Their lawyer, Mr. Havershaw, had said the man—he did not call him a gentleman—her father had lost his money to was a disreputable character, known for goading his victims into playing with him. Her father would have been easy prey. He could not have borne any attack upon his honor as a gentleman—particularly, Cara knew, since he had begun in the last few years to fall short of it. He would have continued playing, Mr. Havershaw had said, betting far more than just the money he had been bringing to him to invest—possibly even wagering Brentwood Crest, she had heard of such things—if some gentleman standing nearby had not intervened.

What had that *gentleman* been doing, laughing and drinking wine while watching her father be robbed of the last of his money? Cara wondered indignantly. For, to Cara, that was what it amounted to—robbery. Her father was no great card player. The number and amount of his losses over the past ten years were bitter proof of that! It was for this reason that she felt justified in her holdups as "Gentleman Jack." She was merely giving the *beau monde* a taste of the medicine it had dealt her poor father—the only difference was that she was not using cards to do her robbing for her. If I had not given it up, I should pay both those "gentlemen" a call as "Gentleman Jack" and put a bullet through them! she thought furiously.

With pain, she recalled the day her father had arrived home after the disastrous card game. He had worn himself and his horse out galloping without rest all the way from London. Never, in his right mind, Cara knew, would he have abused an animal in that manner. It was a measure of the extreme distress he was himself experiencing. He had walked slowly into the hall as if he were in a trance with his hair and coat disheveled and his pants and boots mud-splashed. Her mother had tried to get him to eat something and then put him to bed while Cara and old Harry had tended to the exhausted horse.

Charles Brentwood had gotten up the next morning, still in the silent trance in which he had arrived home, and wandered in and out of the rooms of his house all that day and the two following days. They had managed to get several bowls of soup into him and one or two biscuits but no more. On the third day after his return, he woke up raging something about losing his money and having to return to London to fight someone and get it back, and from that she and her mother got their first inkling of what had gone wrong. Though they tried desperately to restrain him, he put on his riding clothes and raged out the front door to the stable to mount his horse and ride off like a madman in the direction of London.

That was the last time Cara had seen him alive. She had run to find old Harry and send him after her father. Then she had run to scramble into her riding habit and follow old Harry. But even old Harry had been too late. Her father had tried to jump his exhausted horse over a fence, failed, and had broken his neck in the attempt.

It had fallen upon Mr. Havershaw to explain to them the details of what had occurred in London. When she had heard his explanation, Cara had been outraged. She deemed the wealthy people in whose company her father had been playing cards not just robbers but murderers. If it were not for them, Charles Brentwood would still be alive!

It had been a year since her father's death, but, for a moment, Cara's green eyes sparkled with hatred: it was only right that she and her mother should enjoy a London Season at the expense of the *beau monde* and dupe one of its members into providing for them! She sobered instantly. It was enough that she had paid them back by robbing them of some of their fine jewels. She could not allow her hatred to gain the upper hand and cause her to ruin her life or her mother's. Whomever she chose to become her husband must be not only wealthy but kind enough to want to provide for her mother's welfare as well as her own once he learned that she had only the Brentwood name and encumbered estate to join to his own assets. Since they had been living quietly in the country at Brentwood Crest for the last ten years, few people knew of their growing financial difficulties. And she was going to make certain her future husband was thoroughly in love with her and irrevocably engaged to her before she told him!

She had few doubts of her abilities to bring a man to the point of offering for her. She would have had to have been blind not to realize the striking picture she made with her statuesque figure and red hair and green eyes. They should be quite salable on the Marriage Mart, she thought wryly. She sighed. Why could there not exist one gentleman whom she might love just for himself and marry? One who would love her in return without concern for what she would bring to him if they married?

She laughed derisively. Come down from the boughs, girl! she commanded herself. Put those schoolgirl notions out of your head. There is *Maman* to consider, and very likely no such man exists — certainly not among that glittering *ton* set. My marriage shall be a matter of business, and I will consider only the wealthiest of men. And, she finished ruefully, they will probably all be like the ridiculous fops I have held up on the roads!

Unbidden, the image of a tall, dark-haired gentleman in evening dress jumping down from a lighted carriage rose in her mind. He had certainly been no fop. She gave her head a shake. No. That would be the biggest piece of folly for me yet. Better to stay as far away from that particular gentleman as possible.

Gazing around her, Cara realized that she had come to the bend in the road leading to Malton Park while she had been engrossed in her thoughts. She cantered a little farther down the road and then dismounted to walk, slowly searching the ground as she went, toward the spot she judged she had fallen from her horse. But, though she combed the grass on all sides of the spot, she found nothing. Finally when her back had begun to ache and she had still found nothing, she straightened and gave up her search.

With an uneasy feeling in the pit of her stomach, she remounted and turned back toward Brentwood Crest. She would not think about what could happen if the tall gentleman had indeed found her ring. There is not a thing I can do about it now if he did find it, and worrying over it will certainly not help matters, she thought. A sudden notion struck her: but he would not be looking for a woman! She felt reassured.

Faintly hoping that the ring would turn up in some other unlikely place, she urged her horse into a run. She would tell her mother that because it was such a beautiful day she had decided to go for a ride before seeing about the mail.

"We are in luck, *Maman!*" cried Cara, bursting into the sitting room where her mother was seated staring ahead of her with her embroidery spread upon her lap. She started at her daughter's sudden entrance.

"I cannot believe our good fortune! Only hear what Mr. Havershaw has said in his letter! The money from the sale of Father's horse which I had him speculate has made us enough for that Season in London I was wishing for! You must write all your old companions and tell them we shall come up in a month's time and that you will need invitations from all of them to all the *ton* parties so that you may present your *very* marriageable daughter before she may reach an age to be left upon the shelf!"

Instead of laughing at this sally, a small frown creased her mother's forehead.

Cara came close to her mother's side and said softly, "Are you not excited as I am?"

A sigh escaped her mother, "Oh, Cara. I am glad you shall have a Season in London. It is not that. But I had so hoped that you should be able to marry like I did, without regard for monetary considerations. Could we not invest this money as your father was going to do or, or speculate with it again?"

"I am afraid I am not that much of a gambler. I have learned something from Father's mistakes, you see." Lady Brentwood winced. Cara went on quietly, "The chances of doubling our money again, *Maman,* would be slim indeed." I certainly could not keep up my masquerade as "Gentleman Jack" for that length of time! she thought, frowning. I would be certain to be caught, or one of the three of us should get shot. Or killed, and she shuddered, seeing again the dark blood that had seeped through the fingers of the man that old Harry had had to shoot during her last masquerade. But she could not tell her mother this. When her father's horse was put up for sale, it had not brought half what it was worth. Had she really attempted to speculate that pitiful sum as she had told her mother she had, it could not have begun to yield the amount she had gained masquerading as "Gentleman Jack." And it was not as if she had held up people who could not afford it. The loss of a diamond necklace for those she had robbed occasioned only the vexation of having to replace it. She had made certain that she did not ambush the public coaches loaded down with baggage or the dark unmarked hired coaches. She had waited instead for the gaily painted equipages drawn by several pairs of matched horses.

Often she would learn through servants or through her own junkets about the countryside of a party or ball for the *haut ton* to be given in the area. She would then discover the exact location of the house where the party was to take place and make a study of the roads leading into it to decide the best place for a holdup. Her strategy had depended to a large extent on the roads. And when she had decided the place and time, she met with old Harry and Jeb in an old gamekeeper's cottage on the edge of Brentwood Crest and went over the details of her plan with them. They decided then where they would meet to divide the money the jewels would bring once Jeb had fenced them. For old Harry and Jeb deserved their fair share for taking the same risks that she took. They never struck twice in the same place, nor did they meet again until it was time to discuss the next holdup. In this way, Cara felt they had avoided arrest, just as "Gentleman Jack" had, for longer than some of the more unfortunate highwaymen. But she did not care to take that risk again. She already felt they had outworn their good luck with their last masquerade. Only old Harry's good shooting had kept that holdup from turning into a fiasco.

No, she thought, this time we will gamble at the expense of London fools in a game I am sure of winning! Aloud she said, "No, this is the only way out of our difficulties that I can see. It is of no consequence, *Maman*. Indeed, most girls marry for the sake of wealth and position."

Her mother said nothing, and Cara turned to find her staring once again at the sunshine falling through the open French doors onto the parquet floor.

"Besides, a Season in London will be just the thing to cheer you up." And take your mind off Father, Cara added to herself. "Come, we shall have a grand time. Do you not wish to see your old friends again? It has been some years since you saw them last. Perhaps they have gotten fat as butterballs in your absence. Then you can lord that slim figure of yours over them!"

At that, Cara succeeded in making her mother laugh, "Slim figure! I'm afraid I have put on a few extra pounds myself."

"Rubbish!" retorted Cara. For her mother was still a very trim and young-looking forty-three. If anything, she had lost weight in the year of mourning that had passed since her husband's death. In spite of all his faults, she had loved him dearly.

"But you are right, Cara. I am being shamefully dismal. I should love to see my old friends again. I shall go this moment and write to them." She folded up her embroidery and moved to sit at the writing desk.

"And I shall go see Cook about closing up the house. Let me see," Cara said, thinking aloud and moving toward the door, "we do not need to worry overmuch with packing for we do not either of us have many dresses that are still suitable enough to take with us. But I shall need to speak to old Harry and see if he might be able to find some way in which to furbish up the old brougham. Oh! — and *Maman*, Mr. Havershaw said he should have prepared a list of houses we might rent in about two weeks, so we shall very likely go up to London then."

"In two weeks!" exclaimed her mother. "Why, that is too soon. You have said we will not arrive until the end of the month!"

"Ah, but we shall have to visit a dressmaker and give her ample time in which to complete our, have no doubt, stunning new wardrobes! And we will want to have a little time to adjust to the city and be well-rested before we begin our party-going, you know."

"Well, that is certainly true . . . you are right, as always. I don't know how you can be my daughter, Cara. You think of everything!" exclaimed her mother as Cara laughed and went off in the direction of the kitchen to arrange the closing of the house with Cook.

That night, when her mother had retired, Cara sat down at the desk in the sitting room to write her own letter to Mr. Havershaw apprising him of their coming to London for the Season and requesting him to make a list of several houses they might find suitable to rent. Because they were just out of mourning, she asked that the houses on his list be located in the more quiet, if less fashionable, section of the city — which will keep the expense of our rent down, she thought with satisfaction.

Then, to account for their improved financial circumstances, she told him a distant great-aunt of her mother's had died and unexpectedly left her mother a rather large sum of money. I couldn't very well tell him the truth! she thought, grinning. But she asked him not to mention the matter to her mother as she was still feeling the loss of her husband and any mention of death distressed her immeasurably. That ought to prevent his raising the subject to *Maman,* she schemed.

One of the reasons for their coming to London, she continued in the letter, was to raise her mother's spir-

24

its. And *that* much, at least, is true, she thought. No doubt I shall have to do penance sometime for all these whopping lies!

Smiling to herself, she penned her name at the bottom of the page, sanded it, and sealed the letter, taking it up with her to bed to post in the morning.

Two

Julius Wrothby did not relish the jokes and ribald comments that met him on his entrance into his own dining room. But he had expected as much.

He felt like the curtain had gone up the moment they had stepped into the hall of Malton Park. Marion had played her role admirably. Half-fainting and half-fussing over his wound, she had alarmed his major-domo into sending for the doctor and caused enough commotion to bring a crowd of his guests, most of whom had already arrived, flooding into the hallway with avid curiosity stamped on their faces. He had had to have dinner set back and had known when he did so that by the time his arm had been attended to, actress that she was, the Countess Marion Hauterive would have treated all of his guests to some version of their mishap. He would have much preferred to enter quietly, have his valet tend his wound, and play the matter down as much as possible.

As he stood in the doorway arrogantly surveying his guests through his quizzing glass, he realized he was heartily tired of Marion's zeal for the dramatic. It was time to look elsewhere for the pleasures of his female company. When he got back to London, he would buy her another expensive trinket to replace the emeralds and fob her off.

Dispassionately he observed her telling her story to a crowd of male admirers, who had already heard it at least once he'd be bound, and knew she would not go unescorted long. With her flashing black eyes and that raven black hair against her white, soft skin, she might even get one of the poor fools to offer for her, one could never tell. She was a prime'un, he acknowledged, with an appreciative gleam in his dark eyes. Otherwise he would never have troubled himself to take her away from Denby, and he smiled inwardly remembering the look on Giles Denby's face when he'd found the ladybird he'd been wooing had flown his nest at the sight of better prospects. Denby couldn't compete with his own good looks *and* his earldom.

A scowl succeeded his smile. If he had known earlier that the price of the delay caused by his gift of emeralds to Marion after tonight's performance and her impetuous . . . appreciation . . . of it was going to be a holdup and a bullet through his arm, he might have waited until after his dinner party at Malton Park. The scowl softened somewhat as he remembered her manner of showing her gratitude.

He sauntered across the dining-room floor toward the table. Allowing a lazy smile to spread across his face, he drawled a retort to the jokes that had met him at the door. Appreciative snorts of laughter answered him. He sat down, his guests following his example, and outwardly bore with equanimity the jokes made at his expense throughout the meal.

Dully he supposed that his holdup would be the latest *on-dit* until some other poor devil did something to replace it. It wasn't often that a Corinthian such as himself, known for his boxing ability in the ring, was accosted and shot on the very outskirts of his own land. He had to admit there was a certain wry humor in it himself and ground his teeth on the roast lamb he was chewing.

The fingers of his good hand tightened on his fork as he thought of pummeling the highwaymen's leader. He wouldn't last in the ring with me fifteen minutes! he thought, as he remembered how easy it had been for him to unseat the fellow from his horse. He had been surprised when the man had been taken in by his child's trick of dropping the sack of jewelry between his fingers. If it hadn't been for the second man's bullet, things would have gone differently.

Leaning back in his chair, he lifted his wine glass and regarded the ruby lights in the dark red liquid as he delicately swirled the crystal glass. He could wait. It would not be difficult to find out the owner of the seal on the ring the fellow had so stupidly worn. And when he did . . . Smiling lazily with half-closed lids, he glanced at the faces around his table and then tossed off the dark red contents of his glass. Eyeing a footman, he signaled for more wine.

The first two weeks of their arrival in London kept Cara and Lady Brentwood busy choosing a house to rent from the list which Mr. Havershaw had given them, hiring a small staff of servants in addition to Cook and old Harry, and giving the house itself a badly needed, thorough cleaning.

When the new house had been set in order, and everything that could gleam did, they ventured to walk out to Bond Street, learning some of the streets of the city on the way, to the shop of one of the finest dressmakers in London according to the advice of one Elizabeth Dougherty, a companion of Lady Brentwood's younger days.

"Betsy may have been a bit of a madcap when she was young," her mother had said, "but she always knew how to dress. And she says we will want to shop at Madame Diette's. She carries some of the finest cloths in London, and according to Betsy, she knows all the latest modes."

By the end of the day, fitting clothes at Madame Diette's, they were both so tired and stiff from standing stock-still and holding their arms and legs in one position while Madame's seamstresses measured and pinned that they called a hack to carry them back home.

"Oh, my aching feet and arms and legs," moaned Cara as she dropped down onto the soft cushions of the settee in their small new parlor.

"And head," added Lady Brentwood, sinking with a smile into a plump armchair.

"I didn't know being fashionable was so taxing! I vow I haven't the patience for it. I feel like I have enough pent-up energy to gallop for miles, but my muscles are all screaming for a hot bath. And we must go back for more fittings in two weeks!" Cara wailed.

"But those will be the final fittings, my dear, and then we shall be receiving our new wardrobes as they complete them," replied her mother, trying to show her the bright side.

"And then, we shall receive the *bill* for our new wardrobes," Cara countered and moaned again mischievously. "But," she continued quickly, sitting forward on the settee, "You cannot lay a trap without bait. Or put a trifle more delicately," she said, seeing her mother's shocked face, "beautiful clothes make the woman. So I care not a whit how much our new gowns cost since they are going to help me to catch a rich husband!"

"Cara! My love, you must not say such things," re-

29

proved her mother mildly.

"Only in your presence, Mother dear," laughed Cara. "Now I am going to soak this bag of aching bones in a hot bath before dinner, and you, *Maman,* should follow my example." Cara got up from the settee cushions very slowly, pretending to cry out every time she had to move a limb.

Her mother laughed, agreeing, "That is an excellent notion."

The end of the month drew near, and Cara and Lady Brentwood found themselves having a little more time to relax and rest. They had soon settled into a daily routine, often on sunny days walking to Hyde Park for a little exercise. They were also becoming familiar with the sounds of the city—the night sounds in particular. For, at first, neither of them had slept well, being used to the nighttime quiet of the country.

On the last Friday of the month, they returned to Madame Diette's for their final fittings and came out tired once again but very well-pleased with what their new gowns were going to look like when they were completed. Auspiciously they were able to take home with them when they left some of the filmy undergarments and nightclothes and one or two of the simpler day dresses that Madame Diette's girls had already finished.

To their delight, by the time they had reached home with all of their packages, several invitations from some of her mother's friends for informal gatherings in the upcoming week lay waiting for them on the salver in the hall. At last! thought Cara, who, with no high opinion of the *beau monde,* had been worried that her mother's old friends might prove less loyal than Lady Brentwood anticipated and choose not to renew their acquaintance with her.

Contrary to Cara's fears, however, in the weeks following their introductions, she and Lady Brentwood were deluged with invitations of all kinds—from morning carriage rides in the park, afternoon calls, and musicales to dinner parties, rout parties, and balls. In no time, they had acquired a very fashionable set of friends. For none could not love the calm, sweet company of Lady Brentwood, and since Cara, with her fiery beauty and sharp wit, had become the toast of the Season from the moment of her first party, none wanted to be excluded from the *ton* set that had raised her on its pedestal. "We are now *très comme il faut, Maman*," she said, affecting a haughty, cultured tone.

But far from allowing the admiration of the circle of beaux she attracted wherever she went to go to her head, Cara knew it for the fleeting infatuation that it was and regarded it with a derisive eye. To the most profound and heartfelt protestation of love declared by a soulful-eyed swain, she was apt to make a most pithy and unromantic reply in the nature of, "Fustian! Now stop that, Robert, and do be sensible and get up from your knees. You are making a cake of yourself."

Instead of losing her her admirers, such remarks apparently only led them to consider her a greater challenge and made the feat of winning the Incomparable's—for so they had come to call her—heart the more praiseworthy.

Cara was pleased to note a lifting of her mother's spirits as she reacquainted herself with her old companions and caught up on all the events in their lives since the time she had retired from society. Since they had been in London, she had rarely found her mother lost in one of the brown studies that had seemed to

31

descend upon her so often at Brentwood Crest, where everything must remind her of her husband and lead her to ponder on his untimely death.

Cara had also to admit to a lightening of her own spirits. In spite of the cynicism with which she regarded her social success in London, she could not but enjoy the parties of which she had had no experience before and her great abundance of partners. Still, in the back of her mind, she knew her hard-earned capital as well as her time would soon run out. If she did not wish, like the Cinderella she was, to return to her former ignominious condition at the end of the Season, she knew she must quickly single out from her large circle of tinsel admirers those that could be considered sincere in their protestations.

Accordingly in the first few weeks of attending parties, she banished her lingering romantic scruples and, adopting a businesslike frame of mind, coldly narrowed her matrimonial prospects to six gentlemen she felt to be courting her in earnest. And as the weeks progressed, on the basis of their wealth, she ruthlessly narrowed her choices to half that number.

The Baron Richard Llewellyn—easily the most handsome of the three she had settled upon—with his blond curls, blue eyes, and trim figure had attracted her initially with his classic good looks and a wit quite as lively as her own. He was the nearest in age to her of the three gentlemen, being only one or two years older than she, and she often found herself contrasting his youthful gaiety with the staid and rather humorless set of the other two gentlemen. But while Richard seemed to have fallen almost instantly in love with her, he had a volatile, highly romantic nature. His moods changed suddenly and drastically, and she instinctively mistrusted these swings, which neither of the other two gentlemen, if staid, possessed.

The Honorable James Dickson, in his early fifties, with graying hair, pleasant though unexceptional features, and a stocky figure presented the picture of stability. He was old-fashioned, quiet, and as even-tempered as Richard was volatile. Indeed, Cara sometimes wondered if he had any emotions at all, for she had never seen him display anything but punctilious civility. After several weeks' acquaintance with him, he had still shown no desire to move them beyond a formal last name basis, and she, not liking to ask it herself for fear he would think her too forward, had perforce to continue calling him Mr. Dickson.

The last of her three matrimonial prospects, the Viscount Arthur Lyle, also presented a respectable figure in his subdued suits of dark colors and his gallant, soft-spoken manners. In his late forties, he possessed unremarkable brown hair, a somewhat florid complexion, and a small paunch. Though he consistently wore rather more ostentatious jewelry than Cara liked and there often appeared a slight puffiness under his eyes which she thought curious, he had never acted anything but the gentleman before her. Oddly once or twice in his presence she had felt that he was almost too much of a gentleman as though he were merely playing a role, but she had shaken off such thoughts as fanciful and fault-finding when his behavior had continued to be beyond reproach.

Standing in her tidy new bedchamber in a pale lavender wrapper and well-adjusted now to the flurry of London social life, Cara thoughtfully regarded the colorful gowns in the closet before her. Why couldn't, she mused wistfully, Richard, with his good looks and his wit, have, instead of his odious moodiness, Mr. Dickson's evenness of temper and greater wealth? I should marry him on the instant and live happily ever after! she thought dreamily.

Goose! Stop being nonsensical! Mentally, she gave herself a shake and pulled out a sea green taffeta to wear to the theater that night. "This one I think, Ellen," she told her new maid and handed the gown across to her.

"Oh yes, miss, and such a lovely color it'll be on you, too!"

"Thank you, Ellen, but I do not wish to appear but so well tonight. I'm no longer trying to encourage this particular gentleman. Perhaps I should change it for the—"

"Oh, but miss," interrupted Ellen, "you must look well indeed if you're to go to the theater, for from all I've ever heard it's more a place to be seen at than 'tis a place to watch playacting—fine playacting or no, let me tell you."

"Hmm, that is a point, Ellen. I stay with the taffeta then."

As Ellen helped her carefully into the gown, Cara thought of the attractive, blond Richard Llewellyn and couldn't suppress a tingle of excitement. He *was* handsome, and he could be extremely good company. But which of his moods will he be in tonight? she asked herself, and the question dampened her previous excitement.

Too often Richard attended her in moods that were less than pleasant, or, if he started out in good humor, fell pensive or even morose halfway through their evening together. When she would not agree to become engaged to him instantly, when she would not let him make love to her, or when she would refuse to accept any token of his apparently profound feeling for her—all of which he importuned her with at regular intervals—his mood of blithe happiness soured, and he either became melancholy and spent the remainder of the evening tiresomely pleading with her

34

or relapsed into a surly silence before he abruptly bid her adieu and took himself off. Excessively extreme fellow, thought Cara with a slight frown of distaste.

"What's off, miss? Something not laying right?" asked Ellen anxiously, seeing her mistress frown.

"Not a thing, Ellen. I was thinking of something else. The dress sets to perfection, and you've arranged my hair royally. Indeed, if you will hand me my gloves and fan, I will go down now. And," she added, "don't wait up for me. Of a certainty, I can undress myself."

"Yes, miss. Thank you, miss," answered Ellen, bobbing a courtsey.

Gracefully descending the short flight of stairs, Cara thought again of Richard's moods. She knew she was being nonsensical, but they sometimes reminded her uncomfortably of her father's extreme behavior just before he died. Then, too, Richard was only a baron she reminded herself. Viscount Lyle and Mr. Dickson — both considered the best catches of the Season by the matchmaking mamas — were far wealthier than Richard. Though neither cut the romantically handsome figure he did, neither were their moods as changeable as his. Cara began to consider she could no longer seriously regard Richard as a suitor. After tonight, she decided firmly, I shall accept his invitations on vastly fewer occasions.

She had reached the parlor and went in to find her mother and Lady Dougherty enjoying a quiet coze, seated together on the settee. They both looked, on her entrance, the picture of guilt so she was sure she had been the subject of their talk. The corners of her mouth quirked at the comic expression of guilt on the two ladies' faces, but she had no time to twit them on it as Bates, the new butler, chose that moment to show in Richard, who was to escort them all to the theater.

Richard made, as usual, a handsome appearance in

a suit of black velvet that made his blond curls seem even paler. The ruffles of his shirt fell elegantly at his throat and wrists, and he carried an ebony stick in one hand. To Cara's relief, he proved to be in one of his happier moods and kept the ladies entertained throughout the ride to the theater in Lady Dougherty's carriage. Once there, he kept up a running monologue, pointing out members of the *ton* unknown to Cara and Lady Brentwood and regaling the two ladies, abetted by Lady Dougherty, with humorous accounts of some of the more colorful histories. With his satire, he had all three of them smiling and chuckling so that they were almost reluctant when the lights dimmed and the curtains began to rise for the start of the play.

The Lady's Folly opened dramatically with the murder of a wealthy old gentleman by hired assassins. The assassins gave out that the old gentleman's young wife was having him killed so that she could marry her own true love, but at that point the leading lady entered the stage, and the sight of her and the sound of her voice dealt Cara such a shock that she started visibly in her chair and quite lost the thread of the play for a moment. For the leading lady appeared to be none other than the bejeweled occupant of the last carriage Cara had held up! She recovered herself quickly but couldn't prevent herself from staring at the woman with awful fascination, feeling she was back again holding her up as she listened to the woman's familiar voice. The play, though a good one and well-acted by everyone, was quite ruined for her.

At intermission, she was still feeling unnerved. Thus, when Richard asked if the ladies would like to walk outside their box, she readily agreed, though the two older ladies declined. Betsy allowed as how she and Lady Brentwood were content to sit just where they were, and anyone wishing to chat must needs come to them.

So it was just Richard and Cara who left their box to join the fashionable throng of theatergoers mingling in the corridor. But bumped and pushed by the tightly packed crowd, Cara found herself smiling and nodding to acquaintances rather abstractedly and soon began to wish she had remained in the box.

The crush of people, for the play was a popular one, quickly swept them farther than they had meant to go, and after a short time Richard suggested they had best turn around and start back so as not to be caught still in the halls when the second half of the play began.

They were therefore edging their way back against the mainstream of the crowd when a large, well-manicured white hand clapped Richard upon the shoulder and wrenched him about, causing several faces and exclamations of annoyance in the crowd around him. The black hair and white forehead of a tall gentleman showed above the top of Richard's blond head. Cara waited—a difficult thing to do in the jostling crowd—and watched patiently while Richard exclaimed with delight and vigorously pumped the hand of the other gentleman, still obscured from her view by the back of Richard and the crowd.

"Wrothby, you dog! Back from that orgy at Malton Park, eh? I heard about that!"

"It would surprise me more, Llewellyn, my dear fellow, if you told me, rather, that you had *not* heard of that," drawled his friend. "Who are you pining after these days?"

Richard gave him a scowl and ignored his last remark, asking, "How's the arm now?"

"All but healed, naturally. T'was but a scratch."

"The devil it was!" retorted Richard. " 'A scratch'

37

coming from you, old boy, means anything that didn't take your life, I know *you*. But here. There's someone I want you to meet. Cara—"

"I knew it! Your latest *affaire de coeur.* Certainly I'll meet her—present the wench."

"No, Wrothby. That's not the way of it this time. This is different," replied Richard, having the grace to blush. His reputation for being in love with a different female every month was not entirely unjustified. "This is The One," said Richard simply, surprising his friend by describing Cara without his customary lavish compliments.

"Well, lead on. I'll still meet her, even if she believes she may legshackle you!" This remark boomed out over the heads of those standing near but was lost on Richard, for he had swiveled to present Cara and found that she had been obliged to turn away from him and say a few words to a friend of her own and the crowd had jostled her a short distance away. As a result, she had heard none of Richard's badinage with his tall friend, though at first she had been aware of a few faces turned in outrage toward their conversation. She was thus unprepared, when she finished speaking with her friend and felt Richard's hand upon her arm, to turn around, confront the same tall, muscular body—seemingly still in evening dress—and stare up into the same pair of black eyes that had blazed down at her only a scant five or six weeks earlier when she had relieved their owner of his cash and diamond pin.

For the second time that night, Cara started. But the dark eyes were merely regarding her rather cynically, once more, she felt, taking in every detail of her appearance as the gentleman waited for Richard's introduction. Again, despite the nonchalant stance of the man before her, she found herself acutely conscious of the obviously well-toned muscles that filled out his evening clothes to perfection. If I were the type to have the vapors, I would certainly have them now! she thought wildly, feeling the blood surge to her cheeks.

However, since she was not the woman to indulge herself in such poor displays, she thought quickly, assumed a petulant air, and launched into rapid speech. "Oh, Richard! My feet are tired of being stepped on, my mind is reeling with faces, and my mouth sick of being stretched in a smile that shall probably never come off I have held it so long—you must feel so, too! Let us save ourselves further suffering and return to the box before it is time for the curtains to go up again! You will forgive us, sir, this time?" She threw a bright smile over her shoulder in the direction of Richard's friend and started toward their box without waiting for Richard. Providence was with her, for just as the last words tumbled from her mouth, the theater gave the signal indicating that the last acts of the play were about to begin.

Richard, conscious that this behavior was extremely unlike Cara but having observed her rapt attention to the first acts of the play, put it down to anxiety about missing the last acts, and, apologizing, hastily postponed his introductions and rushed off in her wake.

Lord Wrothby raised an eyebrow at this rather rude behavior by Richard's One and Only. "I wonder if my reputation has preceded me?" he mused aloud. But since such abrupt behavior was not uncommon of Richard, his friend merely shrugged his broad shoulders and announced to no one in particular, "Same old Llewellyn," and sauntered off in the direction of his own box.

Feeling as if her cushion were made of her mother's sewing needles, Cara sat through the rest of the play and tried unsuccessfully to curb her imagination, which willfully continued to present her with, and embellish, variations on the theme of her arrest. In her mind's eye, Richard's friend, whose name she did not even know so that she might avoid him in future, kept appearing beside her in their box, recognizing and denouncing her as the villainous "Gentleman Jack," grabbing her by the collar of her dress, and dragging her instantly off to the Authorities to be summarily executed.

Consequently, by the time the play ended, Cara's nerves were jangled and her teeth set on edge. She did her best to rush Richard and the two ladies out of their box, into the corridor, and down the theater stairs in an attempt to escape meeting Richard's friend once more. But the two ladies, absorbed in speaking to friends they had missed during the intermission by remaining in their box, continually held up their progress by stopping to chat until Cara could have boxed both their ears in frustration.

Slowly they approached the large pillars at the entrance to the theater, and Cara began to entertain the hope that she had avoided another encounter. They rounded a pillar, the two older women now becoming aware of Cara's hurry to depart and increasing their pace, and hastened straight into the arms of Lord Wrothby's party, waiting for his carriage on the steps of the theater.

Cara could have screamed with vexation. There was no escape this time without being accounted rude in the extreme and risking, in so doing, raising suspicions which perhaps did not even exist.

"We meet again," drawled Lord Wrothby, calmly observing their hurried approach through his quizzing glass. "If you don't intoduce me this time, Llewellyn, I shall think you a curst jealous fellow with something to hide!" he complained. The narrowed black eyes flitted over Cara appreciatively. "Whatever Lord Llewellyn has told you of me, ladies, I am persuaded he has exaggerated hugely—"

"Even if I'd said anything—which I wouldn't!—the word *exaggeration* in relation to you, Wrothby, has no meaning!" retorted his friend, interrupting.

"You may ascertain," continued Lord Wrothby condescendingly as if he hadn't heard, "from Miss Scogan," and he turned to smile mockingly at a brunette woman standing beside him, "if I have ever acted anything but the gentleman."

"Not toward me at any rate," she replied with disappointment and pouted prettily at him.

He shrugged, giving them a look of innocence, which earned him a playful tap of Lady Dougherty's fan and a chuckle from Lady Brentwood.

Finding this interchange, in general, revolting, and the gentleman's conceit, in particular, offensive, Cara was goaded to exclaim, "I assure you, sir, Richard has said nothing to us about you *or* any reputation you may be furthering—good or bad!"

One black brow shot up in amused acknowledgement of Cara's home thrust.

"Vindicated!" cried Richard, directing a self-righteous glance toward Lord Wrothby and then preventing any further exchange by beginning the introductions.

Cara held her breath and unconsciously caught her lower lip between her teeth as it came her turn and Richard introduced her. But to her profound relief, no gleam of suspicion appeared in the dark eyes of the Earl of Malton, and he gave no show of any special interest in her surname. No denunciation of her followed; no irons were clapped upon her wrists; no one materialized to arrest her and drag her off to the Authorities.

The group chatted a few minutes more and the
split up to depart as their carriages pulled up one aft
the other before the steps. Unimpeded, Cara followe
Lady Dougherty's worthy back into the darkness o
her carriage and, once inside, let go her breath in
soundless sigh of deliverance.

The Earl of Malton, waiting idly for the member
of his party to precede him into his carriage, had tim
to observe Richard hand Cara into Lady Dougherty
barouche.

He brought his quizzing glass up with a sligh
frown of perplexity as he noted Cara's height. Sud
denly, unmistakably, he had the absurd notion that h
had met her somewhere before.

Three

What an excessively bird-witted thing to do! Cara berated herself as their group was driven home. It would have been far better to have gone unnoticed than to have drawn attention to herself and risked raising Lord Wrothby's ire as she had so ill-consider-edly had done.

Although, as she thought back, the Earl of Malton had not appeared offended by her set-down so much as amused by it. A thought she found as irritating as the conceited remarks and smile which had caused her to utter the set-down in the first instance. Hmph! The man probably cannot be embarrassed, she thought. He has been used to having everyone at his beck and call and very likely believes that everything he does is proper simply because he does it! Undoubtedly an aristocrat of aristocrats—never a thought in his head of anyone but himself! And probably just such a one as sat and laughed to see my father robbed! Her lips curled scornfully.

Lady Dougherty's carriage drew up before their house, and both Cara and her mother urged her to come inside—Cara, for the sake of civility, and Lady Brentwood because she genuinely desired to visit with her friend further. But Lady Dougherty declined, explaining that her George was waiting up for her, and she feared he would begin to worry if she didn't arrive home soon.

Richard handed Cara and Lady Brentwood down from her carriage and escorted them inside the house, but he did not stay when he noticed that Lady Brentwood politely began to stifle yawns and Cara's heart did not seem to be in their talk. He put the Incomparable's lack of interest down to weariness and the lateness of the hour and bid the ladies good night.

When Bates had shown Richard safely from the room, Lady Brentwood exclaimed, "La! I thought he would never take my hints and leave." Regarding her daughter's abstracted look, she asked quietly, "Is anything amiss, my love? You did not seem quite yourself tonight."

Cara, feeling a trifle strained after her nerve-wracking evening, shook her head and tried to smile reassuringly back at her mother. She began to gather up her gloves and fan, preparing to retire, since she had no explanations to offer.

Her mother began again tentatively, "If this is not the moment to speak of this, my love, tell me. I thought you would like to know . . ." Cara looked at her inquiringly. "Betsy . . . told me an interesting fact tonight."

Cara smiled slightly and teased, "Come. Out with it! I knew when I caught you two on the settee tonight with your heads together you had married me off to Lord Jack-a-Napes and had me with one grandchild already! Tell me the worst."

Lady Brentwood blushed but smiled herself at the picture the two of them must have made and took Cara's teasing as a sign to continue. "Betsy was concerned that you might have set your cap at Richard, for you have been entertaining him so particularly re-

44

ently. And she wanted me to know . . . well, she said she thought you could do better than Richard, though he *is* a nice young man, and that I should discourage you in that quarter—as if I could if you liked him. But, she thought I should know that . . . and I thought you would want to know . . . that . . . his family is quite as bad off as ours!" she finished, glad that she had gotten it out at last. "Though, of course, she did not put it in just that way as I have not told her of our circumstances."

"Did she indeed!" exclaimed Cara, her spirits reviving and a dangerous glint coming into her green eyes.

"Now, Cara, love," interrupted her mother warningly, "she was only trying to be helpful. You must not fly up into the boughs because a dear friend of mine chose to interest herself in the welfare of my only daughter. You should be flattered."

"Humph!" snorted Cara. "As it happens," she said haughtily, "Lady Dougherty need not have concerned herself. I have already decided that neither Richard's baronetcy nor his moods shall satisfy my expectations of a future husband. Her information, happily, only confirms my decision. You may convey my thanks to her for it at your first convenience," she ended awfully.

"I will do that, my dear," answered her mother, not in the least perturbed by Cara's haughty manner. "Sleep well," she added, her eyes twinkling as her daughter swept majestically out of the room.

The laughter in her blue eyes died, however, a moment later as she began to go round the parlor putting out candles—a custom of hers from their days at Brentwood Crest when they had had no butler—and she thought of the necessity of her daughter's having to consider the wealth of a prospective husband at all. She regretted this condition with all her heart and

worried now that her daughter might have becon
perhaps just a bit — for Cara could never becon
heartless — too mercenary and calculating in her a
proach to the matter of choosing a husband. Feari
she herself was somewhat of a financial burden on h
responsibly minded daughter, she decided she mu
somehow set about a course to relieve her of it.

I wish there were someone who could engage Cara
heart, she thought to herself. She was standing m
tionless, watching the smoke from the candle she ha
just snuffed curl into the air when Bates poked h
head round the parlor door to perform that very o
fice.

Seeing that she had extinguished all but one candl
he gave a shocked, "Madame!" and came to take th
candle snuffer from her in order to finish the job fc
her.

"Oh! I am so sorry, Bates. It's an old habit, yo
see," she declared apologetically and, relinquishin
the device to him, hurried out of the room to escap
his puzzled frown.

Lord Wrothby delivered his companion home fror
the theater and, not feeling tired, had himself se
down at White's to drink a glass or two of port an
converse with whomever he might find there at such
late hour.

As luck would have it, he ran into a large group o
his friends who appeared to have been playing card
for most of the evening and, the earl judged by th
look of their hiccoughing speeches and the libera
amount of back-slapping going on, also appeared tc
have consumed a large quantity of wine. He broke ir
on the group, enduring his back to be pounded, anc
had a glass of wine thrust into his hand and himsel

oasted. Immediately following this, he was asked a question that seemed to have broken up their card game in favor of making a wager, for the betting book was out on the table before them. "Who do you bet on, Wrothby?" came at him from all sides.

Since he had been at Malton Park for some weeks, preferring to kick his heels there waiting for his arm to heal and the brouhaha about it to die down before he returned to London, he had missed Cara's advent on the London scene and knew nothing of her almost instant conquest of the *beau monde*.

"I say she takes Lyle," came one boisterous voice. Several voices dissented this, advocating instead "the Honorable old Dickson." Yet a third faction argued noisily in favor of "the moony Richard."

Shouting, Giles Denby, a stout young man often teased for his cherubicly rosy cheeks and abundance of curly chestnut hair, made himself heard over the arguing and asked again, "Wrothby! Who do you say the Incomparable brings up to scratch?" preparing to enter the earl's answer in the betting book.

When he could be heard, the earl calmly desired someone to enlighten him about the subject of the bet.

He was treated to a great deal of incredulous and slightly inebriated guffawing at his ignorance and then taken aside and given an effusive description which clarified the subject not at all.

He finally asked what her name might be and, when told, realized that he had just met the lady in question not an hour since.

A pretty piece, he acknowledged, a gleam of recognition in his eyes. The spirited set-down she had given him made the corners of his mouth quirk in the beginning of another smile. A piece well worth gentling, he thought with relish.

However, he felt, on the basis of his long-standing friendship with Richard, he could not, in honor bound, dally with his One and Only until Richard had himself thrown her over for someone else. No doubt at most a month hence! And smiling sardonically, the earl bet on Richard as a show of good will and set determinedly about attaining the same happy state of mind his friends had already achieved.

It was not until a week later, returning late from a cockfight in Berkshire, that the earl stepped across his threshold and bethought himself of a matter he hadn't attended to in several days.

He inquired of his major-domo if his secretary hadn't yet retired to send Mr. Mallory to him in the library.

He was seated in his favorite chair stretching his legs out before him and puffing on his pipe ten minutes later when a knock sounded on the door of the library. He called to Hugh Mallory to come in and be seated, and offered the slender young man a glass of port, which he politely declined.

"I trust I do not disturb you at this late hour, Hugh?" asked His Lordship.

"No, my lord. As you see, I had not retired. It is my custom to read a few chapters before going to bed. What is it you wish?" answered Hugh.

"What have you discovered on that seal I gave you to research?"

The young man was silent for a moment recollecting his information and then said, "It belongs to the Brentwood family, sir. According to my understanding, the name will have died out with this generation, for the last heir, a Charles Brentwood, was an only child. He married but had no sons, and he himself has been recently killed in an accident of some kind. He depleted his estate—I believe it is called

Brentwood Crest — sadly through gambling debts. The widow cannot have much to live on."

"Yes," replied His Lordship slowly, thinking aloud, "I remember now. Barely knew him, but that bounder Lyle had him by the shirt points at White's some time ago, playing him for all he was worth — which, apparently, was not much. Couldn't stomach the fellow's fleecing the poor devil." The earl did not add that he had stepped in to play a few hands and win the succeeding rounds from Lyle and then stopped and refused to play further. He had thereby ended the game, sending Brentwood home, without his money to be sure — Lyle had most of that already — but still in possession of his heritage. Lyle, the earl knew, only played when he had the odds stacked highly in his favor. Nor could he be trusted to play an honest game. The earl had even heard it whispered that Lyle had killed the old viscount, another inveterate gambler, in an argument over just such a game of cards and then assumed the role of his son with its title and all its wealth. He supposed it was possible: the viscount took pains to keep his history uncertain.

"A few days later Brentwood was dead," the earl continued aloud. "Devilish odd I thought at the time."

"I believe it was a horsing accident," added Hugh.

"Still damned queer, happening so soon after . . ." mused His Lordship and relapsed into a thoughtful silence.

What Hugh had told him did not bring him much closer to the identity of his highwayman. Brentwood's depletion of his estate could explain the necessity of a son's turning to the road to gain his livelihood, but Brentwood had had no son.

A thief, then? Perhaps Brentwood had had his ring stolen from him or lost it somewhere — even in a card game—before his death? But that wouldn't explain why this highwayman had so stupidly worn it during his holdup, the earl rationalized. Surely he had known, whether he had gained the ring lawfully or not, it could eventually be traced to him? One could not flash such a piece about under the noses of the farmers or the, er, footpad set, without someone's taking notice of it. Why would he wear a piece of jewelry that could send him to the gallows he brooded.

Suddenly realizing that Hugh was patiently waiting, still seated opposite him, His Lordship said abruptly, "Forgive me, Hugh. That is all I wished to know."

"I hope my information has met with your lordship's approval?" asked Hugh.

The earl laughed. "You know damn well it has! But if you think by asking me that in that damned prim tone of yours I shall tell you what this is all about, or why it could not wait until morning, you're out, my boy. Now get out of here and go to the devil!" grinned the earl.

Hugh laughed, too, realizing his ploy had not deceived the earl. Used to being address in such a manner, he replied, "Very well then, my lord. I bid you good night." And still smiling, he bowed and went out.

As the library door shut behind him, the earl returned to his musing. The whole thing did not make sense. Damned sentimental or incredibly vain thing for a highwayman to do, wear another man's ring to hold up a carriage. It smacked of the absurd. Perhaps the fellow was feeble-minded, he thought, giving up his reflections and knocking his pipe out. Well, devil take it! I'll be bound if I'll lose a good night's sleep over it, he exclaimed to himself, and took himself off to bed.

Midmorning the next day, he rose and went down to breakfast, still pondering the matter of the highwayman and his ring. Coming to no conclusions, he gave it up and relegated it again to the back of his mind as he read the papers and ate.

Three-quarters of an hour later, his groom brought round his curricle, and he set off for his boxing salon. It was his habit of a Thursday to give himself a good workout going a few rounds in the ring with Turner, the salon's boxing master.

Concentrating on his left in the midst of his bout with Turner, it suddenly dawned on the earl that he had heard the name Brentwood once before in the last two weeks. Searching his memory quickly, he attached it correctly to Cara and, as soon as he had done so, saw an image of her and remembered the bets being made on the Incomparable at White's. Illogically he then remembered how, after being introduced to her, he had had the peculiar feeling that he had met her before.

He had been throwing punches steadily at Turner throughout the steps of this mental process—indeed they seemed almost to help him think the matter through punch by punch—but then he connected the copper-haired, green-eyed Cara Brentwood with the pitiable, debt-ridden Charles Brentwood, who also had had the same copper hair and green eyes he recalled now, and suddenly felt all the pieces of the puzzle he had been unable to solve for so long fall into place.

He stopped throwing the rapid punches which Turner had been laboring to dodge and halted midstride, stunned by the realization he had just made, exclaiming, "Good God! It cannot be possible!"

Turner, seizing the rare opportunity afforded him, landed the earl a direct uppercut.

But the blow only served to knock the earl several steps backward and drive home the realization. His mind having concluded one problem, it moved on to the next, and the earl shook himself out of his stupor to find Turner rearing back with his right arm, intent on delivering a knock out.

The earl brought his fists up just in time to fend off the blow and then planted Turner a facer of his own that brought the master to the mat instead.

"That's all for me today with *you*, your lordship. You're as fit as you ever were. I only wish all the wine you drink and the hours you keep did as much for me!" complained Turner good-humoredly, rubbing his jaw and walking off to attend to some of the less-strenuous matters of his salon.

His Lordship laughed exultantly, partly at beating Turner and partly at solving the problem of his highwayman's identity. The more he thought about it — preposterous as it seemed — the more satisfied he became that it was the only explanation. And if I'm right, he thought grimly — and one or two more questions to Hugh will put me in the way of it — she shall not cozen Richard nor any other poor devil into marriage with her! Though if what he suspected were true, Richard, with only a baronetcy, had as much chance of winning the jade as a mongrel's flea had. No doubt an earldom would be more to her taste.

Absorbed in his thoughts, he headed toward the baths. He could not take the matter to the Authorities yet, he realized, unless he wanted to be laughed out of Bow Street. They would find it hard to believe a young woman had masqueraded as a man and even more difficult to credit that she had masqueraded as the notorious highwayman, "Gentleman Jack," and then actually held up coaches in that guise! He couldn't blame them if they didn't believe him: it

52

sounded crackbrained even to himself. Without a doubt, he would need irrefutable proof if he expected anyone to believe this story. He had the ring it was true, but that might be explained away.

He halted mid-stride again, suddenly realizing what would occur if he attempted to turn the adventuress in. His lips tightened into a thin line. Unconsciously one hand went to rub his arm where the bullet had entered. He did not care to be roasted a second time! Incensed and frustrated at the thought that she would get away with putting a bullet in him and making him a laughing stock, he continued across the floor toward the baths.

A half-hour later, dressed immaculately in a dark brown superfine coat over buff-colored breeches, he strode out of the salon, leapt up into his curricle, and set off at such a pace his groom had barely enough time to jump up behind him.

Seeing the set of His Lordship's mouth, the groom decided he would keep his own shut.

The earl pulled up in front of his steps sharply, almost tossing his groom over the heads of the two horses, threw the reins at him—apparently without noticing his precarious position—and took the stairs two at a time.

Sending once more for Hugh, he strode into the library and remained pacing back and forth across the length of the room until his secretary arrived.

"On the matter of the Brentwood seal, was there a Brentwood daughter?" he asked peremptorily, not waiting this time for Hugh to seat himself.

"I believe there was," he answered calmly, anticipating his employer's next question. "She would be approximately twenty-three or twenty-four this year."

A chilling, "Ah," was all the reply His Lordship gave to this piece of information. Abruptly he asked,

"Have you a description of her?"

"I am afraid not, my lord." He maintained his silence, waiting for the next question and watching the earl stalk across the room.

"Where is the estate—Brentwood Crest, I think you called it—located?"

"In Somerset, my lord. There is no one living there now, but it hasn't been sold. Though, I don't understand how this can be the case, for I was informed Brentwood had mortgaged it to the hilt. I should have expected it to have gone to auction."

"Should you, indeed," remarked His Lordship quietly. Too quietly for Hugh's liking. Frowning, the earl recollected that Somerset was the county adjoining that of Malton Park. If one did not follow the roads, the distance between the two estates would not be excessive.

"The widow is said to be visiting friends here in London," added Hugh.

"When did they arrive? I assume the daughter is with her," shot His Lordship.

"Yes. Just recently—"

"Exactly, when?"

"I believe they have been here approximately one month. But," he continued a trifle nervously, "again, I do not see where they can have got the funds for this. Perhaps some unexpected windfall—"

But he got no further, for His Lordship exploded, " 'Unexpected windfall' the devil!" stopped short in his pacing, and the black look Hugh particularly disliked in His Lordship descended on his brow. In a moment, he took up his stalking again, the scowl on his face becoming more ominous, but he said nothing further.

As the earl obviously had no further questions for him, Hugh decided it was an opportune moment to withdraw. Noiselessly, he walked to the library door, opened and shut it quietly behind him, and exhaled a soft, "Whew!," glad to have left His Lordship and his black mood on the other side of the door.

Lord Wrothby, on hearing Hugh's answers to his questions, had satisfied himself that Cara was indeed his highwayman.

She shall not get off scot-free! he fumed, silently raging back and forth across the library. Abruptly he slowed his step as the germ of an idea began to take shape in his mind. He remembered an earlier thought. No doubt she *would* prefer an earldom.

I fear, he thought slowly, I am about to become besotted with the wench. I think . . . she shall soon gain a fourth suitor anxious for her hand. So anxious, in fact, that he will brook no other suitors! His eyes hardened. What better way to ruin her game than to prevent her bringing the other poor devils up to scratch?

He rang for his major-domo. "Fetch me Wosso."

When a small, slightly misshapen man presented himself to the earl some five minutes later with a "Yer lor'ship?," the earl said curtly, "A female going by the name of Cara Brentwood. Contrive to observe her movements with your usual, ah, discretion."

With the relish of one who enjoys his line of work, the little man replied, "Right, Guv!," doffed his cap, and was gone.

Catching sight of Brentwood's signet ring where it lay on its side on the top of his desk, the earl strolled over to pick it up. He watched it gleam as he turned it in the light. We'll play *my* game now, my girl! he thought, and smiled, a cold, hard light in his black eyes.

Four

Hours before the fashionable throng would descend on it, Cara was out enjoying the solitary ride in Hyde Park which had become her weekly custom since coming to London. She knew she ought to have old Harry or Ellen accompany her, but she didn't feel herself to be in any particular danger, and she had yet to meet anyone who might cause her embarrassment by carrying tales of it into polite circles. The cost of a little impropriety, to her, was worth the pleasure of the sunny, peaceful quiet of the park when she was free to gallop unrestrainedly, venting some of her restless energy and planning her next strategies in moving her suitors closer to the point of proposing.

Watching the early sun make golden auras of the tree leaves, Cara felt her muscles and her nerves relax as she used the energy that had been building inside her for days to gallop the circumference of the park.

As she completed the circle, she pulled up, smiling happily, her cheeks flushed becomingly, and cantered, allowing both herself and her horse to get their wind back.

"Let's cut straight through this time," she said,

thinking aloud to her horse. She leaned forward to stroke his silky neck and then urged him into a wild, breakneck run, feeling the wind snatch the laugh that broke from her lips as they raced through the middle of the park.

With three-quarters of the park behind her, intent on making the last quarter, she was startled to see a black horse bolt from the trees directly into her path!

She reined in sharply, trying to lead her horse to the side as she did so. Narrowly avoiding a collision, her anger at the stupidity of the other rider flaring, she realized too late, even as she felt herself begin to leave the saddle, that her horse was going to rear in protest at such handling. Out of the corner of her eye, she had only time to see the second horse also rear as his owner, apparently surprised to find her bearing down upon him, pulled up hastily on his own reins.

She landed in a heap, thrown roughly onto the right side of her body.

"I should have thought you could sit a horse better than that," drawled a lazy voice close to her ear, and she felt herself hauled none too gently to her feet.

Dazed, Cara looked up to discover the black eyes of the Earl of Malton looking mockingly down into her own. "You!" she exclaimed, forgetting any pretense at not knowing him. "And *I* should have thought *you* had enough sense to keep your horse out of the paths of other riders!" she snapped back, her green eyes beginning to flash as the dazed feeling left her. "What the deuce—"

But she got no further. Lord Wrothby, steadying her, was assailed by the subtle jasmine scent that

clung to her and by a sudden, overwhelming desir
to kiss the glowing, pink-cheeked face lifted to hi
Unable to think of any reason why he should no
he pulled her into his arms, enfolding her, and
bending his head, kissed her soft lips thoroughl
His hands drew delicious circles over her back an
began to slip down her sides.

Stunned for a moment by his audacity, Cara cam
to life, exclaiming against his mouth and ineffectu
ally struggling to fight herself free of him.

He lifted his mouth from hers, set her free s
suddenly she almost fell, and stepped back, smilin
lazily down at her. "I know you would like to shoo
me for that very pardonable offense, but I hope yo
will restrain yourself . . . *this time*."

Astounded, Cara stared and then, incensed b
yond endurance, threw up a hand willy-nilly to sla
the lazy, knowing look from his face.

The earl dodged and stopped her wrist adroitl
holding it aloft in a hard grip and remarking, "I a
not one of those men who enjoys fighting women
little wildcat. Women are for making love to. Yo
have a decidedly short memory." His black eye
glinted down at her as he held her wrist a momer
longer and then released it. "Shall I refresh it?"

For answer, Cara snatched her arm from him
pivoted on her heel, and stalked furiously to he
horse, cropping the grass not far away.

Trying to muster some semblance of her shattere
dignity, she mounted her animal without a back
ward glance and rode regally off, deliberately no
spurring the beast into a run though she longed t
do so to escape the mocking laughter she continue
to hear long after it had actually stopped.

Street vendors, beginning to come out in forc

now, were surprised to see such a fashionable lady passing at such an unfashionable hour. One or two were uncivil enough to turn their heads and gawk after her, and many more shook their heads wisely and made their guesses about where she was returning from, but none guessed from her sedate pace the tumult of her thoughts and feelings.

Her fury had soon given way to fright and dread as she rode home staring with unseeing eyes before her. The awful phrase, He knows! He knows! repeated itself tirelessly in her brain, punctuated every now and again by the other phrase, What shall I do?! What shall I *do?* which she could have wailed aloud. Worse, outraged as she was by it, she could not rid herself of the feel of the earl's lips and hands, which seemed to have set her on fire at every point he had touched.

Bates remarked on her heightened color as she let herself in, motioning vaguely, in what he presumed to be a wish to have someone attend to her horse, which he could plainly see tethered to the railing out front. He did not, however, deign to corroborate his guess with a question, for he was laboring to build for himself a reputation as one of those elite of elites—the omniscient butler.

Cara headed for the dining room feeling desperately in need of a bracing cup of coffee at the very least. She was brought up short by the sight of Elizabeth Dougherty, seated at the table enjoying a second breakfast (her own cook had provided the first) with her mother and exclaiming, between bites of Cook's good muffins, "I vow, Alicia my dear, 'tis not safe for ladies to drive out alone anymore with all the highwaymen running loose about London!"

Having come too far to retreat gracefully, Cara

continued toward the coffeepot and observed a trifl
grimly, "You are up early, ma'am," addressing Lad
Dougherty, as both ladies greeted her. She poure
herself a cup of coffee and moved to escape to he
room with it, highwaymen being, just at the mo
ment, a subject about which she cared to hear no
the smallest detail.

"Sit down, dear, you will want to hear this," com
manded Lady Dougherty, cutting her flight shor
and continuing, "It's a disgrace, it is, and I'm sure
don't know why the officers don't put a stop to it.

Reluctantly Cara sat, knowing that to refuse t
hear Lady Dougherty's news would be the best wa
in the world to offend that lady.

"My dears. . . ." She paused dramatically, an
Lady Brentwood perceived they were about to hea
the news which had brought her friend over so earl
in the day.

Cara fidgeted, anguishing over her encounter wit
the earl and unconsciously stirring her coffee, th
spoon clinking noisily against the sides of the cup

"My *dears*," repeated Lady Dougherty, starin
pointedly at the offending spoon.

Cara, becoming aware of Lady Dougherty's quel
ing regard, stopped stirring.

"That sweet little Maura—you remember her, Al
cia dear, don't you? She set her cap at Eva
Kirkland of the Drury estates and married him—
though how she brought him to the point I wish
knew! That sweet little thing was on her way to joi
Evan at the Roughton dinner, and she was stoppe
practically in the very streets of London! The ma
took every piece of jewelry she had on! But th
most wonderful part is that he was ever so polite t
her while he did so! She said she would hav

hought she was in her own drawing room by his manner! Can you imagine? Not but what he frightned her to death in spite of it all. He did have a istol, and, you know, she's naught but a mite of a hing.

"Well, she swooned dead away and the fool of a oachman didn't know what else to do but continue n to the Roughtons'. They all thought she was lead at first sight of her!"

"Good heavens!" returned Lady Brentwood, paling.

"Well you may say, my dear, for it might easily ave been one of us!

"Of course, Evan was furious about it. And he as been down to Headquarters twice now ready to un the officers through for not having caught the ellow and taken him straight up to Nob Hill!"

"Why does she believe he was not a common ighwayman?" asked Cara faintly, intrigued in Lady Dougherty's discourse in spite of herself.

"Oh my dear, how should I guess?" replied Lady Dougherty peevishly. "And I must say, I did not hink to ask! What is more to the point, can they get her jewels back?" She looked meaningly from Cara to Lady Brentwood, shaking her head sadly and clucking her tongue, making it plain she did not think so.

"She may have been wearing some pieces she houldn't like to lose. I know I should be prostrate o have my garnet necklace and earrings pinched. Tis not that it's my most expensive set, mind you. I ave many others which are of infinitely more value, can tell you!" Her mouth softened. "But George gave it me just after we were married . . ." She ighed, apparently remembering a pleasant episode

61

in their lives. "He said," she went on dreamily, "t[h]
stones reminded him of my mouth—because [of]
their color I must suppose—and the gold filigr[ee]
chain looked like hundreds of tiny knots to him—
love knots I should like to think—strung one aft[er]
another after another . . . Harrumph!" She bro[ke]
off, chagrined, and recollected herself.

"I know just how you feel, Betsy," said La[dy]
Brentwood, nodding her head, not the least bit embarrassed by her friend's show of emotion.

Cara murmured her assent, suppressing a[n]
amused smile.

"It is only, you see, that one should like to be ab[le]
to get her jewelry back—if 'twere pinched, yo[u]
know," finished Lady Dougherty.

"Rest assured, ma'am, you could get it back on[ce]
it were fenced, though it might take some months [to]
do so," said Cara without thinking, wishing to s[et]
Lady Dougherty's mind at ease.

Both ladies turned to look at her in surprise.

"My dear Cara, I did not know you were su[ch]
a book about highwaymen," commented La[dy]
Dougherty dryly, raising an eyebrow.

"Er—I read of it only recently in the papers,[""]
Cara fabricated hastily, rising and going to pour a[n]
other cup of coffee. "The article spoke of highwaymen and their, er, habits and mentioned sever[al]
holdups which have occurred on the outskirts [of]
London recently. It may be that Maura's was one [of]
them, poor thing," she said, hoping to divert bo[th]
ladies' attention back to Maura and her holdup.

Her strategy succeeded, for Lady Dougherty began again to commiserate with the absent Maura o[n]
her trying experience. While she denounced the ru[n]-
ners for allowing such dreadful experiences to befa[ll]

spectable ladies of breeding, Cara bid her mother
dieu with a silent wave and made good her escape.
Her mind anxiously returned to the Earl of Malton
s she mounted the stairs and went to her room to
eady herself for a morning call she hoped to receive
rom Mr. Dickson.

What *must* I do? And how dare he *kiss* me! she
thought, her cheeks burning. She heard again his
mocking laughter, and her hand itched to succeed in
slapping that smiling face. If that is not just like a
lord! she thought, scowling, the whole of the *beau
monde* suddenly telescoping into the single pre-
sumptuous figure of the Earl of Malton. If she
could best him in this business of highwaymen, she
would have bested the *ton* and avenged her father.
Lose, and she should go to prison or worse. She
shuddered.

But I shall not lose! she vowed. I shall think of
something, some way in which I may rid myself of
the problem of the Earl of Malton.

She sighed unhappily. If only he did not have
father's ring! If I could just get that back—Hold!
she thought, almost exclaiming aloud as an idea
that had been all but staring her in the face struck
her. Why not? she argued. Why *not* steal it back? It
could not be any more dangerous than holding up a
carriage—indeed, I should think it to be a sight eas-
er and safer since I shan't attempt it while the earl
s even in his apartments!

She should wait till he went out, some night when
there was not much moon and his servants should
have retired. Perhaps old Harry might be persuaded
to be her lookout, for she wouldn't countenance any
notions of his stealing it for her as she well knew he
was going to suggest. He was the one who had a

family to look after — what if he should be caugh
Her chin went up, and she grinned as she though
One should do one's own dirty work! A lookou
however, might not be a bad notion. At any rat
she was going to have to present the matter to o
Harry just so.

She then set the problem aside, having reache
what she considered a promising plan of action i
the hour and a half it had taken her to bathe the
change with Ellen's help into a pale blue dimity. Th
dress lent her a deceptively gentle air in the softne:
of its color, and she nodded her head approvingly :
her reflection and glanced at the clock on the mar
tel. She had spent rather more time than she shoul
have done in changing, for the morning was no
half gone. She had wanted to be ready and waitin
in the event that Mr. Dickson presented himself. Sh
therefore rushed Ellen throughout the dressing c
her curls.

When Ellen had finally finished, she sped dow
the stairs and fidgeted from the parlor to the ha
and back again, waiting expectantly. Since Mr. Dick
son had presented himself every morning now fo
the past week, she was tolerably certain that thi
morning would be no exception.

She was proven correct a moment later when th
knocker was heard to thump heavily against th
front door.

Bates punctiliously showed Mr. Dickson into th
parlor.

Cara fairly pounced upon him and dragged hin
to the settee in her happiness to see that he was in
deed setting up a regular pattern of morning calls
considering this to be an excellent sign of progres
in their courtship.

After sundry pleasantries of polite conversation, they rose from the settee and went for a sedate drive that was, after her unsettling encounter with the earl, most acceptably soothing in its nicety and uneventfulness.

Had she but known it, it was to be the last such drive she was to enjoy with Mr. Dickson for some time. For the next morning, though Mr. Dickson presented himself just as he had the morning before, there was another knock upon the parlor door just as they had once again risen from the settee.

The door swung open, and Bates announced, "Lord Wrothby!" as that gentleman sauntered across the threshold.

Nonplussed, Cara blushed remembering the previous morning. She observed, too, resentfully, that the events of that last meeting appeared to cause the earl not the smallest embarrassment in approaching her now. Indeed, she could believe he had forgotten his disgraceful behavior! She recovered herself quickly, however, and after only the slightest of pauses introduced the two gentlemen. Explaining to Lord Wrothby that she and Mr. Dickson had been about to go out, she politely implied that he had interrupted them and should come back another time.

Lord Wrothby, fully aware of her implications, brazenly ignored them. He clapped Mr. Dickson jovially upon the back and invited himself along. "What do you drive, old man?" he asked.

"A phaeton, sir," answered Mr. Dickson formally.

"Room for all of us, easily," declared Lord Wrothby. "Shall we go?" he asked, blithely disregarding the long faces of the two before him.

For James Dickson was no happier to see the earl than Cara. He had taken to calling upon her in the morning because at that time of day she was never surrounded by the circle of admirers that gathered around her everywhere she went. Slower in wit and shy by nature, he found it very difficult to gain her attention or hold a conversation with her in the presence of all those admirers. They distracted him with their bantering remarks from what he had been about to say to her, and he considered their interruptions rude in the extreme. Inevitably, he gave up, slightly annoyed, and removed himself from the crowd around her, hoping to catch her more privately at some later time.

His morning calls had been the perfect answer to his problem. Her usual circle of admirers, being younger, kept their beds later in the morning, sleeping after the previous night's indulgences. During his morning calls, he had found he could enjoy a pleasant, quiet chat with her free from silly, rude interruptions. The sight of Lord Wrothby during what he had come to consider *his* time with Cara filled him with misgivings. He was certain when she compared His Lordship's dashing appearance to that of his own rather more sedate style, he would come off the loser.

As they walked outside, he saw Lord Wrothby expertly maneuver himself to hand Cara up into his own phaeton and then take the seat beside her. A spirit of gloom descended upon him as he got in and seated himself opposite them, facing backward — a manner in which he detested riding because it was apt to make him ill. To make matters worse, Lord Wrothby increased his discomfort by directing his driver to "pick up the pace a little, can't you?"

Fortunately when they reached the park, Mr. Dickson's driver was forced to slow the phaeton to accommodate the many other riders and drivers enjoying the day's bright sunshine. But for his master the damage was already done. Though Cara did her best to keep him included in the conversation, he was increasingly hard-pressed to answer her in anything more than brief phrases and monosyllables, for his stomach had become decidedly nauseous.

Observing Mr. Dickson go slightly green about the gills and wishing to give him time in which to recover himself, Cara reluctantly turned her attention to the earl. "London is quite a city," she remarked lightly, purposely keeping the conversation on a general topic, "to house Parliament as well as the shops and merchants of Bond Street and yet retain something of the country." She indicated the park around them.

The earl agreed, surprised by her observation. Most women of his acquaintance cared only for the city's shops and the latest fashions that issued from them.

"I don't believe you have been in London long, Miss Brentwood? Are you just up for the London Season?" he returned pleasantly, steering the conversation back toward specifics.

She looked at him searchingly but saw only polite inquiry, mixed with what appeared to be a characteristic cynicism in his dark eyes. Guardedly, she answered, "I felt a change would benefit my mother's health. We . . . lost my father somewhat recently, under rather . . . rather unfortunate circumstances."

Her bald statement caught the earl off guard. But he answered with equal frankness, surprising Cara in turn, "Yes, I am aware. An unfortunate accident." His simple tone expressed all that was necessary.

Oddly Cara felt none of the awkwardness that

mention of her father's death usually caused. She was grateful, too, that the earl did not ask her to explain the "unfortunate circumstances."

The earl frowned. He found himself in the rare position of feeling excessively sympathetic toward an adventuress whose every word must be suspect and whom he had absolutely no wish to feel sorry for. Even Marion, formidable actress that she was, had never been able to elicit any emotion from him which he had not already been predisposed to feel. A very practiced jade indeed! he thought, appreciating Cara's skill. He decided that a little charm on his part would not be amiss and deftly turned the conversation.

"Do you attend Lady Harrows's musicale tonight, Miss Brentwood?"

"Why yes, but—forgive me, surely such a function is beneath your notice?" she replied, her green eyes beginning to twinkle.

He had to laugh at that, acknowledging her reading of him. Musicales did not number at the top of his list of entertainment. "I have attended one or two, I'll have you know. In point of fact, I've heard tonight's singer, one Madame Valparaiso."

"Indeed? And what may be your informed opinion of her talent?" Cara asked sweetly.

"Informed enough to know better than to attend a second time! Normally the singers that Lady Harrows engages are the very pink of the profession, for Lady Harrows used to sing herself at one time." He shook his head solemnly. "But even the best of us make mistakes—with the exception of myself, naturally!" He grinned at her, and Cara threw a glance skyward in mild disgust. "And Madame Valparaiso is assuredly one of Lady Harrows's!" Assuming a reflective air, he said, "One might say that she croaked, warbled—perhaps, yes, even yodeled. But *sing,* she did not!"

"Oh sir!" said Cara, laughing, genuinely amused at this description, "You are too harsh! I daresay it is difficult even to croak!"

He shook his head adamantly. "Ah, you have pity, my good woman, because you did not attend. Had you had to sit through two hours of that veritable torture, you would, er, sing," and Cara groaned at his pun, "a different tune!"

"You sat through two *hours* of her!" she asked sympathetically.

"Certainly not! I conveniently remembered a prior engagement that required my presence elsewhere. I merely state that if you *had—*"

"Gammon, sir!" interrupted Cara, chuckling.

"Not in the least!" returned the earl, grinning. He went on to tell her about some of the better and more famous talents who had performed for Lady Harrows, and it became obvious to Cara that, surprisingly, he was quite knowledgeable on the subject.

Mr. Dickson's driver began to take them around the other side of the park.

The earl, thinking the time ripe to discomfit his little adventuress, smiled lazily down at Cara and remarked, "I see you have relaxed that iron guard you had upon yourself at the outset of this drive."

Cara stiffened. She laughed, this time uncomfortably. She would have to remember how perceptive he was.

"Odd," he observed blandly, "you do not appear to be the ordinary rather empty-headed female socialite that I find so wearying." His dark eyes gleamed.

"Tell me, Miss Brentwood, how does the *freedom* of such country living as I am persuaded you are used to compare to living here in the city?" He brought his quizzing glass up. "No doubt you find all the meticulous rules of London social life . . . constraining?"

Cara looked at him sharply. His black eyes mocked her. She glanced quickly at Mr. Dickson. There was still a greenish cast to his skin, and he sat with his eyes closed. Thankfully he did not appear to be attending. But clearly he should also be of no help to her in diverting the subject.

Shifting uncomfortably against the phaeton's cushions, Cara gave a short laugh of irritation and evaded the earl's question. "Surely, Lord Wrothby, on such a beautiful day as this we can think of a less bookish subject to discuss? I vow I should have to write a treatise on that one!"

"No doubt you find a discussion of rules, or, ah, *laws,* Miss Brentwood, a tedious subject?" he asked softly, his black eyes glinting under the lazy, half-closed lids.

Cara did not at all care for the turn the conversation was taking, and she liked even less the small cynical smile that seemed to have grown more pronounced on His Lordship's face. Her previous delight in the earl's humor faded. Now why has he decided to play the boor? Cara wondered crossly. He has been quite good company up till now! Making an effort to remain pleasant and wishing he might return to his former amiable self, she asked in a low voice, "I am not sure I take your meaning?"

He leaned close, his eyes glinting wickedly, and said, "I think you take it very well, my dear. But I

70

will make it plainer. How does the subject of highwaymen appeal to you?"

"It doesn't!" she snapped, recoiling. Searching for any excuse to relieve the situation and courteously remove her attention from the earl, Cara spotted an elderly friend of her mother's not far off.

"Oh, look! There is Lady Beaufort," she declared loudly, trying to rouse Mr. Dickson. "I have not seen her in an age. We simply must go and say hello to her!" And not waiting for the earl to signal the driver, she directed him herself to drive them over to Lady Beaufort's carriage and stop there so that she might greet her.

But Lady Beaufort, having exchanged pleasantries with her, drove off all too soon, and Cara heard the earl say close to her ear, "Come. I find your company entertaining when it is not on the wrong side of a pistol. Give over whatever corkbrained schemes you have devised—for they are corkbrained, I assure you!—and let me set you up in your own little apartment, anywhere in the city you like. I shall see that you have everything your greedy little heart desires, and we will speak no more of highwaymen." One hand traveled up to set an unruly curl back in place.

Cara repulsed his hand as if it had bitten her and, blushing hotly, stared at him in mortification. He thought her a—a—lightskirt! And he was so certain of her, sitting before her smiling complacently, nay, patronizingly, waiting for her to *accept!* Of all the conceit! she fumed. The supreme arrogance of the man! Her green eyes sparkled with anger as she racked her brain for words cutting enough to express her outrage.

Providentially out of the corner of her eye, she

saw a figure on horseback canter up beside the carriage. Knowing Mr. Dickson to be still unequal to the task of coming to her aid and not caring who it might be in her patent desire to deliver the earl a set-down, she ignored the entire subject of highwaymen and consequent mistresses and behaved for the benefit of all who might be watching them as if he had merely invited her to attend Lady Harrows's musicale that evening. "Oh, my lord, I *am* sorry," she answered, in a gleeful tone which bespoke no regret at all. "I cannot. I am already engaged *with my mother,*" she emphasized pointedly, her green eyes flashing, "to entertain the good Viscount here and some few friends at a dinner party we are giving tonight. You know Viscount Lyle?" she finished, a slight smile curving her lips as she watched her words wipe the expectant smile from the earl's face.

It was replaced with a look of faint incredulity, and then his brows snapped together in a black line and he clamped his mouth shut in suppressed anger. He hadn't expected the jade to turn him down, much less his wealth, and he certainly hadn't been prepared for her to do it in such an unpleasantly public manner!

"I am sorry. Another time, perhaps?" she added sweetly in a tone that made the earl wish to crook his fingers about her pretty neck.

There! thought Cara. That should take you down a peg, you odious man!

The viscount, quick to realize he had been favored over the earl, filled the breach. "We are acquainted."

To Cara's polite inquiry if the Viscount Lyle were known to him, Mr. Dickson could only nod his head miserably in the affirmative.

"Sir, you will not have forgotten you are to dine at our home tonight at eight, will you?" asked Cara.

The viscount pretended to look shocked. "I could never do that, my dear Cara," he answered gallantly.

"Until tonight then, sir," she said, irritated by his suave playacting. "It is time I returned home. I have many things yet to do to prepare for this evening."

His black eyes blazing with anger, the earl looked into Cara's green eyes, still sparkling with the heat of battle, and said sardonically, "I am sure you do. Your servant, Lyle!" he said curtly and impatiently signaled Mr. Dickson's driver to turn the phaeton around.

The three returned, in a silence bristling with unspoken emotions, to Cara's house. She fussed over Mr. Dickson a moment before stepping down from the carriage and then politely expressed the hope that he would be feeling better and call upon her again tomorrow.

He gave her a feeble smile and mumbled something indistinguishable.

The earl, stiff with anger, bid his own grim goodbye to Mr. Dickson and handed her to her door. In a voice heavy with sarcasm, he said, "I hope your dinner may be as successful as the time you have obviously taken in planning it!" and giving a short bark of laughter he turned on his heel, marched to his curricle, and drove off at a speed that caused his groom to roll his eyes toward heaven and cross himself fervently.

As Bates opened the door, Cara walked in feeling very pleased with herself, satisfied that she had delivered the Earl of Malton a much deserved setdown. He will certainly keep his distance from me after this! she thought, chuckling again at the jut of his chin as he had whipped up his horses and raced off.

Curiously she was conscious of a tiny feeling of disappointment. Ignoring it, she thought dryly, No doubt, no one has ever snubbed that one before. And high time someone did too! Mistress, *indeed!* she snorted. But she had no time to stand congratulating herself over the earl if she hoped to have everything ready for a small party to sit down at eight that evening.

Picking the mail up from the salver on her way through the hall, she asked, "Where can I find my mother, Bates?"

"She's out with Lady Sheldon and some friends, miss," he replied with dignity.

"Oh drat!" excalimed Cara, passing on into the dining room and forgetting the presence of Bates behind her.

Bates did not so far forget himself as to start at his mistress's rude exclamation, but his eyebrows shot up involuntarily. Auspiciously, however, her back was turned to him.

Cara sat down at the table and quickly sifted through the invitations and calling cards that had accumulated in her absence. Well, I cannot wait for her return, she thought. I haven't really enough time as it is.

An invitation caught her eye. A picnic! she exclaimed to herself as she scanned the card. What a capital idea! I shall write Lady Marston and accept — but tomorrow shall be time enough for that. Right now, I must go and see to the menu for tonight.

Mentally listing the things she must do to prepare for her dinner party, she rose and went into the kitchen. Diplomatically she changed the York ham her mother had ordered for the two of them to raised pigeon pie and told Cook to add four places. Then, because she well-knew from her days at Brentwood Crest — when she had helped in the kitchen and her father had brought home an unexpected guest — how disruptive it was to have the menu changed only a few short hours before the meal was to be served, she blatantly flattered Cook and told her she might have free rein over what she served as the side dishes. She left the large woman beaming with her flattery and busily cogitating an opportunity to express her creativity.

She then hurried into the parlor and composed two notes at the escritoire there. Their contents were much the same, saying only that she knew it was extremely short notice, but she hoped her friends had no other engagements and would forgive her and make one of a small dinner party she found herself in the necessity of having to put together at the last minute. Promising each of them good company but purposely giving them no explanations, she sealed her notes with wafers. That ought to bring them, she thought wickedly, and gave them to Bates to have them delivered immediately — one to Lady Dougherty and her husband and one to Captain Perkins, a tart, white-haired old gentleman who had become an especial friend of hers.

All three, she felt, were close-enough friends that she might count upon them to come in this emergency. George will not like it above half, she laughed to herself, but I've no doubt Betsy, agog with questions, will bring him! Besides, I am certain he shall like Captain Perkins enormously. She was equally sure Captain Perkins wouldn't fail her, for she knew him to hold her in great affection.

She had now only to prepare the dining-room table attractively with candles and an arrangement of fresh flowers and explain matters to her mother when she came in, which Lady Brentwood did very shortly thereafter.

She clicked her tongue sadly over her daughter's hasty temper but apparently felt it was not the moment to scold if they were to get Cara out of her scrape and set about helping her daughter finish the table preparations.

By the time that was accomplished, they had just enough time to have a bath and change their dresses before their guests were due to arrive.

Lady Dougherty and her husband were the first to be admitted, arriving a full ten minutes before eight in order, Cara suspected, for Lady Dougherty to try and pump an explanation out of her mother before the other guests arrived. Captain Perkins was announced promptly at eight o'clock, and the viscount several minutes later, and they all went in to dinner.

George Dougherty had indeed looked glum on his entrance but, as Cara had foreseen, was soon laughing heartily with everyone else at the tart humor of Captain Perkins and enjoying second helpings that did credit to Cook's ingenuity.

When the meal was over, Cara got out a deck of cards, and they struck up a rousing game of loo, passing the remainder of the evening most enjoyably.

"All in all," crowed Cara to her mother after the door had closed on their last guest, "I should say the dinner came off without a hitch." As well, she thought spitefully, remembering the earl's last words to her, as if it had been planned for weeks!

"Thank goodness for the Doughertys and Captain Perkins," replied Lady Brentwood pointedly.

"Yes," agreed Cara absently as they went up the stairs together to retire. The only mar in the evening, she reflected, had been in the attentions of Viscount Lyle. He had been just a shade more familiar than she liked, and she had frequently, throughout the meal and the game of loo, looked up to discover him staring at her with eyes that were unnervingly bright over the puffy circles beneath them. My own fault I suppose, she reproved herself, for the off-hand manner in which I invited him. Well, he is said to be rich as Croesus, and I do not doubt, should the need arise, I would be very capable of restraining his attentions, she thought, and dismissed him from her mind.

A knock sounded at the front door.

Lady Brentwood stopped and turned in surprise to Cara. She also stopped, shrugging back at her mother in equal surprise, as they heard Bates go to answer the door.

There were low voices and then Bates appeared at the foot of the stairs and announced very nearly in his usual dignified tone (though he privately thought it very far from usual and slightly indecent at such a late hour), *"These* have just arrived for Miss Cara." He held up a vase of red jasmines.

"Oh no," groaned Cara and descended the stairs to take the flowers from Bates.

Bates discreetly withdrew.

"Who are they from?" asked Lady Brentwood curiously.

"Lord Wrothby," replied Cara, reading the card that was attached. "A very pretty note," she said appreciatively. "He is apologizing to *me* for *his* behavior!" She strode out of the hall taking the flowers with her.

"Surely that is a good thing?" her mother asked bewilderedly of her daughter's receding back.

"No, it is not," Cara answered, coming back into the hall several moments later and climbing the stairs again. "For I do not believe he means it in the least!" she said angrily.

Since her mother had no idea why the Earl of Malton should put himself to the trouble of writing an apology he did not mean, she merely nodded her head, for a moment hoping that Cara might enlighten her.

When Cara said nothing further, Lady Brentwood remarked, "Well, they shall certainly look lovely on the dining-room table," at a loss to understand her daughter's displeasure.

"They are in the kitchen," said Cara brusquely. "Cook may do whatever she likes with them!"

This statement appeared to bereft Lady Brentwood of speech, for she exclaimed, "In the *kitchen—!*" and turned at the top of the stairs to look at her daughter in astonishment.

But, anger still in her eyes, Cara only wished her mother good night and entered her bedchamber, shutting the door behind her with a firm click.

Lady Brentwood knew from long years of experience that no amount of coaxing would make Cara tell her what was wrong before she was ready, so she, too, frowning thoughtfully, retired to her bedchamber.

Cara allowed Ellen to assist her out of her dark emerald silk before shooing her off to help her mother. Once the maid had gone, an anxious frown appeared on her brow.

The earl had ruined her drive with Mr. Dickson. In terms of their courtship, she had made absolutely no progress with him today, incapacitated as he had been. Worse, the earl's insufferable behavior toward her—she couldn't be sure how much of it Mr. Dickson had or had not observed—might have caused Mr. Dickson to doubt the success of his courtship of her. She would just have to wait and see.

She pressed her lips together, growing angry again as she remembered the earl's insulting proposal. She was not foolish enough to believe his apology sincere. But why he should take such pains, after her deliberate snub, too, she could not fathom.

She pulled on a white cambric nightdress and got into bed. Why, she asked herself, knowing that I played the highwayman, should he behave as if he wished to court me instead of denouncing me to the Authorities?

She fluffed her pillow violently and lay down, staring up into the darkness. What could the man be up to?

Five

Cara came awake suddenly the next morning, frightened by a nightmare in which the earl, dressed in the uniform of a constable, had pursued her through the streets of London and finally cornered her against a wall at the end of a dark cobblestoned lane. At his, "I hereby ARREST you in the name of—!" she woke to find herself half out of bed with tiny beads of perspiration dotting her forehead.

"This cannot go on," she said in a voice of determination. "Old Harry and I must make plans." She rose, frowning, and rang for Ellen.

Soaking in the warm, scented water, Cara listened to the maid chatter as her dress was laid out and felt the last wisps of fear caused by her nightmare recede. Her body relaxed, and her mind began to formulate several ideas for burgling the earl's apartments.

She descended the stairs in an embroidered peach cambric feeling very much more the thing after her bath, and sat down to breakfast cheerfully with her mother revolving several now well-formed plans on how she and old Harry might go about the burglary.

Thus it was that all thoughts of a morning call from Mr. Dickson slipped completely from her mind. She left immediately after breakfast to go and confer with old Harry and thereby missed Mr. Dickson when he arrived a quarter of an hour later.

He got down from his phaeton only to be met at the door by Bates with the information that Miss Brentwood was out and it was not known when she was expected to return.

Reflecting dejectedly that it was probably Lord Wrothby who had supplanted him again, he climbed back into his carriage and directed his driver to take him to his club where he might consider this new rival for Cara's affections with the aid of a strong cup of tea and the advice, should he desire it, of his good friend Lord Dougherty, who was very likely to be there at that hour of the morning.

When Cara returned to the house that afternoon and was informed that Mr. Dickson had called, she frowned, biting her lower lip in vexation for allowing herself to be so remiss as to forget about him entirely. But she had to admit that the morning had been well-spent in spite of missing him.

Old Harry had been easier to persuade than she had expected. He had had news of his own to tell her: runners had been nosing about Brentwood Crest and asking neighbors a lot of meddlesome questions. He had felt, as she had, that if they might just get the ring back the only link between them and the holdups would vanish. Then let the runners quiz till they were blue in the face! 'Twould do them no good without proof.

So they were agreed. The quicker they got the ring back, the safer they would both be, and old Harry had fallen to planning with her with as much enthusiasm as she could have wished.

Now, once he had gleaned the information they

needed, they had naught to do but wait for a moonless night. Cara frowned. She felt old Harry had the lion's share of the work to do, but he was right. He could ask more questions about the earl's household without arousing suspicion than she could. So she would gather the materials they would require, and when he learned of a night the Earl of Malton would be away from home, providing the moon was slight, he would signal her.

With the ring back in her possession, the earl would pose no threat, for he would no longer have a shred of evidence. Then, as he would surely realize, it would be merely a matter of his word against hers, and she imagined most would find it difficult to credit that she had held up a carriage without strong proof of it.

She laughed out loud, imagining the look upon the earl's face when he discovered the ring gone. It had been worth missing Mr. Dickson, just this once, to set her worries to rest. She sighed, much satisfied. She almost felt like she had the ring back already!

Due, perhaps, to that fact, she found that she enjoyed herself enormously that evening at young Lady Camrose's party. Although as she had suspected, Mr. Dickson and Viscount Lyle had not been included among the guests, quite a number of her usual circle of admirers had, and she delighted in the quick verbal play, bandying words back and forth with them, which she was usually forced to forego in the conservative company of Mr. Dickson and the rather studied company of the viscount.

Before the night was much advanced, however, a sense of anxiety, caused by the time she felt herself to be wasting since neither gentleman was there, assailed her. Trying to ignore it, Cara caught sight of the Earl of Malton on the other side of the room.

Almost as if she had called to him, he finished speaking with a jovial and absurdly curly-haired young gentleman and looked up, pompously turning his quizzing glass upon those around him as if deciding whom he would speak with next. Observing that she watched him, he swept her an ironic bow and began to saunter across the floor to her.

Cara blushed firily and averted her eyes, mentally berating herself for getting caught at observing him.

"Your two swains not here tonight, Miss Brentwood?" he mocked, coming to her side.

"I don't know whom you mean, Lord Wrothby," she answered sweetly.

"Why, the scintillating Mr. Dickson and the suave Viscount, of course," he drawled.

"I don't believe so, now that you bring it to my attention."

"Ah. Then I need not exert myself," he remarked, appearing, if possible, even more relaxed.

Astonished, Cara gasped, "Do you mean you are *trying* to drive them away from me?"

"Surely that is obvious, Miss Brentwood?" he replied softly. He came very close to her, his eyes gleaming sardonically and one arm rising as if he would put it about her waist, and continued in a caressing tone, "I do not intend to share you with them."

Cara escaped his arm with the smooth, practiced movement she had had to develop since coming to London. She faced him and said distinctly, "You will do me the favor, Lord Wrothby, not to speak to me as if I were a chucklehead. I am not so foolish as to be taken in by such flummery." Turning on her heel, she marched off to where she could see Lady Brentwood sitting some little distance away, absorbed in talking with a friend.

And *that* ought to belie any intimacy between us, she thought, if anyone did remark us. She glanced over her shoulder to see how the earl had taken her departure and discovered him to be still staring after her, his eyes gleaming with appreciative laughter and an odd little smile upon his face. Incensed that he should be laughing at her, she whisked herself back around and thereafter took pains to avoid him for the remainder of the evening.

The next morning Cara rose early, eager to begin work again on Mr. Dickson. She attired herself in a pale green gown which just set off her hair and eyes and, knowing herself to look her best, went down to eat a sustaining breakfast and wait impatiently for Mr. Dickson's arrival.

She watched the clock on the parlor mantel tick maddeningly on and finally began picking up periodicals, flipping through them, and then throwing them down to jump up at intervals and stride worriedly back and forth across the room. When, at half past eleven, Mr. Dickson had still not put in an appearance, it became apparent that he was not coming.

Drat Lord Wrothby! Cara thought furiously, her worry changing to anger as she considered it was probably the earl's fault that Mr. Dickson had today broken his habitual morning calls. It was not in the least a good sign, and Cara felt keenly that her time was slipping through her fingers like the proverbial sands through the hourglass. What *can* I do? she thought, her anger changing back to worry.

Abruptly she stopped her pacing and went to the

parlor window to stare down at the carriages passing in the street below. If only I might see Mr. Dickson tonight, she mused, I could set things to right in a moment. But the party she was attending that evening was again that of a younger set, and she doubted seriously whether he would be included. I cannot very well send for him, which means I must wait until he calls again. She groaned inwardly at the thought, for she was not very optimistic about when that might be, by now knowing well Mr. Dickson's timidity. Unless . . . I may see him at something later in the week — Lady Banridge's party perhaps.

Cara felt her anger at the earl return. She in no way liked having her control over the situation removed and left, as it were, to chance, for she did not at all depend upon Mr. Dickson to pursue matters between them.

Plague take the earl! she thought again. "I hope his grays may toss him on his head!" she said aloud, and, attaching several more quite unladylike epithets to that dark head, she gave up upon Mr. Dickson for the day and went off to distract herself in doing something useful by paying some of the bills she and her mother had so far incurred.

Two days later, as Cara went about her usual morning activities listening intently all the while for the heavy knocker to sound against the front door and hoping against hope it would be Mr. Dickson, she was indeed gratified to hear it.

It was not, however, Mr. Dickson but Viscount Lyle who had come to take her for a drive in the park and prove to himself, as well as to all the wagging tongues, that neither Dickson nor Wrothby had yet cut him out of her affections.

Far from being disappointed that her visitor was not Mr. Dickson, Cara was equally glad to drive out with the viscount and herself prove to the odious Lord Wrothby, should he accost her, that he had not driven away at least one of her serious suitors.

She had been driving with the viscount in the park for nearly a quarter of an hour, alternately nodding to acquaintances and catching up on what the viscount had been doing in the interval since her dinner party, when they both observed the Earl of Malton, astride his beautiful black stallion, bearing down upon them with two friends in tow.

"Ah, Viscount Lyle," he hailed them when they were within speaking distance, "and the acclaimed Miss Brentwood. Are you acquainted with Lord Mercer and Miss Quincy?" He indicated his friends. "We are just about to go on a tour of some of the more unusual older residences in London. Miss Quincy," he addressed a tiny, blond young woman, "Miss Brentwood is also new to the city and, I am persuaded, would like nothing better than to join us." Cara's eyebrows shot up in amazement at this piece of information, and the earl threw her a lazy smile.

Miss Quincy exclaimed, "Oh! But she must come with us then!" and spurred her horse round to Cara's side of the viscount's carriage, thinking she had found someone of similar background and interests. Lapsing into a thick country brogue, she began talking excitely of the things she had done so far on her first visit to London. "For I want to see and do simply *everything!*" she breathed ingenuously and, without pausing, launched into a detailed description of her life at home in Macclesfield.

Cara began to understand all too well the earl's

smile. I should have known! she groaned inwardly. She regarded the earl with narrowed eyes as Miss Quincy prattled on beside her.

Lord Mercer, sitting his horse with as straight a back as any riding master could have wished, nodded politely in acknowledgement of the introductions and wondered why the earl should wish to invite Viscount Lyle, about whom he had heard quite a few unsavory stories, along with them. Naively he supposed it had something to do with the viscount's beautiful companion. He was, at any rate, inordinately grateful that the earl should take so much trouble for his country cousin, whom he knew to be not quite up to the mark — at least, not *yet* she wasn't, he thought loyally.

Under the circumstances, the viscount, without being boorish, had no choice but to acquiesce, which he did, cursing the earl roundly under his breath.

For his part, the earl, knowing himself to be irritating both Cara and the viscount, enjoyed the situation immensely and led the group off on the most circuitous route about the back streets of London he could devise.

At one of the frequent stops before old houses — a magnificent old building that truly had some architectural merit — the earl gave its history and then brought his horse round to break in upon Miss Quincy's chatter. Pointedly he drawled, "Enjoying yourself, Miss Brentwood?"

"Oh yes, indeed!" she replied and smiled politely as she allowed a vision of the earl in the most awful fate she could invent for him — wedded to the prolix Miss Quincy — to occupy her imagination.

"I felt certain you would be," he grinned and left

her to the unceasing Miss Quincy to go back to the front of the group and lead them on to view another house.

Cara sighed and turned her attention reluctantly back to the young woman.

"Do you suppose people really *live* in that house?" Miss Quincy asked in awed tones.

Five houses later, the earl took mercy upon Cara and, announcing their tour at an end, began to lead the group back toward the park.

Seeing Miss Quincy direct a question to the viscount and take her horse around the carriage to walk between him and Lord Mercer, the earl brought his horse up beside Cara again. He was silent for several minutes, merely keeping his horse level with the carriage.

Finally in a voice that hinted at laughter, he said, "You deserved that, you know—payment for that rarified set-down you gave me the other day."

Surprised, Cara looked up to see the dark eyes twinkling at her, for once with no trace of cynicism or mockery in them. Her own eyes flashed dangerously as she remembered the proposal that had preceded her set-down. "That is a matter of opinion, Lord Wrothby!"

"Come," he invited, apparently enjoying provoking her, "I have forgiven you—I have even sent flowers, for which I have received no thanks, I might add. Can you not forgive me?"

"You have an ulterior motive," Cara accused. The earl laughed. Her next remark, however, rankled. "And I don't believe for a moment you have truly forgiven me." She looked pointedly at his shoulder.

The earl ignored her glance and went on as if he hadn't heard her. "I do not even require flowers—or, perhaps, only one, ah, particular flower," he said wickedly.

"Oh!" Cara flushed and averted her face. "I shall not dignify that last abominable remark with an answer," she said haughtily.

"Coming it a bit too strong, my girl," chuckled the earl, smiling at her hauteur.

But Cara was not destined to hear what else the earl might have said, for just then Miss Quincy descended upon them and kept up a seemingly breathless monologue all the way back to the park.

Once there, the earl immediately made good his escape. "Gentlemen, ladies," he excused himself, "I have business with my lawyer that must be attended to. I hope you will forgive me if I take my leave of you."

"Another convenient 'prior engagement', Lord Wrothby?" Cara asked quizzically as he began to move off.

The earl threw her a grin and urged his horse into a canter.

The four of them were left rather awkwardly together to watch him disappear among the crowd of milling carriages and riders. Fortunately for Cara, Lord Mercer felt that without the earl the viscount was not, despite his beautiful companion, the best company for his cousin and soon politely took his leave of them and bore Miss Quincy, still talking happily, off with him.

Curiously, instead of being angry with the earl, Cara felt quite in charity with him. A sentiment echoed, if she had but known it, by the earl as he had departed.

Each had given as good as he had got, each had discomfited the other, and their contest of sallies had ended in a draw. Thus each had been left with the satisfying feeling of having faced off with a worthy opponent and come off tolerably well.

Paradoxically Cara almost wished she might have enjoyed the earl's company a trifle longer, without the vexing presence of Miss Quincy, to be sure.

But, glancing at the viscount's cold countenance, she promptly forgot the wish as she realized that somehow she must erase the tedious effect of the earl's tour. The viscount must be left feeling that he had enjoyed his morning's drive with her. Consequently she asked him if he would not like to drive round the park once more before he took her home. By concentrating all her attention on him and teasing him gently, she had him smiling at her in good humor once more and promising to call upon her again in the next day or two by the time they pulled up before her front door.

As Bates closed the front door upon the viscount's retreating back, Cara allowed a smug smile to curve her lips. She was excessively pleased with the progress she was making with the viscount.

As she walked, however, into the dining room picking up the mail and glancing through the invitations, it was not the viscount's bright hazel eyes she was remembering but Lord Wrothby's twinkling black ones.

Six

Cara was standing by the parlor window looking out and occasionally turning back to carry on a desultory conversation with Lady Brentwood, who was sitting in one of the comfortable overstuffed chairs working on her embroidery.

"Thunder and turf! I don't believe it!" she cried involuntarily and then faced her mother and stated in tones of patent disbelief, "Mr. Dickson has just driven up in his phaeton."

"Oh, Cara, I am so glad," answered her mother. The front door knocker sounded heavily as if to confirm that her daughter wasn't dreaming.

"There's no need to sound that relieved," Cara teased. "I know I've not been the best of company lately, but I didn't think I'd been an ogre."

"My dear you know I didn't mean—" began her mother apologetically and then saw the glint in Cara's green eyes. "You are . . . roasting me!" she cried indignantly, using one of Cara's words.

"I am—with infinite pleasure," Cara agreed, smiling mischievously.

"I should have sold you to the gypsies long ago," retorted her mother, surprising Cara into a laugh.

"A rare hit, *Maman,*" she acknowledged appreciatively.

Bates came to the doorway and announced, "The Honorable Mr. Dickson," and withdrew.

That gentleman came nervously into the room and stopped. "Good afternoon, ladies," he began.

Lord Dougherty, on being asked for his opinion, had advised him to "run with the bit between your teeth, man, until the filly throws you!" which Mr. Dickson had taken to mean that he might continue to court Miss Brentwood with an eye toward success. But now that he was here, he could not for the life of him think what to say next.

Observing this, Cara took matters out of his hands. "Mr. Dickson, what a *most* pleasant surprise," she said in her very warmest tone. Then, to make her point clearly to him, she stated simply, "I have missed you lately."

Mr. Dickson turned pink.

Hah! Cara exulted silently, thinking of the earl. You lost that battle, Lord Wrothby. He is back in spite of you! And now, I shall make up for all the time you've cost me, she continued to herself, thinking nothing of the fact that she was addressing a person who was not physically present in the room.

Skillfully she maneuvered Mr. Dickson into suggesting that they take a walk while allowing him the impression that it had been his own idea. Inviting her mother to come along, Cara fixed her with a look that told her in no uncertain terms she didn't expect her to accept.

Lady Brentwood, her cough sounding suspiciously like laughter, politely declined the offer, and, stammering his goodbye, Mr. Dickson felt himself swept out of the house and down the front steps.

Brazenly putting her arm through his, Cara started down the street with him. Not giving an awkward silence a chance to develop, she turned toward Mr. Dickson and asked playfully, "And what very important business have you been attending to that has kept you so long away from me?" She gave him a pouting look and fixed her large green eyes on him, appearing to be awaiting the pearls of wisdom that could only fall from his lips.

He blushed again and bashfully related a long-winded, rather disjointed account of his activities over the last week. To Cara it sounded as if he hadn't been doing much of anything except attending his club and talking to Lord Dougherty.

By the time he began to bring a halting speech that could only loosely be termed an account to an end, they had reached the park. Cara continued to stroll on, pulling him along, admiring the flowers and the lush green trees, and confiding to him anything she could think of to flatter him and build his confidence where she was concerned.

Too soon for her liking, afraid he had tired her, he suggested that they turn back. Equally afraid that she had tired *him,* she agreed, and they began to retrace their steps, Cara drawing him out and getting him to talk about some of his younger days.

"Why, it is Miss Brentwood! And, I do believe, Mr. Dickson," broke in a familiar drawl, and there followed the sound of a carriage pulling up.

Dismayed, Cara spun round to see the Earl of Malton, resplendent in a dark green coat over almond pantaloons, looking her insolently up and down through his quizzing glass from the height of his curricle. Beside him sat a pretty older woman engaged in patting her light brown curls back in to place while she observed Cara with a measuring look.

Oh rot! thought Cara. How does he always manage to discover me here? One would think he had either some sixth sense or very good spies!

"I vow, Julius, your dear one does not look at all happy to see you. What have you been doing to her?"

Smiling, the earl introduced his companion to Cara and Mr. Dickson, "The infamous Lady Laval."

"Don't be silly," she answered, objecting mildly to his epithet. She tapped his arm smartly with her fan and commanded, "Your hand, please. I want to get down."

Answering Lady Laval's question, the earl smiled mockingly at Cara and replied, "I fear I have been remiss in my attendance upon her, and she has been reduced to walking out with Dickson here." Jumping down as he spoke, he clapped Mr. Dickson roughly on the shoulder and gave him a friendly shake.

"How do you do, ma'am. How do you do again, Wrothby, t'be sure," responded Mr. Dickson civilly, wondering glumly if he were going to be forever plagued by the Earl of Malton every time he went out in Miss Brentwood's company.

"Julius!" commanded Lady Laval again, recalling the earl to help her down from his carriage. He sauntered round the curricle and handed her down.

"So this is the Incomparable! I have been wanting to meet you, my dear. You are, just as they say, very beautiful!" she said, causing Cara to blush.

Turning to Mr. Dickson, the lady advised, "You must not mind Lord Wrothby today, Mr. Dickson. He is being a devil. Rather, we should all have pity on the poor boy because he hasn't the self-restraint we do!" She threw a mock glare at the object of her dig, who merely grinned broadly back at her.

"I myself," she continued, "am already quite out of patience with him. I was conversing contentedly with my own friends when what must this madman do but dash up in his racing carriage and drag me away from them. And for what? To talk with me? No! To come and disturb you two poor children! And I am sorry for it, but here we are, and you may as well make the best of it."

"Besides," she said, addressing Cara's chagrined expression, "if it is out of the regular, tedious routine of things, there is something to be said for it surely?" Ordinarily Cara would have agreed with her. "Don't be cross," she scolded Cara lightly. "I am an old married lady—*happily* married, I might point out—and you shall have him back soon enough." She linked arms with Mr. Dickson and began to stroll off, saying, "We shall only accompany you a little ways to wherever it was you were walking. You were heading south, were you not?" But Mr. Dickson's answer could not be heard.

Left standing with the earl, Cara faced him and asked caustically, "Did you have to promise her your best matched pair to get her to help you?"

He chuckled. "A masterful piece of strategy, don't you agree? Lady Laval is an old friend of mine. As I once, er, helped her out of a sad scrape, she would stoop to any level for me," he smiled blandly down at her, "—though I must admit this took some coaxing on my part. She didn't think descending upon you two lovebirds in very good taste.

"But I convinced her you really would not mind because you had much rather be with me in the first place." Cara choked. "And then you go and pull such a long face!" he chided mockingly. "You

95

will have her believing you *do* prefer that stuffed shirt—"

"I do!" Cara interrupted hotly.

"Depend upon it, I shall have some explaining to do when she gets me alone again!" He sighed loudly and bent an aggrieved look upon her.

Cara glared back at him and finally had to laugh in exasperation. "Really, Lord Wrothby, you are insufferable!" She began to walk after Lady Laval and Mr. Dickson.

"Mort!" the earl called, beginning to walk with her. His groom appeared to take the reins of the curricle and follow at a discreet distance. "So I am often told," the earl answered and grinned at her.

In spite of herself, Cara found herself smiling back. "Tell me something, Lord Wrothby. How do you manage to accost me *every* time I come to the park?"

Without hesitation, the earl replied matter-of-factly, "I employ spies," and grinned again.

Cara gasped. Though she had thought it earlier, she hadn't really believed it. She didn't think she believed it now, either. "Oh, do stop talking fustian! What stuff!"

The earl tried a second answer. "Fate?"

Cara laughed. "Now that I might believe. No doubt, Lady Fate is exacting penance for some, er, rather large untruths I told some time ago," she teased without thinking.

As if she had reminded him of something unpleasant, the earl's eyes narrowed, and he looked at her intently, "Oh? And what might they have been?" he asked softly.

Something in the way he looked at her made Cara nervously increase her pace to catch up with the others. "Oh, the . . . the . . . usual little white lies," she stammered uneasily, mentally cursing herself for letting her tongue run away with her.

"Ah . . . I should turn you over to the runners, Miss Brentwood," he replied slowly.

"What!" Cara gasped.

"For telling little white lies," he answered deliberately. "My dear Miss Brentwood," he said solicitously, "you look quite alarmed. Whatever is the matter? You are not going to faint?" His arm went round her and brought her close in a clasp so tight she would have sworn he was trying to squeeze the breath from her rather than steady her against fainting.

Taken aback, her eyes flew to his face and received the shock of his black eyes blazing furiously down at her.

Exasperatingly, in the midst of his anger, the earl felt an absurd desire to kiss her again. His angry gaze raked her lips.

His mouth only inches away from her own, keenly aware of the hard, muscled arm that held her, Cara felt as if he burnt her. The blood rushed to her cheeks, and she started to struggle.

"There is no need," he said coldly, instantly letting her go. She staggered, striving to regain her balance.

"Don't feel well, Miss Brentwood?" Mr. Dickson's blunt question broke in.

Lady Laval came up behind him saying, "I wish you two will stop dawdl—" and stopped abruptly as she viewed the two faces before her. "Julius, you *are* wicked! Depend upon it, Mr. Dickson, he has been making love to poor Miss Brentwood, and it is that which has upset her."

As if to confirm this, the earl allowed a roguish

smile to curve his lips.

Cara, not in the least wishing Mr. Dickson to think this, interrupted vehemently, "No! Indeed, that is *not — !*"

But Lady Laval already had perceived her mistake as well as the frown that had appeared on Mr. Dickson's face and amended hastily, "No, no, of course not. Truly Mr. Dickson, you are too gullible. I was but joking with you. No doubt the sun has merely made Miss Brentwood feel a trifle faint as it frequently does me, is this not so, Miss Brentwood?" she asked, and Cara quickly agreed. "The thing to be done is to get you back home immediately."

"Come, Miss Brentwood," the earl commanded, smiling mockingly and presenting his arm. "I'll deliver you home posthaste!"

Cara glared at him. She had not the smallest notion of moving an inch in the direction of his curricle.

"No, Julius, indeed you shall not!" vetoed Lady Laval, considering him the cause of the small scene and also glaring at him. "We shall all walk very quickly en masse to Miss Brentwood's home, for Mr. Dickson has only just told me it is not far from here. Julius! You shall walk with me, if you please!" she ended.

Thus, she felt, scotching any rumors which might result from the amused passersby, Lady Laval peremptorily commanded Mr. Dickson and Cara to walk ahead of her, put her arm through the earl's, and set the group off at a brisk pace to travel rather silently the remaining distance to Cara's residence.

When they arrived, she said, "No, my dear, you have endured enough trials for today. We shall certainly not go in. Your poor mama! Come, Julius,

98

we are going now. Julius!" she repeated sharply, as the earl showed an alarming tendency to continue being abominable and enter with Cara.

"Mr. Dickson? Do you come with us?" she demanded.

Fearing to offend Lady Laval by not going with her, although he could not for the life of him see where she intended him to sit in a vehicle that seated two people at best but also fearing to offend Cara by not staying with her, Mr. Dickson hesitated and was lost.

Cara stated, rather than asked, in a tone which told him the opportunity for choice was past, "Oh, surely you will stay and dine with us, Mr. Dickson."

In the face of such a request, he felt he could not leave without causing the greater offense and apologetically declined to accompany the earl and Lady Laval.

"Come then, Julius," sniffed that lady and swept majestically toward the curricle.

The earl came to take Cara's hand in his own and raise it to his lips. To her mortification, he held it there a moment longer than was quite proper and then released it. He bowed.

"Sure you won't come, Dickson old boy?" he asked again. "We should take you up somewhere, never fear!" Receiving a shake of Mr. Dickson's head, he bent a languishing glance upon Cara and went to hand Lady Laval back up into his curricle.

As the two drove off, it took an effort of the severest discipline for Cara to quash an impulse to stick out her tongue at the earl's exquisitely tailored back. Masking her anger, she turned to Mr. Dickson with a rueful smile. "I wish all gentlemen might have *your* manners, Mr. Dickson." She ushered him through the doorway, with every intention of keeping him captive, entertaining him to be sure, until it should be dinner-time. "I don't know what I should do if I were continually called upon to keep gentlemen like the Earl of Malton from making their unwelcome advances!"

Lady Brentwood, hearing voices and wondering who might have arrived, came into the hallway in time to hear this last remark. Having a very notion of what her daughter *would* do, she repressed a smile and greeted them with commendable gravity.

Several hours later found Mr. Dickson leaving the Brentwood residence fully satisfied as far as his stomach was concerned. He had been plied with marinated sole, French beans, sweet rolls, and comfits. But as far as his mind was concerned, he found himself hopelessly confused.

Cara, seeing him to the front door, felt his confusion and could have shaken him for it. Haven't I flattered the breeches off him? she thought to herself with irritation. Ye gods, I've all but proposed to him! How could he be in doubt? Plague take Lord Wrothby — it is all *his* fault! — With his idiotic, mooning faces and his indecent hand-kissing! Men! she thought with vexation, lumping all her problems with both the earl and Mr. Dickson together in that one word.

"When shall I see you again?" she asked, trying hard to sound wistful. Receiving his vague mumble of an answer, she decided not to press him and, shutting the door, snorted again in disgust, "Men!"

She retraced her steps to join her mother in the parlor unconsciously putting her fingers up to touch her lips. They still felt as if the earl had seared them with his own.

Mr. Dickson climbed into his phaeton, and it started off with a small lurch. Prompted by her question, he ponderously began to review his recent calls upon Miss Brentwood.

At times, it seemed to him that she got along famously with the Earl of Malton. Yet at other times, it appeared equally that she couldn't stand the sight of the poor devil, and then the two of them seemed to have what looked very much—very much, indeed—like a lover's spat. Add to that the fact that there was never an inordinate amount of time between when Miss Brentwood was getting along with the earl and when she wasn't—and he confessed himself at a stand to unravel the matter at all. For if he could not ascertain the earl's standing with Miss Brentwood, he certainly did not see how he could ascertain his own standing with her.

Not being a gentleman given to lengthy meditations, he supposed, since he had yet to experience anything but pleasantries and a nice regard of himself from her, he would continue to court her. However, if he was going to keep on running up against the earl, who seemed positively to *like* causing a ruckus, every time he wished to see Miss Brentwood, he was not at all sure he thought Miss Brentwood's company, enjoyable though it was, worth the embarrassment the two of them usually caused him.

She should behave more like her mother, he reflected, admiring Lady Brentwood's calm and slowly getting down from his carriage to enter his house. His mind now became occupied with thoughts of the soft feather bed onto which he would soon lay his comfortably drowsy body.

Seven

Plague take him, he is a black-eyed devil! He *is* keeping me from fixing either Mr. Dickson's or Viscount Lyle's affections! Cara thought furiously, clenching her hands into fists at the sides of her delicate rose print gown and stamping one kid-slippered foot. She was referring to the Earl of Malton.

She had just returned from riding in Hyde Park with Michael Vennard, a notorious lady's man, who requently made one of her circle of admirers. Although the Earl of Malton, astride his glossy black horse, had observed her ride with Michael back and forth across the park twice under his very nose, he had done no more than doff his hat to her and watch her ride by with a mocking smile upon his lips.

Depend upon it, he knows that Michael hasn't the least notion in his head of offering for anyone! It is only when I am with Mr. Dickson or Viscount Lyle, whom he knows to be on the point of offering for me, that he intrudes, first making poor Mr. Dickson positively ill and then vexing poor Viscount Lyle, not to mention me with silly little Miss Quincy!

Cara thought in frustration, running down a mental list of the earl's offenses within the past several weeks.

How shall I ever bring either one of them up to scratch with that—with Lord Wrothby forever interrupting? And that, no doubt, is exactly what he would like in order to be revenged upon me! Oh, I wish old Harry had *killed* him instead of merely pinking him in the shoulder! she raged—knowing full well she did not in the least wish such a bloodthirsty thing—and called several shockingly unladylike epithets down upon the earl's dark head.

If I thought he was at all deceived in my past, I should bring him to the point, marry the devil, and then take inordinate pleasure in revealing to him how I had duped him! Cara thought, a wicked smile playing round her mouth.

The smile lost some of its malice as she thought wryly, I could imagine worse fates than to be the wife of the wealthy Earl of Malton. But that is the outside of absurdity! she rebuked herself scornfully.

She challenged the earl silently. I shall thwart you yet! I *shall* get that ring back and bring them both up to scratch, wait and see! Then she flounced upstairs to choose the ball gown she was going to wear to Lady Gannon's dance that night at which she fully expected to see both Mr. Dickson and Viscount Lyle.

The day passed uneventfully, and shortly after nine o'clock that evening, Cara, in a diaphanous white gown shot with tiny silver threads, and Lady Brentwood, dressed becomingly in mauve satin, were set down before Lady Gannon's front door. As the old brougham lumbered off, Cara leaned close, taking care not to crush either dress, and brushed her mother's cheek with a light kiss. "We shall outshine them all!" she whispered to bolster her mother's confidence just before they stepped inside, and Lady Gannon's major-domo announced them. Her mother had expressed some slight trepidation earlier as she had considered the substantial number of people that they had heard were to attend Lady Gannon's ball.

Lady Brentwood smiled back at her daughter in quick appreciation and thought again, as she had on more than one occasion throughout her life, that she, as mother, should have been the one to say something of the sort to Cara instead of the other way round. But she had no time in which to reflect further as Lady Gannon came bustling up to them in a royal blue sarcenet gown that very skillfully hid her large girth. She kindly took them in tow and had soon introduced them to quite a few people they had not already known.

Delighted to find that the earl was nowhere in evidence, Cara stayed with Lady Brentwood, chatting with their new acquaintances until she judged it past time that Mr. Dickson would have arrived and determined to go and search him out.

She asked her mother if she should like to accompany her. But Lady Brentwood had spotted her friends, Lady Dougherty and Lady Beaufort, talking together a short distance away and declared she would go and speak with them. Accordingly, mother and daughter split up, agreeing to meet again later in the evening.

Cara found Mr. Dickson easily in an adjoining room that had been set up so that those who did not wish to dance might play cards. But she was disappointed to see that he had already become engaged in a game of whist. She gained his attention, nodding to him and smiling, but could do no more for the moment.

Observing her to be without a partner, Lord Mercer, whom she had not seen since the day she had taken the earl's dubious tour, separated himself from the crowd and came to ask her if she would be interested in playing a game of piquet with him.

Deciding that piquet was as good a pastime as any while she waited for Mr. Dickson's game to end, she agreed with pleasure.

They seated themselves, and Lord Mercer picked up a deck of cards and began to shuffle them. He had just finished dealing and looked up to smile across the table at her when he seemed to notice someone behind her. A perplexed frown appeared on his face, followed swiftly by an expression of comprehension, and then begging her pardon apologetically he said, "Pray excuse me, Miss Brentwood. Would you mind terribly if Lord Wrothby stood in for me? It seems my cousin is in need of my assistance."

Dumbfounded, Cara watched Lord Mercer vacate his chair to the earl, who slid smoothly into his seat, picked up his friend's hand, studied it and threw down a card, saying imperatively, "Certainly she will not. *Your* play, Miss Brentwood," his black eyes gleaming blackly.

On the point of getting up, Cara found she couldn't ignore the challenge in his voice or the exceptional hand of cards she had been dealt and sat down again. She threw down a card and took the earl's play, her green eyes sparkling with relish. "Need I even ask if Miss Quincy truly desired his assistance?" she asked sarcastically.

"You needn't," replied the earl.

"Then Lord Mercer did not know that he was unnecessarily going to her aid?"

"Oh, I daresay by the time he arrives his aid will be most necessary," stated the earl knowingly.

"Humph!" Little ninnyhammer, thought Cara. But the earl was very likely right. "You are wasting your time here, Lord Wrothby. As you can see, Mr. Dickson is occupied, and I make no doubt Lord Mercer is not in the market for a wife," she remarked acidly.

"I'll lay you a monkey you're right, Miss Brentwood," he agreed rudely. "Shall we put it down to the strong attraction of your arresting company?"

"*Oh!* Look to your cards, Lord Wrothby," she retorted, "for I am assuredly going to trounce you!" And at more than this nonsensical game of cards, she added to herself, giving him a meaning look.

"I am trembling in my boots, Miss Brentwood," the earl returned, grinning.

Intent on the battle between them, the earl and Cara played swiftly and quietly. For several minutes all that could be heard was the tiny slap of cards as each laid one down to take or lose the trick.

The game was decided at last with a loud "Hah!" from Cara, which caused several heads, including Mr. Dickson's she realized with chagrin, to turn in their direction.

"That, Lord Wrothby," she said, lowering her voice and referring to her win, "allows me now to leave and remain unaccosted, no matter whom I may keep company with for the remainder of the evening! Agreed?"

But the earl merely sat back in his chair and regarded her with a small, insolent smile.

Receiving nothing but his continued leer for answer, Cara gave him a speaking glance and stood, turning her back on him, her fingers wanting badly to crook themselves about his throat. Knowing the earl as she was beginning to, she decided it would be wiser to wait for Mr. Dickson in the main room than in the earl's unpredictable proximity. That move would upset any notions he might be entertaining about joining them when Mr. Dickson finished playing.

Threading her way through to the main room again, Cara discovered Lady Brentwood not far from where she had left her, still talking to Lady Dougherty and Lady Beaufort. She stopped to greet her mother's friends and chat for a moment before continuing on through the crowd to the ballroom.

Once there, it did not take long for her dance card to become filled with the names of gentlemen wishing to dance with her. She saved several dances out for Mr. Dickson and the viscount, whom she had not yet seen but whose habit she knew it was not to arrive until late in the evening, and went sailing off in the arms of Michael Vennard, who had managed to attain the first place on her card.

Watching for Mr. Dickson from the dance floor, Cara saw him emerge a half-hour later from the crowd at the doorway and stand along the edge of the dance floor looking, she hoped, for herself. When the quadrille she was performing ended, she had her partner escort her to Mr. Dickson so that she might show him which dances she had saved for him.

As she drew near, he rewarded her with a pleasant, if a trifle shy, smile. "I didn't forget you, Mr Dickson," she smiled back at him. She pointed to the dances on her card beside which she had written in his name.

"M-Most obliged, I'm sure," he answered, as if he were a little surprised at her show of favor.

Now why should that surprise him? Cara asked herself with irritation. Was it too bold of me for him? But she had no time to say more to him, for another gentleman had appeared to whirl her off into the next dance.

She gave a tiny sigh that went unperceived by her partner. How tired I am of watching out for Mr. Dickson's very particular sensibilities! "Yes, Lady Gannon gives a lovely ball," she agreed aloud, smiling at her partner's inquiry. I must bring one of them up to scratch soon before I lose my patience altogether, box somebody's ears — and here her partner's features altered remarkably for a moment to resemble Mr. Dickson's — and ruin the whole game!

'Tis Mr. Dickson's dance now, she thought, bolstering herself for another siege as the present dance came to an end and her partner took her back to Lady Brentwood, who, liking to watch the dancing, had entered the ballroom and sat down among the other mothers.

"*Maman!* When did you come in?"

"Just now," replied Lady Brentwood, smiling. "You look as though you are having a good time, my love."

"Well, I should hope I do not look like I am having a bad time! And what of you?" Cara fixed her mother with a penetrating stare. "I don't believe I can tell just from looking at you, *Maman.*"

108

"Well, and I should hope I do not wear my emotions upon my sleeves!" rejoined Lady Brentwood.

Cara grinned back at her. "Oh, you are quick tonight, *Maman!* Has Betsy been riling you up?!"

Her mother smiled but only shook her head.

Mr. Dickson, who had merely waited patiently at the edge of the dance floor, now approached to claim his dance and courteously presented his arm to lead her out onto the floor.

"I think not, Dickson, old boy. This one is mine," stated the Earl of Malton cheerfully, swooping down upon Cara from nowhere.

"You are mistak—!" Cara protested.

But the earl had clasped the hand she had been in the act of laying on Mr. Dickson's arm and now caught her up in his arms, swinging her out onto the floor in perfect rhythm with the waltz the orchestra had just struck up: they were the first couple upon the floor.

Cara's cheeks flamed, whether more in embarrassment or anger she couldn't decide.

Mr. Dickson, left standing awkwardly by himself, looked around in confusion and explained to Lady Brentwood, sitting just behind him, "Thought Miss Brentwood told me earlier she'd marked me down for this'un."

Lady Brentwood, feeling for Mr. Dickson, got up and came to stand next to him. "I should not worry if I were you, Mr. Dickson. The Earl of Malton is . . . is . . . not himself tonight," she smiled, trying to imply subtly that the earl, not Dickson, should be held responsible.

Mr. Dickson smiled back at her gratefully and found himself looking into the most understanding pair of blue eyes he had ever beheld. "Just as well—

don't really waltz, you know," he admitted shyly and smiled again. "D'you care to sit down?" he asked indicating the chair she had just vacated.

Lady Brentwood's eyes twinkled merrily as she replied, "An excellent notion!" and suited action to words.

An action that was not lost on the earl, who noted it with calculating satisfaction and smiled as he whirled Cara in smooth circles about the dance floor.

Cara teetered dangerously for several minutes, wrestling an overwhelming desire to box His Lordship's ears smartly and leave him standing in the middle of the floor to dance with himself. She was aided in mastering this desire when she would have withdrawn her hands from his and found that she could not break the grip that held her as lightly as it did firmly. At this realization, her head snapped up, her green eyes sparkling with suppressed anger, to find the earl observing her efforts with his lazy, infuriating smile.

"One would think you did not wish to dance with me, Cara," he complained provokingly. "I may call you Cara? I do feel we know each other well enough now. And Brentwood is such a long surname—unmistakable, to be sure," he added softly. "But such an effort," he complained again.

At his insinuation, Cara snapped, "Of a certainty, you may not!" She bit her lip, controlling her temper with an effort, and asked sweetly, "Aren't you afraid the hostesses of Almack's shall see you behave as you've just done, Lord Wrothby, and bar you from attending their parties?"

He gave a derisive laugh and replied bluntly, "No. I have far too much money. And I am—a bachelor." He smiled cynically down at her.

Her thrust having gone wide of the mark, not annoyed the earl at all, Cara said in a tight voice, "This is the end of the dance, Lord Wrothby. Kindly take me back to Mr. Dickson and my mother."

"—And do not dare to bother me again tonight!" finished the earl mockingly.

She gave him a smoldering glance and walked ahead of him refusing to be baited into an answer.

His soft chuckle followed her.

Mr. Dickson was waiting, chatting contentedly with Lady Brentwood.

The earl bowed to the two of them, smiled mockingly at Cara, and disappeared into the crowd of guests.

If Mr. Dickson felt any animosity toward the earl for usurping his dance with Cara, he did not show it.

"That is one gentleman who, I am certain, must always get his way," remarked Lady Brentwood.

"Do not sound so awed!" returned Cara sharply.

Lady Brentwood looked at her daughter in surprise.

Instantly Cara apologized. "I'm sorry, *Maman*. It is just that he is an excessively disagreeable fellow and puts me out of all patience!" she exclaimed. "Come, Mr. Dickson! Let us dance, and you must be your most delightful self and make me forget him completely!"

Mr. Dickson looked doubtful but gave her his arm, and they moved away from Lady Brentwood onto the floor, thereby cutting an astonished Lord Carleton out of his dance in Cara's determination to give Mr. Dickson his.

Lady Dougherty came to sit down in the chair

next to Lady Brentwood. "My dearest Alicia," she began in a scandalized whisper, "I remarked Lord Wrothby's atrocious behavior toward Cara just now. *Such* bad manners! Tut, tut. Some gentlemen think because they are rich as Croesus they may behave any which way. I vow I know ostlers with better manners than the Earl of Malton!" She then proceeded, to her listener's dismay, to recount the entire incident, criticizing the earl's behavior at every point just as if Lady Brentwood had not witnessed it herself only a moment before.

When she had finished, she paused and lowered her voice to impart the information which had brought her to her friend's side. "My dear, only guess what I have learned! Don't look now, but that gentleman over there by the door — just entering. Now he is standing beside Lord Weypourth — there! He is a *runner,* my dear!" she breathed.

Gratifying her friend, Lady Brentwood's eyebrows rose in surprise.

While Lady Dougherty began her whispered speculations, the Viscount Lyle, having arrived a short time before, strolled through Lady Gannon's guests until he spotted Cara in the ballroom just coming off the dance floor again.

"Good evening, sir!" Cara exclaimed as he approached. "It was getting so late I had given you up!" she said playfully.

He placed a damp hand upon her shoulder and answered with an unmistakable ring of sincerity, "I would never miss an opportunity to see you, my dear." She cast her lashes down modestly and fidgeted beneath his moist palm. "Have I fallen so far into your black books that you shall not give me a dance?"

"Not at all, my good sir. You are, on the contrary, so high in my estimation that I have saved you two dances!" She slipped smoothly out of his grasp. "And I see that this," she indicated the strains of music beginning to be heard, "must be one of them, for no one has descended upon me yet to claim it!" She dug into her riticule for her dance card to check her supposition but looked up again quickly, her brows snapping together, as she heard a deep, familiar voice boom, *"Miss Brentwood.* I do believe this is my dance. Evening, Viscount," it continued pleasantly. "You'll excuse us? Shall we, *Miss Brentwood?"* invited the Earl of Malton, emphasizing her name tiresomely. Without waiting for an answer, he hooked his arm through hers and pulled her off.

Cara threw a rueful glance behind her at the viscount, having learnt from her first dance with the earl that there was now no hope of escape.

The viscount looked first surprised and then angry as he was left standing, like Mr. Dickson before him, awkwardly by himself.

Cara compressed her lips and did her best to mask her anger and appear, at least, pleasant. She could not, however, keep herself from remonstrating icily, "Lord Wrothby, you will gain a shockingly boorish reputation among your fellows if you go on in this vein. I wish you will stop cutting them out of dances I am convinced you do not desire!"

After which remark she averted her face and retreated into stony silence. She answered the earl only when he addressed a direct question to her and then only in monosyllables. For, she rationalized, showing Lord Wrothby his absurd antics infuriate me will do me no good at all and very likely *encour-*

113

age him!

"Ah, I have it!" exclaimed the earl, shamelessly striving to goad her into breaking her silence. "I have bethought myself, Miss Brentwood, of a piece of information you cannot fail to find diverting. Do you observe the short gentleman in that disgusting waistcoat standing against the far wall?" Her face remained averted. "I have it on the best authority in the world, Miss Brentwood, that he is a runner!"

"Ahh, I see I have your full attention now," he remarked dryly, as Cara blanched and her eyes flew to the gentleman in question.

He was leaning back against the wall, engaged in surveying the crowd about him and looking bored in the extreme.

"It seems the runners think," went on the earl, "that this latest highwayman who skulks about the outskirts of London has his base in Somerset County. Is not *your* home in Somerset County, Miss Brentwood?" he asked mockingly.

Cara stared back at him, her green eyes sparkling wrathfully, a flush staining her cheeks. In a low voice, she flung at him, "Oh! How I should dearly love to shoot you!" At the unexpectedness of which the earl threw back his head and laughed heartily in genuine amusement.

"—*Again!*" she added furiously and thought, Laugh while you can, my good lord, for you shall not have that ring for very much longer! And then we shall see who shall laugh! Then she clamped her lips together and mulishly refused to utter another word for the remainder of the dance, for she had almost flung that thought at his head, too!

Observing her determined face, the earl's eyes narrowed thoughtfully, but he said nothing.

Several moments later, during which Cara had not vouchsafed even a monosyllable in answer to the earl's efforts, he remarked, still with an eye toward provoking her, "I was not aware, Miss Brentwood, that you were, er, such a scintillating conversationalist. Perhaps," he mused, "I have been unjust to Mr. Dickson?!"

Cara would not have deigned to answer but for the fact that she saw he was taking her back to Lady Brentwood. "I will go back to the Viscount, if you please!" she snapped.

Sardonically he replied, "And I should take you, my dear Miss Brentwood and help nature to render a little poetic justice, but I'll warrant even *you* do not deserve the Viscount Lyle!"

Realizing he was in earnest, Cara looked up at him in surprise.

"It is wiser, practiced as you may think yourself, my dear, if I take you back to your mother," he said with a cynical smile.

"Why, whatever do you mean?" she asked. But they had arrived before Lady Brentwood, and he merely bowed formally and disappeared again into the crowd.

The viscount, however, was not to be thwarted so easily. As Cara surreptitiously regarded the runner from behind a knot of guests, the viscount made his way through the dancers to Cara's side. He greeted Lady Brentwood and smoothly suggested that they all go for something to drink.

Cara withdrew her uneasy thoughts and glance from the runner, who still appeared mightily bored, and gave the viscount a searching look. Was it her imagination or did the puffiness under his eyes seem more pronounced than usual?

Viscount Lyle smiled pleasantly at her. "Come, my dearest Cara. A glass of ratafia will put you back in countenance," he said.

Cara blinked and gave herself a mental shake. She was letting her imagination run away with her. The earl was simply trying to kick up another dust with his silly remarks about the viscount. Sour grapes, she told herself, because I put a bullet through him and he cannot endure the thought of it!

A tiny smile began to play about the corners of her mouth. And soon old Harry and I shall contrive to get Father's ring back and throw his nose even farther out of joint! That thought improved her mood considerably, and her anger at the earl faded. She returned the viscount's smile and almost laughed out loud. Wouldn't it rankle when the Earl of Malton no longer had anything to threaten her with! She shot another glance at the runner, still leaning against the wall but engaged now in regarding the nails on one hand, and decided she need not concern herself unduly over him.

"You are quite right, Viscount," she said. Though he had not looked it, she'd wager the viscount had been as angry with the earl as she. If the viscount were going to dismiss the earl's behavior, so could she. She tossed her red curls. The best thing to do now, she concluded, giving him another smile, was to entertain the Viscount Lyle.

She hooked her arm through Lady Brentwood's, achieving a measure of her former good humor. "What of it, *Maman*. Shall we go?" she asked Lady Brentwood, who smiled and nodded her agreement a trifle absently. But *not*, Cara thought, suppressing a small grimace of distaste, for a glass of ratafia!

Not until she was standing in the next room sip-

116

ping a glass of champagne did Cara realize appreciatively how clever the viscount had been in his suggestion. Under the indisputable aegis of her mother, he had maneuvered her away from any more interruptions in the form of prospective dance partners.

The three stood chatting comfortably until the viscount finally remarked with a ponderous attempt at humor, "I had better take her back, Lady Brentwood, don't you think, before a federation of her admirers comes in search of her?"

Lady Brentwood smiled politely.

He walked with them back to the ballroom and took his leave of them. "I shall go, I think, and play a few hands of cards." He smiled at Cara. "In the unlikely event you weary of dancing, my dear, you may find me at the tables."

"Don't forget I have you down for at least one more dance, Viscount, just before the last. You must make certain to tear yourself away for it, else I shall be dreadfully disappointed!" Cara teased and sat down beside Lady Brentwood.

"*Maman!*" she exclaimed then, turning to look curiously at her mother. "Are you going to woolgather all the evening?" You have scarce uttered a word this past hour."

Lady Brentwood blushed guiltily but did not try to offer any explanation as she could see a young gentleman, his course set determinedly upon Cara, approaching.

Lord Carleton, concluding that the Incomparable was not keeping strictly to her dance card, had decided to lay claim to the dance he had been bumped from earlier.

From her vantage point on the dance floor, Cara

117

listened to Lord Carleton with half an ear and could not help but observe distastefully that the earl stood up twice with an attractive blonde and once more with a small, pretty dark-haired girl. With some surprise, she saw him take the brunette back to Richard Llewellyn.

Over the past few weeks, trying not to make it appear so, Cara had been studiously avoiding any proximity to Richard that would require more than a polite nod across the distance. Now she considered that if Richard were enamored of this dark-haired chit, she might safely relax her guard and take up something of his company again.

She watched the earl saunter out of the ballroom and relegated him to the devil for his insinuations and his threats, and then promptly forgot him in her enjoyment of alternating between dancing with one of her horde of admirers and sitting and conversing lightheartedly with her mother and Mr. Dickson. Curiously Mr. Dickson appeared equally content to simply sit beside her mother, watch the dancing, and wait for her to return. A contentment which Cara could not but feel was rather poor-spirited of him.

Thus the evening wore happily on for all concerned. As it neared its end, the viscount abruptly recollected his dance with Cara and pulled out his fob watch to look at the time. Hurriedly, for he would almost be late, he gathered his winnings from the baize table before him and excused himself despite more than one disgruntled frown at his departure.

The Earl of Malton remarked him pass and waited only a moment before he, too, excused himself from his circle and took a shorter route to the viscount's destination.

Just as the viscount reached out to touch Cara's shoulder, a familiar, hateful voice boomed, "Miss Brentwood! This is my dance I believe!" and the Earl of Malton, with an all too active gleam in his dark eyes, clamped a hand on her arm and started out onto the floor with her.

Mr. Dickson's mouth flew open.

Lady Brentwood was appalled.

Cara's eyebrows shot up in disbelief and in muted, furious tones she began to object.

Viscount Lyle cut her short in a cold voice that carried over the conversations of those standing nearby and had the effect of stopping them. "You err, Wrothby. The lady is engaged to me for this one!"

The earl turned, swinging Cara bodily with him, and fixed the viscount with a steely eye. Slowly, in the most languid and affable of tones, he repeated, "I believe this is *my* dance," leaving no doubt in the minds of either Cara or the viscount that he cared not a whit whose dance it was — he intended to have it.

Heads began to turn and stare as those standing closest began to interest themselves in what had all the makings of a delicious new *on-dit*.

Cara, unused to being this kind of center of attention, became acutely conscious of the growing number of amused onlookers. She took one look at the earl's face and knew he harbored no compunctions about causing a scene of horrid proportions — indeed, he looked to be enjoying himself hugely! She judged the viscount her only hope and swiftly laid her free hand on his arm and drew him in, as if the three of them were the best of old friends. In an

119

urgent undertone, she said, "Please, Viscount, you would not come to sword points here, surely?" and anxiously indicated their amused observers with a nod of her head.

An angry flush suffused the viscount's face. He no more than Cara wished to be the latest subject of the scandalmongers. He gave a disdainful shrug, too violent to be convincing, and brusquely replied, "Naturally not. *I* should not wish to subject you to such a scene!" His lips came together in a white line, and he turned on his heel and strode out of the ballroom.

A smug smile played about the corners of the earl's mouth. Nodding to Lady Brentwood and Mr. Dickson, who nodded faintly back at him, he continued smoothly with Cara in tow to the dance floor.

Cara stared after the viscount. Not content with putting Mr. Dickson off, she thought furiously, struggling to contain her rage, he has now begun in earnest on Viscount Lyle!

The earl asked reasonably, "Well, what else could he do after that very empassioned plea you made him?"

And that was the last straw. Cara, who had sorely tried all evening to keep her temper, lost it. "You . . ."

Observing her, the earl clasped her lithe body tightly and swung them both from the ballroom out a convenient French doorway.

In the dark, flower-scented garden Cara burst out, "inSUFFer—!"

Neatly silencing her, the earl crushed her lips under his own.

For a moment all Cara felt was the pleasant, insistance of the earl's lips and the security of the strong arms around her. Then her brain coldly tallied the audacity of this, the earl's last iniquity, with all he'd done that evening.

Through a haze of rising fury, she thought she heard him groan her name. Then she felt his arms relax their hold and begin to drop as her own limbs came to life. Struggling free, she felt one of her hands fly up, almost of its own volition, and deliver a resounding slap. Staggering back from him, she stood, her breath coming quickly between her lips, her green eyes, if they could have been seen, sparkling wrathfully. Then she picked up her skirts and haughtily reentered the ballroom.

The astonished Lord Wrothby muttered, "Wildcat!" rubbed his jaw, and then grinned crookedly into the darkness. It was going to be extremely interesting to tame one Miss Cara Brentwood.

Cara's cold rage carried her, head held high, back across the ballroom through the crowd that was beginning to break up as guests took leave of one another and began to move toward the door. Silently fuming at the earl and calling down every epithet she could think of upon him, she did not on her approach particularly remark the tranquil attitude of Mr. Dickson, still seated cozily next to her mother.

Lady Brentwood, however, immediately noticed the two angry spots of color in her daughter's cheeks, but she refrained from commenting upon them in Mr. Dickson's presence. "Mr. Dickson has very kindly offered to convey us home, Cara," she stated calmly, reading her daughter's state of mind accurately and giving her a moment in which to compose herself before she need speak. "I've sent a note to have old Harry waved on."

121

Cara nodded, taking several deep breaths to try to regain control of her temper. She succeeded only in giving Mr. Dickson a rather pinched smile.

He returned her one of perplexity wondering if he had, without meaning to, in some way upset her, for she did indeed look upset, even to him.

"Well then, are we all ready?" asked Cara finally, a little too brightly.

"I believe so," corroborated her mother, and they began to follow the other guests in the direction of Lady Gannon's front door.

Much to everyone's impatience, with the exception of Mr. Dickson, it took some twenty minutes to reach the entrance due to the crowd that had attended the ball, and several minutes more before Mr. Dickson's carriage was brought round. During that time, Mr. Dickson thoroughly enjoyed himself as he and Lady Brentwood kept up a steady conversation, interjected by occasional comments from a rather tight-lipped Cara.

As soon as Mr. Dickson had seen them inside their door, Lady Brentwood addressed the matter and pleaded, "Cara, I know something has occurred to overset you. Can't you tell me what it is?"

But Cara only shook her head and replied brusquely, "I'm not very good company just at the moment, *Maman*. I think I shall go on up to bed."

Her rage now abated, draining her in the process, she mounted the stairs like a somnambulist and, upon entering her bedchamber, threw herself full length across her bed.

The irony of her situation had struck her forcibly.

Here is one of the most handsome, wealthy, eligible bachelors of *any* Seaon, she thought slowly, seeing the Earl of Malton before her, with his perfectly

122

odious smile. He appears to have more than the usual backbone common to men of the aristocracy and more in his brainbox besides the latest color of vest or style of cravat. And he is excessively good company, when he chooses to be, she reflected, a tiny smile playing about her mouth.

A frown replaced the smile. And what am I doing? she asked herself. I spend all evening long fencing with him while I try to prod poor, dense Mr. Dickson and paunchy, damp-handed, *puffy*-eyed Viscount Lyle into proposing to me. Lord, but I'm a fool! It is the Earl of Malton I *should* be trying to marry!

The trouble is, just when he is at his most charming, and I begin to enjoy myself and relax my guard a trifle, he slips in some horrid barb about highwaymen and recalls me to the fact that he could and very likely would dearly love to turn me over to the runners! Indeed, I cannot fathom why he plays at courting me instead of doing so! It would have been but a simple matter to have turned me in to the runner at Lady Gannon's tonight, she remembered, a chill running up her spine. I shouldn't even be *in* his company, much less enjoy it!

And then what do I do but slap him! A groan escaped her. Nothing could have been more calculated to send him to the runners! Lord, I am a fool!

Three tears began to run, one hotly after the other, down her cheeks and trickle saltily into the corners of her mouth. Why did it have to be *him* I held up? Or, if it had to be him, why did I have to lose Father's ring? Without that he should never have known it was me! she asked herself futilely.

She dragged herself up off the bed, brushing the tears furiously from her cheeks, and limply began to undo her gown, crushed sadly from lying across the bed. At any rate, she thought, he will not have Father's ring much longer, and then I need never worry about the runners or him again!

But that thought, instead of lightening her mood, made her feel more blue-deviled than ever.

Eight

Three nights later, Bates entered the parlor where Cara and Lady Brentwood were divesting themselves of their light shawls as they had just come in from an Assembly some five minutes before. As neither Mr. Dickson nor Viscount Lyle had been among the young set which had attended the Assembly, Cara was feeling somewhat vexed, considering it a profitless, if pleasant, evening. Impassively Bates held out a small salver to Cara.

She dropped her shawl onto the settee and gathered her own necklace with its small gold intaglio from the salver with a surprised air and exclaimed, "Why Bates, where did you get this? I looked for it only yesterday without the smallest success." Guiltily she felt the old excitement that used to assail her before the holdup of a carriage rise in the pit of her stomach. The necklace was the arranged signal from old Harry that the Earl of Malton would be away from home the following evening.

Waiting only to be asked, Bates replied, "Old Harry, miss, sent it round. He said he found it in the stables."

"The chain your father gave you, Cara?" asked Lady Brentwood, looking up from her shawl.

Cara nodded, fastening the chain round her neck again. "Thank you, Bates."

"Certainly, miss." He withdrew.

"I know how you should hate to lose that, my dear," said Lady Brentwood. "How fortunate that old Harry found it."

Almost as much as I hate having lost Father's ring, thought Cara, determining to remove the chain before she set out the next evening. Aloud, she agreed absent-mindedly, "Yes. 'Tis one of my favorite pieces."

"Well, I'm going on, my dear. Good night," said Lady Brentwood. She came to give Cara a kiss, waking her from her brown study.

"A capital idea, *Maman*," Cara sighed, accompanying her out of the parlor. The two climbed the stairs together and said good night at the top.

Lady Brentwood enjoyed herself hugely the next day at Lady McArdle's tea and also at the small dinner party given for her that evening by Lady Fairbury, another of her old friends. Cara should have, too, but for the fact that she was sorely trying to conceal the mounting restlessness and anticipation that threatened any time those twenty-four hours to make her jump from her chair and post home to change her dress and be off to retrieve her father's ring.

With a sigh of relief, she observed Lady Brentwood indicate she was preparing to make their farewells to Lady Fairbury and went to add her own thanks to those of her mother's.

They returned home at last shortly thereafter, and Cara, successfully appearing her usual self despite her mounting excitement, accompanied her mother up the stairs to bed once again.

"I won't trouble Ellen tonight, *Maman*. Tell her she may go to bed when she's done with you." By the time Ellen helped her mother and then came to her, she could have herself out of the simple dress she was wearing.

"All right, my dear. Sleep well."

Once on the other side of her bedroom door, Cara began to tear at the tiny buttons on her dress. In what seemed to her like hours, it fell to the floor in a circle about her feet. She stepped over it and in a comparatively few short minutes had donned her father's old pants and shirt. She swung on his cloak and tied it about her neck.

Watching her dark-clothed figure in the mirror, with its white face and large dark eyes, she twisted her red hair up into a bun and pulled the worn hat over it once again. Then she turned from the glass, snatched up her candles, stuffing them into the pockets of the cloak, and tipped in her boots to listen at the door.

Some ten minutes later, she heard Ellen shut her mother's door and go down. Once she and her mother went to bed, the servants were not long in following suit, and the house quickly went dark. But she waited a quarter of an hour longer to be certain no one was still up. Then she opened her bedchamber door quietly and peered out into the darkness.

Swiftly she felt her way down the stairs through the dining room to the kitchen and shot back the bolt on the servants' door, grimacing at its loud scrape in the silence. She pulled the door to and tried to quell the wild butterflies in her stomach, hoping fervently that the earl's household would take to their beds as quickly as her own had.

A small, misshapen figure, obscured in the portico of a residence he neither owned nor intended to enter any time that evening if he could help it, observed Cara walk the short distance from the back of her house to the corner.

A second, stocky figure on horseback arrived a moment later, leading a second horse. Cara was seen to mount, confer briefly with her partner, and then set off with him, remarkably in the very direction the observer himself had traveled not too many hours earlier.

Like as no', considered the small man, rubbing the scraggly stubble on his chin, this 'ere's wha' 'is lor-'ship's been waitin' t'ear. He set off then himself.

Cara and old Harry arrived before the earl's residence and settled themselves out of sight on the far side of the gardens. They waited well past midnight until the household had been dark for some time, with the exception of a single candle in a portion of the house which looked to be almost separate from the earl's apartments. When this last window finally went dark, they left their horses and stole to the servants' entrance.

With a hand that shook slightly, old Harry used the key he had wheedled away from its owner on pretexts he had refused to tell Cara and swung the door open. Straining to see him in the dark, Cara shut the door behind them and followed him down a close hallway more by the feel of his presence ahead of her than by any ability to see him. Thus when he stopped abruptly at the end of the hallway, she bumped into him. He reached back to pat her arm reassringly, and they waited, listening for sounds that anyone might still be up.

Cara dug in the pockets of her cloak and brought out matches and candles. She lit one and handed it to old Harry. Turning first right then left then twice again to the right, only making one wrong turn, they wound quietly through the servants' hallways and came to the main rooms.

Old Harry jerked his thumb, indicating he would go round to the left. Cara nodded and put her candle to his, watching the wick take the flame. She would

128

search the rooms to their right.

She looked at old Harry over her candle, her eyes worried and dark, and mouthed, "Hurry!" The earl was not due back from the boxing meet he had gone to attend until the early hours of the morning, but the candles were throwing their shadows eerily over the strange furnishings, and her heart was thumping unpleasantly. She wanted to be gone. Old Harry's face in the candlelight mirrored her sentiment.

They separated, each moving swiftly and silently through the rooms on the first floor searching drawers, shelves, and any other furniture which seemed a likely place for the earl to have secreted her father's ring.

They met again, completing their search of the first floor, outside the earl's library. Cara raised her eyebrows inquiringly. Old Harry shook his head and pointed into the library. Cara shook her own head, beginning to feel faintly alarmed. "It must be with his jewelry then!" she hissed.

"Ye're sure it weren't in ther'?" he whispered back, walking into the earl's library and eyeing the important-looking papers spread out across the desk. This was obviously where the earl attended to his private business.

Cara followed him in and closed the heavy library door quietly behind them. "I looked in all the drawers—I looked everywhere! It has got to be in his jewelry chest. I'm going to look upstairs—"

"Aye, an' I'll look through this mess ag'in."

"And if it's not there . . ." Cara's whisper trailed off.

Old Harry looked at her sharply. "We'll not be crossin' they bridge jest yet, if'n ye please. G'on—I'll meet ye at th' bottom o' th' stairs."

Cara nodded and hurried out of the library, taking

care to open and close the door gently.

Let it be in his jewelry chest — Lord, let it be there! she prayed as she gingerly climbed the unfamiliar stairs.

Systematically she searched the second-floor apartments, saving what she guessed were the earl's personal rooms until last. Not daring to hope, she entered the bedroom, made a thorough search of its furniture, and crossed to his dressing room.

She rummaged through the brushes and discarded cravats on his dressing table and found, with a leap of excitement, his jewelry chest. A moment later, she snapped it shut again in vexation, having found naught but a series of diamond studs, several of his own rings, and one gold earring. Wouldn't you know it! she thought in disgust as she viewed the earring, surprised for a moment from her purpose.

She drummed the tips of her fingers lightly on the carved mahogany surface of His Lordship's box and tried to think where else he might have put her father's ring.

She returned to the bedroom and searched the mantel; above the fireplace but found nothing. Turning from the mantel in disappointment, she stood with her back to the warmth of the glowing coals which had been left for the earl against the chill of the morning hours.

Struck by the sight of the large fourposter bed, she thought, Of course! Under his pillows! Excitedly she went to lean one knee on the bed and slide a hand beneath both pillows. But, again, she found nothing.

Straightening, she sat down in dejection on the edge of the bed. It is not here, she thought, unless he keeps it in a strongbox and, heavens! breaking into that, even if we found it, would certainly be beyond us.

She ran her eye over each piece of furniture in the

room, certain she had not overlooked any but wishing that she had if it would offer another place to search.

In desperation, she bounced from the bed and ran back to his dressing table, rifling through the objects on the top of it. It *has* to be here, she thought wildly, after all the risk we have taken!

But a moment later, having exhausted the jewelry chest, the objects on the top of the table, and the contents of the drawers a second time, she had to acknowledge that it was not. She let fall a comb, her heart sinking, and heard the small clink as it hit the table. In the act of lifting her candle to go and rejoin old Harry, she froze.

"You will put the candle down on the dresser, my good fellow, and turn around slowly, keeping your hands exactly where they are unless you wish me to blow a hole through you," said an indifferent voice.

A cold sweat washed over her as she did as she was told and turned around to stare with awful fascination at the tall form of the Earl of Malton looming in the doorway, his pistol aimed at her heart. She had the wits to keep her head down so that the shadow of her hat might fall across her features.

"Back in there." He waved the pistol, indicating the bedroom.

Unconsciously she glanced toward the doorway.

"Don't look for help from that quarter. He is quite incapacitated." Careful to keep his pistol aimed at her, the earl divested himself of his cloak and tail coat.

He seated himself comfortably in the chair beside the fireplace and stretched out his legs to the warmth of the coals. Then he chuckled. "And now, let us see what I have cornered." In the candlelight, his eyes seemed black recesses.

"You will oblige me, please, by removing your cloak."

Cara's mouth flew open in surprise, but she shut it again immediately. Hoping she might keep the earl in ignorance of her identity if she did not speak, she untied the cloak and let it drop to the floor.

"And now the shirt."

Thinking she could not have heard aright, Cara stared, unmoving.

"The shirt," the earl repeated, enunciating distinctly. *"Now."* The pistol was cocked.

Her fingers flew to the top button on her shirt and, fumbling, began to unbutton. Blushing firily, her green eyes shooting daggers at him beneath the brim of her worn hat, Cara opened the shirt and painfully shrugged one and then the other white shoulder from the sleeves.

"Leave it!" commanded the earl as Cara began to draw the shirt before her.

An angry sob escaped her, and she threw the shirt to the floor, eyes blazing at him, a lovely slim figure bare to the waist of her dark breeches.

The earl rose from his chair and began to advance upon her, his pistol aimed pointedly at her heart.

Cara backed toward the chest of drawers, her large dark eyes fixed upon his face, her heart thumping against her ribs, the hair on the back of her neck prickling. Wildly she wondered if the earl were finally going to even the score and kill her, thinking she had meant to rob him in earnest this time. For that must, she realized, with a sick feeling in the pit of her stomach, be how her presence in his house at this hour, dressed so, must appear to him.

Coming level with her, he reached out and grasped her right wrist, pulling her inexorably to him. Raising his pistol before her frightened eyes, he carefully released the hammer back into place and laid the weapon down on top of the crumpled ties that adorned the top of his chest of drawers. He caught her left wrist, rising to strike at him, pushed it behind her body to join the other in his large clasp, and ran his free hand caressingly over both her hips. "What," he asked softly, "no pistol tonight, Miss Brentwood?"

Deliberately he knocked the hat from her head and observed the red curls escape the bun and slip slowly down her back.

Irrelevantly Cara watched the hat flutter down to rest on the floor near her shirt.

The earl's hand came down, warm, on her bare shoulder and slid caressingly up her throat.

He forced her chin up: flashing green eyes met glinting black ones.

The light Cara now saw in the earl's eyes frightened her far worse than the pistol he had aimed at her heart. Through lips that were suddenly dry, she stammered, "Wh—what—"

"—Am I going to do?" the earl finished for her, with a mocking smile. "But you know already, Miss Brentwood. I do not fight—or shoot—women." His eyes gleamed blackly.

"There are far more pleasant . . . things . . . one may do with them." His lips came down on hers, and his hand ran gently back down the column of her throat. His fingertips stroked the skin along her collarbone, and then his large palm came down upon the satin skin of her breasts, abrading them with its passes to set them tingling.

His mouth left her lips throbbing and followed the path his hand had taken, fastening, when he reached them, on the tight buds of her nipples and teasing them until for the first time in her life Cara thought she was going to faint.

He tore a groan from both of them and began to sweep her toward the large fourposter bed.

As Cara heard their mingled sound and felt his direction, something inside her snapped. "Stop! Stop, please—*Don't!*"

Startled, the earl stopped, raising his head to find that her face had gone very white and her green eyes, abnormally large in her ashen face, stared up into his own with one of the most desperate, pleading looks with which he had ever been fixed in the whole of his life. The sight came as a decidedly unpleasant shock, and he then perceived that she was trembling in his arms from the top of her pretty, curly red head to the tips of what were undoubtedly equally well-formed toes.

He swore.

So softly he had to strain to hear it, her lashes dark on her pale cheek, Cara said, "Lord Wrothby, p-please! I—I am not what you think me!"

The earl's brows snapped together in a black scowl. This was not at all the manner in which practiced, sophisticated adventuresses behaved, and his grasp on her slackened.

Feeling it, Cara saw her opportunity and seized it without the smallest hesitation. She wrenched herself free and fled, snatching her clothes from the floor on the run and dodging, with a decidedly hunted air, through the door.

She left the Earl of Malton standing nonplussed in the middle of his bedroom floor, wanting to call out after her as he saw her hesitate in the instant before she disappeared into the darkness, "To the left! The stairs are to your left—dammit!"

He then walked unhurriedly over to the chair he had vacated earlier, sat down in it, crossing one elegant Hessian boot over the other, and proceeded to frown into the red coals glowing in the fireplace.

Left to himself in the earl's library, as comfortable

as one may be when one is trussed tightly to a chair, old Harry had begun to doze off. But he came awake with a start when he heard someone come flying down the stairs making an unholy racket as he or she did so, apparently tripping judging by the sound of it, and landing with a loud thud, followed by an equally loud "Ow!" at the bottom.

Then there was a protracted silence.

He had just begun to think whoever had fallen down the stairs had picked himself up more quietly and gone off when a loud, hissed "Harry!" made him start again, and he recognized Miss Cara's voice.

He made as much noise as he judged prudent through the handkerchief that covered his mouth, fearing to bring the whole household down on them if they were not already about it. Why they were not, after all the clatter Miss Cara had just made, was beyond him, but he was not one to look gift horses in the mouth.

Cara, in her unnerved state, listening for sounds of pursuit from the earl's bedchamber, had no trouble in detecting old Harry's mumbles. She burst into the library, her clothes disheveled and a look upon her face which gave old Harry a sudden mental picture of the Earl of Malton at the head of a company of white-aproned cooks and black-liveried major-domos brandishing carving knives and forks and heavy silver trays.

He quite forgot the image of the nonchalant earl who had earlier calmly walked in on him going through the drawers of his desk, several hours before by rights he should have been home, and very efficiently, though without any marked harshness, tied him to the chair.

His fright was further increased when he observed Miss Cara wield the scissors she rummaged from the

135

earl's desk on his ropes and knots with an alacrity and imprecision that threatened to remove fingers from his hands and gore portions of his body he considered essential to him. Indeed, observing her made him think the very devil himself was after them!

She snipped the last rope that held his feet to the chair in two at the same moment he managed to untie the handkerchief covering his mouth—it, apparently not having been a priority to her—and ask, "Did you get it?"

To which she whispered fiercely, "There's no *time*! Come *on!*" and dragged him, hopping on first one foot and then the other and running—like a child! he thought aggrievedly, at *his* age!—as he tried to kick off lengths of rope still dangerously twined about his feet back out of the library through the servants' quarters the way they had come.

Only when they had reached the kitchen door to Cara's house again, having ridden quickly and silently, was anything said.

Cara threw her right leg over the pommel and slid down her horse's warm flank. She held the reins up to old Harry and looked toward his face through the darkness, searching for some explantion to give him.

Finally she shrugged and said tonelessly, "It wasn't there. I didn't get it." She turned to put her hand on the door, opening it.

Old Harry's soft statement, more to himself than her, stayed her. "It'll end with the death of ye. Or they'll clap ye in th' lockup. Ye're like a moth to the flame."

Then Cara swung inside, and old Harry turned the horses' heads.

Nine

A bright, warm stream of sunshine falling across her face woke Cara the next morning. She turned her head on the pillow and looked out of her windows. The sun was well advanced in a cloudlessly blue sky, but she didn't care.

She had not got the ring back. She flushed. And the earl had treated her as if she were some . . . some . . . lightskirt! She pulled the covers over her head. She felt as if she would die of mortification or, and this was the more likely, search out the Earl of Malton on the instant and shoot him where he stood for all to see and the runners to clap her up without the smallest pause for thought! She gritted her teeth until they squeaked. It was best not to refine on the matter at all.

She threw off the covers and sat up. The household, settled into midmorning duties, seemed unnaturally quiet. Her mother, she knew, had already gone out, being engaged to Lady Parmell for a visit to Lady Granton this morning.

She swung her legs over the side of the bed and winced as pain shot through her side. Pulling her nightgown away, she saw that most of her left hip had turned an ugly blue-black color, bruised in last night's fall down the stairs. "Oh Lord," she groaned, gloomily observing the extent of it for several minutes.

Thus reminded of the earl again, her lip curled, and she thought, He is a true member of the *ton*. No real gentleman would have behaved in that fashion and taken such advantage! But no lady would have gone to his apartments in such a manner, at such an hour! her own fair-mindedness asserted. Blushing furiously, she had to admit to herself that she had only got what she deserved, and she might well have got a good deal more than that. She remembered her own moan. She had been betrayed into returning his ardor with some lusty feelings of her own she hadn't known she was capable of until that moment.

She rose to put on her wrapper, her skin tingling again where the earl had touched her and her cheeks burning. But he had stopped when she had asked him to. How many other men would have? And now that she considered the matter, she judged he had not attempted to stop her flight. For he could easily have called his servants to apprehend them if he had desired to do so. Not to mention the constable—or the runners! She shivered. Why he had not done either she did not know.

And it doesn't signify now! She rang for Ellen. What is more to the purpose, she told herself, a martial light coming into her eyes, is to guess where he does keep the ring and contrive another plan to relieve him of it!

For being, as her father had always called her, of a stubborn persuasion, she had not in the least given up on the notion of getting the ring back and laying her worries to rest. Where the earl's reception might have paralyzed a lesser woman with mortification, it merely raised Cara's fighting hackles and made her the more determined to meet what she considered in the nature of a further challenge and achieve her objective. The only question troubling her was how to proceed since she did not know the ring's whereabouts.

"Come in," she called, in answer to the knock on the door.

"There, and that's longer than I've ever known you sleep, Miss Cara," said Ellen, bustling in and going to set up her bath.

"I hope you made the best of your time then, for I don't expect to repeat the occurrence!" replied Cara testily.

Ellen laughed. "That I did, miss. T'be sure!"

"What dress today, Ellen? I shall be at home, I think." She needed time to think and resolve how best to get that ring back.

She and Ellen then entered into a heated discussion of the merits of a rather severe poplin dress Cara favored over the worked muslin Ellen championed in which Cara should have to wait for Ellen to do up the intricate closings and arrange the pleats which gave the dress its charm. Ellen, winning, pointed out that it "looks just a bit more the thing, Miss Cara, in case one of your gentlemen should call."

Cara wished wistfully as she stepped into the warm bath water that that might be a real concern, but she didn't think so after the treatment both Mr. Dickson and Viscount Lyle had received at the hands of That Wretch and herself, though to be sure she had been an unwilling accomplice at Lady Gannon's ball.

As it turned out, however, Ellen's choice was the better one, for just after a rather solitary luncheon, Cara's gloomy thoughts were diverted from That Wretch by the sound of the front-door knocker.

A few moments later, to her pleasant surprise, Bates announced Mr. Dickson.

"Mr. Dickson, I didn't expect to be honored with your company again quiet so soon—how nice!" she said candidly, leading him to sit down on the settee. His arrival improved her mood a hundredfold, for she took his appearance, almost in the teeth of the earl's boorishness at Lady Gannon's, to denote a considerable regard for her.

She was not, however, going to put it to the test. "But I vow I am feeling the heat dreadfully today. Would you mind terribly if we remained here and did not go out?" I refuse to go to the park and give the earl the smallest chance to interfere! she told herself, smiling with rather steely eyes at Mr. Dickson.

Although Mr. Dickson didn't feel it was particularly warm, he was always ready to make allowances for the delicacy of a lady's constitution. "C-Certainly, Miss Brentwood," he acceded. Then he was silent.

He had no topic of conversation ready to present for discussion and had Lady Brentwood been there he would have had no need of one. He didn't know himself why he was there. He had certainly been quite overset by the actions of Lord Wrothby and Cara at the Gannon ball. Yet the discomfort they had caused him had been equally balanced by the pleasure he had derived seated in Lady Brentwood's quiet, amiable company. He had also enjoyed sitting between Lady Brentwood and Cara when she sat out, himself alternately the object and mediator of the bantering remarks that flew between mother and daughter.

Upon reflection, he had concluded tentatively that, barring Lord Wrothby, it had been one of the most relaxed and enjoyable evenings of his life. So pleasant, in fact, that it had motivated him to blindly present himself again today in hopes of having the experience repeated. But so far, he was conscious only of a feeling of uneasiness that was beginning to increase as the large green eyes across from him regarded him steadily, expecting him to say something further. He began to fidget and shift about uncomfortably on the settee cushions.

Used to being entertained, the Incomparable realized his plight at last and spoke again of the weather. She elaborated on that theme for several minutes seeking some topic which might set him at ease.

Inventing freely, she remarked, "Lord Dougherty has been admiring your browns. Did he tell you?" knowing full well he hadn't because, in fact, he had said the exact opposite. But she considered horses a safe topic of conversation on which Mr. Dickson would find it easy and stimulating to converse and on which she had some little knowledge herself.

But there, however, she was out. Mr. Dickson, if it had been known, did not give the flip of a guinea for what kind of horseflesh walked between the shafts of his carriages so long as they drew them and were unexcitable, hardy beasts. He had no interest whatever in racing horses and would not have raced his even had they been prime goers, as indeed, Lord Dougherty had remarked disparagingly, they were not.

But dense though he might at times be, it had been borne in upon Mr. Dickson that a proper gentleman took an interest in and could talk with a certain amount of knowledge about horseflesh in general and his own in particular, so he began a long, tedious description of his browns, their points — which were negligible, as Cara well knew — and where, when, and from whom he had acquired them.

He filled his account with tips he thought might prove useful to Cara should she ever find herself in the market for a horse, but they only showed her appallingly that she herself knew infinitely more of the subject than he did. She very wisely refrained from making him cogni-

141

zant of this fact, however, and answered appropriately at intervals to show that she understood.

In the midst of this decription, both Cara and Mr. Dickson wondering why their conversation was not going as well as it had the night of Lady Gannon's ball, the parlor door opened and Lady Brentwood walked in. "Hello, my dear. Mr. Dickson, how good of you to call again." She gave them both her gentle smile and continued, "Bates told me you had not had any refreshment yet, so I asked him to bring in some tea and scones. You can stay, Mr. Dickson?" she confirmed.

"C-Certainly, Lady Brentwood," he replied, growing almost visibly more comfortable under that calm, understanding blue gaze.

Lady Brentwood seated herself and began to tell them delightedly about a skit Lady Granton's children had just put on for her during her visit.

Unperceived by either Cara or Mr. Dickson, the tense atmosphere between them began to dissolve. One after the other, they relaxed and leaned back comfortably in their seats.

"The children were adorable in themselves—handsome and extremely well-mannered. May is doing an excellent job of raising them—they will not be at all like *my* unruly daughter when they grow up!" she teased fondly.

"*Maman!*" Cara objected, laughing. Her green eyes twinkling, Cara turned to Mr. Dickson and protested, "You see what I must put up with—maligned! And before a guest, too!" She turned back toward her mother and pretended to glare at her. Lady Brentwood had the grace to blush, but laughed unrepentantly. At her laugh, Cara observed, "I did not get it all from Father!" and laughed again with her mother.

142

Smiling absurdly, Mr. Dickson merely looked from one to the other and basked in the affectionate rapport only too obviously evidenced by their teasing.

Just then Bates came in bringing the tea and scones, and the remainder of Mr. Dickson's visit proceeded as pleasantly for all concerned as it had on the evening of Lady Gannon's ball.

Mr. Dickson took his leave an hour later feeling so lighthearted and pleased with their company that he beamed at them both and began to calculate eagerly when next he might see Lady Brentwood—and Cara, t'be sure—something that had never occurred to him to do before.

Both ladies, in quite as good spirits as he, saw him cordially to the door. Lady Brentwood had simply enjoyed, she told herself, his shy but receptive company while Cara congratulated herself on erasing all the doubts Lord Wrothby had raised in his mind.

As soon as the door was shut upon Mr. Dickson, Cara gave a spiteful crow. I've outdone him! she thought with glee, imagining the earl's expression the next time he discovered her with Mr. Dickson. It was more than obvious to her, and should be to the earl as well, that Mr. Dickson was now quite on the point of proposing. For, in the satisfying aftermath of Mr. Dickson's call, Cara had completely forgotten the strained beginning of it.

Catching her perplexed mother round the waist, Cara whirled them both out of the hallway into the dining room in her delight. Now she need only worry about the viscount and that little matter of the ring.

Leaving Lady Brentwood gasping, she went off, her eyes snapping, to cogitate that last, perpetually it seemed, vexing problem.

But though she considered it often in the course of the following days, at the end of the week she was no nearer a solution and a good deal more provoked with the earl for having dwelled on the problem so long.

On her way to her own bedchamber to dress for Lady Wycliffe's drum that evening, Cara knocked and stuck her head round her mother's door to ask what she was wearing.

Lady Brentwood looked around Ellen, skillfully arranging her hair, and told her, and Cara continued to her room considering which of her own dresses she should choose.

Two and a half-hours later, dressed becomingly in pale yellow silk and violet jaconet, Cara and Lady Brentwood greeted Lord and Lady Wycliffe genially and followed the stream of guests moving through their foyer into the large, attractively decorated room beyond.

Lady Dougherty left her husband's side to hail Lady Brentwood as they entered. She waved Cara on affably as she came up to them, saying, "The young gentlemen are waiting, I know!"

Assuming she wished to speak privately with her mother, Cara smiled politely back at her and continued on toward Mr. Dickson, whom she could see standing several paces in front of her. "Good evening, Mr. Dickson," she greeted him, smiling and watching an older gentleman who had been standing with him move off through the crowd. "I hope I did not frighten off Lord Albright?"

"Good evening, Miss Brentwood." His eyes lit and then, the glow dying, darted behind her to where Lady Brentwood remained standing with Lady Dougherty. "No, no, b'lieve he had something t'tell his wife."

"You are a very poor fibber, Mr. Dickson. 'Something to tell his wife,' indeed!" she teased, but the shy smile of greeting on Mr. Dickson's face had disappeared, and he was beginning to blush and look uncomfortable. Blast my miserable tongue! thought Cara.

Wishing to set him back at ease, she continued hurriedly, "My mother tells me you are something of a gardener. What kind of plants do you grow?"

Much to her surprise, she seemed to have hit upon a topic that was close to Mr. Dickson's heart. For he began to talk at length in as animated a tone as she had ever heard him speak. And for the better part of an hour, he went on in meticulous detail about the care and maintenance of the many different kinds of flowers, lilies and gentians in particular, he had planted.

At the end of an hour, much as Cara herself liked flowers, she didn't wish to hear another little-known fact about their fertilizing, pruning, or transplanting, lilies and gentians in particular, and hinted as subtly as she knew how that they should, perhaps, go and dance.

Her subtlety was lost on Mr. Dickson. She listened to a few more minutes of flowers and then gently laid a hand on his sleeve and stopped him.

He flushed with embarrassment and stammered, "S-s'pose I've jawed y'r ear off about m'gardens."

Thinking it best to ignore the whole issue, Cara merely said, "Listen, Mr. Dickson! Do you hear that music? It is an especial favorite of mine. Please say you'll dance it with me?" She fixed him with large pleading green eyes.

Always willing to oblige a lady's request, he replied, "C-Certainly, Miss Brentwood," now nervously conscious that he had been rattling on about flowers for a long time—probably *too* long.

They moved through the crowd into the Wycliffe's ballroom and joined the dancers already on the dance floor.

Mr. Dickson, still guiltily aware that he had overstepped the bounds of good manners, became mute and awkward in consequence and tensely stepped all over Cara's toes and the hem of her pale yellow gown in a way that he had not previously done.

Guessing the reason for his clumsiness, Cara wished he could forget it and, when he apparently couldn't, felt like boxing his ears for such extreme silliness.

They remained on the floor for the next dance, in which Cara was subjected to the same nervously apoplectic treatment, and when, at the end of it, she discovered that Lady Brentwood had seated herself among the onlooking mamas, she dragged Mr. Dickson willy-nilly over to her mother's side implicitly begging Lady Brentwood with her eyes to come to her aid in dealing with him.

Complying with her daughter's unspoken plea, Lady Brentwood realized that she found it not only a very easy service to render but also a most enjoyable one.

Mr. Dickson, finding himself once again looking into Lady Brentwood's understanding blue eyes and breathing in, or so it seemed to him, her gentle demeanor, so in contrast to that of her daughter's rather challenging air, relaxed and became the lighthearted self of his Monday afternoon call.

Cara spent another rather more pleasant hour in company with Mr. Dickson and her mother, and then, spotting the Viscount Lyle, unaware that she attended and moving toward the card room, excused herself to go and further the viscount's courtship. Dispiritedly dodging through the Wycliffes' guests, she wondered if it would always take Mr. Dickson so long to warm up to her.

Approaching the entrance to the card room, Cara slipped behind two gentlemen heatedly arguing the points of their respective horses. As she passed behind them, she suddenly realized that she had not caught sight of the irritating Lord Wrothby all evening and concluded with a joyous gurgle of laughter that he had not attended the Wycliffes' drum.

She put out her hand to touch the viscount lightly on the arm.

The viscount turned in some surprise, though when he saw who it was, his bright hazel eyes lit with pleasure and swept lingeringly over her figure.

"Would you care to lose a game or two of piquet to me?" she challenged, blushing in spite of herself under his gaze.

"I believe I'll chance it," replied the viscount, smiling slightly.

Seating themselves, the viscount picked up a deck of cards and began to shuffle them expertly. They played several hands during which Cara felt nervously that the viscount appeared a trifle bored.

He did nothing to allay her suspicion by daring her a moment later, "Shall we add a little spice to the game and make a wager?"

"Why not?" Cara answered, taking up his challenge after only the slightest of pauses.

"I will play to claim that handkerchief I can just see," he said silkily, and Cara followed his eyes to the front of her dress where the lace edge of her handkerchief peeped from the low-cut neckline of her dress. She had slipped it there when she had gotten warm dancing with Mr. Dickson and forgotten it.

She blushed but returned calmly enough, "Done. And I shall play for one of your gloves."

The viscount raised his eyebrows and asked humorously, "Only one?"

"Only one," Cara stated firmly. In explanation, she added wickedly, *"One* glove is of no use to its owner save to serve as a reminder of the card game in which he lost its mate!"

The viscount smiled good-humoredly, dealt the cards, and then, looking at her intently, remarked, "Prepare to lose, my dear Cara!"

Smiling back at him, she retorted, "We shall see, Viscount!"

But the viscount proved to be right. Several games later, they played their last hand, and Cara threw down her final card exclaiming, "Faugh! I am usually a much better player."

The viscount laughed indulgently and soothed, "Come, don't be upset. I find I am unequaled at piquet. Ah . . . Shall we take a breath of fresh air . . so that I may claim my prize?"

Cara dug her fingernails into her palms and gritted her teeth, but she was no welsher. At least he wasn't going to claim her handkerchief in full view of everyone in the card room. Appreciating his discretion, she replied, "Of course."

He drew her hand through his arm, and they strolled toward Lady Wycliffe's arbor.

Lord! thought Cara in embarrassment. All the indecency of the wager now struck her.

They left the lights behind and stepped into the cool pine-scented darkness, and she was reminded of another night when she had entered a dark garden. How Lord Wrothby should laugh if he knew of this! she thought in mortification.

The viscount had come to a stop in front of her and turned around in the shadows.

"Let us do this as quickly as possible," Cara said, admitting, "I am not a good loser." She smiled ruefully into the darkness.

The viscount put out one hand, in answer, drawing her closer, and Cara inhaled sharply. With the other hand, he reached, brushing gently against her soft flesh, to tug the lacy handkerchief from its place.

Blushing hotly, Cara exhaled, "That will cure me of making such wagers in future, sir, I assure you!" Her right hand fluttered to cover the hollow between her breasts as if in protection. "Shall we go back?" she asked, beginning, without waiting for his answer, to retrace their steps.

"Of course." He lifted the delicate lace and held it to his nose. A moment later he had pocketed it and moved to follow her.

Inside once more, Cara strained to catch a glimpse of Lady Brentwood among the crowd of guests. "My mother will wish to depart soon, Viscount, I am certain. It is getting rather late." She had had quite enough of Lady Wycliffe's drum.

Why couldn't that wretch of an earl have appeared before I made that harebrained wager? He shows up often enough when I don't want him to! she thought crossly, finding no irony in the fact that she was at that moment blaming Lord Wrothby for *not* doing what she usually blamed him for doing.

"I do understand," Viscount Lyle replied, to Cara's further annoyance, smiling. "Allow me to escort you to her. I believe I see her." He held out his arm again as he spoke and, leading her in a somewhat haphazard fashion through the crowd, brought her to Lady Brentwood, who was still, to Cara's mild surprise, in company with Mr. Dickson.

The viscount acknowledged his rival with a curt nod of his head and addressed Lady Brentwood. "Good evening, madame. Cara has informed me that you would desire to depart soon. May I put my carriage at your convenience?"

Mr. Dickson made a small grimace. He had meant to say that very thing, but, engrossed as he had become in his conversation with Lady Brentwood, he had forgotten.

At the Viscount Lyle's offer, one of Lady Brentwood's eyebrows rose a fraction, and she looked toward Cara. Receiving a slight nod, she answered, "We should like that, sir."

The four chatted a little while longer, and then the two ladies politely took their leave of Mr. Dickson and went, accompanied by the viscount, to retrieve their shawls and depart.

When they had arrived home, Cara thanked the viscount prettily for conveying them and expressed an anticipation she did not at that moment, if truth be told, feel for their next meeting.

"I, too, my dear Cara, hope I may have the pleasure of your company again *very* soon," he said, taking her hand and kissing it. "Until then."

Cara smiled for him and closed the front door upon his retreating figure. She then commented darkly on the evils of taking gentlemen up on their cheeky wagers and flounced off to bed.

But she found that she was not the least bit sleepy and remained pacing back and forth across her bedchamber floor in her nightgown for some time.

By all appearances, the viscount's wager among them, she would soon have the pleasure and relief of not one but two proposals of marriage. But which should I accept? she asked herself. They are equal in almost everything. Mr. Dickson is reputed to be quite as wealthy as Viscount Lyle, and certainly neither outshines the other in terms of features.

The viscount, perhaps, holds the more prestigious position because of his title. That certainly weighs in his favor. Then, too, in terms of personality, though I haven't spent quite as much time with the viscount as I have with Mr. Dickson, I do feel the viscount is the more assertive of the two, she thought.

Both gentlemen seemed to be reserved by nature, but Mr. Dickson's shy hesitancy and tendency to vascillate over decisions she often found vexing. She had not found those characteristics to be part of the viscount's makeup. If anything, Viscount Lyle was more apt to be too opinionated, she mused, leaning toward preferring him.

Illogically, though she was pleased, she did not feel as exultant as she thought she would now that she felt she had her two suitors firmly ensnared. In fact, upon further reflection, she was conscious of a pang of disappointment. The one person she would have wanted to lord the accomplishment over, particularly after his horrid behavior to her the last time she had seen him, had not been present to acknowledge it. She shrugged off her disappointment and thought triumphantly, He might still have the ring, but I've won the game!

She stopped pacing and climbed into bed. Blowing out her candle, she lay back on her pillows and closed her eyes.

Mr. Dickson's tedious monologue on lilies and gentians stole into her memory and began to echo in her head. Then she saw a shadowy Viscount Lyle reach out for her handkerchief and felt his fingers brush the top of her breasts again. Those long fingernails of his! she remembered with distaste, blushing again in embarrassment. She scowled into the darkness.

Sleep was a long time in coming that night.

Ten

Cara twirled happily before her mirror and watched her skirts spread about her in a wide, dark red circle. The color set off her burnished curls daringly and made her skin appear very fair, but she wasn't thinking of that as she surveyed herself in the glass.

No one, she had heard several different people say, wanted to be excluded from any party given by Lady Fairbury, so she knew that the Earl of Malton would be there trying, she made no doubt, with every opportunity that arose to ruin her present state of success with Mr. Dickson and Viscount Lyle.

But I shall be ready for you tonight, my lord, Cara challenged her reflection in the mirror. After such conduct as you have shown, I should put nothing past you! Her color rose as she remembered their last meeting. She put it forcibly out of mind.

Smiling softly to herself, she bit her lips gently to turn them rosy. " 'Tis a good thing Lady Fairbury is an old friend of *Maman's!* she thought. So confident was she that the plan she had in mind would thwart any machinations of the earl's, she had to resist a strong urge to shout "Hah!" at the earl's imagined features in the glass. Contenting herself with another smile, she smoothed an unruly curl and passed out of her bedchamber to descend the stairs, having almost forgotten the Honorable Mr. Dickson and the Viscount Lyle in her eagerness to frustrate the Earl of Malton.

Lady Dougherty, with a resigned George Dougherty seated bside her, pulled up in her carriage outside the Brentwood residence, and Cara, in fine fettle anticipating her meeting with the earl, came away from the parlor window, remarking, "Here is Betsy—the major proponent of gossip in the city. Without her, London should be lost! Or rather, it should be as dull as life in the country!"

Lady Brentwood put aside the periodical she had been leafing through and stood up. She frowned at her daughter and reproved, "Cara, that is not a very becoming thing to say."

"Perhaps not, but you will admit, at least, it is true!" retorted Cara.

Lady Brentwood had to suppress a smile. Betsy did love a good scandal—as long as she was not involved in it! Shaking her head but glad her daughter was in such good spirits, Lady Brentwood linked her arm through Cara's saying, "Come along, my outspoken daughter. If you are going to be so hard on poor Betsy, let us at least not keep her waiting!"

"Poor Betsy, my eye," snorted Cara and was gratified to hear what sounded very like a muffled laugh from her mother as they left the house and were met by George Dougherty, just coming heavily up the steps.

"Ah, a good evenin' to ye, ladies, I'm sure," he greeted them. He escorted them back down the steps and handed them chivalrously into the carriage.

Lady Dougherty's strident voice welcomed them

saying, "I made sure you would not mind, Alicia, my not getting down to come and fetch you when we should only be getting right back in a moment later." Not waiting for Lady Brentwood's murmur of assent, Lady Dougherty thumped the floor of the carriage imperiously with her husband's cane, her signal to the coachman to set off.

They arrived at Lady Fairbury's some fifteen minutes later, and Cara and Lady Brentwood proceeded to spend their first forty-five minutes agreeably mingling among her guests with Lord and Lady Dougherty. Cara had spotted Mr. Dickson early on, but she considered it only polite to remain some little time with the Doughertys. After forty-five minutes, however, she considered the amenities observed and dragged Lady Brentwood off with her to surreptitiously wind her way over to Mr. Dickson, having every intention, once there, of monopolizing his attention.

She was pleased to see his face light up at the sight of her, and the three of them enjoyed a merry conversation for the better part of an hour. Remarking an ormolu clock that stood behind Mr. Dickson and realizing it would soon be time to sit down to the light supper that Lady Fairbury had indicated on her invitation, Cara felt it was the moment to put her plan into action. She had not yet seen Lord Wrothby among the guests, but he had a provoking habit of appearing not to be in attendance and then popping up at the most disadvantageous moments. Lady Fairbury, too, had probably finished greeting even her latest guests at the door by now.

Cara excused herself for a moment from her mother and Mr. Dickson and went to draw her hostess off into an anteroom. "Dear Lady Fairbury, I

154

have the greatest favor to ask of you. I am a very bold piece, I know, even to approach you, but it has become a matter of Necessity," she said candidly. "I should simply love to be seated next to Mr. Dickson during supper. I am certain I should enjoy your delicacies that much more." She smiled. "Is there *any*—?"

Motherly Lady Fairbury had nodded her head solicitously as she listened to Cara's request. Now she held up one hand and interrupted with, "No need to go on, my dear. I know exactly what you mean," and carried her instantly off to the supper room to help her attend to the matter.

Cara watched her place, with a knowing smile, their name-plates side by side on her table and began to thank her profusely.

Lady Fairbury stopped her with a light touch on the arm. "I once asked a hostess of mine for a similar favor, my dear—the old harridan turned me down." She winked at Cara and continued roguishly, glancing in her husband's direction. "But I got him anyway!"

Cara laughed and bent to place an affectionate kiss on Lady Fairbury's cheek before she started back toward her mother and Mr. Dickson. As she went, she acknowledged that what she had done was as audacious as anything the earl had done at Lady Gannon's ball. I don't care! she thought, tossing her red-gold curls. He has set the rules—no holds barred! and she smiled to herself with smug satisfaction. Reaching Mr. Dickson and Lady Brentwood again, she joined in their conversation and began once more to lavish attention and encouragement upon Mr. Dickson, who, she did not notice, appeared not to have missed her in the least.

155

Lady Fairbury, keeping punctually to her schedule, soon announced it was time to sit down to supper, and Mr. Dickson, gallantly offering an arm to each Brentwood lady, escorted both to the supper room.

Reading the nameplates before each place, they passed slowly down the long row of chairs at the table and came to those Cara had visited earlier with Lady Fairbury. Cara allowed Mr. Dickson to announce her place. He moved a chair farther, and she waited expectantly for him to read out his own name.

"Lord Wrothby," he announced, and her eyebrows shot up in shock. She sprang forward to read the little card herself. Neatly lettered upon it were the two words: *Lord Wrothby.*

"If I am correct, you and Lady Brentwood are seated farther down, Dickson, old chap," drawled a voice behind Cara, and she whirled to face the earl, waving lazily with his quizzing glass toward the end of the table.

Her temper rising, Cara watched Mr. Dickson yield his place to the earl politely, unsuspecting of the injustice done him, and travel the length of the table to sit with Lady Brentwood in the very last seats, where she knew the earl had purposely placed him.

In his stocky, retreating figure, she saw all her painstaking effort go for naught. The realization that that effort was so conservative in comparison to the earl's brass as to make her appear silly only exacerbated her feelings.

She sat down hard in her own seat as the earl seated himself next to her. Who was it had said *exaggeration* in relation to the earl had no meaning? Richard? Oh, what did it matter who had said it!

She tossed her head and looked incredulously at the earl.

Lord Wrothby gave her his blandest smile.

She returned him a scathing glare. "At least I *asked* her!" she snapped and turned a furious shoulder upon him.

He leaned toward her and said aggravatingly, "You know you did not want to sit next to that stuffed shirt."

"Why, here is Viscount Lyle!" To her delight, she observed Viscount Lyle just sitting down heavily to her right on the other side of the balding gentleman opposite her. "Hello Viscount Lyle," she called, making a point of his presence for the earl's benefit.

The earl's eyes twinkled appreciatively. "To be sure—Good evening to you, Lyle!"

Viscount Lyle nodded back, allowing some of his displeasure to show in his face. He did not care for the earl, nor did he like having such attention drawn to himself.

"And there is Miss Britmeyer, too, on the other side of him—hello!" continued the earl, irritatingly in Cara's vein. "Let me make Miss Brentwood known to you, Miss Britmeyer."

Miss Britmeyer nodded coldly, enviously eyeing Cara's seat next to the earl.

Cara returned a pleasant smile and recognized the blonde Lord Wrothby had danced with at Lady Gannon's ball. She might have my chair and welcome! Cara thought with vexation.

She turned to concentrate her attention on Lord Sinclair, sitting on the other side of her, and started a moment later as the earl boomed, "You don't hunt, do you, Miss Brentwood?" She opened her mouth to answer that, indeed, she had been used to go with her father in his younger days, but the earl gave her no opportunity to speak.

Including those near him and Lord Sinclair in particular in his look, he continued loudly, "I love to hunt myself. Anything and everything." He threw her a sidelong glance and went on, "That's the thing for which I used to get in most of my trouble when I was young. I would be out shooting when I was supposed to be inside studying. Why, I remember once I came down from school early, before Christmas vacation had started, but I didn't go home. I went to our lodge near *Somerset —* " he emphasized.

The thin balding gentleman opposite Cara, who had been looking rather bored, began to pay attention.

The earl threw another mocking glance at Cara and continued, " — and hunted until my folks expected me at home. My father didn't find out about that one for some time, but when he did . . . !" The earl raised his eyebrows expressively. His listeners chuckled.

"I hope he thrashed you soundly," Cara retorted in a low voice.

The earl ignored her. "What have you added to your illustrious collection of heads recently, Lord Sinclair? I know you are an avid hunter all year round," asked the earl, succeeding in starting Lord Sinclair off on his favorite topic.

"Well," Lord Sinclair began and cleared his deep voice, "just t'other day, I shot me a . . ."

"There'll be no stopping him now," chuckled the earl. "Don't you find these mushrooms a trifle overdone?" He glanced toward the end of the table as he spoke and observed with complacency that Mr. Dickson and Lady Brentwood seemed to be etting along famously.

"You did that on purpose," accused Cara.

"Nonsense. I had nothing to do with the preparation of this meal," he answered, deliberately misunderstanding her and passing a cold collation of meats. "Now. What topic shall *we* converse on? I am nowledgeable on a great many subjects *ladies* enjoy discussing," he said patronizingly, trying to provoke her.

"I do not wish to talk to you at all," declared Cara oldly and popped a mushroom into her mouth to mphasize her point and absolve the mushrooms.

"Overdone, aren't they. I did warn you," he admonished mildly. "If you have an attack of indigestion later, you will have only yourself to thank. Now et me see. You would, I know, enjoy a discussion of dresses," he condescended. "Yours I will state right off becomes you immensely. That red sets off your hair surprisingly well and the . . . creaminess . . . of your skin admirably."

The creamy skin became suffused with pink, and ts owner almost choked on her mushroom.

"But take Miss Fanshawe's dress," continued the earl, bringing his quizzing glass up to survey Miss Fanshawe, seated farther down the table to their left. "She has not had the good sense to choose a color hat becomes her. Probably that dragon of a mother's doing. I have never known anyone to look well in puce," he mused inconsequentially, letting fall his quizzing glass. "With Miss Fanshawe's blond coloring, delicate bone structure, and shy nature," he pronounced, "I should certainly have chosen a cloth n the pink family. There again, that's where your choice of that burgundy suits your, er, *bold* personality.

"Of course, Miss Fanshawe is not nearly so well endowed as you," he persisted exasperatingly, "but we cannot fault her for that. And a skillful seamstress can sometimes address that problem. Perhaps you should give her mother the name of yours? I can tell you have engaged an excellent seamstress because that dress nearly molds itself to the delicious curves of your body," he approved, raising his quizzing glass again to survey Cara insolently.

He let it drop and gave her a whimsical look. "Although, I do believe I prefer the outfit you were wearing on the occasion of our last meeting — even after I had altered it, of course!"

"*Stop!*" hissed Cara, her cheeks burning. "No doubt you have dressed many a mistress in your day, but I do not wish to be the beneficiary of what you have learned!" she whispered.

"Hmm. It would appear you do not enjoy this topic," complained the earl with a mock puzzled expression. "Odd. Perhaps you would rather discuss why you choose to encourage the attentions of a dull stick like Dickson? Or Lyle there?" he asked wickedly, nodding in the viscount's direction and smiling genially at him.

"How dare *you*, of all people — !" spluttered Cara.

Catching his name, the viscount looked up and returned a suspicious nod.

"It cannot be because you love them," finished the earl, his eyes glinting.

Cara lowered her voice and continued furiously, "You, who treat ladies as if they were common trollops!"

The earl's brows snapped together in a black line, and his lips tightened. A moment later, only the hard, angry gleam in his eyes showed that her retort ad gone home. "Miss Brentwood, Miss Brentwood. Do calm down!" he declared loudly, taking up one of her hands and patting it vigorously. "She gets so excited about the plight of the poor working children, you know," he explained to those around them. He bestowed a look of great sympathy upon her.

Speechless, Cara snatched her hand from his and turned her shoulder upon him again. There was a titter from those around them, and the earl shrugged innocently. Cara pressed her lips together tightly, afraid she should say something before all these people she would regret heartily.

Prompted by a remark he had heard on the other side of him, Lord Sinclair broke off reminiscing about his boar's head and directed a question to the gentleman opposite Cara. Thinking he wouldn't be heard over the noise of the plates, he shouted, "Callahan! I say there, Callahan!" Having diverted the man's attention from Cara and the earl and gained everyone else's within carrying distance of his voice, he lowered it, a trifle red about the ears, and asked bluntly, "Harrumph! Um . . . Thought this sort of affair was out of your line. What *are* you doing here?"

The balding gentleman cleared his throat in a manner calculated to capture any remaining wandering attention and returned pompously, "My men and I are here at the express wish of Her Ladyship—an Unpleasant Incident having come to her ears—for the protection of her guests, both while they are attending her party as well as after they should leave it."

"Are you indeed, sir!" exclaimed Lord Sinclair. His voice was lost as he turned to direct a remark to someone farther up the table on his other side. A burst of laughter followed his remark. He turned back to Callahan. "I'd like to know how you're going to do that! What do you plan to do, man, when all of us stand up at midnight and call for our carriages?" Another burst of laughter from those around Cara followed this remark, and Mr. Callahan flushed.

A dreadful suspicion began to grow in Cara' mind.

Observing her expression, the earl confirmed it "Mr. Callahan, Miss Brentwood," he explained mockingly amidst the laughter, "is Chief at Scotland Yard."

"I-Indeed?" stammered Cara, blanching, and trying to sound indifferent.

Waiting until he could be heard again, Mr. Callahan put up his chin and sniffed, "We have our ways, Lord Sinclair." He rounded on the earl then, correcting him disdainfully, "And I'm sure I wish I might be, sir, but in point of fact it is merely over the runners."

"My apologies, sir. You fellows are all rather, er, difficult to keep straight."

Snickers followed the earl's remark.

Mr. Callahan regarded him with dislike. "You may talk down your nose at me all you like, my lord," and he turned to look pointedly at Lord Sinclair before he made his remark general, continuing angrily, "but my runners do a demme—yer pardon, ladies, I'm sure!—good job of protecting just such ungrateful, fancy gents as yerself who can't defend themselves any better that what a—!" He recalled himself to where he was. "—Any better than what a baby could!"

"My dear fellow—" began the earl, perceiving that

162

Mr. Callahan had achieved a high dudgeon, but Lord Sinclair interrupted him.

"Here! There's some that way, but Lord Wrothby ain't—"

Mr. Callahan cut him short. "And what's more, my good lords, it's one of yer own that's preying on you!" he finished triumphantly. He said no more, beginning to consider in the abrupt silence that had fallen if perhaps he had been indiscreet to make that last remark.

"Oh no!" burst out Lord Sinclair, not able to resist the opportunity for a good joke. "So you, sir, in point of fact, have attended in order to spy upon us hoping to catch the poor devil out" and he began to laugh heartily, amid smiles from those around him.

"That would not be unheard of, sir. He might be seated at this very table," replied Callahan primly, retreating behind an official air.

"La, sir," remarked Miss Britmeyer, "that is not in the least humorous," pretending a maidenly alarm. Several other ladies agreed with her.

"Indeed!" boomed the earl, "It might even be good Viscount Lyle here. Where were you, Lyle, last Tuesday eve when Lady Rockingham was, er, relieved of her sapphires out on the old Stanton road?"

Laughter broke out anew at this remark, and Lord Sinclair roared.

"One might easily ask the Earl of Malton the same question," parried the viscount coldly, keeping his anger well-hidden.

Cara threw the viscount a look of sympathy.

Catching her look, the earl observed, "But one might well ask where any of us were, even the ladies!"

Cara's eyebrows shot up in shock.

163

But even Mr. Callahan laughed at that, watchin the earl eye Miss Britmeyer suspiciously.

She beamed back at the earl, delighted at his no tice.

The earl let his suspicious regard rest on severa other ladies before he brought it to bear on Cara "Where were you, for instance, Miss Brentwood?" h asked mockingly.

Her cheeks flamed.

"Really, sir, you are ridiculous," simpered Mr. Cal lahan, laughing on though others were now begin ning to return to their former conversations. "Th very idea that such a fine lady — so *delicate* — c-coul handle a weapon, a horse, b-bring down a carri — oh *no!*"

He realized he was the only person still laughin, and endeavored to contain himself. But apparentl he felt he had to ask, "Wh-Where should she kee her pistol, sir — eh? Beneath her skirts?" and gave final guffaw in the face of several shocked frown from the ladies sitting close enough to have over heard such an improper remark.

"Where indeed?" asked the earl harshly.

Cara forced a laugh, her cheeks still stained wit color, and agreed with Mr. Callahan. She decided th fool merited a Cheltenham drama for unwittingl taking her side. "La, sir! If it were not so absurd t'would be fearfully terrifying — to be all alone, ou in the dark without a candle — *by myself,*" she re peated to be sure he got her point. "I vow the ver; subject of highwaymen makes me tremble!"

It was the earl's eyebrows which shot up now, and for a brief moment he looked as though he woul throw back his head and give a shout of laughter.

Cara gave a shudder for Mr. Callahan's benefit. "

don't care a jot what these gentlemen say, Mr. Callahan, I am excessively glad of you and your runners!" Wonder writ large upon his face, the earl watched as Cara leaned forward and blinked her large green eyes innocently at Mr. Callahan, noting out of the corner of them that guests were rising farther up the table. "Why, you ought to be awarded some kind of medal!" she pronounced.

She watched her praise reduce Mr. Callahan to blushing, stammering imbecility. Then she delivered the *coup de grace*. "Would you — could I — impose upon you, sir, to grant me your arm and put your great skill to poor use in helping me to find my mother?" She pushed back her chair as she spoke and stood.

Shaking out her skirts, one slippered foot tapping impatiently, she waited for him to hurry the interminable distance round the table to her side.

"I declare all this talk of holdups has made me quite faint-hearted," she said plaintively as he approached.

He clucked his tongue and offered his arm, saying, "There, there, my dear. No need to worry yourself . . ."

As he reassured her, she turned to bestow a bland smile of her own upon the earl. Then she took Mr. Callahan's arm and sailed out of the inordinately vexing presence of the Earl of Malton, set, despite what Mr. Callahan might think, on searching out the Honorable Mr. Dickson.

"A performance worthy of Marion Hauterive herself!" exclaimed the earl softly and grinned appreciatively.

Miss Britmeyer was the only one to hear the chuckle that escaped the earl. Surreptitiously, she watched him rise and saunter, a smile still on his face, after Cara and Mr. Callahan.

Calculating the distance admirably, she politely took the viscount's proffered arm. At the door, however, she contrived to make both gentlemen believe they had bumped her into the earl and in the ensuing confusion of amenities pulled her hand from the viscount's arm and placed it daintily upon the earl's.

To the viscount's annoyance, she then tripped happily off with the earl, who threw an offensive knowing grin behind him.

The viscount's eyes narrowed, and he swore softly under his breath. Then he started toward the card rooms to assuage his vanity.

Cara found Mr. Dickson talking animatedly with her mother. Lady Brentwood laughed at something he had been saying as Cara and her escort came up to them.

"M-Miss Brentwood!" exclaimed Mr. Dickson, a shadow of guilt flitting across his face.

Still nettled by the earl's behavior, Cara performed hasty introductions and did not notice Mr. Dickson's expression. "Here you are! We have been looking all over for you." She thanked Mr. Callahan prettily, dismissing him.

"Happy to be of service, Yer Ladyship. Now remember—don't you worry. My men and I shall be looking out for you." He bowed himself off.

I sincerely hope not! thought Cara, grimacing at her mother. Not knowing the cause of the grimace, Lady Brentwood returned a puzzled look, but Cara did not care to explain. "Shall we make up a faro bank?" she asked brightly and carried them both off to the cardrooms. They did not, however, meet the viscount there, for he had long since won his stake in the main room where the play was general and moved with it into one of the smaller, quieter rooms where the betting was enticingly higher.

Drat him, drat him, drat Lord Wrothby! Cara fumed, seated before a baize table and holding a deck of cards in her hands. *I cannot credit the effrontery he had to switch the nameplates!* She turned over the top card and slapped it down upon the table in answer to Lady Brentwood's call.

Where were you? she mimicked the Earl silently. *One might well ask where any of us were, even the ladies!* She ground her teeth. *Where were you Miss Brentwood? The gall of the man!*

She slapped down another card, this time in answer to a call by Mr. Dickson. *Switching Lady Fairbury's nameplates indeed! Why did I not foresee that? I vow he is capable of anything, and I am an absolute nodcock who deserves to be dragged fifty miles behind a horse for not anticipating such an occurrence!*

"Mr. Dickson, would you care to keep the bank?" she asked sweetly. He motioned for her to ask Lady Brentwood first. Lady Brentwood smiled back at him and shook her head as Cara asked, *"Maman?"* Cara looked inquiringly back at Mr. Dickson.

"Don't mind if I do," he answered, and Cara passed him the deck of cards.

Noticing his pile of winnings, she exclaimed in genuine surprise, "Why, Mr. Dickson—you are on a streak tonight!" So incensed with the earl and angry at her own shortsightedness, she hadn't been paying the least bit of attention to whether he won or lost his calls. She glanced at her mother and discovered that she, too, had a small pile of coins before her. *"Maman!* You too? I can see I have some catching up to do." Recalling herself sharply to the game, Cara made a bet on the top card of the deck.

Mr. Dickson flipped it over. He gave her an apologetic smile. Cara bit her lip in frustration and felt like boxing his ears. She smiled charmingly back at him instead and mentally cursed the earl.

A little over an hour later, Mr. Dickson suggested it was getting late. "Not your night, Miss Brentwood," he said, rising. He and Lady Brentwood collected their winnings.

"Unlucky at cards, lucky at love," remarked Lady Brentwood, smiling at Cara.

Mr. Dickson, watching Lady Brentwood gather up her coins, unaccountably turned pink.

Cara gave her mother a rueful smile and replied, "That remains to be seen, *Maman*." Glancing at Mr. Dickson, she noted with pleasant surprise his pink color. He felt her regard and turned, if it were possible, even pinker. Well, perhaps the earl hasn't ruined me after all, Cara thought as she observed Mr. Dickson's pinkness, and her mood improved considerably as the three of them went to take their leave of Lady Fairbury.

To Cara's annoyance, as they approached the entrance, she saw the earl and Miss Britmeyer come out of an anteroom that issued off Lady Fairbury's foyer. They stopped, Miss Britmeyer standing suggestively close to the earl.

Several steps ahead of Lady Brentwood and Mr. Dickson, Cara looked for an alternate path to the door and found none. He must be standing upon the hem of her skirts! she thought indignantly. Heaven only knows what they were doing in there!

Close enough now to see one of Miss Britmeyer's fingers tracing a gentle pattern on the earl's sleeve,

Cara could not help overhearing her ask prettily, "Shall you attend Lady Concord's State Dinner, do you think? I shall be there."

"Then I should be a fool not to," replied the earl, somewhat cynically, Cara thought.

But then, when wasn't the Earl of Malton cynical? Cara wondered, hurrying past before the earl should look up and discover her. Lord, but Miss Britmeyer was shockingly fast!

Miss Britmeyer, hastily putting a proper distance between herself and the earl, looked up to see the back of Cara and nodded to Lady Brentwood and Mr. Dickson. She smiled. If someone had had to see her standing so close to the earl, she could not have chosen a more perfect candidate than Miss Brentwood!

At the door, Cara held her breath, afraid her hostess would remark on her unusual request. But Lady Fairbury had not noticed that her good intentions had gone awry. Absorbed in the duties of hostess, she only remembered Cara's request now that she saw her again and merely gave Cara's hand a little knowing squeeze as she said goodbye.

Cara smiled at her gratefully and returned her squeeze. After all, she thought fairly, following her mother into Mr. Dickson's carriage, it is not *her* fault my plan didn't come off as it was supposed to.

She began to seethe anew over the earl's audacity and frowned into the darkness wondering what Mr. Dickson had thought about her supping next to the earl. Very likely, he hadn't considered it. Who one supped with didn't signify, she hoped, and she had spent a great deal of time in Mr. Dickson's company before the meal. It was the time she had spent with him after the supper that worried her. She was afraid

169

she had appeared rather distracted and wondered now if Mr. Dickson had noticed.

I must contrive more time alone with him soon to be sure this evening has not raised his absurd doubts again. Perhaps, she mused, I should have him to dinner?

Mr. Dickson's driver pulled up before the Brentwood residence with a small lurch. They had all been rather silent on the ride home.

"Do come in for a few moments at least, Mr. Dickson," Cara urged.

He cleared his throat noisily. "I should like to I'm sure, Miss Brentwood, but you see—truth is, it's getting on t'be m'bedtime." He handed them down from his carriage, delivered them to the door, and descended the steps again.

Bates closed the door after him, and Cara snorted, "Poo! It is barely ten o'clock!"

But Lady Brentwood only smiled enigmatically at her and passed on into the parlor.

Cara stood in the hallway a moment thinking. Even *Maman* does not retire quite this early. Mr. Dickson surely would not tell a fib—she could not bring herself even to think the word *lie* in relation to him—would he? she doubted. Wondering apprehensively if the earl's interference had caused more damage to Mr. Dickson's suit than she had thought, Cara slowly followed her mother into the parlor.

She sank down on the settee. Neither lady felt like talking.

"You are tired, *Maman*? Too many balls and dinner parties?" asked Cara finally, noticing her mother's reticence.

"Oh—no, no, my dear." She smiled and shrugged, indicating there was no particular reason for her silence.

170

Cara frowned. After a pause, she asked bluntly, "Is it Father? You are not worrying about what he would think of your going to all these parties? For you know, *Maman,* he of all people would've wanted you to be happy."

A faint blush rose guiltily in Lady Brentwood's cheeks. Her daughter was entirely too close to the mark. "Oh my dear, I know. You are right." She rose and came to give Cara a kiss. "Perhaps I *am* just a little tired, my love. I think I will take Mr. Dickson's—I think I will go on up to bed."

She stopped at the door and turned to look at Cara queerly. "You know that I love you very, *very* much, my dearest?"

"But of course, *Maman,* don't be silly."

"Sleep well, then."

Cara frowned again as Lady Brentwood passed from the room. Of a certainty, *something* was troubling her mother. Cara got up and rang for Bates.

"A glass of chablis, Bates, please," she said, on his entrance.

"Very good, miss." He withdrew.

Most shocking! he thought, scandalized. Young ladies drinking wine! And at such an hour, too! What was the aristocracy coming to? He allowed himself several *tsks* before he swung open the kitchen door and delivered his request to Cook.

She, he noticed, did not appear surprised. Used to Miss Cara's freakishness b'now, more than like. But there, he had heard that country folk had some strange habits. Mayhap this was one of them.

He retraced his steps and schooled his features into a poker face as he knocked and reentered the parlor.

"Thank you, Bates. I think that will be all," Cara

171

said absentmindedly. She came to take the glass from him and continue to sit in a chair closer to the fireplace.

Bates inclined his head with dignity. Very correctly, he closed the parlor door gently behind him. No fool country fashions were going to get the better of his butling!

Cara sipped her wine and stared into the fire. The warmth of it felt good through the thin silk of her evening gown. She supposed she ought to fetch her shawl, but now she was settled she didn't feel like getting up again even to ring for Bates.

She puzzled over what else might be worrying her mother. But she could think of nothing else that might have upset Lady Brentwood. Indeed, until tonight, she had appeared content with their new lives. Something, perhaps some spiteful remark, must have occurred this evening to bring Father to mind, Cara decided—very likely while I was occupied with that odious Lord Wrothby! Fresh anger washed over her.

Moodily she wondered for the hundredth time where Lord Wrothby did keep her father's ring. Of a certainty, it hadn't been in his apartments.

Oh, how I should dearly love to shoot him! she thought, frowning. Her first sight of the earl, standing in the yellow lantern light beside his rocking carriage, rose before her eyes, and she gasped as the idea struck her.

The wine she was sipping took the wrong course, down her windpipe. He keeps it with him! Of course if it is not in his house, he must carry it with him! She choked, coughing violently, her eyes watering. All I have to do is hold him up—again!

She smiled wickedly, several crocodile tears spilling down her cheeks. Transferring her chablis to the other hand, she pulled her handkerchief from her sleeve with her free hand and wiped at them. It is so absurdly simple that I am a cod's head not to have thought of it days ago! she told herself.

She began to plan then, considering every detail. If she could catch him again, returning home after some party, alone this time . . .

Her wine glass had stood empty for three-quarters of an hour, and the fire glowed in a bed of embers when she finally uncurled herself, cold and stiff, from the chair and rose to go to bed.

Her plans did not include old Harry. She could not ask for his help again. Seeing him tied up that last time had acted like a dash of cold water in her face. If the earl had chosen to call a constable that night, regardless of what would have happened to her, old Harry would have been thrown in prison — or worse. Cara blanched at the thought. She was not going to let him run that risk again.

She grinned. Though she suspected he had begun to harbor doubts of her sanity, she was certain if she asked him he would help her. So she was not going to ask.

Now all I need do is choose the place, which depends wholly upon learning the earl's schedule — and take care that that blasted Mr. Callahan is not watching over me as he declared he would! she thought with a shiver of fear. But very likely he, like the *ton,* could be counted upon not to mean his protestations.

She left the parlor and stifled a yawn as she climbed the candlelit stairway. How could Mr. Callahan possibly, she wondered sleepily, even with all of his men, watch over all of Lady Fairbury's guests? And there is no reason he should single out the silly, frightened chit I hope I appeared to him for special services. All the same, I shall have to keep an eye out.

She passed into her bedchamber and closed the door softly, leaning back against it for a moment and relishing her plan to hold up the Earl of Malton. Ohh, what a pleasure it shall be! She chuckled. Just the earl's kind of brass, too.

Eleven

Shall you attend Lady Concord's State Dinner, do you think? I shall be there, whispered the dulcet tones of Miss Britmeyer. Cara woke, the sun at its usual position in her window. *Then I should be a fool not to . . .*

She shook off the last vestiges of sleep, an idea taking shape in her brain. If the earl were indeed going to Lady Concord's dinner, her manor might just be the perfect place to relieve him of her father's ring!

Cara lay under the covers and remembered several snatches of complaints she had heard over the last week about how far out of the city Lady Concord's residence was. She hadn't paid much attention to them at the time, suspecting the complaints of being merely another way for their speakers to let one know they were attending the fête. But she had gathered that an invitation to Lady Concord's State Dinner was something to be envied and the thought of turning it down not to be considered — no matter how far out of the city one had to travel to attend it. The farther out it was the better for her purposes. And the earl would certainly go, even were Miss Britmeyer not going to be there, as *she* no doubt knew very well!

It is not hard to guess how she wrangled an invitation to it! Cara thought with a curl of her lip. She stretched and rose, crossing to the window to stand in the warm sunshine and look out. She had also heard one or two rather blatant jokes about Lord Concord's eye for pretty women.

I am *glad* I was not invited to watch her hang all over both of them as I am certain she will manage to do! she thought coming away from the window and ringing for Ellen. It was going to be a beautiful day and she needed a very good map.

With Ellen's help, Cara hurried into a lavender walking dress and just under half an hour later ran lightly down the steps to join her mother for breakfast.

"Do you need anything, *Maman?*" Cara asked, when they had finished. "I have an errand to run, down to Bond Street."

"I don't believ—"

"Doesn't Madame Diette still have to send round the reticule to match your rose satin ballgown? I may as well stop in and ask if it is ready as I shall be down there. You might want to wear that gown to Lady Cranton's ball."

"Oh! Yes, indeed. I had almost forgotten. Though, I don't think I am going to wear that dress to May's," Lady Brentwood mused. "But," she said with a smile, "do get it if it is ready, for I might want to change my mind."

"I shan't be long," Cara said, dropping a kiss on Lady Brentwood's cheek. She was relieved to note that her mother seemed to be her usual self this morning.

176

4 FREE BOOKS

TO GET YOUR 4 FREE BOOKS WORTH $18.00 — MAIL IN THE FREE BOOK CERTIFICATE T O D A Y

Fill in the Free Book Certificate below, and we'll send your FREE BOOKS to you as soon as we receive it.

If the certificate is missing below, write to: Zebra Home Subscription Service, Inc., P.O. Box 5214, 120 Brighton Road, Clifton, New Jersey 07015-5214.

FREE BOOK CERTIFICATE

4 FREE BOOKS

ZEBRA HOME SUBSCRIPTION SERVICE, INC.

YES! Please start my subscription to Zebra Historical Romances and send me my first 4 books absolutely FREE. I understand that each month I may preview four new Zebra Historical Romances free for 10 days. If I'm not satisfied with them, I may return the four books within 10 days and owe nothing. Otherwise, I will pay the low preferred subscriber's price of just $3.75 each; a total of $15.00, *a savings off the publisher's price of $3.00.* I may return any shipment and I may cancel this subscription at any time. There is no obligation to buy any shipment and there are no shipping, handling or other hidden charges. Regardless of what I decide, the four free books are mine to keep.

NAME

ADDRESS _____ APT

CITY _____ STATE _____ ZIP

TELEPHONE ( )

SIGNATURE _____ (if under 18, parent or guardian must sign)

Terms, offer and prices subject to change without notice. Subscription subject to acceptance by Zebra Books. Zebra Books reserves the right to reject any order or cancel any subscription.

ZB0893

ZEBRA HOME SUBSCRIPTION
SERVICE, INC.
120 BRIGHTON ROAD
P.O. Box 5214
CLIFTON, NEW JERSEY 07015-5214

AFFIX
STAMP
HERE

Old Harry soon drew up before the front door in the old brougham, and Cara and Ellen set off to search out the best map of London and environs Cara could find.

When they returned an hour and a half later, Cara was pleased to find that Mr. Dickson had called in her absence quite as he had been used to do. She sent Ellen upstairs to deposit her packages, one in her mother's room, for the reticule had indeed been ready, and the other in her own room for later study, and joined Lady Brentwood and Mr. Dickson in the parlor.

On her entrance, Mr. Dickson blushingly suggested both ladies come for a ride in his phaeton.

Lady Brentwood would have declined, but Mr. Dickson stammered a second invitation, and Cara, taking her cue from him, insisted, feeling both that his invitation was another good sign of his intentions toward herself and that, since her mother would probably accompany them frequently after the wedding, he might as well start becoming used to the notion.

Consequently, they all set out, Lady Brentwood making it a point to sit with her back to the horses so that Cara and Mr. Dickson might sit together. Mr. Dickson's man drove them, stopping twice so that they might chat with Lady Beaufort and the Doughertys, around the park during which time all three thoroughly enjoyed themselves in twitting one another on some ridiculous habit they each possessed or some embarrassing situation they had witnessed the others engaged in. To Cara's surprise, Mr. Dickson not only held his own in the conversation but told several tales on himself that made her laugh out loud.

177

"I have a good one," Cara said after laughing at one of Mr. Dickson's, "but I can't tell it," she teased, coloring as she thought of the viscount and her wager with him.

"Oh, that is too bad of her, don't you think, Mr. Dickson?" protested her mother. "Who is embarrassed by it?" she wheedled.

"Me, and that's all I'm going to tell you," laughed Cara. Both Lady Brentwood and Mr. Dickson tried diligently for several minutes to get Cara to disclose her story.

"Stubborn child!" accused Lady Brentwood in mock irritation, finally giving up. "It is no use, Mr. Dickson," she said, shaking her head at him to indicate he also should stop trying. "When she decides she isn't going to tell you something, you may believe me that even another excruciating series of dress fittings, like the ones we endured when we first arrived here, wouldn't drag it out of her!"

Cara and her mother both laughed in remembrance, somewhat to Mr. Dickson's perplexity, since he had never had to endure such an ordeal, and then went off again describing each other's absurd habits for Mr. Dickson's benefit. As each was careful to mention only habits that the other was well-aware made her a figure of fun, they all returned to the house in quite as good humor with one another as they had been when they had left it.

It wasn't until they pulled up before the house again that Cara realized with a shock that the earl hadn't interrupted them once during their drive! The realization struck her with considerable unpleasantness, and a small frown appeared between her brows as she tried to divine what this new strategy might mean—for that had to be what his absence signified.

178

He has decided to throw up his preposturous romantic campaign and turn me in! she concluded, an icy coldness washing over her. She gulped and took a deep breath. You are letting your imagination run away with you — don't be a goose! she commanded herself. If he had done that they would surely have come for me by now.

She looked quickly to her left and right, almost expecting to see Mr. Callahan and his men converging on her. Seeing no one of such an official nature, she heaved a silent sigh. Surely they would have, she assured herself, which must mean he cannot have told them — yet, at any rate. She tried to attend to what her mother and Mr. Dickson were saying.

Apparently Lady Brentwood had suggested Mr. Dickson come inside for refreshment of some kind, for she was looking at Cara and Mr. Dickson inquiringly. Cara hastily agreed and looked to Mr. Dickson, who beamed at both ladies and accepted in an extremely pleased tone of voice. The sooner I get that ring back, the better everything shall be! thought Cara grimly.

Mr. Dickson handed the ladies down from his carriage, and they went inside, Lady Brentwood allowing the other two to precede her into the parlor in order to inform Bates of what they required.

Cara, preoccupied with anxious thoughts about the earl, strode into the room and flung herself down upon the settee. She failed to notice that Mr. Dickson, seating himself stiffly in a chair, had regained his old nervousness.

He sat, sliding his hands up and down upon the thighs of his pants' legs in a hopeless attempt to find them a position that would indicate, even if he didn't feel so, that he was at his ease. He cleared his throat, preparing to ask Cara if the weather were bothering her today. Fortunately for him, since his question would have made it abundantly plain to Cara that he was more than a little uncomfortable for the simple reason that had the weather been bothering her it was to be assumed she would not have gone out in it, Lady Brentwood came into the parlor just then.

Without appearing even to realize his discomfort, she set him instantly back at ease. Her entrance, too, Mr. Dickson observed irrelevantly, brought Cara out of her brown study.

A pleasant forty-five minutes later, Mr. Dickson, declaring happily he should like a dance with both of them at Lady Cranton's ball, took his leave of them and was driven off in his phaeton.

As they closed the front door upon him, Cara remembered her mother's purse. "Oh! Madame Diette had done with your reticule, *Maman*, and I brought it home with me. Ellen has taken it upstairs."

"Well and good then. Now I may change my mind if I wish. I think I shall just go and have a look at it this very minute. Have you looked at it? Come and see," she invited, starting for her bedchamber and humming softly.

Cara followed her mother upstairs, smiling in spite of her worries. It was good to see her mother so obviously happy.

When Lady Brentwood had exclaimed over Madame Diette's handiwork and declared herself satisfied with the purse, Cara excused herself and went to her own room to unwrap her own package.

It did not take her many minutes' study to realize with surprise that Lady Concord's residence was only on the outskirts of London! Lord, she thought scornfully, these Londoners had me thinking it was

180

almost to Brentwood Crest! The proximity, she could see, was going to make it easier than she had expected, if a trifle more dangerous, to hold up the Earl of Malton there.

Believing that the earl might have changed his tactics, Cara found it difficult in the extreme to wait, with rising trepidation, the week remaining before Lady Concord's dinner.

But the day arrived at last and dawned clear and sunny. Cara woke very early and was unable to go back to sleep. She got up and, pulling her wrapper about her, went to sit in her window seat and watch the sun, just risen, burn away the last wisps and lengths of light pink and dark purple clouds.

At her usual hour, she rang for Ellen. She did not wish this day remembered for any departure of hers from her usual practice. Consequently she went with Lady Brentwood that morning as planned to call on Lady Dougherty.

When they had done with their visit, Lady Dougherty gave them an excellent lunch, and then the Brentwood ladies returned home to spend a quiet afternoon. Lady Dougherty was to call for Lady Brentwood again that evening to attend another of Lady Harrows's musicales, and Lady Winnipeg and her two daughters were engaged to take Cara up with them to a rout.

For Cara, the hours in the interim before dinner seemed to crawl. She went over her route out of the city three times and studied her entire plan again with an eye toward any dangers she might still have overlooked. Then she tried to rest, to no avail. She was far too wrought up.

When dinnertime finally approached, she dressed with her usual care, quite as if she were really going to attend a rout, and went downstairs. But she was finding it difficult to ignore the excitement beginning to roil in her stomach and harder still to force herself to eat her usual dinner. For one of the most dangerous parts of her plan lay just after dinner when it would appear that Lady Winnipeg and her daughters were late. That good lady had no notion that she and her offspring were engaged to Cara, being from start to finish a Banbury tale told to gain Cara the evening free.

At last the dishes were removed, and Lady Dougherty arrived. Cara had an anxious moment fearing that the two ladies would indeed wait as they declared they would for Lady Winnipeg to arrive and take her up. But, wisely, she played on Lady Dougherty's own anxieties by pointing out that they should both be in Lady Harrows's black books if they caused Distraction by coming in late.

Lady Brentwood, who would have prevailed against Cara, bowed to the combined forces of Cara and Lady Dougherty, for she did not wish to cause her friend any embarrassment. She was persuaded into leaving before Lady Winnipeg arrived, but not before she had uttered several strong pronouncements on that lady's ideas of promptness.

Both Lady Dougherty and Cara breathed a sigh of relief as the two ladies went out the door, Cara still assuring her mother that she should have no difficulty in getting up in Lady Winnipeg's carriage, this once, without her watchful eye. She stood on the steps and waved them out of sight and then returned inside to delegate Bates a task that would keep the entire household occupied in the kitchen for the better part of the night.

Then she retired to the parlor, appearing to wait

for Lady Winnipeg but, in actuality, only waiting for the servants to get well into the task she had set them before she slipped up to her room and undid hooks and eyes to remove her dress and don her father's old clothes.

I vow this *is* the last time! she told herself, pushing her hair up under the hat. It shall be, for I intend to get that confounded ring back tonight!

She swung on her cloak, felt the weight of her pistol in its pocket with satisfaction, and went to listen at her door. Hearing nothing, she stole out, locking the door behind her, and waited again, listening at the top of the stairs. Then she stole down the staircase and out her own front door.

She walked briskly to the corner where she could see a boy walking the horse she had engaged a day ago under the streetlamp. She grunted at him in male fashion and, taking the reins from him, swung herself up into the saddle. As indifferently as several men she had observed, she tossed him a gold coin and cantered off, her horse's shoes making entirely too much noise for her taste as they rang on the cobblestones.

Following the course she had plotted down the less-traveled streets, she wound her way out of the city, and a half an hour's easy gallop under a rising crescent moon brought her within sight of Lady Concord's manor.

Brightly lit and situated on the highest knoll of the rolling countryside, it stood out against the sky like a jewel. Guests, Cara could see, had already begun to arrive. She bit her lip and wished she might have been in place earlier. She had wanted to watch for the earl's crested carriage and be certain he had attended. But there was nothing she could do now about the time Lady Dougherty and her mother had cost her. She stayed her horse under the trees and continued to watch the lanterns of two carriages travel, blinking in and out of sight, a narrow, curving lane that ran toward the manor. Wondering if Lady Concord had asked Mr. Callahan to her State Dinner, she could not help smiling at the thought. She could not imagine him, in his plain dark suit, sitting down to all that pomp. She sobered and spurred her horse forward through the trees as a sudden notion pushed all thought of Mr. Callahan from her mind: she could still watch for the earl's carriage. She had never known him yet be among the first to arrive anywhere!

In fact, his was one of the last carriages to drive through the gateposts before Lady Concord's manor. Cara smiled as she observed the gold of his crest gleam under the flambeaux from her vantage point through the tree limbs. Now she was certain he had attended.

Enjoy your dinner, Lord Wrothby, she thought, almost doffing her hat as the earl's carriage rolled past into the darkness of the drive. For you will surely have the indigestion later!

She waited, watching several more carriages drive through after the earl's, but when after half an hour no more carriages had appeared, she judged all the guests had arrived and turned her horse's head away from the gates.

She had ample time now while they ate to search for the most advantageous point on Lady Concord's road to stop the earl. Allowing her horse to pick his way through the trees, she directed him back toward the road now and again with a gentle tug on the reins. Such a point had to remain out of sight of other carriages which might be traveling behind the earl's, for a good fifteen minutes. It should also be a point easily attained and departed, for the holdup itself must needs be accomplished very quickly.

In the end, she decided upon a piece of road that followed a series of particularly sharp curves about a mile after Lady Concord's road had forked onto the county road. The land was flat there and the border of trees that separated the county road from a field dense but not very wide. She could watch for the earl's carriage at the fork, parallel its travel down the field, cut through the border of trees, and catch it just after the bends in the road forced it to slow, making it easier and quicker to bring to a halt at her shot. Then she could bolt back through the trees and cross the field to the safety of the wood on the other side. Doubling back through the wood, she would then circle east and approach the city from an innocent direction, arousing, she hoped, no suspicions.

Knowing she had several hours yet before Lady Concord's dinner should be over, she tested her plan walking her horse several times from the fork down the field, cutting through the trees, and returning to the fork. As she did so, she memorized the slope of the land along her projected course. When she felt she knew the course well enough, she branched out and spent the remaining time exploring the countryside adjacent to her projected course. She kept her movements quiet throughout and circumscribed to the edges of the field where, should chance bring a late passerby—or someone who came by more design—she would not be easily observed.

Finally when her bones had begun to ache and her legs to cramp from sitting in the saddle so long, despite getting down at intervals to walk and stretch, she judged it time that guests would soon begin to depart. Pulling her mask from the pocket of her cloak, she slipped it on and went to conceal herself at the fork.

Half an hour later, carriages indeed began to emerge between the stone pillars that marked the entrance to Lady Concord's road. Butterflies assailed Cara's stomach, and the beating of her heart began to pound in her ears as she watched them roll past and disappear. She noted with a measure of relief that Lady Concord's road had spaced them nicely. For the fear of having another carriage roll up upon her in the midst of the holdup had been always at the back of her mind.

Miss Britmeyer's charms must be formidable, she thought with a sardonic little smile when the earl's carriage had not appeared some thirty-five minutes later. Lord! I hope he does not decide to take her up with him and carry her home! She wiped her moist palms on her pants' legs, growing impatient. She leaned forward and ran her hand over her horse's smooth neck. Any moment now, any moment, she told him silently.

Good lord, why doesn't the wretch come *on?* she thought. It's been fifteen minutes, if it's been an hour—not another carriage has gone by! She sighed, wiping her right hand on her pants again. He was nearly the last to arrive, and it would appear he is going to be the very last to leave. It shan't hurt, however, to have most of the other carriages already gone home, she rationalized.

Ten minutes later, another carriage pulled through the pillars and revealed, at last, as it passed on her right, the earl's crest on the paneling between its lanterns.

Instantly Cara backed her horse from her position in the midst of a tight cluster of trunks, limbs, and foliage and dodged as quickly as she dared with safety in the slight moonlight through the trees to the edge of the field. Once on the field, she urged her horse into a breakneck gallop.

As the earl's carriage pulled onto the county road, a small, dark figure darted from the trees. It ran alongside the carriage for a moment and then leaped, one arm outstretched toward the door handle.

The earl, lying back against his cushions in the semi-darkness inside the carriage was startled to see the door fly open and a small man cannonball in at his feet.

"Your ingenuity and verve, Wosso, I see, know no bounds. I congratulate you. *Don't* spoil the shine, please," remarked the earl, removing his Hessians from danger as the little man scrambled from the floor of the carriage.

"Thanks, Guv," replied Wosso, grinning and slapping at his clothes as if such action would remove their dirt.

The information he then delivered made the earl's eyebrows rise in a frown of surprise. But without so much as a pause, he took up his cane and struck the ceiling of the carriage once. Whatever crackbrained notion the chit had, she was going to discover it routed.

The carriage was already slowing as he rolled the window down and stuck his head out to call, "Stop her, Thomas."

"Here, m'lord?" asked his driver, doing as he was bid despite his question. "What if another carriage—?"

"Get over as far as you can and then unhitch the leader," interrupted the earl, as if he were making the most common of requests. "I'll wager there aren't many behind us."

"Unhitch the—! But m'lord—!"

"Now, Thomas." His Lordship's head disappeared inside the carriage.

He saw that Wosso had already pulled his pistol from the side pocket and was priming it. "Why do I feel you are hanging out for more gold, little man?" he remarked, his lips curving into a smile. Wosso chuckled.

"Ho, there," called a voice a moment later.

"Devil take it!" growled the earl and laid his head back against the cushions, closing his eyes in exasperation.

"Cain't yer pull that thing over any fu'ther?" called the voice again.

"Not without going o'er in the ditch I cain't, nor you could neither!" retorted Thomas from the horses' heads, already flustered by the earl's request. "What d'you care for, there's room and plenty for ten such hacks as your'n to pass!"

"Hacks—!" Whatever the other driver was about to say was cut short by a sharp command from within the other carriage. The driver thought better of his anger and started his horses with a testy, "Giddap then! I'm coming through."

"You've a foot on either side, at least. I could've been by twice by now," goaded Thomas.

The second driver spared an eye from his wheels to glare at Thomas as he rolled past.

Thomas glared back, raising his voice as the carriage distanced itself. "And no, we don't need yer help, thank yer very much!"

"Thomas!" commanded the earl.

Muttering, Thomas went back to unhitching the earl's horse.

"All right and tight, Guv," said Wosso, holding out the pistol.

"Ah." The earl took the pistol and demanded again, "Thomas!" He needed to be off. He flung open the carriage door and jumped down. "Tho—!"

"There! He's ready, he's ready, m'lord!"

"Thank you, Thomas," returned the earl politely. He took the reins from the driver and swung himself up. "I will see you at home." He turned the horse and galloped for the trees at the side of the road.

"Aye, an' you will," grumbled Thomas, staring after him, "in despite of yer queer starts."

Cara, waiting in the middle of the county road, thought grimly, Good lord, it is taking him a year to come those turns!

She walked her horse in a large circle, returning to her place in the middle of the road. Frowning, she decided, I will give him five minutes more. If he is longer than that, it can only be because something has gone off.

Just as she was ready to give it up she saw the carriage appear around the bend before her.

Her heart began to pound. "Thank heaven—at last!" she exclaimed softly. She raised her pistol, aiming carefully at the driver, her mouth set, her eyes glittering behind her mask. A little farther, she thought, calculating the distance. *Now!* She fired.

The carriage had begun to gather speed as it had finished the turn, but it slowed now ludicrously, as if the reins had been cut and the carriage left to roll, horseless, as far as it might. For the driver had seen Cara at the same moment she had sent a bullet whizzing expertly past his right ear. It had left no doubt in his mind about the nature of her intentions.

He threw up his hands. "Don't shoot! Don't shoot me!" he cried, and as an afterthought he bent to frantically unhook his blunderbuss and throw it over the side of the carriage. Then he threw his hands back up and stared, pop-eyed, as she closed the distance between them.

"Get down," she growled.

Instantly he threw himself over the side in a manner reminiscent of the blunderbuss.

"Open it." She waved her pistol toward the door of the carriage. When he had done so, she leveled her pistol at his nose and growled again, "Leave us!"

He did not have to be told twice. He started with surprise, crossed himself at this unforseen stroke of luck, and loped off down the road without a backward glance for his master.

Cara spurred her horse to the door of the carriage. She could hear the scratch of the driver's boots in the dirt as he ran for the curve in the unnatural quiet. She dropped all pretense and, aiming her pistol at the dark figure inside the carriage, commanded, "I will have the ring, my lord, with no games this time, if you please. Consider yourself fortunate I don't shoot you where you sit for the liberties you have taken!"

Something about this highwayman's voice made the figure in the carriage think better of killing him. He relaxed the grip he had been tightening on the trigger of the pistol concealed in his coat pocket. "I presume it is my onyx you refer to," remarked the Viscount Lyle calmly. "It is the single ring I

190

value." He slipped it off his long white middle finger as he spoke and held it out.

Good lord, *it is the Viscount!* thought Cara with horror. But how—? It don't signify. Take the ring like a real highwayman and muddle through it later: it is past time to be off! she thought in rapid succession. For she was certain she had seen the earl's crest. That meant there was at least one more carriage to be accounted for, and the Lord only knew how many other people besides!

The thought of the earl rolling up upon this scene was too much for her. Wordlessly she snatched the ring from the viscount's palm, reined her horse around, and spurred him into a gallop.

Once she was out of sight of the carriage, she left the county road, backtracking at a dangerous pace through the trees toward the field and the safety of the wood on the other side.

The viscount was left to sit musing in the half-light of his coach lanterns until his driver's call and the sound of another carriage rolling up behind his own roused him from his brown study.

His driver's head appear in the doorway. "I weren't jest makin' off, m'lor'. I brung back 'elp. An' we've sent th' earl's t'other man ridin' 'ell for leather up the manor, m'lor'," he said obsequiously, hoping to placate.

"You fool," replied the viscount softly.

"B-Beg pardon, m'lor'?"

"The Earl of Malton?" shot the viscount, fastening on the single piece of information in his driver's speech he had found interesting. He had paid no attention before to the carriage they had passed earlier beyond noticing a delay.

"Y-yes m'lor', an' we've sent—"

191

"I heard you. Keep a still tongue in your head."

"Yes, m'lor'."

The viscount frowned thoughtfully. "Yesss, most interesting." After a moment, he remarked curtly, more to himself than his driver, "We shall have to wait for him to return, I suppose."

"Yes, m'lor'." When the viscount said nothing further, his driver bowed and withdrew from the doorway. It would be wiser to wait in company with the earl's man.

One long finger of the viscount's folded hands tapped with slow irritation as he listened to his driver walk back to the earl's carriage.

Happily they did not have long to wait. Thomas, whom Wosso had told bluntly would be the more presentable of the two of them, rode up soon after in a flurry of hooves. He had brought four other men with him.

"Where is Viscount Lyle?" called Lord Concord testily. He had no particular liking for the viscount and did not at all relish having to come out in the early hours of the morning to his aid. In a just world, he felt, he should have been in his bed digesting his dinner and dropping off to sleep.

The viscount emerged from the dark opening of his carriage.

Lord Concord and a second gentleman dismounted and met him between the two carriages.

"You are not hurt, sir, I take it?" asked Lord Concord, running his eye over the viscount's portly figure and cutting to the heart of the matter. This business could quite possibly take all morning.

"Mr. Callahan," greeted the viscount.

"Viscount Lyle," acknowledged Mr. Callahan.

"Oh, to be sure. But you know each other already

it seems," apologized Lord Concord.

Mr. Callahan jerked a thumb toward the other two men on horseback. "My men."

Viscount Lyle answered Lord Concord's question. "Not in the least. Indeed, I would prefer you gentlemen had not been disturbed. My man, I fear, bolted and sent for you on his own accord." The viscount shrugged. "I think we may all go home to our beds."

This remark made Lord Concord brighten and look on the viscount in a far more positive light. He clapped the viscount on the shoulder. "Well done of you, Lyle! They didn't get much then?" Now he saw the prospect of his bed appear closer, he was inclined to remember his manners.

"No."

At the smile that accompanied the viscount's answer, Lord Concord's dislike returned. Devil! He has murdered the wretch! he thought and looked toward the ditch expecting to discover the body.

"I'd like an account, sir, for the books if it's all the same to you," said Mr. Callahan.

Lord Concord gave Mr. Callahan a look of disgust. The man was determined to keep him from his bed!

"Forgive me, it is not all the same to me," answered the viscount pleasantly. "I thank you for your concern, sir, but nothing of any great moment was taken, and I was not hurt. Only my servant has been caught out in a great piece of foolishness which has unnecessarily disturbed you gentlemen. For that, he shall be dismissed." The viscount began to move toward his carriage. He snapped his fingers at his driver and motioned him to get up on the box.

His driver did not move. As he was to be dismissed, he was weighing the temptation to quit the viscount's service on the instant. Then his better judgment asserted itself. The viscount was not one to run afoul of. His memory provided him with two very good examples for not quitting, and he came to life and did as he was bid.

"But, sir," began Mr. Callahan, refusing to let the matter drop.

"My apologies again, gentlemen. Good night," said the viscount firmly and turned his back on them and got up into his carriage.

His driver waited sullenly to see the carriage door shut and then started the horses.

"Well, that's it then, Callahan. I'm for home and my bed," sighed Lord Concord, remounting.

"We'll just have a look about here a little, sir, if you don't mind. You never know what may be turned up," said Mr. Callahan. "Johnson, attend His Lordship home."

"Not necessary, not necessary," blustered His Lordship.

"To be on the safe side, my lord, if you don't mind. We can't be too careful."

"Oh, very well." He set off, Johnson following.

Mr. Callahan addressed Thomas and Wosso, sitting on the driver's box of the earl's carriage. "You two might keep an eye out as well." Thomas nodded.

"Where's your other leader?" asked Mr. Callahan sharply, finally putting his finger on what had been bothering him about the earl's equipage. "And where's your master, now I think of it?"

Wosso cut Thomas short. "Leader went lame, Gu—sir. 'Is Lor'ship's gone on wit' 'im."

"Your master took him?" asked Mr. Callahan, frowning.

Thomas, also frowning at Wosso, looked to see

194

what he was going to say to that.

"Yessir, 'e's a bit queer thet way, sir, about 'is horses, yer know," said Wosso.

From what Mr. Callahan had seen of the earl at Lady Fairbury's supper, he didn't find this hard to credit. He nodded and turned his attention to his men.

Considering themselves dismissed, Thomas clicked his tongue at the horses. He held his peace, looking as if he were going to burst, until he thought they were out of earshot. Then he gave Wosso a speaking glance and opened his mouth to demand what *that* Banbury tale was all about.

Wosso clapped a dirty hand over his lips and whispered fiercely, "Jest a little fu'ther, if ye doan mind, Tom old boy. Ye'd be amazed how th' sounds kin carry."

When he judged it safe, he removed his hand and, though he grinned all the while, listened politely, allowing Thomas to vent his spleen to his heart's content. Then he blithely explained his first Banbury tale to Thomas's satisfaction with a second. For, in his experience, the fewer people who knew of havey-cavey doings, the fewer people got rolled up for 'em.

The earl, trusting the little man's information implicitly, ambled south through the trees with only the infrequent snap of a stick or swish of a limb returning to place to herald his presence.

He saw what he was looking for well before he heard the soft thud of hooves that accompanied it: the white of a shirt glimmered rhythmically, presumably as someone's cloak fell open and shut, weaving toward him through the dark shapes of the tree trunks. As he had been told to expect, the wisp of white changed direction as he watched and began to angle east, still coming toward him.

A slow smile spread across the earl's features in the darkness, and he moved to become part of the outline of a large tree.

Cara was intent on making the open field and crossing it as swiftly as her horse could carry her to the safety of the wood. She hadn't the slightest idea how the earl had managed his switch with the viscount or why the viscount might have chosen to go along with any harebrained notion of the Earl of Malton's, but she was not going to be caught by the earl, or anyone else who might be skulking about, puzzling over the matter here. She concentrated on riding and achieved a pace that barely allowed her to stay in the saddle avoiding limbs she perceived through the darkness only at the last possible moment.

She pulled up at the edge of the field winded and stopped inside the line of trees to rest her horse and nervously survey the open expanse before her. Lord! she thought, her breath still coming quickly, but I've got to fly across that! What an easy mark I'll—!

Her thought ended in a faint scream as another horse soundlessly separated itself from the trees in her peripheral vision, bumped alongside her, and its rider enfolded her from behind, clamping a hand over her mouth. The grasp around her tightened as he lifted powerfully, almost succeeding in dragging her from her saddle across to his own.

Cara, her eyes wide, her heart hammering in her chest, lay still in her assailant's arms and waited, fighting to contain the scream that was rising in her throat. A scream could easily bring more trouble than aid.

Her body was given another pull, which also failed

196

to dislodge her from her saddle. Then the earl's voice, with an irritated chuckle, ordered softy, "Let go of your stirrups, dammit!"

Cara's scream came out in a gasp of relief. An angry, muffled "No!" was heard from behind the earl's palm. She squirmed violently, pinioned in the earl's arms.

The earl chuckled again. "It is all one to me. This position is a sight more uncomfortable for you, stretched across two saddles, than it is for me, I'll be bound." He made as if to settle himself more comfortably in his saddle. "We will sit here all night if need be."

Cara digested this information for a long moment. His grasp on her did not appear to be loosening. With a muffled "All right!" she capitulated, relaxing the toes of her boots.

Removing the hand over her mouth, the earl pulled her across to his saddle. "I am wondering, Miss Brentwood," he remarked dryly, "why a lady might be out at this hour, alone, dressed in the rig you've got on."

"It's none of your business!"

"Yes, but there are, I'm afraid, certain, er, indignities one must suffer if one insists on plying your particular trade — which, by the by, my girl, I should give up if I were you." His hand moved down the front of her cloak as he spoke and passed beneath it to run intimately over her body.

"Oh!" Cara gasped, blushing hotly in the darkness. Her lawn shirt offered little protection from his searching fingers. She squirmed again.

"And what might this be?" He pulled the viscount's ring from her breeches' pocket, peering at it and turning it between his fingers. "I perceive you

197

are starting a collection?" he asked rudely and slipped the ring into his coat pocket.

"Give it back! It is not yours!"

"Nor yours."

"Stop!" she gasped again, as his hand returned beneath her cloak. She struggled, but he had found what he searched for.

He pulled the pistol from her belt and slipped it after the ring. "You will admit a degree of difficulty, Miss Brentwood, in recognizing a woman dressed as you are as a lady?"

"No!" Her fair-mindedness asserted itself. She tossed her head. "Oh, very well, yes then! But—"

She got no further. The earl cradled her roughly and brought his mouth down on hers, stopping her words. His hand came back to rest against her stomach, lying warmly over the spot her pistol hilt had occupied only a moment before.

It took Cara, lost in the sensation of the earl's lips, fully a minute to realize what that pleasant warmth was.

The earl raised his head abruptly, clamping his hand back over Cara's mouth and listening.

Butterflies fluttered to life in her stomach as Cara raised her hand and pulled with irritation at the earl's fingers. There was no need; she had heard the sounds, too: the distinct jingle of harnesses and the murmur of voices.

"Callahan and his men, I'll be bound! The fools must have ridden to the manor with it," the earl exclaimed softly. He smiled crookedly down at Cara. "You have landed me in the briars this time and no mistake, chit."

Cara saw only the white flash of his teeth in the darkness. Her heart had begun to pound again. "Quickly! We must split up and try to out run them! Let *go!*" she whispered fiercely, trying to shake off the earl's grip.

"Little fool! It is too late for that—do exactly as I say!" He shook her, and she stopped trying to loosen his grasp. "Get back on your horse and wait here. Don't make a sound! When you hear my shot, ride like the very devil and go *home.*" He pulled her pistol from his pocket and pushed it into her hand. "I hope you do not need this."

He made as if to swing her to the ground, but Cara stayed him, holding to the front of his coat with both hands. "What are *you* going to do?" she shot.

"I am going to reward their efforts with a little sport!"

"But why should y—?"

"Now go! Before I change my mind and hand you over to them!" He dropped her to the ground, and she felt him turn his horse.

By the time she had remounted, he had melted into the darkness. She pulled up close to a large trunk, hoping to pass as the earl had done, for a tree. Her heart in her mouth and the hair on the back of her neck rising, she listened to the runners plod closer and closer.

Just as she saw, with horror, the pale oval of a face not four trees distant and feared the earl had saved himself and abandoned her to her just fate, she heard his shot.

There was an instant of silence as the runners froze, listening. Then shouting and hallooing broke out, and the pale oval heading in her direction blinked out as its owner wheeled to join his comrades, already galloping off in the opposite direction in hot pursuit.

She waited, not moving a muscle. When the stillness around her continued unbroken, she let go her breath, moved swiftly from the protection of the trees, and spurred her horse into a hard gallop to the south and home.

Lord! she thought, the wind whipping at her eyelashes and making her worn hat flap. If they catch him, it will be on my head!

A chill that had nothing to do with the wind ran up her spine.

Twelve

Cara waited in an agony of suspense for two excruciating days, fearing to read or hear of the earl's capture and emprisonment. Curiously her anxiety over the earl's welfare pushed all thoughts of the ring—and her failure to get it back—from her mind. When, after two days, she continued to learn nothing of any capture or emprisonment, her fear for the earl began to abate. And on the third morning after the holdup, Lady Dougherty obligingly presented herself and settled the question.

Cara, never so glad to see anyone as Lady Dougherty, surprised her mother with the genuine smile and open arms with which she greeted that lady. She pounced upon her before Bates was through announcing her and pulled her to the settee, even sitting down on the edge of it next to her. She then proceeded to pump her for all the gossip she could muster. But among all the *on-dits* that lady had to relate the earl's name never once crossed her lips.

So, Cara mused, I must suppose he got away. For news of the Earl of Malton's arrest would run like quicksilver, she was certain. If Elizabeth Dougherty hadn't a whisper of such news, it could only be because there wasn't any. Well! He might have let one know! she thought, vexed.

"I declare I feel like a pressed orange," complained Lady Dougherty, giving Cara a look of undisguised suspicion.

"Good heavens, Cara," said Lady Brentwood, unable to keep from laughing at the face Lady Dougherty gave her daughter, "What is it? You will make Betsy think I raised you in the stables. Indeed, Betsy, I have taught her better manners if she would only use them!"

Cara hastily returned her attention to Lady Dougherty. "I beg your pardon, ma'am. I did not mean t—"

"Oh pish, tush, my dear. 'Tis all right, Alicia. The young ones will be young ones," Lady Dougherty cut her off. "I gather I did not give you the news you wished to hear," she added dryly to Cara.

Cara had the grace to blush. "Oh, I believe you did, ma'am. It was nothing of moment. Perhaps you should like to stay to lunch, Lady Dougherty?" Cara invited, politely changing the subject.

"Don't freeze me, my dear. I shan't ask you any more questions. I don't mind if I do, as my George would say. I hope you may be having those delightful little ham rolls I enjoyed so much last time?" she queried.

It was left to Lady Brentwood to reply as they rose and walked to the dining room, for she could see that Cara's thoughts had wandered again. "No, but we are having a turtle soup that I think you shall like just as well. It is one of May Cranton's recipes, which she lent me only recently. She said she serves it before the rabbit at her larger dinners, for it has the most convenient quality of being so filling."

"My dear, she didn't!" exclaimed Lady Dougherty. "I have been trying to wheedle that recipe out of her these past two years!" Lady Dougherty looked at her friend admiringly. "You don't think I might have just a glimpse of it?" she asked wistfully.

Lady Brentwood's eyebrows rose ever so slightly.

Lady Dougherty sighed, "I did not think so."

Lady Brentwood patted her hand before she seated herself at the table. "But I will speak to May and see if perhaps she will give it to you herself," she said consolingly.

"Cara Brentwood!" exclaimed Lady Dougherty, giving vent to her feelings in rapping the table before Cara's place with her fan. "Stop that! It is the height of rudeness to woolgather in the presence of Company!"

Guiltily Cara returned her attention to the two ladies and did her best throughout the meal to keep her attention on the subject at hand. She succeeded tolerably well, having only two brief lapses which Lady Brentwood pretended not to notice, and Lady Dougherty, thankfully, did not notice at all. It would not do to raise Elizabeth Dougherty's curiosity.

But when the luncheon dishes had been removed and the two ladies began to ready themselves to visit Lady Jamieson and a niece she was bringing out, Cara begged off saying she had a slight headache.

Lady Dougherty raised an eyebrow.

Lady Brentwood put her shawl down on a dining-room chair, a tiny frown apparent between her brows.

Cara came to gather it up and place it back in her hands. "But you must go, *Maman*, for I shall only feel worse if you stay on my account."

Knowing the truth of this from her own experience, Lady Brentwood reluctantly agreed. "I will go only if you promise me, Cara, you will lie down and rest," she demanded.

"I promise, *Maman*," replied Cara meekly, smiling slightly as she saw the ladies to the front door.

Lady Brentwood sighed as she went down the front steps behind Lady Dougherty. "I don't believe for a moment she will really lie down," she told herself.

"Never fear, Alicia," said Lady Dougherty, catching the remark. With an effort she heaved herself up into her barouche and looked at her friend. "I make no doubt she will be right as a trivit before time for May's ball tonight," she said dryly.

"I hope you may be right, Betsy," returned Lady Brentwood doubtfully, getting in lightly after her friend.

Lady Dougherty then pounded the ceiling with her sunshade, and the two were driven off.

Cara, however, did go up to her room with some notion of resting. She did in fact have a small headache, for her body had not yet quite caught up for the night's sleep she had foregone to hold up the earl. But she sat down in the window seat upon entering her room and promptly forgot about lying down, so immersed did she become in puzzling, not for the first time in the past three days, over how Lord Wrothby had managed to switch his carriage for the viscount's, to know her escape route, and why he of all people—someone she had been in the habit of regarding as The Enemy—had elected to rescue her from the very men he ought to have wanted to turn her over to. Instead, he had risked his own safety in leading them on a goose chase! Somehow, not having got the ring back seemed very much

ess important than that fact, and she forgot the
ing.

She played with a ribbon on the front of her dress
and wondered idly if Lord Wrothby had taken leave
of his senses. Her memory betrayed her, and she felt
he soft, warm insistence of the earl's lips against her
own. Then she saw the mocking look in his glinting,
half-lidded black eyes. Does he give that look to
Miss Britmeyer, she wondered irrelevantly, or reserve
t for me?

Her thoughts were interrupted by the sight of the
Viscount Lyle, leading a second horse, coming down
he street below her window. She watched him tether
the two horses and disappear from view as he
climbed the front steps.

A moment later, she heard the knocker bang heavily. Oddly, though it was an excellent sign for the viscount to be stopping in so informally, she did not at
all wish to see him.

Reluctantly she got up from the window seat,
smoothed her skirts, and went to meet him in the
parlor.

"Arthur! How nice. I did not imagine when you
said you would see me again soon that it would be
quite this soon!" she greeted him.

He looked neat and respectable in a riding coat of
dark blue serge, which succeeded in hiding his
paunch. Exhibiting, true to his custom, several rings,
he took a pinch of snuff from an ornate box in his
right hand.

Cara looked away uncomfortably from the bare
spot on his middle finger. She noticed again with
shiver of distaste the viscount's immaculate long fingernails. They were as well-manicured as a woman's.

Echoing her sentiment, he said, "How nice it is to

find you at home at this hour of the afternoon, my dear Cara. I trust I do not inconvenience you. I've brought a second horse with me in the hope you might condescend to ride a little with me?"

"I should like nothing better," she answered, putting on an engaging smile and trying to convince herself as much as him. "Of all things I miss in living here instead of at Brentwood Crest, I think the one I miss the most is my regular junkets on horseback about the countryside. Driving in the park is not quite the same thing," she declared ruefully.

"That problem is easily remedied, my dear. Allow me to reserve Ginny, my bay mare, for your personal use. No, no," he protested, putting up a jeweled hand to wave away her expostulations. "I insist. Whenever you feel the desire to ride in future, you have only to send a note round to my stables and one of my grooms will deliver her here to you. You will only," he continued firmly, when Cara attempted again to demur, "crush the tender sentiments I am persuaded you must know I feel for you if you will not avail yourself of my offer."

"You are too kind, sir," murmured Cara, casting her lashes down charmingly.

"Perhaps, if it is not hoping too much, you might also desire my company on one or two of your rides." He took her hand in his, turned it over, and kissed the palm.

"You may be sure of it," she replied, allowing her hand to rest a moment in his before drawing it away. "It will take me but a moment to change. I shall send Bates to procure you some refreshment while you wait."

The viscount bowed his head in acknowledgement, and Cara, stopping to ask Bates to bring the viscount a glass of Madeira and send Ellen to her, hurried up the stairs to change into her riding habit.

Some fifteen minutes later, she returned with a smile she did not in the least feel and asked, "Shall we go?"

"Of course."

Cara told Bates when her mother could expect her back, and they set out walking their horses down Triton Street, which the viscount said soon led out of the city, and turned into a country road.

The day was sunny and warm with a pleasant breeze, and Cara soon allowed Ginny to break into a canter. She wished she might give Ginny her head and gallop until they were both winded, but she refrained in deference to the viscount, sitting his horse rather stiffly.

Half an hour later, the viscount slowed and pointed to a large hill with several shade trees suggesting that there was a pleasing vista of London from the top of it. He proved to be right, and when Cara had exclaimed over the view and looked to her satisfaction, the viscount dismounted and brought out a blanket and proceeded to spread it on the springy grass beneath the trees. Then he laid out a loaf of bread, a cloth of cheese, and a flask of wine for a small picnic.

"Ah, you are a romantic at heart, Arthur," Cara teased, also dismounting and going to seat herself on the blanket and help him. "But this puts me in mind of the Marstons' picnic. Do you go to it?"

He sat down heavily next to her, rather closer than she liked, but she permitted it in order to further an atmosphere of intimacy. "I do indeed and should desire no greater pleasure than to escort you and Lady Brentwood if that favor hasn't already been bestowed on another."

"Not at all, we should love to go with you."

Cara ate little, only sipping her wine. The turtle soup she had had at luncheon had been quite as filling as Lady Cranton had predicted.

They talked desultorily as the viscount ate. He, at least, Cara noted, seemed to enjoy their intimacy even if she herself often found her thoughts wandering back to the earl and his puzzling behavior.

I do not see, now, whether he has Father's ring or not, how he might turn me in to the runners, she mused, and became aware that the viscount had fallen silent. She felt rather than saw him shift imperceptibly and knew he was about to kiss her.

Illogically she jumped up, feeling a sudden loathing to be kissed by him, and, trying to make it appear she was still in ignorance of his intention, strolled a short distance away to stand in the sunshine and look back out over the countryside.

The viscount was surprised by her sudden move but rose himself to follow her, inexorably set on achieving his purpose.

His stubborn determination communicated itself to her through his slow step behind her. With an unreasoning fear lest she be drawn within the circle of those long fingernails, Cara made a banal observation on the view and would have hurried over to untie Ginny from the limbs of the trees.

But the viscount, as she passed, put out a quick hand, exerting a gentle pressure on her arm to convey that he wished her to stop. "In a moment, my dear. I have something of import I wish to speak to you about first."

Cara regarded the long, white hand upon her arm and reluctantly raised her eyes to the intensity of the viscount's eyes. They did not waver from her face.

He took up her other hand, pulling her round to face him. He smiled slightly. "I fear I shall not ask this so well as your other admirers might, my dearest Cara, for this question is not one that comes easily to my lips, but . . . I feel that you are not . . . unaware of my regard for you?" Cara nodded, unable to look away from his bright eyes. "Would you do me the honor to become my . . . wife?"

"Ohh, Arthur, last week, three days ago even—!" Cara groaned and then governed her unruly tongue. "I—you—oh, I don't know!" she cried. He watched the play of emotions across her face. "Please, today is . . . is not a good day to ask me. I—I must be tired. I . . . have had the headache all day—" she ended lamely. "I—I cannot give you an answer today. I must have time to think things through. Forgive me, I know I am behaving stupidly, but I must have time to think! Might—may I give you an answer tomorrow or—or the next day?" She tore her eyes from his.

He released her, retaining one hand and patting it. "Very well, my dear. I understand, perhaps better than you think."

"You are very generous, Arthur." Her lashes dark against her cheeks, she stared irrelevantly at her right hand, caught fast between the viscount's own.

"Shall we go back, my dear?" he asked lightly, letting go her hand. "I shall wait, of course, before I broach the matter to Lady Brentwood."

"Yes, of course," Cara answered mechanically. She turned and hurried to her horse. She was appalled at herself. To have such a proposal made to her—by the Viscount, her preferred choice—and to have bumbled it as she just had! *Why on earth didn't I just say yes?* she asked herself, nonplussed.

If she was more silent on the ride home than was her custom, the viscount courteously appeared not to notice it. He resumed his usual amiable demeanor, and they alternately cantered and walked their horses back to Cara's house.

At the door, she thanked him for the use of Ginny, preferring not to mention his proposal again, though the thought of it was foremost, she felt, in both their minds. She bid him adieu.

The viscount raised her hand to his lips, turning it over as he did so, to kiss the palm sensuously. In a soft, passionate voice, he remarked, "You need have no scruples, you know, my dear."

Not sure she had heard aright, Cara looked up quickly to see his catlike eyes burning with the passion his voice had hinted at. He let her hand drop and turned to walk unhurriedly back down the steps, leaving Cara to stare after him.

Frowning over his odd behavior, she entered the hall and closed the front door slowly behind her, leaning back against it for a moment.

Bates appeared to inform her that Mr. Dickson had called while she was gone out and was, in fact, still in the parlor, waiting, with Lady Brentwood.

Cara nodded and went to join them. "Lord, when it rains, it pours," she muttered. She did not wish, just at the moment, to see Mr. Dickson any more than she had wanted to see the viscount.

Laughter met her as she opened the door and hesitated there, forcibly struck by the absurdly happy looks upon the unguarded faces before her in the moment it took them to realize she stood there.

She smiled and proceeded across the room, mentally condemning herself for a fool not to have guessed sooner what the cause of Mr. Dickson's lack of initiative in her mother's absence was. And a very good cause it was, too! she thought, observing with approval her mother's pale blonde hair becomingly arranged around her oval face, smiling now with amusement.

Lady Brentwood's blue eyes lit in delight as she saw who had entered the room. "Cara, at last! Here is poor James waiting the better part of an hour for you, entertaining me when I should've been entertaining him! You must hear his last anecdote—what do you call it, sir?"

"Well, I guess—guess I should have to call it James's Faux Pas, but I doubt Miss Brentwood would care t'hear it . . . or . . . or . . . would you?" he faltered, trailing off into silence. He also had exclaimed when he had seen Cara enter, but not with the same look of pleasant surprise her mother had shown. His face had fallen ludicrously, and Cara could have laughed out loud at it as he perceived that his visit with Lady Brentwood must be ended now that the supposed object of his visit had arrived. But he strove valiantly to conceal his feelings.

The use of his first name by her mother was not lost on Cara. Taking matters into her own hands, she stopped before them and pleaded, "Oh, Mr. Dickson, I hope you will not think too poorly of me, but I've just returned from a ride, and I fear it has made me ready only for a nap. You know how easily we women tire—I should be frightful company just now." Lady Brentwood's eyebrows shot up at this uncharacteristic avowal. "But I beg you will stay and continue to entertain my mother, for I vow I haven't seen her look this radiant nor heard her laugh as I did a moment ago in quite some time."

Mr. Dickson blushed rosily and began to stammer, "Oh—no, couldn't, not if you can't—"

"Mr. Dickson," Cara said in stentorian tones, using the viscount's argument, "If you leave now on my account, I shall have to conclude that you are sadly put out with me *and* my mother." She gave him a downcast look.

"Oh no, Miss Brentwood. Know I could never be put out with either of you. You could never offend me," he repeated, anxious to have her believe him.

"Then you'll stay?" she asked hopefully.

"Should be d'lighted to stay, if your mother—"

"Good! I know I leave her in good company. I only wish," and here she pretended to stifle a yawn, "I could keep my eyes open and stay, too. We shall see you at the Marstons' picnic, shall we not?" she asked, seeing him nod, but not waiting for his answer to walk back across the room, turn at the door to smile at the two of them, and wave, pulling the door shut behind her.

I suppose I should be wildly jealous, she thought, walking thoughtfully toward the stairs. But the truth is I do find Mr. Dickson a dashed dull stick—now who was it described him that way? Oh yes! The inimitable Earl of Malton! Firmly she put him out of her mind as she ascended the stairs.

In her room, she changed out of her sunflower yellow riding habit and into her lavender wrapper. Lord, what a tangle, she thought. *Why* didn't I accept Viscount Lyle?! she asked herself again. I have worked so hard only for that!

She moved to stand before a small bookcase and abstractedly pull a book from its shelves. Taking it back to the window seat, she sank down and opened it, to all appearances, reading.

Twenty minutes later, Lady Brentwood knocked at her door and receiving an answer, entered. "What," she demanded, "was all that—that," she searched for a word, *"gammon* you told poor Mr. Dickson just now?"

Smiling, Cara answered innocently, "Gammon?"

"You may have fooled him, my dear, but I know you too well. The day you tire easily or need a nap after a ride about the country, no matter *whose* company you've been in—sheer humbug!" She sat down in the dainty armchair near the bed and waited for an explanation.

Cara laughed and said, "Caught out. I'll come clean then. The day was so warm and so sunny and the ride so exhilerating that I did not feel at all like coming inside nor sitting clapped up in a stuffy parlor with a stuf—I mean, with Mr. Dickson, money or no money."

"That is why you are clapped up in your room reading, no doubt!" retorted Lady Brentwood. Cara had the grace to look embarrassed. Getting to the heart of the matter, her mother continued in some surprise, "My dear, I thought you liked Mr. Dickson?"

"Oh, I'm sure I do," replied Cara airily, giving her mother just the opposite impression. "But he is too often not so . . . spontaneous as I could wish him."

"Mmm." Lady Brentwood digested this new piece of information and gave her daughter a suspicious look as if she did not quite believe all that had been told her.

They sat in a comfortable silence for several minutes, both immersed in their own thoughts. Each had a tiny frown between her brows, but for entirely different reasons. Lady Brentwood was thinking of

213

the Honorable Mr. Dickson; Cara of the Viscount Lyle.

At last, Lady Brentwood shook herself back to reality and regarded her daughter. It was unusual for Cara to sit silently for so long. She noticed the slight shadows beneath her unseeing eyes and asked, "How is your headache, my love?"

Cara shrugged.

"You look as though you should try to rest before tonight," she said and then sighed. "But I don't suppose you will."

Surprising her, Cara answered, "On the contrary, I think I will. I feel quite fagged to death."

Instead of pleasing her mother as one might have expected, this answer worried her more than if Cara had refused, as expected. It was unusual in the extreme for Cara to retire in the middle of the afternoon and even more so for her to admit to weariness. "Can I do anything, Cara?" asked her mother with concern

"No, *Maman*, it is only a very little headache. Please don't worry about me." She met her mother's eyes and then looked away, out the window.

"Nothing you care to talk about, I see," commented Lady Brentwood ironically. She rose and came toward her daughter.

"Indeed, *Maman*, it is nothing. I am sorry to vex you. Please, don't worry."

"Oh Cara, Cara. You will be the death of me yet!" her mother scolded. She bent to place a kiss in the red-gold curls. "A little rest often works wonders, my dear," she remarked and went out with a thoughtful look on her face.

As the door closed, Cara laid her book aside and went to lie down in the middle of the big fourposter bed. She rolled onto her side, putting her elbow under her head. She didn't think she could sleep, but she might at least rest.

Her mother might have Mr. Dickson and welcome, she thought. They did seem to suit each other. Her eyelids drooped. She remembered his monologues on gentians and horses, and with an expression somewhere between a smile and a grimace, acknowledged, We should very likely have made each other miserable.

As her weary body overpowered her mind, she thought sleepily, That leaves the viscount. His white fingers with their long manicured nails rose before her. I suppose I shall have to say yes.

Then, for no particular reason, she remembered the earl's clean, masculine scent and the secure sensation of being wrapped in his arms, and her eyes closed.

Thirteen

"Oh!" Cara woke with the warmth of the earl's lips against her own.

Ellen was standing over her in the dusk and shaking her lightly. "The missus sent me to tell you 'twill be dinnertime soon, miss," she said apologetically.

"Yes. What is . . . the time, Ellen?" Groggily Cara struggled to wake up. Her sleep, haunted as it had been by the earl's mocking smile, had not refreshed her.

"Half past six, Miss."

"Then I've time for a bath."

"Yes, miss." Ellen bobbed a curtsey and moved away from the bed.

Cara closed her eyes again and lay back to wait for Ellen's signal.

A short time later, feeling somewhat less groggy after a cool bath and wearing a simple blue gown, she descended the stairs to the dining room

Coming from the parlor, her mother met her, scrutinizing her face. "I'm not at all sure you look any more rested than when you went up," she declared.

Cara smiled wanly. "A good dinner is all I need now to put me in the right of things."

"Well, Cook's will be good," predicted Lady Brentwood.

A heartening dinner of veal tenderloins removed the last of Cara's grogginess, and she teased, "I feel decidedly much more the thing, *Maman*. You shall not have to go alone tonight after all!"

Lady Brentwood raised a derisive eyebrow and exclaimed, "As if I thought you would miss a ball! I believe you would have to be on your deathbed first!"

"Quite so!" answered Cara, her spirits reviving. Very likely she would meet the earl tonight at Lady Cranton's ball since the Season was nearing its close, and there would not be many more functions.

In some indescribable manner, she felt the chase on which he had led the runners had put their relationship on a different footing. What the new one might be she was certain she did not know, but she was intrigued to see how the earl would behave toward her tonight.

"Madame, I believe I shall dazzle the hordes with my white lustring," announced Cara. It was a daring gown because of the décolletage, quite her lowest, and the contrast of the white against the flaming color of her hair. "What will you?" she asked, waxing Elizabethan.

"The rose satin, I have decided. My, that meal certainly did quite a bit for you!"

"Indeed! I am in fighting fettle now! Come—"

"Fighting fettle?" interrupted her mother doubtfully.

"Quite! Let us adjourn to our bedchambers and adorn ourselves!" She offered Lady Brentwood an arm and promenaded with her out of the dining room and up to her mother's bedchamber.

"I shall leave you here, madame," said Cara formally, depositing her mother, laughing, in the chair before her dressing table and leaving her to the capable ministrations of Ellen. "Be good enough to send your maid to me when you have done." She abandoned her formal pose, dropped a kiss on her mother's cheek, and ran out of the room chuckling.

"Minx!" called Lady Brentwood after her.

Some time later, the two climbed into the old brougham and proceeded toward the residence of Lady Cranton, an especial friend of Lady Brentwood's from her younger days.

"Will any of her daughters attend tonight?" asked Cara idly. She had remembered the Viscount Lyle. Very likely he would also be present tonight.

"Cara!" exclaimed Lady Brentwood in surprise. "You know I told you even her eldest daughter isn't old enough to be properly out until next year!"

"Oh yes, forgive me, *Maman*. I'm afraid I was thinking of something else."

"Yes, I see!" She went on, overlooking Cara's rudeness. "She said she was going to indulge them and allow them all, even the little ones, to come down—for she dotes on them, you know. She feels it can do no one any harm if they attend for an hour, and it may help their manners considerably, and I daresay I agree with her."

Lady Brentwood was quiet a moment in the darkness of the carriage. Then she said in a low voice, "I only wish I might have done as much for you, my love."

Cara was surprised at this reference to her mother's old life. She had hoped all their partygoing had helped her mother to put that life behind her. Fool! she told herself, Of course *Maman* could not forget that quickly. It is still too soon . . . but I see no reason to let that memory spoil tonight. Adopting a droll tone, she said, "Well! And as you can see, I have been suffering terribly these last few weeks because I simply did not know *how* to go on."

They both laughed, Cara a little cynically. It was quite plain to anyone from the number of admirers that constantly encircled her that she knew precisely how to go on.

There was no time to say more, for at that moment the old brougham came to a stop, and a footman pulled open the door and let down the steps.

May Cranton greeted her friend at the entrance with warm affection, introduced her to her husband whom Lady Brentwood had not met on her previous visit, and professed herself delighted to meet, in return, her friend's only daughter. Promising to introduce Cara to her own children as soon as her duties greeting guests might be over, she allowed them to continue on into the drawing room and turned back to graciously receive her next guest.

As they joined the stream of entering guests, Mr. Dickson, having apparently been waiting for them, singled them out. Precariously carrying two glasses of ratafia as he dodged people who threatened to bump into him, he came up to them saying, "Saw you come in, 'n thought you might like something to drink."

Exclaiming at his thoughtfulness, the ladies accepted the glasses and watched him disappear into the crowd again to reappear several minutes later carrying a glass of punch for himself.

The three soon fell into the same bantering vein of conversation that had occupied them earlier that afternoon, Mr. Dickson and Lady Brentwood apparently thoroughly entertained. Cara alone began to feel, though she tried not to admit it to herself, a trifle bored with their gentle stories and teasing.

Just then Mr. Dickson sighted George Dougherty and his wife entering and hailed them through the crowd. When they did not respond, he excused himself saying, "I'll just go and get them."

In his absence, Lady Brentwood teased, "Who is it you are looking for so eagerly, my dear? That is the third time you've done that since we arrived."

Caught in the middle of surveying the guests around her, Cara started and snapped her attention guiltily back to her mother to find blue eyes regarding her with curiosity.

"Why, no one! I was, er, merely approximating the number of guests present here tonight," she fabricated. Seeing her mother's eyes light with amusement, she knew she had not deceived her and added with some belligerence, "There are nearly three hundred people here already!"

"Indeed?" commented her mother politely, still smiling.

Mr. Dickson returned with the Doughertys in tow, and greetings went all around. The conversation was resumed, and Cara, listening with only half an ear, realized with a shock that it was Lord Wrothby that she had, in fact, unconciously been searching for. Even now, she half-expected him to emerge from the crowd of guests before her and challenge her in some audacious manner. She gave herself an irritated shake and brought her wandering attention forcibly back to the group around her.

"Where is Lord Wrothby tonight?" asked Lady Dougherty in an ostensibly sympathetic tone of voice, almost reading Cara's thoughts.

"I'm sure I don't know," replied Cara airily, shrugging her shoulders.

"There's a cockfight out in Lancaster County tonight. Mayhap he's at that," suggested Lord Dougherty. His wife sniffed loudly in disapproval. "It'd be more to such a man's taste than this frill, I'd guess." He was quiet a moment thinking and then added with some relish, "B'George, I wish I were there m'self!" Everyone except his wife laughed at this admission.

Giving him a meaning frown, Lady Dougherty said curtly, "Nonsense! You know you don't wish the Brentwoods, nor James, to think you would enjoy such a barbarous sport!" The two Brentwood ladies hid their smiles.

"I don't believe I should bother m'self overmuch on that, m'dear. Ladies are a bit too delicate to understand why a man might like such a sport, beggin' your pardon, ladies, I'm sure," he addressed the Brentwoods. "And as for James here, I *know* he don't care b'cause he's kept me company at a couple of 'em!"

Lady Dougherty turned a scandalized face upon Mr. Dickson and exclaimed, "James! Really!"

Mr. Dickson gave her a sheepish grin and began to blush as he stammered, "No, no, Betsy, that ain't the way of it at all! Was just keepin' George company. I wasn't enjoyin' it! 'Deed if I'd known what he was takin' me to, I wouldn't have gone with him!" He looked anxiously from Lady Dougherty to the Brentwood ladies and back to Lady Dougherty.

"Stand your ground, man. Stand your ground," directed Lord Dougherty.

Lady Dougherty still appeared scandalized, but Cara was having trouble controlling her laughter.

Taking pity on him, Lady Brentwood changed the subject. "There is May again, Cara. Perhaps she is through with her hostess duties by now." Lady Dougherty's expression changed to one of curiosity. "She promised to introduce her delightful children to Cara when she was through," Lady Brentwood explained.

"She allowed her children to attend?" Lady Dougherty queried, aghast. At Lady Brentwood's delicately raised eyebrow, however, she amended her tone. "Harrumph! How . . . *quaint.* By all means, do let us meet them," she agreed.

"Quite! Bring on the little blighters," said her husband cheerily, glad to have his wife's ire placated.

Still pink, Mr. Dickson murmured his concurrence.

"May!" Lady Brentwood called, catching Lady Cranton's attention as she drifted through her guests checking to see that all their needs were being met. On her approach, Lady Brentwood asked, "May, have you a moment to spare now? I should like Cara to meet your children if you have time."

Lady Cranton beamed back at her exclaiming, "Yes indeed!" and immediately sent a footman to fetch them. They were soon to be seen trooping together behind the footman through their mother's guests and causing a stir among them as they came, for they were, as Lady Brentwood had said, all eight of them—from the eldest daughter down to the youngest son—extremely handsome children.

Lady Cranton, regarding them proudly, introduced them to Lady Brentwood's group, and each child bowed or curtsied, appropriate to his or her gender. Cara declared herself charmed to meet them, as indeed she was, and Lady Brentwood told them again

222

how much she had enjoyed the skit they had put on for her on her previous visit. They thanked her prettily and chatted with the grownups a few minutes longer before their mama declared they had disturbed Lady Brentwood and her friends long enough, and carried them off to present them to some of her other guests.

When they had gone, even Lady Dougherty had to exclaim over their manners. "I vow when the youngest one made his tiny bow I quite wanted to pick him up and hug him to death!" she said, putting her handkerchief to the corners of her eyes. Cara's lips quirked in amusement at this.

"There, there, m'dear," comforted her husband. Lady Dougherty allowed him to put his arm about her ample frame—which required some maneuvering on his part. "Don't you be turning on the waterworks now," he said gruffly.

"Oh, George!" was the answer he received, but she allowed him to keep his arm about her.

"P'rhaps we should move on into the ballroom for a dance or two," suggested Mr. Dickson, nervously observing Lady Dougherty's brimming eyes and desirous of avoiding any further confrontations with her.

"A capital idea!" exclaimed Cara, restless and somewhat bored. She looked round the crowd of guests again, still half expecting the earl to appear. If I stop expecting him to show up, that is just when he will surprise me and appear out of nowhere, she thought. She wasn't sure if that would be a good thing or not. She had agreed with Mr. Dickson, hoping a little music and dancing would take her mind off the earl altogether and give her something to do with herself.

Moving slowly through the mingling guests, the five of them threaded their way, stopping frequently for one or the other of them to speak to a friend, into the ballroom.

Lady Dougherty immediately spotted a dowager friend of hers she had not had an opportunity to confer with recently and seated herself beside her with a hearty greeting.

Judging himself on his own, Lord Dougherty promptly asked Cara to dance, which left Mr. Dickson to ask Lady Brentwood. Something he did with no apparent disappointment at being cut out of a dance with Cara by his friend. In fact, one might almost have said he appeared eager to dance with Lady Brentwood.

Lady Dougherty, seeing the dowager's eyes widen, looked behind her and observed with a lowering brow what her husband was up to. Commanding herself to remember to give him a piece of her mind at the first opportunity, she turned back with a loud "Harrumph!" to her friend and resumed what she had been saying.

Blissfully ignorant of his impending doom, Lord Dougherty happily switched off with Mr. Dickson, and the two gentlemen monopolized the two Brentwood ladies for three dances. Lord Dougherty's luck then ran out, and he chanced to be coming off the dance floor with Cara to await Mr. Dickson and Lady Brentwood at the same moment that Lady Dougherty happened to look up from her conversation. She excused herself from her friend and stepped briskly over to grasp him above the elbow.

"Aha! You don't mind, I'm sure, Cara," she stated rather than asked through her teeth, surprising both

Cara and Lord Dougherty, neither of whom had seen her approach.

Lord Dougherty started as if he'd been shot while his wife, without waiting for either of them to vouchsafe an answer, proceeded to drag him back onto the dance floor.

Cara could not help the burst of laughter which escaped her before she could restrain it at the sight of poor George Dougherty's genuinely puzzled face—which earned her a glare from Lady Dougherty.

As his wife dragged him off, he could be heard declaring, "But Betsy, m'dear! You've told me I don't know how many times that you don't dance!"

His heartfelt declaration caused Cara to lose her control, and she burst out in another peal of musical laughter. Wishing there were someone with whom she might share the laugh, she could not help looking again for the earl, expecting he might saunter up and make some caustic remark showing he had enjoyed it as much as she. But she was disappointed. There was only Michael Vennard, mincing his way toward her, seemingly to ask her to dance.

Eyeing his ridiculously high shirt points, she felt her heart sink. She did not feel in the mood for Michael's somewhat conceited dandyism, but neither did she wish to hurt his rather sensitive feelings, so she smiled at him and accepted his arm courteously, if unenthusiastically.

Listening to Michael discourse on himself when the quadrille permitted, Cara suddenly felt thoroughly bored with the whole evening. Forgetting that Viscount Lyle would be expecting an answer to his proposal, she determined that once the dance was over she would go in search of him. The very thought of returning to Mr. Dickson's and her mother's gentle conversation made her feel as though she might scream. The viscount's company, while not so challenging as the earl's, would at least, she thought, remembering her wagered handkerchief, present some measure of stimulation, and it was late enough now for him to have arrived.

The quadrille came to an end, and Michael escorted her back to where her mother and Mr. Dickson were standing and talking to George Dougherty. Lady Dougherty had, apparently, returned to continue her coze with her friend. Cara curtsied, regarding Michael with a slight curl of her lip as he bowed over her hand, kissed it, then minced off in the direction of an an attractive blonde.

Before another of her admirers descended upon her for the next dance, Cara excused herself from the circle, judging the card rooms the best place to begin her search for the viscount.

As she moved off into the crowd, she felt a hand grasp her arm and propel her toward an adjacent antechamber. Looking up quickly, she saw the Earl of Malton, eyes glinting, at her elbow. "Why—hello!" she exclaimed, pleased. "What—where are we going? Is something the matter?" she asked, now observing the rather grim set of his mouth while he still said nothing.

The earl had attended Lady Cranton's ball for the express purpose of putting a flea in Cara's ear. Nodding to several friends as he passed, he steered Cara into the antechamber and shut the door.

"You silly little chit! You will get your pretty head blown off if you do not stop these corkbrained masquerades!" he rounded on her.

Stung, Cara protested, "But I didn't! I mean, I

226

aven't—! Not since I've seen y—!"

The earl didn't listen. "You are playing a game more dangerous than any card game your father played! Callahan appears bumble-fingered, but he's no fool! You shall not have the whip hand very much longer, I can tell you! I must have windmills in my head to be leading your runners on wild goose chases!"

Trying to restrain her temper, Cara said icily, "Have the goodness to tell me what you are talking about!"

"Lord and Lady Peirce up on Markham Hill last night! And if I hear of another one, my girl, I *shall* turn you over to the runners—if only to keep someone from putting a bullet through you!" He walked quickly toward the door, opening it.

"What difference is it to you if I do get my head blown off!" Cara flared, losing her temper. "You high-handed, arrogant, interfering—!"

"Don't think because I haven't I won't!" he tossed over his shoulder and strode out. Why the devil he didn't just let her get herself killed he did not know and, not being in the mood for a ball, left immediately for his club.

Her eyes flashing, Cara stood staring at the open door. She took several turns about the room trying to calm herself. Then she, too, left, almost desperately redoubling her efforts to find the Viscount Lyle, having forgotten, in her anger, all about his proposal.

With a groan of vexation, she caught sight of Lady Dougherty talking with Lady Beaufort and attempted to cut a wide swath around her. But the sharp-eyed Betsy, whose vision had frequently been likened to that of an eagle's, had spotted her and

called out loudly. Cara chose the lesser evil—prefer
ring to go over and hear what she had to say rathe
than keep hearing her name called above the head
of the other guests.

"My dear," Lady Dougherty began, laying he
hand earnestly on Cara's arm, apparently having for
given her for dancing with Lord Dougherty. "I knew
you should want to know." She turned to Lady
Beaufort and explained, "The Earl of Malton ha
been simply accosting her at every party she's beer
to of late!"

Lady Beaufort's bushy white eyebrows went up in
disapproval, and she clucked her tongue sympatheti
cally. "Though," she said, cocking her head to one
side, "I am not certain I should not like that."

Biting back the words that leapt to her tongue
Cara waited politely, one slippered foot tapping im
patiently.

Lady Dougherty continued conspiratorily, "I've
just had it on the best authority, my dear—I won't
say whose—that Lord Wrothby cannot distress you
tonight. He's in the country at his estate, Malton
Park, of course, and has been for nearly a week
now—debauching himself, I make no doubt," she
added in a scandalized tone, "with his cronies and
heaven only knows how many—" She broke off to
glance protectively at Lady Beaufort and then fin
ished awfully, "You-Know-Whats!"

Lady Beaufort looked, a puzzled expression upon
her face, from Lady Dougherty to Cara back to
Lady Dougherty.

Cara's eyebrows flew up, and, containing herself
with an effort, she said bluntly, "That is a complete
faradiddle, Lady Dougherty, for I have just seen
That Wret—Lord Wrothby not a moment since!"

228

Surprise writ large upon her face, Lady Dougherty took a moment to absorb this.

Before she might prepare a barrage of questions, Cara made good her escape. "Pray excuse me, Lady Dougherty, there is Captain Perkins waving at me; I have not spoken to him in an age!"

Lady Dougherty, who prided herself on the fact that her information was always correct, turned to Lady Beaufort and was heard to exclaim, "Just you wait until I see that Liza MacIntosh again! How very fortunate 'twas only Cara I told!"

As Cara joined Captain Perkins, he said, "Good evening, Miss Brentwood! I thought I should save you from putting yourself to the lie!"

She looked at him curiously, one eyebrow rising.

"I am normally reluctant to interrupt other people's conversations, but in this instance I felt sure if I did not one would shortly be made up!

"I am in your debt then, sir. Was it so obvious?" she asked ruefully.

"Oh no!" He looked pointedly at her foot, still giving an infrequent tap. "Restraint, Miss Brentwood, is—"

"—The better part of valor, sir, I know. But I should ascribe both those qualities to you before myself, I'm certain!"

"Blue-deviled, are we?"

"Oh no, sir," she answered, only confirming Captain Perkins's opinion.

They chatted several minutes more, and then Captain Perkins declared he had served his purpose and sent her off into the crowd again.

Cara found the Viscount Lyle easily, standing beside the tables from which glasses of champagne were dispensed, a glass of the yellow bubbly drink in his hand. He welcomed Cara cordially, a question obvious in his bright, catlike eyes.

Instantly Cara remembered his proposal and floundering in her greeting, wished heartily that she had remained in the company of her mother and Mr. Dickson. Eventually, she knew, she must accept the viscount, yet she could not bring herself to say the words.

After an awkward pause, she stammered through the relation of some piece of trivia, and the viscount, perceptively gathering that she still had not made up her mind, considered it wiser not to press her at the moment for an answer.

After twenty minutes of careful conversation with the viscount, Cara could have screamed with the tediousness of it. But she did not like to offend the viscount by departing his company so soon after seeking it out. Instead, she assumed a demure pose, strangely in contrast to her true mood, and suggested prettily that the viscount might, perhaps, like to dance.

He interpreted her invitation as she had intended, as a sign of her forthcoming decision and nodded, pleased, his cat eyes gleaming as he suavely presented his arm to escort her to the ballroom.

When they entered, she looked idly to see if either her mother or Mr. Dickson were present, but she did not feel she could in reality expect them still to be dancing together since she had been gone from them for nearly an hour.

The viscount lead her out on the floor as the music struck up again, and Cara glided easily in his arms, her mood improved simply to be moving about. The viscount was a better dancer than Mr. Dickson but not, however, quite as polished as Lord

Wrothby, who moved liquidly to the music almost as if he were himself a strain of it. Absurdly the thought of the earl made Cara notice that the viscount held her closer and tighter than she liked. A tiny frown appeared between her brows. Of a sudden, the picture of his long, rather rapacious-looking fingernails rose to her mind and would not be banished. In her concentration to do so, she missed a step and caused them both to stumble. "Indeed, I am sorry, Arthur!" she apologized.

But the viscount only smiled in a manner which brought the picture forcibly back to her mind, held her the tiniest bit closer, and continued in the dance steps. All of which served, quite in contrast to his intent, to increase Cara's vexation with the evening in general and the viscount in particular.

They danced the following two dances as well, for, when he asked her, though she was beginning to feel as if she were hobbled, she adamantly did not wish to sit down and rest. She did not feel she could tolerate more tiresome conversations and infinitely preferred the exercise of moving in rhythm to the orchestra to sitting inactively and merely watching the dancers.

When the third dance ended, Cara saw Lady Brentwood enter the ballroom with Mr. Dickson and stand along the edge of the dancers to wait for her. And quite suddenly, Cara felt she had had enough.

Laying her hand gently on the viscount's arm, she suggested that they stop and attempt to leave before the rest of the guests and the crush of carriages that would attend their departure. Assuming his acquiescence, she did not wait for his answer but turned and hurried off the dance floor just as the last dance was beginning.

"Oh! We made it!" she exclaimed, putting on a smile as she came up to her mother and Mr. Dickson.

"May I have the honor of escorting Lady Brentwood and yourself home?" offered Viscount, puffing slightly from his exertions in his attempt to keep up with Cara.

Lady Brentwood interrupted Cara, rushing to accept and make good their escape before the dance ended and it became impossible to move through the crowd. "I'm afraid Mr. Dickson has already offered, Viscount Lyle." She smiled pleasantly. "Perhaps another time."

Having beaten the viscount to the jump this time, Mr. Dickson smiled quietly to himself.

"But you may certainly escort us to the door," appended Cara, mollifying him as she saw his lips set into rather a thin line. She looked at Lady Brentwood and Mr. Dickson inquiringly. "Shall we go?"

They smiled and nodded their agreement, Mr. Dickson not appearing in the least upset, Lady Brentwood noted, when Cara proceeded to put her arm through the viscount's and lead the way through the crowd.

In her haste to leave, Cara hurried the viscount in and out among people, causing the two of them to arrive at the entrance well before Lady Brentwood and Mr. Dickson. She was obliged to stand making small talk — something she depised to do above all things — and tried to control the impatient tapping of her foot as she waited.

The other couple emerged, finally, from the crowd, and the viscount saw them out to Mr. Dickson's carriage, pointedly remarking on his anticipation of conveying the two ladies to the Marstons' picnic and bidding them all good night.

The carriage door closed and the horses started off, and Cara leaned her head back against the cushions, wearily letting Lady Brentwood entertain Mr. Dickson without her. Both, provokingly, appeared to be in very good spirits.

I wish *I* felt as jolly, Cara thought, becoming blue-deviled. What a tiresome ball! I hope I may never attend another like it!

She did not like to think of how pleased she had been to see the earl—until he had started his addle-pated tirade! His parting words began to echo unpleasantly in her head: *"Don't think because I haven't I won't!"* She was not at all certain he had not meant that—and she remembered, he still had the ring!

It was a subdued Cara that got down with Lady Brentwood and, thanking Mr.Dickson, abstractedly bid him good night.

Mr. Dickson, however, absorbed as he was in the pair of blue eyes smiling beside her, did not appear to notice Cara's preoccupation.

Lost in her thoughts, Cara mounted the steps and entered the house, leaving Mr. Dickson to escort Lady Brentwood to the door and say his goodbyes.

Fourteen

At eleven o'clock Saturday morning, the viscount's chaise pulled up before the Brentwoods' door, and the Viscount Lyle stepped awkwardly down. His bejeweled hands pulled slightly at his waistcoat where it had risen over his stomach, and he climbed the stairs heavily and let fall the heavy brass knocker.

Bates promptly swung the door open and showed him into the parlor where the viscount found both ladies looking cool in their pastel dresses and anticipating the Marstons' picnic. They rose as Bates announced him.

To her mother's pleasant greeting, Cara added her own, pointedly bestowing a warm smile upon him. For, having decided it was silly in the extreme to continue putting off the inevitable, she had ignored the malaise she felt at the idea and determined to accept his hand today at the picnic.

With the sun shining down on them, they set off in tolerably good spirits in the viscount's well-sprung chaise and were soon out of the city bowling along the thoroughfare on the forty-five minute drive to the Marstons' home. Pulling up in the long drive shortly after twelve noon, they discovered they were not by far the first to arrive. A crowd of people was to be seen already mingling on the green expanse of lawns before the imposing Tudor building that was the Marstons' home.

Plump, short Lord Marston, with his gray shock of hair ruffled as if he had run his fingers through it several times, greeted them as the viscount handed the ladies down from his chaise. "Hello there! Glad you could come, glad you could come! Elsa is shut up in the kitchen directing those dishes you see coming out over there." He pointed with a chubby finger. "But I wouldn't advise trying to pay your respects to her just yet," he laughed. "She'll be out here to visit a little later. Meantime, you come on out to the lawn, see the rest of the guests, and I'll fetch you your lemonade."

He looked up suddenly at the sound of another carriage pulling up his drive. "Whup-bup," he sputtered, "p'rhaps you could get the ladies their lemonade, Lyle, I see I've some more guests to welcome. We've already brought it out—you can see it in the bowls at the ends of those tables." He slapped the viscount on the back and was off to greet his new arrivals.

The viscount gave him an irritated look and steered the two ladies, chuckling to see the little man so obviously enjoying himself, toward the lemonade.

As the viscount ladled the liquid into ornate crystal cups, Cara surveyed the crowd.

"I am curious to know who you are looking for," said a voice close behind her, and she turned to find Richard Llewellyn with a wistful smile on his face. "I am persuaded it cannot be me."

"Richard! I was not looking for anyone in particular," she denied primly. "You're a pleasant surprise! I have been intending to speak with you, but I haven't seen you since the Gannon ball. What have you been doing with yourself?" She remembered the dark-haired girl the earl had escorted back to him.

"As if you couldn't have if you had desired it," he chided. "Coming it a bit too strong, my girl!"

Cara laughed, a mischievous gleam lighting her eyes and making them appear very green. "Well, I'll lay you a monkey you've fallen head over ears in love with someone else by now. Come—out with it! Who are you making your pretty speeches to now?"

Richard smiled. *"Touché,* Cara. A thrust to the heart. As it happens—"

"Aha! As it happens, you do, you rogue!" Cara interrupted.

"As it happens, I have my eye on a delightful girl—one Janie, by name, whom I took up when the devastating Cara Brentwood would not deign to acknowledge my existence." He dropped his jesting manner and became suddenly serious. Lowering his voice, he said, "But she is in no way a match for the Incomparable. If you would have me, I'd marry you in an instant."

"Don't, Richard," murmured Cara, pained at the sincerity she heard in his voice. "We really should not suit, you know."

"Don't, Richard, don't, Richard," he repeated brusquely, and Cara feared he was about to treat her to one of his surly moods. But he surprised her by continuing in his former jovial manner. "Don't spoil a pleasant day and a happy occasion by becoming blue-deviled—that's what Janie says to me. All right, I won't. But I shall carry you off under the very noses of Lady Brentwood and the viscount here to introduce you to the dear girl." He shot the viscount a provoking smile and took her arm in his, pulling her off, protesting and laughing, across the lawn to where a diminutive girl with dark brown hair and large pansy brown eyes was standing, talking animatedly and waving her small hands excitedly before several people. The viscount, holding two glasses of lemonade and staring coldly after them, was left to converse with Lady Brentwood.

The brunette broke off in alarm as Richard dragged Cara up beside them. "Richard, what are you up to now, you naughty thing?"

He assumed a dramatic pose and said darkly, "I have abducted her from under the very nose of Viscount Lyle—the Incomparable!" Returning to his former light tone, he then blurted, "Miss Cara Brentwood, I should like to present you to Miss Janie De Witt."

Miss DeWitt's face broke into a smile of pleasure, and she exclaimed, "Oh, Miss Brentwood—Cara— may I call you Cara? I have been dying to meet you since this, this . . . *Richard,* for I cannot seem to think of a rude name to call him," she shot a mischievous glance at him, "is forever going on about your accomplishments and holding them up to me. He thinks I am not quite up to snuff, you know, for I live in the country. I tell him not everyone can be perfect, but now that I have met you and know you just a little I can watch what you do—if you won't mind, that is—and see how I should go on and maybe please this . . . *Richard* . . . a little better."

She paused for breath, and Cara, amused at this artless confession, answered, "Janie—and you must certainly call me Cara—I can see we shall suit famously! I do *not* know what this rogue is about telling you such fibs about me! I assure you I am the greatest scapegrace imaginable, and you would be far better off to choose some other lady as a model for your behavior! And, as far as I am concerned, for up until recently I, too, lived in the country, you are *quite* up to snuff," she finished, pretending to give Richard a quelling glance.

Janie beamed at her and turned to face Richard triumphantly, "Hah! What do you say to *that*, Richard? You . . . rogue," she added hesitantly, testing Cara's name for him. "No. I do not think he is quite a rogue," she mused. "He is something else, a . . . oh, I don't know! I shall think of something yet. You shan't get off, Richard!" she teased.

He laughed. "I know when I'm bested. For siding with the enemy, Cara, I should refuse to return you to the infamous viscount."

"Oh no, Richard. You mustn't do that!" cried Janie. "After she has been so nice—never! I shall come, too. We will both take her back where you got her," she said, linking her arms through Cara's and Richard's and starting off. The bluntness of her last remark made both Cara and Richard laugh. "What's the matter with you two?" She brought them bumping to a stop. "Have I done it again?" she wailed.

"See what I mean?" asked Richard of Cara.

"Cara! You have gone over to the other side," accused Janie, viewing Cara's mirth. "Can't a person say anything?"

"Never mind. Never mind," soothed Cara, still smiling as, arms linked, they started off across the lawn once more.

In Cara's absence, the viscount and Lady Brentwood had been joined by Mr. Dickson. He and her mother appeared to be having an enjoyable con-

238

versation, but Cara was guiltily aware that the viscount appeared bored and annoyed.

"Here she is back again, Lyle. Don't look so put out. I had dire need of her presence elsewhere, but the office has been performed, and you may now have her back, you lucky devil," announced Richard pompously. He had no more liking for the viscount than had the earl. "What do you see in this fellow, Cara?" he asked, not above needling the viscount.

Putting Richard's dislike of the viscount down to resentment at his being preferred by her, Cara made her apologies to the viscount and her mother and introduced Janie around the circle they had now formed. By the time she had accomplished this, luncheon was being announced, and they all moved off in the direction of the tables to pick up their plates and sample the delicious dishes they had been smelling since their arrival. Richard and Janie volunteered to gather enough chairs together to seat their group after they had gotten their food and returned in ample time to move down the buffet with their friends.

By the time all the guests had eaten, some of the gentlemen having gone back to the tables two and three times, it was difficult to tell from the empty dishes remaining on the buffet that there had been a sumptuous spread of food there only an hour or so earlier.

Lady Marston, rosy and flushed from her efforts, declared herself to be well-pleased. She then, instead of relaxing and resting as one might have expected her to do after her hectic morning in the kitchen, set about appointing several gentlemen to help her organize the different games she had planned for the afternoon's entertainment: various card games for the older guests, hide and seek and Blindman's Bluff for the young children, and teams of croquet for the older children and the rest of the adults.

In the midst of this organization, there came the sound of wheels on the gravel of the driveway. Heads began to turn to see who the latecomer was. Cara, also, looked up to see a bright yellow and black trap flying up the drive at what seemed a wreckless speed.

"That would be Wrothby—the devil!" exclaimed Richard.

Sending up a cloud of dust behind it, the trap pulled up shortly, and the Earl of Malton was seen to leap down and hold out his arms for the lady who was seated beside him. He caught her easily, drew her hand over his arm, and the two came striding across the lawn, the lady struggling to keep pace with the earl and still laughing and pink-cheeked from her wild ride.

Cara regarded this ostentatious display with a curl of her lip. He *would* have to make the grand entrance, she thought in disgust, eyeing the wind-blown curls which only served to make their owner appear more entrancing.

Lady Marston quickly finished her delegations and called her eldest daughter over to answer any further questions the gentlemen might have in setting up the games. Then she went to greet the earl, a favorite of hers, saying, "Julius, you wicked boy, to come so late! See, you have got just what you deserved, too, for we have all eaten with excellent appetites and the food is quite gone," she teased.

"Lady Marston, nothing could have persuaded me to miss your picnic," he asserted loudly, taking her hand between his own. He gave her the smile that had made many a matchmaking mama forgive him for leading a recalcitrant daughter into foolish behavior. "I should have been here at the start, ma'am, in time to enjoy all the delicacies (which no one else's cook may rival!) but for the fact that one of my horses threw a shoe. There is nothing for it, madame," he said mournfully, "once your horse has thrown a shoe. You have no choice but to stop and have another fitted. And if you are fortunate, you will be near a town when it happens. I, Lady Marston, was nigh ten miles from the nearest town. Miss Britmeyer," he indicated his companion, "was the soul of good humor about it all."

Lady Marston listened to this account with growing concern. She exclaimed, "Oh, you poor boy. Well, we would not let you starve in any case! Come along, the both of you, and we'll get Cook to find you something good to eat—what a terrible thing! And just the day you'd set out for my picnic, too. It's a wonder you both weren't killed!" Still clucking over their mishap, she carried them off to the kitchen.

"Pulled it off," said Richard admiringly. "What a complete hand."

"What utter humbug!" retorted Cara, snorting with disbelief.

"I'm sure if I did that you'd say I'd disgraced you," pouted Janie to Richard.

"Disgraceful display, I agree," grated the viscount.

"Because *you* could not pull it off half so well as that!" rejoined Richard, addressing Janie.

"D'mean you don't b'lieve he really threw a shoe?" asked Mr. Dickson, his doubt mirrored on Lady Brentwood's face.

Cara choked and exclaimed angrily, "I'm sure I for one could not care less whether he did or not! He has already received far more attention than he deserves. Come and let us play!"

Lady Brentwood, as well as the viscount, observed this outburst with frowning surprise as Cara flung off, leading the way to where guests were being divided up into teams for croquet.

"Quite right," agreed Richard, nodding his head and following, pulling Janie along behind him.

The rest of the group followed slowly, Mr. Dickson lingering behind with Lady Brentwood who had seen the Doughertys heading in their direction and waited for them to catch up. The viscount was left to walk on alone, the frown still upon his face.

As he came level with them, George Dougherty slapped Mr. Dickson heartily on the back and said jovially, "I've talked Betsy into playing a game with me — but she'd have a better time if you two was t'join us and make up a team of doubles."

"He just wants to play gentlemen against the ladies, Alicia," remarked Lady Dougherty, with a patronizing smile at her husband, as she came up behind him.

Lady Brentwood smiled back at her, and the four of them walked on to where mallets were being handed round, balls produced, and games begun. Several courses had been marked with wickets so that more than one game might be played at the same time.

Determined not to pay any more attention to the earl, Cara threw herself into her game. She soon succeeded in forgetting him in her absorption on the struggle between her own team — made up of the viscount, Janie, and Richard — and the opposing team to win the game.

Her own team won, taking ten minutes to rest and

efresh themselves with cups of cool lemonade before preparing to play the next team, for Lady Marton had set up a round robin tournament.

One match later, Cara's green eyes were sparkling and her cheeks flushed from the exertion and excitement of winning the first two games. Discussing their winning strategy, her team went for another cup of lemonade and then prepared to play their third game. But the viscount, having exerted himself already more than he cared to, decided to step out, and another person was substituted in his place.

"Oh, it is too bad of you!" cried Cara on learning what he had done. "You will ruin our winning streak!"

"I assure you, my dear, I am easily replaced *in croquet*," he emphasized. "Sit out with me—you are looking a bit hot and flustered yourself. We will take a stroll through the gardens, where it is shaded and cool."

"Never!" she retorted, laughing. "Hot and flustered or not, I'm in this to the death!" She finished her lemonade and, with the light of battle in her eyes, hurried off to join the others.

The frown, having grown more marked, reappeared between the viscount's brows.

Whether or not it was because the viscount was no longer playing or simply because the players by now were beginning to tire, Cara's team lost their third match.

"Deuce take it! If only we could have won this last game we could have trounced Julius in the next," grinned Richard, losing with a good grace and causing everyone to laugh.

"Take care he don't hear you, Richard," warned Lord Dougherty jovially, returning from the matches

243

he and Mr. Dickson had just won.

"Indeed yes, I am certain he would consider that a personal challenge!" agreed Lady Dougherty, venting some of her spleen on the absent Earl. "But, i would have been far more courteous of you to le Alicia win one game at least, George," she went on apparently continuing the conversation her husband had walked away from.

"You don't let me win at whist!" he retorted.

"Though we only played two games, I will admi to being a little weary," Lady Brentwood confessed interrupting.

"Me too," sighed Janie.

"Shall I bring you ladies a chair t'sit on?" inquired Mr. Dickson and, receiving nods, went off while the six continued to talk. He lead the group back to his cluster of chairs, and the ladies sat down and fanned themselves while the gentlemen went to procure something more to drink. They found they had to wait in a short line, for they were not the only ones with that idea in mind.

"My apologies, Cara. I did not dream my playing would make such a difference," said the viscount suavely, walking up with a cup of punch for her. "Excuse my boorishness, ladies. I am afraid I am not one of those people who can juggle more than one cup in each hand."

Lady Brentwood and Janie nodded pleasantly.

Lady Dougherty raised her eyebrows disdainfully and looked away—the viscount was not a favorite of hers.

Cara, irritated that he should assume their loss was due to his absence, though she herself had jokingly intimated as much earlier, felt like boxing his ears. Instead, she accepted the punch and swallowed er irritation, saying gaily, "Oh, I expect you were ight earlier, Arthur. I fear we had already played our est games and were hot and tired when we started his last one."

The gentlemen returned, carrying drinks for all our ladies.

Lord Dougherty handed his wife her punch. Glad o get off his feet, he sat down with an audible 'Ahh," which earned him a pinch from his wife, almost costing him his own punch.

Richard, a step ahead of Mr. Dickson, realized first that with the viscount seated they would be a chair short and, with a sly smile at the ladies, slid into the last free chair.

A moment later, Mr. Dickson, with his hands precariously full of three drinks, realized too late the situation and stood looking from one to the other of them with a woebegone face. Everyone burst out laughing.

Cara rose. "Here is my chair, poor Mr. Dickson," she laughed. "What an ungrateful lot, for you put the chairs together in the first place!"

The viscount saw his opportunity. "Perhaps, if you are not too tired, you would care to take that stroll through the gardens now, my dear?" he asked pleasantly.

"Oh, a capital idea, Arthur! It is reputed to be quite beautiful. I will just take that cup of punch though, Mr. Dickson. Thank you. All that croquet has made me frightfully thirsty."

The viscount linked his arm loosely through hers, and they ambled off toward the gardens at the side of the house.

Richard scowled after them. "What is it she sees in him?" he asked irritably. Janie looked quickly at

Richard. " 'Pon my word, he has the worst reputa tion at White's you can imagine."

This remark brought a frown to Lady Brentwood' brow. She determined to remember to ask her daugh ter about it later.

"Do you care so much, Richard?" murmured Jani wistfully.

Richard looked surprised. "Don't be a goosecap Janie! I'd have said the same thing were you or an other gently bred woman with him," he said harshl Lightening his tone then, he declared, "Come on let's go watch Wrothby burn them. Excuse us, ladies Your servant, gentlemen," he said politely, pullin; Janie to her feet and leading her off in the directior of the final croquet matches.

Cara had entered the Marstons' well-kept garden still arm in arm with the viscount. She was quiet finishing her punch, as they strolled along the nar row, green walkways that turned and intersected much like a maze.

They chatted desultorily, breathing in the fain aroma of honeysuckle and roses mingled with that o green leaves, until the viscount, too, became quiet He slowed, regarding the bright hair and the lon; lashes, dark against the creamy skin, and his finger: tightened on her arm.

He turned her to face him and remarked, "M; dear, I think it is time for an answer."

Cara looked away from him. "Oh, you are right of course." It was a subject she did not care to think about just at that particular moment amid the lush vibrant greens and delicate pastels of the garden.

"You need play the innocent with me no longer my dear. I fear I begin to weary of the game."

Cara looked back at him sharply.

"You did not think I give up my rings so easily to real highwaymen, surely?"

She gasped in horror.

"I gave it you as an engagement ring. Why do you still play games?" His cat eyes narrowed. He looked into her eyes as if he would read her very soul and guessed softly, "Unless it is an earldom you are waiting for—is that it?" He shook her, breathing in the intoxicating scent of jasmine that always clung to her. "I will change your mind!" One arm came up swiftly behind her and, grasping the nape of her neck, he pulled her mouth roughly to his. The other hand slid down her arm to her waist, pinched the soft flesh there famililarly, and dropped to the small of her back, pressing her body intimately against his own.

Outraged by the hot, wet mouth covering her own, Cara tried vainly to move her head and push him away and discovered herself caught fast in a viselike grip. Her arms were neatly pinned to her sides and her head unable to move even a fraction to escape the rapacious lips bruising her own.

She opened her mouth to scream at him and felt, to her horror, his thick tongue push into her mouth!

Neither of them heard the click of heels approaching on the flagstones.

For one instant Cara remained still, frozen in the fear that she was subject to whatever the viscount chose to do to her. Then it hit her that her feet were free. Knowing her kid slippers could not hurt the viscount's foot through the heavy boot he wore, she swung her foot back awkwardly and delivered a hard kick to his shin.

The viscount yelped in surprise, releasing her to grab at his hurt leg. Cara fell back and began to hobble painfully to the stone bench nearby.

Laughter rang out behind them.

At the end of the walkway stood the Earl of Malton, laughing heartily at the scene he had just come upon. "By George, Lyle, you have met your match this time!" he exclaimed.

"Oh no!" Cara groaned in dismay and continued to hobble toward the bench. She sank down onto the hard stone, setting her punch glass, on which her grip had only tightened, down on the ground and rubbed her throbbing toes through her slipper.

The viscount glowered at him and ground, "Always interfering, eh, Wrothby? What do you want!"

"Do forgive my ill manners, Lyle, in barging in upon your, er, tender moment," he drawled sardonically. "I came at the bidding of the lady's mother to deliver her a message." He flicked an imaginary piece of dust from his sleeve and looked up, the anger in his eyes visible only an instant before the sleepy lids drooped to veil it once more.

"Deliver it and begone!" grated the viscount.

"I think not," said the earl softly. His lips curled into an unpleasant smile.

Cara shivered and said a silent prayer that that smile was not directed at her.

The viscount stood glaring at the earl. The earl's boxing prowess was well-known. Then he barked, "This is the last time you interfere with me, Wrothby!" turned on his heel, and walked quickly down the shadowed walkway.

Ignoring the earl, Cara looked down at her lap, mortified to have been discovered in such a scene.

Disregarding her embarrassment, the earl chuckled and said, "He is irate this time and no mistake!"

He came to sit down on the end of the bench and

lifted Cara's hurt foot to his lap. As he drew off the kid slipper, she tried to pull her foot away. "Don't be missish," he scolded. "It don't become you. Besides, in a salon, you would pay handsomely for the massage I am about to give your toes." He grinned, "Some of Turner's best—owns a boxing salon, you see," he explained, "and knows all there is to know about massaging sore parts of the body, head to toe." Chatting on easily about nothing in particular while his fingers expertly eased her crimped toes, the earl allowed Cara to collect herself.

A short time later, he gave her foot a last pat and drew her slipper back on. "Time I got you back to Lady Brentwood. She said she was ready to return home. Come," he said kindly when she remained silent and unmoving. "I think you will find that Lyle has departed."

The earl saw again the image of Cara's graceful figure molded tightly against the portly body of the viscount and was surprised by the violent emotions that rose with it. He frowned.

"Th-Thank you, Lord Wrothby," answered Cara, astonished at his kindness.

"Smooth your hair," he ordered. "I do not want anyone to think *I* ruffled you!"

She gave him a weak smile and murmured, "No, that would spoil your reputation!"

"Ah," he said wickedly, "now I know you are feeling better." He gave her his arm, and they passed in silence out of the green shadows of the garden and into the watery sunshine of late afternoon.

"There you are! We were beginning to think the gardens had eaten you," exclaimed Miss Britmeyer acidly, seated in company with Lady Brentwood, Mr. Dickson, and Lady Beaufort. The Doughertys had, apparently, moved off.

Three pairs of eyes were turned on them.

Cara blushed vividly, opening her mouth to explain.

"No, only one of us," replied the earl cheerfully, cutting Cara off.

Since she wasn't certain what explanation she had been about to give, Cara gratefully closed her mouth again and allowed the earl to prevaricate as he chose.

"Viscount Lyle has been, er, called away and had to deprive us of his company. He asked me to make his apologies to you, Lady Brentwood, for being unable to convey you home. I would put my carriage at the disposal of you and Miss Brentwood, but, as you see, I have room for only one passenger. Mr. Dickson, however, I feel sure, will offer you the use of his carriage, won't you, Dickson?"

Mr. Dickson gave him a puzzled look, but always gallant, replied, "Of course — happy to oblige."

"Called away, the devil!" retorted Miss Britmeyer, shaking her golden curls. "You sent him away is closer to the mark! What did he do?" She looked suspiciously at Cara, who blushed again.

The earl turned a quelling glance upon her. Then to Lady Brentwood he remarked, "I believe we will take our leave now as well, ma'am. May I give you my arm?"

Surprised, Lady Brentwood took his arm after only the slightest of pauses. "Why — yes!" She tugged surreptitiously at Mr. Dickson's coat to indicate he should come also.

The earl turned back to Miss Britmeyer, wide-eyed with surprise. "It will take but a moment to convey our thanks to the Marstons," he said and began to move off with Lady Brentwood.

"Are we *all* ready to leave?" asked Mr. Dickson, starting, with Cara, to follow the earl and Lady Brentwood.

"I'm not," stated Lady Beaufort flatly, having just listened to the queerest conversation in which it had seemed to her that none of the conversants had had the least idea what any of the others were talking about.

Refusing to be left behind, Miss Britmeyer cried, "I will come with you!" picked up her skirts, and ran to catch up.

Lady Beaufort, deciding she was, perhaps, getting older than she had thought, went to surround herself with some of her own peers.

Cara had confined her eyes to her immediate circle, not wishing to encounter the viscount's over-bright gaze. But she raised them as they crossed the lawn and realized that quite a few of the guests appeared to have already departed—the viscount among them, she decided with relief.

They found both Marstons seated near the buffet tables, relaxing at last among a small group of intimates. They thanked them, exchanged several pleasanteries with the group surrounding them, and then moved off in the direction of the carriages.

"Well, I s'pose we're all ready t'leave." Mr. Dickson stated again as they all stood before his coach in an awkward silence.

"We are ready if you are ready, James," answered Lady Brentwood quietly.

The earl reliquished her arm, and Mr. Dickson handed Lady Brentwood and then Cara, blushing again as she felt the earl's eyes upon her, inside and followed them in. His driver slapped the reins, and they started off sedately down the drive.

Not long after, the earl, driving to an inch, passed them in a blur of yellow and black, waving his whip at them as he went out of sight around a bend in the road.

Fifteen

Cara sank back onto the plump blue cushions of Mr. Dickson's coach and left her mother to carry on a conversation with Mr. Dickson — James, to her mother, she corrected herself wryly. With *James's* coachman driving, she knew she was doomed to every bit of forty-five minutes, and probably longer, to reach home.

She put her head back, pretending to fall asleep. Undoubtedly the earl would get Miss Britmeyer home in record time. Limply Cara wished she might trade places with her — perched excitingly above the ground, traveling at a breathtaking speed, and sitting in close proximity to the earl, the sole recipient of his attention and wit. Bah! she thought, It will all be wasted on her. From what I saw of her, she has nothing to recommend her except perhaps her yellow curls — the tossing of which she has certainly perfected into an art! Cara scoffed disdainfully.

Does he give *her* those mocking looks? Or does he reserve for me because of my, er, masquerades? she wondered.

She saw again the attractive picture Miss Britmeyer made shaking back her golden curls, and she shifted petulantly against the carriage cushions. The same, seemingly causeless, feelings of restlessness, boredom, and disappointment which had dogged her throughout the week since Lady Cranton's ball descended upon her once more, and she shifted again trying to find a more comfortable position against the cushions.

Well, it would appear I have botched everything, she thought miserably. I put Richard off, I lost Mr. Dickson, and I won't have Arthur—how *could* I have let him deceive me like that!

She remembered now the many hints he had unwittingly given her. But she had refused to recognize them despite warnings from several people. Her own willful blindness disgusted her.

Dully she watched the lush green trees along the roadside and was glad of the growing darkness inside the carriage. As if to match her mood, the trees began to appear almost black.

Lord Wrothby didn't help matters any, either, she thought accusingly, trying to refuel her old anger at him. Interrupting my conversations, stealing dances, switching nameplates! But she found she could not muster the same rage toward him she had once felt.

True, the earl had ruined Mr. Dickson's courtship of her. She was certain that a great deal of Mr. Dickson's initial shift in affection from herself to her mother had been caused by the earl's interference—which had rendered herself unavailable. But she could not forget the fact that, with the opportunity before him, he had not handed her over to Callahan and his men but had risked his own safety instead. Nor could she forget his kindness after his timely intercession—accidental though it had been—that afternoon. What might have occurred if her mother had not sent him when she did, she did not like to refine on. She could not but feel that she owed the earl her gratitude.

She felt herself grow hot again at the thought of the viscount's familiar embrace and tried to push the memory away from her. Very likely, she thought distastefully, the puffiness under Arthur's eyes and, indeed, even their peculiar brightness can be explained by practices I much prefer not to think about!

She curled her lip as she remembered what she had read concerning certain parties for the select members of the *ton,* who indulged themselves in the consumption of drugs such as opium. Groups that were also reputed for unusual practices in their intimate relations, she remembered, recalling his pinch. She shivered and refused to allow her thoughts to go further in that direction.

I suppose, she conceded dolefully, Lord Wrothby has won. His romantic strategy has succeeded, for I have now no hope that I can see of becoming affianced at all, much less by the end of the Season. There is not enough time remaining to bring anyone else up to scratch, and even to even try at this late date, I am certain, would appear exceedingly queer, since I have encouraged Mr. Dickson and (ugh!) the viscount so particularly—not to mention the earl's feigned interest in me! He has run simply everyone off, she concluded, and sighed audibly.

What am I to do? she asked herself, discovering she had developed a pounding megrim, then succumbed to a fit of the dismals in all its intensity. She had never liked to find herself without some course of action ready to execute, but that was exactly the position she now perceived herself to be in, having had the promising courtships she had been so confident of only two days earlier washed, as it were, like so much bulwark away from her. Mr. Dickson, she could not in all honesty fault. It was easy to see how one couldn't help falling in love with her mother. But the viscount and the earl were a different matter.

Her thoughts returned to the blonde Miss Britmeyer with a feeling closely akin, though Cara would never have admitted it, to jealousy. And alternately upbraiding herself for bringing the viscount's attentions down upon her own head and upbraiding the earl, nonsensically, just for being the earl, she endured the remainder of the long, tedious trip home.

When Mr. Dickson's coachman pulled his horses up in front of their house, her megrim had developed into mammoth proportions until she felt like someone was inside her head wielding a sledgehammer at her temples. She waited impatiently, teeth on edge, for Mr. Dickson to climb slowly down and hand them to the front door. Since she did not feel very grateful for a ride she considered to have vied with the speed of a snail, compared — most unjustly — to the ride she imagined Miss Britmeyer had experienced, it wasn't surprising that she forgot to thank him. She said goodbye curtly and preceeded her mother smartly into the house.

As Bates shut the door behind Lady Brentwood, she asked her daughter innocently, "Did you have a good time, my dear?" preparing to open a conversation about the viscount and ask Cara if she were aware of the reputation Richard had mentioned. Not illogically, she felt that when she did so her daughter would then explain the strange conversation that had taken place prior to their departure from the Marstons'.

Thus she was greatly astonished when her daughter turned on the last stair, glowered at her, and announced, "*I* am going to bed," in tones of heartfelt gloom and, turning back around, picked up her skirts and clumped dolefully up the stairs.

"Oh dear," sighed Lady Brentwood, "I have said the wrong thing."

Had Cara but known it, she would have been delighted to learn that Miss Britmeyer had not enjoyed her ride home with the earl half as much as Cara had imagined she had. For instead of devoting his attention wholeheartedly to Miss Britmeyer as he normally did, the earl had been downright preoccupied with thoughts that plainly had little to do with her. He had actually seemed to forget her presence entirely and had driven his trap accordingly.

Miss Britmeyer had been unpleasantly jiggled and bounced against her side of the trap in a most undignified manner. The air whipping by her face had caused her eyes to tear, and on more than one occasion she had felt the hair on the back of her neck crawl as the earl took hairpin turns at a speed she knew must land them, their bodies mangled beyond description, in the ditch.

However, she feared lowering the earl's opinion of herself more than she feared his speed, so, feeling uncomfortable and ridiculous, she merely clung to the side of the trap and tried, employing every wile she knew to start any kind of conversation that might bring his attention back to her. But to her chagrin, she received no reply at all to show he had even heard her leading statements and only absentminded, monosyllabic answers to her questions.

She did not regain his attention, in fact, until they had raced up the drive to her home, and he seemed to wake out of his brown study by himself and become aware of his taciturnity. He then returned to his usual charming self, and only then, in the last few minutes of her ride, did Miss Britmeyer truly enjoy herself.

Had she been able to read the earl's thoughts, she might have spared herself considerable effort and discomfort. The earl had lead Cara's runners on as good a chase as they were ever likely to get, and when he had tired of the game at last and lost them, he had been halfway to Malton Park. Deciding it would be just as well to go on and put up there for the night as to return to London, he had slept through the whole of the following day and risen to eat a restorative dinner, none the worse for his wild chase of the night before. But sitting over his port before the fire in his favorite chair, he had had the leisure and solitude to ask himself why he might have done such a corkbrained thing in the first place. He certainly had not set out from his carriage with the notion of rescuing his highwayman!

For, in that action, he, like Cara, had perceived a change in the footing of his relationship with her. At the time, he had laid it down uneasily to the lure of the game and the test of seeing if he could lead and then escape his pursuers, and returned the next day to London. He had then been told of Lord and Lady Peirce's holdup—a scant week after he had helped her escape!—and gone to Lady Cranton's ball to put a flea in Cara's ear, restraining himself with difficulty from throttling her.

But the question she had thrown at him as he had left for his club had rankled for the remainder of the evening and the whole of the next day. It was too closely akin to the first question he had asked himself and found only an uneasy answer to. He did not know why he didn't just let her get her foolish head blown off, and when, this time, he couldn't find even an uncertain answer, he decided to invite a large company of his friends, Miss Britmeyer among them, back down to Malton Park to help him forget the matter.

But, having spent the past several days in company with Miss Britmeyer, he had reached much the same conclusion of her that it had taken Cara only a few minutes' study to determine. And though the attractive, blonde Miss Britmeyer had indeed behaved royally that very morning in the circumstance of his horse's thrown shoe — which had not, as Cara had thought, been a Banbury tale — without quite being able to put his thumb on why, the earl had begun to notice a distinct lack about Miss Britmeyer. Some air, some indefinable spark of something was decidedly missing.

Without realizing it, in his weeks of plaguing Cara, the earl had begun to appreciate the quick defiant flash of her green eyes and the honest retorts which were as apt to make him laugh as they were to peg him, putting him neatly in his place, and make him furious.

Reflecting as he drove his companion home, he had begun to realize that Miss Britmeyer, like most of the ladies of his acquaintance, simply did not think as fast as Cara did and was more likely to yield in the face of his sallies, not being able to muster a good retort. Having thought this, he then also remembered, in contrast to Cara's constant rather piquing desire to be rid of him, that Miss Britmeyer on several occasions, today among them, had shown herself to be a good deal more possessive than he was willing to tolerate.

The earl had always been aware that Cara was different from other women — what other woman of his acquaintance would even entertain the notion of robbing in the guise of an infamous highwaymen to support herself, much less carry the notion out! Successfully, too, he had to concede with a grudging measure of admiration. But as he raced his trap, comparing Cara to Miss Britmeyer as well as the other women he knew, the earl slowly began to comprehend not only just how different Cara was but also the fact that he might find that difference *attractive*. The idea was astounding, and once he had arrived at it he found, surprisingly, that he couldn't take his mind off of it or Cara.

He remembered the sight of her lithe body pressed tightly against the viscount's corpulence as he had come upon them in the Marstons' gardens, and his lips unconsciously tightened into a grim line. She had appeared to him at first to be willingly embracing Lyle. That thought still rankled, and the earl found himself, as he drove, examining a third question much like the other two: why should he care at all that Cara should want to kiss the Viscount Lyle?

He had only searched her out, he told himself, because he had feared Lyle might indeed take advantage of her in the seclusion of the gardens. Having only recently witnessed the viscount exit a club of a most unsavory celebrity, the earl needed no further convincing of the truth of Lyle's unscrupulous reputation. But he had doubted very much if Cara were aware of it. At such a late hour in the afternoon, when most guests were more likely to be departing than taking a stroll through the gardens, there was no telling what the viscount might or might not have attempted.

But, the earl objected, not quite ready to accept

he astonishing idea that he was, in fact, very attracted to Cara, he would have gone to check on the safety of *any* woman he had known to be in that situation — and a moment later admitted candidly that he had been quite a bit more interested in the well-being of that particular fiery-headed woman than he would have been in just any woman. Had he not been, he knew he wouldn't have taken such pains, when Richard had mentioned her whereabouts, to leave Miss Britmeyer with Lady Brentwood, Mr. Dickson, and the Doughertys to ensure that he was the only witness of Cara's foolhardiness, if indeed that's what her trip to the gardens turned out to be.

Contrary to what one might have thought, the fact that she had been proved foolish did not lessen the earl's growing appreciation of her in the least. He knew numerous women who, finding themselves in Cara's position would simply have fainted or allowed themselves, through fear, to be mauled. The earl smiled crookedly and his black eyes twinkled as he recalled Cara's resourceful kick.

Then his brows had risen as he recalled what she had next done. At the end of it all, she had won his admiration outright by simply sitting calmly down to rub her toes and take a few deep gulps of breath to regain her composure. At that same point, every other woman the earl could think of would have treated him to a fit of the vapors, either because she really had them or because she felt like she *ought* to have them to prove her femininity. Whereas a display of the vapors would have disgusted him, the fact that Cara had not indulged in them had assured her of his sympathy like nothing else she could have done.

When he thought of it, he realized she had kept her head with the runners after them, too. He had then found himself in the peculiar position of admir ing one whom he had been in the habit of regarding as That Adventuress. Forced, in the light of his re flections, to resolve that the pistol-wielding, copper headed Miss Brentwood was not, perhaps, quite the villainess he had heretofore made her out, the earl took the last dangerous step toward falling in love with her.

He had then become guiltily conscious of the pres ence of Miss Britmeyer and the fact that he had been neglecting her sadly and turned toward her and done his best to entertain her in the last few minutes of the drive.

Cara, had she been privileged to learn that the earl's opinion of her had undergone a change for the better, would have been delighted, though she would never have expressed it. As it was, however, not privy to the earl's reflections, she rose the next morning in little better spirits than she had gone to bed the night before.

Listlessly she descended the stairs to breakfast and found that the eggs and ham she usually enjoyed with such a hearty appetite tasted bland and were hard to swallow, and she left most of them on her plate.

Observing this unusual occurence and remember ing her behavior of the night before, Lady Brentwood asked worriedly, "You are not sickening for something I hope, my dear? How do you feel?"

"Oh—no. I feel fine, *Maman*," she replied wanly, creating just the opposite impression on her mother.

Lady Brentwood decided to brave the questions she had put off the night before. "Cara, I am troubled by something that Richard Llewellyn said yesterday about Viscount Lyle. He did not seem to hold him in a very great respect and claimed outright that he had a bad reputation among the gentlemen. At the time, I did not like to question him so particularly before so many people. But I did want you, if you were not already aware of it, to—"

Cara interrupted her brusquely, "Arthur Lyle has already borne out everything Richard intimated. I will not distress you by telling you details. Suffice it to say that I would not allow Viscount Lyle to attend me again under any circumstances!" Her creamy skin became suffused with pink at the thought of the viscount's handling, and her green eyes burned with anger as she faced Lady Brentwood. Dropping her gaze and her voice, which had risen with the violence of her emotions, she added wearily, "I only wish I had listened to Richard sooner." She left her mother to guess, with more accuracy than she knew, what the viscount's offense had been.

"You will say I am just saying this now it is already proven, but I have never really liked that gentleman."

"He is no gentleman!" stated Cara vehemently.

Lady Brentwood rose from the table and came to stand behind Cara, putting her hands comfortingly on her shoulders. She began to knead the tense muscles lightly, putting Cara in mind of the recent massage her sore toes had received. But instead of raising her spirits, this thought lowered them.

He probably would have done the same thing for any other poor creature he had found in Arthur's clutches, she thought. If I saw him tomorrow, he would probably still be the same vexing impediment to my future that he's been all along—just because I pinched a small diamond pin and a few guineas from him!

Or maybe he wouldn't, she thought suddenly since he seems to have achieved his revenge. Now he will very likely cut me dead, she thought gloomily.

Lady Brentwood broke in on her thoughts. "Then that is what that ridiculous conversation just before we left the Marstons' was all about," she asked.

"Yes. If you hadn't sent Lord Wrothby when you did, Lady Marston's guests would have received more entertainment than they had bargained for," Cara answered, grimacing.

"Sent Lord Wrothby?" repeated her mother blankly.

"Why, yes. He said you sent him to tell me that you were ready to go." At her mother's continued blank look, she went on, "And when we came from the gardens that's the next thing you said—you told Mr. Dickson we were ready to leave."

"There was nothing else to say!" exclaimed Lady Brentwood. "No one knew what anyone else was talking about! Everyone was trying to save face—except perhaps Miss Britmeyer. You had gone into the gardens with the Viscount, he had disappeared, and here you were returning on the earl's arm. And *he* was talking about leaving and offering us seats in his trap, of all things, and telling me James would offer us seats in his carriage! The earl was obviously steering us toward departing, and, since it seemed for your benefit, I acquiesced. But I would never have sent him to get you, my love."

Cara acknowledged the truth of this latter statement to herself. Since coming to London had been her own idea, her mother had usually been content to remain wherever they were until Cara herself suggested they leave. "Well, if you didn't send him," she said slowly, thinking aloud, "then he came on his own as if . . . as if he expected Arthur to—" she stopped abruptly, realizing the extent of the danger she had been in. "Then he made that up about your sending him and . . . and manipulated all of us!" concluded Cara angrily, some of her old resentment at the earl's high-handed ways rising again.

"It would seem that Viscount Lyle may be counted upon to live up to his poor reputation," answered Lady Brentwood sensibly, refusing to be angry with the earl. Pointing out the truth of the matter, she continued, "And I would say Lord Wrothby deserves your thanks rather than your anger, Cara. He shall certainly receive mine the next time I see him."

They were both silent, thinking, for several moments.

Cara wondered what to think of the earl's considerate actions. If it had been anyone else, she might have thought he had some personal interest in her welfare. But since it was the earl, she was puzzled. Perhaps his rescue had been merely another facet of his romantic campaign against her? But that doesn't make any sense! she thought irritably.

He would simply have gone to see about any woman in that circumstance, she decided, and then was surprised at herself for attributing such a noble characteristic to the earl. But though she wouldn't have admitted it, in her heart of hearts she had known, and refused to recognize, that the earl's nature was as sincere and altruistic as Arthur's was sly and self-centered.

Involuntarily she remembered the earl's kisses, and the ghost of a smile curved her lips.

For her own part, Lady Brentwood was thinking

about Mr. Dickson and wondering if it was an opportune moment to bring him into the conversation. Deciding now was as good a time as any, she took a deep breath and asked softly, "Cara, are your affections very much engaged by Mr. Dickson?"

Startled out of her reverie, Cara answered, "Lord, no, *Maman*. I gave him up to you ages ago."

Lady Brentwood looked astonished. "Then you are certain you do not care for him *at all?*" she asked again incredulously.

"I do not care a fig for him, *Maman*. I never did. He simply had a lot of money and a malleable temperament. Even so, I found him a dashed duler—sedate. And I do wish he would hurry up and ask you to marry him so that I could be assured of the future of at least one of us!" she exclaimed testily.

Lady Brentwood heaved a sigh of relief. "He has," she replied calmly.

"What!"

"He *has* asked me to marry him. Yesterday at the picnic."

"Well, what did you say? What did you say?!" questioned Cara, jumping out of her chair to turn and face her mother expectantly.

"He wanted to explain matters to you before we regarded anything as settled, but I asked him if I might do that, which he did not at all like—but I felt I ought to be the one to do that, you see. And after I told him of our financial difficulties—"

"You told him that *then?*" groaned Cara, slapping a hand to her forehead.

"Of course I did. I could not deceive him, Cara." She resumed quietly, "After I told him that, and he still would have me—"

"Whew," breathed Cara, half seriously and half in jest.

"—I said I would have to see how you felt—"

"Stuff!" exclaimed Cara. "I don't give a fiddle for Mr. Dickson," she repeated, "and you needn't ask me anything. You're of age," she teased, smiling.

"But I should not wish to marry anyone you disliked excessively, my dear or anyone you did not wish me to marry—for some other reason."

"You could never do that," replied Cara quickly and gave her mother a kiss on the cheek and hugged her fiercely.

"For I expect you to live with us until you get married yourself, you know, my dear, and then I expect you to visit us often," exhorted Lady Brentwood.

"I think you and *James* shall suit perfectly, *Maman*. And I will live with you as long as you like and then visit you more often than you can stand me!"

"Ugh. Don't break my bones, please!" laughed her mother as Cara continued to hug her. "He probably was a little too dull for you, my love. But he will be just right for me, for I am a little dull, too, you know. Well! I'm glad that's settled. Now—"

"You are *not* dull," Cara interrupted. "Now, you can run give James his answer and get the poor devil off tenterhooks!" she teased.

"Well, as a matter of fact, he did suggest that he might call this morning to take us driving in his phaeton and—"

"And see how I took the news, eh?" Cara broke in again. "I've a mind to enact him a Cheltenham drama," she said with a wicked gleam making her eyes greener than ever.

"No—and I could give him my answer then," finished her mother. "Don't you dare to scare poor

James with your play-acting! He will be certain to take you seriously!" laughed Lady Brentwood. "And now, I had best go and put on something presentable." She gave Cara a kiss and a smile that made her look years younger and hurried out of the dining room.

Her mother's news should have dispersed the gloom that had descended on Cara the night before but, watching her mother leave the room in such transports, served merely to increase it. She had become used, in the months since her father's death, to the need for deciding and arranging her own as well as her mother's future. Now that need no longer existed. But instead of making her feel relieved and delighted as she ought to, the thought made her feel more disheartened than ever.

Her mother's future appeared decisively and neatly—and even happily—wrapped up. Her own was none of those things. True, she was no longer a Cinderella striving frantically against the twelve o'clock chime that would return her to the penury of Brentwood Crest. And Lady Brentwood had assured her that Mr. Dickson would provide for her. But in spite of her mother's assurance, Cara did not feel she could be comfortable living as a poor relation—for, in essence, that's what she would be—on Mr. Dickson's generosity.

I suppose I am disappointed that I am not the one getting married, she thought candidly. Though, by rights, I should be deliriously happy now that I may take my time and marry someone I care something for. Still, she could not make herself feel happy.

I shall have to take up some cause or, better yet, procure some kind of *honest* employment so that I may set up a household of my own, she thought gloomily, going off to the parlor to look at the paper and discover what employment she could expect to find.

Mr. Dickson was shown in a quarter of an hour later, and her mother came in on his heels. She looked charming in a pale blue silk that was the exact color of her eyes.

Mr. Dickson appeared as nervous as Cara had ever seen him. For several minutes he made small talk and fidgeted about the room, sitting down on the settee and then standing up, only to sit down again. Finally he blurted, "Well, I . . . well . . . guess we're off for a drive. Care to come along, Miss Brentwood?"

Both Cara and Lady Brentwood hid their smiles. But Cara returned seriously, "No. Not today, Mr. Dickson. Perhaps another day. I imagine you have some things to say which are not for my ears."

Mr. Dickson blushed rosily and stammered his goodbye.

Her blue eyes twinkling merrily, her mother smiled at Cara, rather pinkly, and also bid her goodbye.

Not long after they had left, Cara was still seated in the parlor perusing the newspaper when the knocker banged heavily against the front door. She heard Bates's dignified step in the hall and then heard him say, "I will see if she is at home."

She waited, wondering curiously who it might be. Bates usually showed any visitor into the parlor if either she or her mother were at home.

Stony-eyed, he appeared at the parlor door and announced emotionlessly, "The Viscount Arthur Lyle brings you his apologies. He is at the door with Ginny and begs you will ride out with him and allow him To Explain."

Cara was stunned. The pure effrontery of the

man! she thought, her anger rising swiftly and her green eyes beginning to flash fire. *"Explain!"* she choked.

Keeping his face expressionless, Bates hoped fervently his mistress was not the type to throw things.

"The devil he will! Tell him I consider a visit from him in the nature of an insult! I do not wish to see him now nor in the future, and if he dares to call again he will find no one at home!" she snapped.

"Very good, miss," replied Bates dispassionately and left the room, priding himself upon the fact that he did not hurry in the slightest despite his fear that objects from the parlor tables would begin whizzing past his ears at any moment.

Seething, Cara went to the window and watched the viscount descend the front steps.

Scowling visibly, he mounted his horse and, leading Ginny, trotted down the street in the opposite direction.

Fuming and muttering, Cara strode back and forth across the parlor floor.

At length, she calmed down and returned to the paper. But as she opened it back up, it occurred to her to wonder how Bates had known she would not want the viscount shown in. It had scarcely been one day since the change in the viscount's status!

She chuckled in spite of herself. You may be able to cozen the *ton,* she thought, but you will never succeed in putting anything past their servants!

Then her smile faded, and she returned to the depressing prospects of the paper.

Sixteen

The beginning of a new week did little to improve Cara's mood. She felt as though all her goals had been removed without her having had the satisfaction of attaining any of them, and she had found no advertisements in the paper for any employment more feasible than governess.

Monday afternoon found her sitting in the parlor staring into space with the newspaper open upon her lap. I do not really desire a governess position, she mused, but I suppose I would rather take one than burden Mr. Dickson with my dependency. She brought her attention back to the page before her and unenthusiastically circled an advertisement with her pen. She sighed. Something else to remember not to tell *Maman*, she warned herself—at least, not until after the wedding. She would worry herself sick over it and never cease trying to make me change my mind.

Cara smiled fondly. Her mother was indefatigable when it came to getting people to do things that were good for them—whether they inconvenienced herself or not. In this case, Cara felt to live with her mother and her new husband just after they were married would be too much of an intrusion. She had no intention of doing that. Her smile faded, and a serious look replaced it as she folded the newspaper and took it over to the escritoire with her to inquire into some of the more promising governess positions.

The remainder of Tuesday, then Wednesday and Thursday dragged by without lifting her depression, and whether or not by consensus in observation of the Season's beginning to close, no one in the Brentwoods' acquaintance held any kind of party on those days.

The only ripple of excitement came with an early visit Thursday from Lady Dougherty, agog with the news that Mr. Callahan had apprehended "the gentle highwayman." This news did much to set the minds of Lady Dougherty and Lady Brentwood at ease but nothing at all to improve Cara's state of mind. *Having got him, Mr. Callahan's next step will very likely be to take me!* Cara thought dismally.

On Friday, there was Lady Onslow's soiree, and Cara, though still feeling dispirited, dressed for it with meticulous care. *I will not close the Season looking downtrodden!* she lectured her reflection fiercely, *particularly* if the Earl of Malton is going to attend! Deliberately she chose an elaborate emerald gown that made the color of her hair and eyes prominent.

Several hours later, she stepped into Lady Onslow's entrance hall and scanned her guests for the sight of the earl's tall form. But she was disappointed. Though her usual admirers flocked to create a lively group around her, the earl, she concluded, must have returned to his estate, for he was nowhere in evidence. This conclusion added to the general lowness of her spirits and made it harder for her to keep pace with the animated, jocular young bloods surrounding her. But, determined not to care if the earl arrived or not, she turned her back upon the door and made every effort to appear as though she were having the best of times and, in so doing, missed his tardy entrance some twenty minutes later.

Greeting the Onslows, who received him cordially, he addressed several friends as he moved to take his place among the guests. He spotted Cara immediately, grinning as he thought, I could not very well miss her in that rig! and availed himself of the opportunity to observe her in an unguarded moment.

With satisfaction, he noted the intimacy that Mr. Dickson and Lady Brentwood, standing beside Cara, seemed to exhibit. But he decided that Cara herself appeared somewhat woebegone, though she was acting happy enough, surrounded by her horde of admiring dandies. He frowned slightly and then determined that he should derive great enjoyment from snatching her from her group of gentlemen and carrying her off to where he could see couples beginning informally to dance.

He began to saunter across the room with the express purpose of nettling her, knowing it the best way to revive her particular spirits.

A strong hand clapped him on the shoulder, and he turned to see Lord Huntingdon, a good friend of his whom he had not seen for some time, grinning at him.

"Huntingdon!" he exclaimed, and, grinning himself, the earl pounded his friend on the back. "How have you been, old boy? I see they let you back into England. Why haven't you been round to visit me, curse you?" he added, as it occurred to him he ought to be insulted.

"One at a time, Wrothby! One at a time! I haven't

yet been back forty-eight hours," his friend protested, laughing. "M'mother and m'sister—you know Sophie—dragged me to this, or, be assured, you wouldn't see me now, either!"

"Poor devil," the earl sympathized. Changing the subject, he asked, "How did you find the Peninsula?"

His friend gave him a meaningful look and, lowering his voice, talked seriously for several minutes.

The earl's face soon took on an expression equal in seriousness to that of his friend's.

They were interrupted by Lord Dougherty, who burst between them, draping an arm conspiratorially about each. Quite as bad a gossip as his wife with news that concerned his intimates, he was agog with the news of Mr. Dickson's impending marriage, which his friend had just happily told him on the condition that he first promise to keep his mummer shut about it.

"What the dev—! Dougherty!" both gentlemen exclaimed, startled by his sudden descent, for they had both been engrossed in their discussion of military affairs.

"How d'ye do, gentlemen. Huntingdon, glad to see you're back in one piece. Gentlemen," he repeated urgently and looked to each side to see that no one was close enough to overhear him. "I've just heard the greatest piece of news! But you mustn't spread it about if I tell you." The earl raised an eyebrow and directed an amused glance at Lord Huntingdon.

In mock tones of sincerity, Lord Huntingdon, grinning back at the earl, said, "You may depend upon us, Dougherty."

Lord Dougherty could keep his news inside no

longer. "Dickson's offered for the Brentwood woman!" he whispered excitedly and waited for their reactions.

He was not disappointed.

"WHAT?!" barked the earl, his brows snapping together instantly with what he considered a decidedly unpleasant piece of news.

At his friend's exclamation, Lord Huntingdon looked blankly from Lord Dougherty to the earl. The news meant nothing to one who had been out of the country for close to eight months. "Who is she?" asked Lord Huntingdon.

Lord Dougherty nodded his white head vigorously at the earl's stunned disbelief. His news was receiving just the reaction he had hoped for, and he was enjoying himself hugely. "Yes, sir, they haven't set the date yet, but it's official and you'll see the banns in the paper soon enough. James is to marry Lady Brentwood," he said again, in the voice of one commiserating with the doomed fate of a friend.

"Who is she?" Lord Huntingdon asked again, looking from one of his friends to the other for an explanation of this, apparently, explosive information.

The earl snapped his attention abruptly back to Lord Dougherty. "Did you say *Lady* Brentwood? It is the *mother* who is to wed Dickson?" he demanded.

"I did. Most certainly," answered Lord Dougherty, becoming irritated now as he perceived that the importance of his news was, for some reason, decreasing in the earl's view. "James—Dickson—is—going—to—marry—Alicia—Brentwood," he stated, enunciating crisply as if he were talking to a singularly dull child.

The earl's brows relaxed, and he broke into laughter and slapped Lord Dougherty delightedly on the back, making him take a step forward to regain his balance. "Well, why didn't you say so, man!" Lord Dougherty directed another irritated glance at him. "Nothing to concern yourself over, Huntingdon. Just a rather charming older woman marrying a rather stuf—ahem! Er, a friend of Dougherty's here. Now where were we?"

With a look of disgust at this belittlement of his news, Lord Dougherty sniffed loudly and stumped off to enlighten someone who would be a deal more appreciative, and the two friends resumed their earlier conversation.

They parted amicably a quarter of an hour later, each promising to call upon the other in the near future and take up their discussion again in more private surroundings.

The earl pumped the hand of his friend and continued on his way toward Cara, whom he could still see laughing and standing some distance away in her circle of admirers. Eyeing the high shirt points of several gentlemen in the group, the earl curled his lip as he sidestepped a couple bent on a collision course with him.

Suddenly he checked. It struck him that perhaps Cara's long face was due to the information Lord Dougherty had just told him. For the first time since he had met her, he recognized that Cara might, quite possibly, have really been in love with the staid Dickson—the earl could never fathom why any woman loved a particular man. He became guiltily conscious of the fact that it was due to his own interference that Dickson had become acquainted with Lady Brentwood and then apparently transferred his affections to her. And with a shock, he realized he had succeeded. By anyone's standards, his revenge was now complete!

The shadow of a smile flew across his face. He was fairly certain that Cara would no longer consider the viscount a suitor after the incident at the Marstons'. And he knew for a fact that Richard was now seriously courting Janie DeWitt with an eye toward becoming legshackled to her.

The earl told himself he ought to be boasting over the fact that he had blighted Cara's chances at a marriage that Season. But, observing her joyless face and lackluster eyes, the momentary thrill of attaining his revenge began to sour, and his mouth soon held the distinct taste of ashes.

How the devil could she love a damned stuffed shirt like Dickson! he muttered, and, with a look of anger and irritation, he wheeled abruptly and went instead deliberately to steal Miss Britmeyer from beneath the noses of two young men arguing over who the rightful owner of her next dance was.

Engaged in conversation, Cara had turned slightly and became aware out of the corner of her eye of the earl's tall form standing stationary several yards away. Nonchalantly turning round a moment later, she was in perfect time to see him whip the only-too-willing Miss Britmeyer away from her two gentlemen, as he had used to drag herself, and out onto the dance floor.

Her spirits plunged. So! she railed silently, anger boiling up inside her, he has no more use for me now he's got his revenge! And, not being able to countenance the sight of Miss Britmeyer's blonde curls bouncing against the earl's dark coat, Cara turned her back in cold fury on the impromptu dance floor and launched into speech.

Choosing the two most handsome gentlemen in the circle about her, she commanded petulantly, "John! Pete! I declare I have grown infernally hot in this crush. I simply *must* get some fresh air." The two pink spots of anger on her cheeks supported her claim. She smiled demurely at the group around her and said, "Gentlemen, you will excuse us for a few moments, I feel certain."

Laughing gaily at the protests and exclamations of envy for the two she had chosen, Cara linked arms with her escorts and majestically led the way toward Lady Onslow's garden. She threw a smoldering look behind her in the earl's direction and stepped through.

Had the earl seen the look she threw him, he might not have entertained the notion that Cara was enamored of the Honorable Mr. Dickson quite so seriously. But the earl, busy spinning Miss Britmeyer to the end of their dance, found his attention captured prettily by that lady when the music stopped.

Miss Britmeyer, once she had the earl's attention, was not about to relinquish it. Shrewdly, as she had accepted his offer to dance, she had taken note of Cara's whereabouts. When the dance ended, she steered the earl as quickly as she dared as far from her rival's proximity as possible, with every intention of maintaining that distance for the rest of the evening.

The earl looked about him once to see what effect, if any, his dance with Miss Britmeyer might have had on Cara and, catching no sight of her, decided somberly that his behaviour must be a matter of complete indifference to her. And in that event, Miss Britmeyer's company was as entertaining as any other woman's, and he allowed her to guide him into he next room to see how her mother did.

Outside, Cara had stood as many witticisms and puns from her two escorts as she was able, not feeling in the least mood for such things. Tapping a slippered toe impatiently, she considered it time to reenter the main room.

She lead the way with an angry flourish and entered as regally as she had left, hoping fervently that the earl might witness her come back in with her two handsome escorts in tow. But, though her admirers soon collected round her again, her hope was frustrated, for the earl was nowhere to be seen. This fact, quite instead of lessening Cara's efforts to appear as if she were having a wonderful time, only made her redouble them. For if the earl should come upon her unawares a second time, she wanted it to be abundantly clear to him that she was going on very well without his company—seeing no irony at all in the fact that she was not.

"How was the air?" teased one of her admirers, causing chuckles among the rest of the circle.

Cara smiled saucily and retorted, "Quite fresh!" Laughter broke out at her answer. She continued, "And I find that it has made me frightfully thirsty—"

"I know what's coming now," interrupted another gentleman, to more chuckles round the group.

Cara turned on him with a mock glare, "Then perhaps *you* will be good enough to procure me—"

"Something to drink?!" he finished for her, elbowing his friend at guessing correctly. He looked round the circle and said triumphantly, "But, of course. See, gentlemen? I anticipate the Incomparable's every whim!"

Several retorts in the nature of "Doing it up too

brown, McDowell!" and, "Why aren't you engaged to her then?" followed him as he disappeared into the crowd of guests to obtain Cara's drink.

Cara gave another gay laugh and said in a teasing voice, "You are all just jealous that I didn't ask *you* to bring me my drink!"

Instantly, returning her teasing, several gentlemen, smiling and nudging their friends to join in, replied, "I am!"; "So am I!"; "I know I am!"; "I am, too!"

Pretending to be taken in by them, Cara tossed her copper curls, put on a feigned smug smile, and retorted, "I *knew* it!" causing the gentlemen to roar with laughter at her pretended conceit.

McDowell then returned with a glass for her, and she groaned inwardly as she accepted what looked to be ratafia. She suppressed an urge to wrinkle her nose and sipped delicately, confirming her suspicion.

I should have known! This makes my evening complete! she thought, mentally raining a string of unladylike epithets down on McDowell's blissfully ignorant head. What I should really like is a good, strong glass of claret. But were I to send him back for it, I should quite probably shock these upstanding, aristocratic young gentlemen so badly they should hold me in disgrace forever after! Heaven knows I can't do that! she thought derisively. Aloud, she smiled and teased, "At last! I thought I should faint with thirst!"

Always quick to respond, McDowell assumed a haughty pose and looked down his nose to answer, "What is *time* if I might procure the nectar of the gods for you, madame?"

Groans met him from all sides, and Cara raised her eyebrows in patent incredulity.

"Peasants!" he retorted, at which everyone, including McDowell, laughed.

After another hour of acting as if she were enjoying herself and straining to keep up with the bantering remarks that flew around her, Cara began to feel a dull throb grow in the back of her head.

Choosing another gentleman to escort her, she excused herself to go in search of her mother and Mr. Dickson to see if they would consider departing. "The Honorable Mr. Dickson, gentlemen," she explained apologetically, "I fear, has already this evening wished several times for his bed. He retires early, you see, as, no doubt, your mothers wish you would do!" And with that parting sally, amid chuckles and laughter, she left them.

Moving dully through Lady Onslow's guests into the adjoining room, she did not, in truth, expect much opposition from either Lady Brentwood or Mr. Dickson.

She caught a sudden view of Miss Britmeyer's golden curls and couldn't stop herself from looking to see if the earl was still keeping her company. She craned around several people in front of her and received the unpleasant sight of the earl smiling down into that lady's provocatively upturned face.

Involuntarily giving out a small "Oh!" she desperately scanned the crowd for her mother and Mr. Dickson. Judging them not to be in that room, she retreated swiftly to the main room — her escort recklessly dodging people in his effort to keep up with her — and spotted her mother standing with Mr. Dickson in the far corner.

"Whew! You are the devil to keep up with, Miss Brentwood!" exclaimed her escort, arriving before Lady Brentwood and Mr. Dickson several instants after her. "How d'you do, ma'am, sir," he addressed them.

But Cara only laughed at him with a merriment she did not feel and performed the introductions. After a few minutes more of polite conversation, during which Cara strove valiantly to control her anxiety to be gone, she turned to her escort and thanked him for accompanying her, thereby dismissing him to return to his friends.

Immediately after he left, she remarked, "Mr. Dickson, I know it is approaching the hour at which you retire." She faced her mother inquiringly, *"Maman?* If you are ready to leave, I am."

Surprised that Cara would wish to leave so early, Lady Brentwood only nodded and replied, "All right, my dear."

And several minutes later found the three taking their leave of the Onslows and waiting somewhat silently for Mr. Dickson's carriage to be brought round.

An hour after Cara had departed, Miss Britmeyer suggested that the earl take her home. Not having glimpsed Cara, happy or unhappy, recently, the earl saw no reason to stay and indifferently acquiesced.

As Miss Britmeyer went to collect her widowed mother, engrossed at the card tables, the earl reflected that, at any rate, Miss Britmeyer's company had kept his mind from dwelling upon a certain fiery young woman who, incredibly, appeared to prefer a stuffed old goat to himself—the senseless chit! And after several other thoughts in this vein, Miss Britmeyer returned with her mother reluctantly in tow and linked her arm through his for everyone to see as they exited.

When they reached her residence some fifteen minutes later, Miss Britmeyer leaned gently into the earl so that he might feel the soft contours of her body and asked, "Should you like to come in for a little while, Lord Wrothby?"

Not in the habit of disappointing ladies, the earl, again, could think of no reason why he shouldn't and lazily smiled his acceptance in the glow of his carriage lanterns. He had a strong suspicion that Lady Britmeyer would quickly retire once they had entered.

He helped the ladies down and escorted them into the house. But as he followed Miss Britmeyer's blonde head into her sitting room, he found himself wishing, instead of looking forward as he once would have done to a pleasant hour of intimate company, that the curls that preceded him were not yellow but red.

Seventeen

Cara dropped her shawl on the settee and sank down after it. She felt drained. Putting one hand to her throbbing temple, she declared, "I cannot bear another such party! I vow that is the last one I shall attend!"

"Oh, Cara, I know you do not mean that. The Season is nearly over!" exclaimed Lady Brentwood, shocked. If anything, her daughter had appeared to her to be having almost too gay a time. "Is it Betsy? Has she said something tonight which has offended you?" she asked, when Cara did not appear to have changed her mind.

"Oh, it wasn't Lady Dougherty in particular. It is just that . . : Oh! I have had quite enough of the *ton* to last me the rest of my life!" Cara cried.

"Then you were not having a good time tonight when you looked so gay and so happ—?"

"No!" Cara burst out and, on the verge of tears, ran for her bedchamber.

Her daughter's reasons for her announcement made no more sense to Lady Brentwood than the announcement itself, though she was aware of Cara's animosity toward the members of the aristocracy since her husband's death. Having learned something of human nature in general and her daughter's in particular during her forty-odd years, she decided there was very likely more to Cara's outburst than a simple dislike of the aristocracy. She resolved to observe her daughter a bit more closely the next time they were out — provided, of course, she could persuade Cara to rescind her decision and there *was* a next time out. But of her own ability to persuade her — Lady Brentwood had to admit it, if only to herself — stubborn child, she had more than a little doubt. She shook her head and absent-mindedly picked up the candle snuffer.

Bates stuck his head inside the parlor and, knocking dramatically to be sure Lady Brentwood heard his approach, proceeded smartly into the room. He held out a dignified palm for the snuffer and, looking at the ceiling, suggested politely, "I'll just do that for you, Madame."

Lady Brentwood started at his knock. "Wh — Bates! Of course, I was thinking of something else." She blushed faintly and turned to go upstairs. "Good night, Bates."

"Good night, Madame." Bates had a good idea of what was occupying his mistress's thoughts. The young miss's exit would have been hard to miss even if he hadn't been keeping a close eye on the parlor.

He had to be grateful to her, though, for she had left the parlor door open, making it easier for him to catch the mistress before she put out a single candle. On too many occasions recently, he had entered the parlor to snuff the candles and found himself in total darkness — but not tonight! He smiled, extremely pleased with himself. Slowly but surely he *would* break the mistress of her habit of snuffing the candles!

I know what I'd do to her if she were one o' mine, he told himself, his thoughts reverting again to his young mistress—and so should she! But there, he philosophized, the Quality never did know how to raise their young'uns, and, as they aren't paying me to, it's no business of mine.

Ahh! he breathed, having extinguished the last candle.

When Cara came down the next morning, a trifle later than usual for her, she sought out her mother and apologized profusely for her behavior the night before.

Wisely Lady Brentwood refrained from commenting on her daughter's decision. Any efforts at persuasion just then, she knew, would only serve to make Cara the more determined.

But two mornings later, sitting at the breakfast table with Cara, Lady Brentwood took pains to make the party she had attended with Mr. Dickson and the Doughertys the night before sound a great deal more entertaining than it had actually been. Then she administered a little coaxing. She was met with silence, but she knew she had planted a seed or two of doubt in the mind of her stubborn offspring about the wisdom of her decision.

And, in fact, it took only twenty-four hours for that seed to bear fruit. Lying on her bed the next afternoon, ostensibly reading, Cara suddenly looked up and threw the book violently across the room. It struck the wall harmlessly with a loud *smack* and slid to rest open-faced upon the floor. This is nonsensical! she told herself severely. I am verily wallowing in self-pity!

I am not the only girl who hasn't achieved the marriage she desired and worked for, and no doubt I won't be the last! Morever, I am, absurdly, making myself miserable because I have escaped having to marry someone I did not at all care for merely for the sake of his wealth! I should be the happiest person alive, she pointed out to herself. Now I may take my time, have another Season—or two!—and become affianced to someone for whom I feel a decided affection.

With a pang, the earl of Malton rose to her mind. But she dismissed him immediately. Forget him! she commanded herself harshly, recalling his behavior at Lady Onslow's soiree. As *Maman* would say, there are many other gentlemen. Surely I can discover someone else to interest me!

Squelching any lingering thoughts of the earl, she got up from her bed and went to pour water out into a basin and bathe her face. I am heartily tired of my own dull company! she thought and reached blindly for a towel and dried her face.

Going to her closet, she pulled out a rucked white muslin and, walking back to the bed, laid it down there. I have had as much sleep as I can stand—I couldn't sleep another wink if I tried!

She let her wrapper fall and stepped into the white dress. I *will* look upon the bright side of things and enjoy the last of this Season's parties as *Maman* always meant for me to enjoy its first—with no cares or worries about making a wealthy liaison. So there, Lord Wrothby!

She finished buttoning the last button, tied her sash tolerably well, and, picking up her hat and two shawls, rang for Ellen and marched down the stairs.

Ellen met her in the hall, her eyes falling scandalously on Cara's sash. As the maid began to remonstrate with her, Cara pushed a shawl into her hands and dragged her willy-nilly out the door to revel in the fresh air and bright sunshine on a liberating walk around the neighborhood.

When she returned, glowing from her exertion, she discovered her mother on her way into the kitchen to see how dinner was progressing.

At the sight of her, Lady Brentwood's worried expression vanished, and in a relieved voice, she remarked lightly, "Oh! There you are. I didn't know what had become of you—whether you had decided to commit hara-kiri or not." She regarded her daughter tentatively.

Cara laughed and gave her mother a kiss. "I am sorry, *Maman*. I should have left you a note. Nevertheless! You will, I'm sure, be overjoyed to learn that I have decided to resume attending parties, and you and James shall have the pleasure of my entrancing company at the Doughertys' rout tonight."

"Oh, that *is* good news, Cara. What has changed your mind? No!—Don't tell me," she said, changing her own mind. "I don't want to know. Your decision to stop going to parties made positively no sense to me in the first place, so I am quite certain your reason to start again shall make very little more." She hugged her daughter and smiled. "I am simply glad you are coming. I missed you."

"What about poor Mr. Dickson?" teased Cara.

"Well, you are back to normal, I see," retorted Lady Brentwood. "You *know* what I meant! Now let me go and see to dinner, or we may not have any."

"And I had better go and see what I'm to wear tonight, or you and James shall have to go by yourselves after all." Lady Brentwood then continued on her way to the kitchen, and Cara went to stand thoughtfully before her closet.

Hours later, after a delicious dinner of marinated fillet of sole, Cara stood before her mirror, gave herself an indifferent approval of the pale gold gown she wore and turned away, leaving her bedchamber. As she descended the stairs, she still felt an underlying gloom threatening to break out again the first time something chanced to go wrong or the earl happened to put in an appearance — particularly, as seemed likely, if he had Miss Britmeyer on his arm.

Oh! I hope he shall not be there! she thought vehemently, grimacing. Immediately she scolded herself. Don't be so faint-hearted! If he *is* there, I will simply treat him as civilly as I would anyone else, and there's an end to it!

Lady Brentwood and Mr. Dickson were waiting for her in the hall, and they all proceeded out the door and into Mr. Dickson's carriage.

Due to Cara's rather last-minute decision to attend, they arrived late, and the rout was already in full swing. They greeted the Doughertys genially, Lady Brentwood complimenting her friend on her gown, which contrived to make her ample proportions appear thinner.

Pleased, Lady Dougherty beamed back at her and promised to come and find them after all her guests had been welcomed.

As they moved past his wife, Lord Dougherty pumped the two ladies' hands in greeting and pounded Mr. Dickson cheerfully on the back.

Mr. Dickson attempted to pass on into his friend's house and received a sharp dig in the side and a blatant wink. "How's the happy couple?" asked Lord Dougherty in a loud whisper.

He would have continued on the subject, but Mr. Dickson frowned him into silence and whispered back only a little less loudly than Lord Dougherty had done, "S'pose t'keep your mummer *shut* about that!"

His friend looked stricken and then smiled sheepishly. "So I was! Very sorry, very sorry, indeed!"

The two Brentwood ladies had moved on, but since the conversation had been conducted very nearly at normal voice level and neither was in the least deaf, they heard the whole of it.

Cara opened her mouth to twit Mr. Dickson on it but caught the shake of her mother's head and so, though she wore a wide grin, refrained from making any comment.

Much as Lady Brentwood had calmly assumed, her daughter's wide smile was lost on her dear, if slightly obtuse, future husband.

Turning this way and that among the crowd to chat with their respective friends, the three passed a pleasant hour mingling among Lady Dougherty's guests. Cara, still feeling irresolute about coming at all, had preferred to remain in company with her mother and Mr. Dickson rather than seek out any of her gentlemen friends, as she might have done, and set up the core to which her circle of admirers usually gravitated.

She was amused to bump into Miss Britmeyer in the course of their mingling and, greeting her politely, was even disposed to be pleasant, noting quickly that the earl was not with her. On a previous night I could easily have snatched her bald! thought Cara, her green eyes sparkling with merriment as she watched Miss Britmeyer give her a considering glance. The corners of her mouth quirked as she reflected that Miss Britmeyer had, on occasion, very probably felt the same.

Having had quite enough of her rival, Miss Britmeyer moved off saying, "Well, I must go and see how my mother is getting on."

"I don't believe that for one moment," Cara remarked, when she was out of earshot. She watched Miss Britmeyer make her way toward a group of gentlemen and stop. "Ha! I was right!" she cried, looking triumphantly toward Lady Brentwood and Mr. Dickson. Her expression turned to one of mild disgust. Smiling quietly at each other, her mother and Mr. Dickson were oblivious of her.

When they showed no signs of coming out of their abstraction, Cara leaned close to them and announced, "You two had better stop that mooning at each other, or you'll leave no doubt in anyone's mind about your engagement!"

The two before her started and looked up. With an alarmed expression, Mr. Dickson blurted, "No! Mustn't know till the banns come out."

Lady Brentwood, with an expression of benign indifference, murmured, "I don't care *what* others may think."

Laughing at Mr. Dickson's expression and nodding in approval of her mother's attitude, Cara praised, "That's a Brentwood for you!" and then stopped abruptly, her own expression frozen ludicrously.

It was Lady Brentwood's turn to become alarmed. "What is it? Cara? What's the matter?!"

"Lady Dougherty—!" Cara choked, watching Lady Dougherty make her way steadily toward her, and then, with a prodigious effort of will power, Cara changed her expression to one of polite indifference.

"But what can be wrong with Betsy's com—?" began Lady Brentwood and stopped abruptly as she watched the transformation in her daughter's features and suddenly realized what must be the cause not only of Cara's immediate dismay but of her recent moody behavior as well.

Mr. Dickson merely looked from mother to daughter in bewilderment.

Lady Dougherty approached with Lord Wrothby in tow. He was smiling blandly, his eyes half-lidded.

Cara was almost certain his eyes were gleaming under their heavy lids with enjoyment at her situation.

In the tone of a mother who is in part teasing and in part sincerely scolding her child, Lady Dougherty came up saying, "Cara, I have brought this wicked young man over to you the moment he set foot in my house so that he might get whatever it is he apparently *must* say to provoke you off his chest *now* while I am with the two of you. I cannot have him cause some, some spectacle or other, later, when he finds himself—or is it *plans*, Lord Wrothby?" she asked, giving him a meaning look—"running across you later, unattended by either myself or your mother!" She paused to catch her breath. "For—tut, tut—we *all* know, Lord Wrothby, how you love to cause scandals, don't we?" and she looked toward her listeners for corroboration.

Only Mr. Dickson, always ready to acquiesce, nodded his head in agreement. Then, realizing that what Lady Dougherty had just said sounded rather in the nature of an insult, a moment later he shook his head in the opposite direction.

Receiving no encouragement from Cara or Lady Brentwood, Lady Dougherty went relentlessly on, tapping the earl smartly on the arm with her fan to emphasize her point. "But not, Lord Wrothby, I re-

292

peat — *not* in *my* house!" she finished awfully.

Cara's eyes sparkled appreciatively at the limitless opportunities afforded her to roast the earl in what Lady Dougherty had just said. But she merely bit her lip and maintained an impassive silence.

"Betsy, I am certain the earl does not purposely set out to cause, er, scandals," chided Lady Brentwood mildly.

There was an obvious gleam of amusement in the earl's black eyes as he agreed, "No ma'am, indeed I do not, Lady Dougherty. They just seem to, ah, happen . . . when I am by!"

He was enjoying himself hugely, Cara knew, and she was sorely tempted to deliver a rejoinder that might take him down a peg. Instead, she bit her lip again, keeping her witticisms to herself and repressing a smile as he continued to bait Lady Dougherty.

Unmollified, Lady Dougherty went on, "But the fact is they *do* happen! Now, Lord Wrothby. If you have anything you wish to say to Miss Brentwood this evening which you think she might consider even remotely unsettling, I wish you will say it now!"

Looking directly at Cara, his eyes glinting, the earl protested meekly, "Indeed, Lady Dougherty, I do not!"

Cara averted her gaze and looked quickly at Lady Dougherty's shining wood floor. She was not, however, able to avoid hearing the tone of his voice and gave a choked cough which sounded decidedly like a laugh.

"Well then! Let us all consider the matter closed," concluded Lady Dougherty. "And, dear boy," she added, tapping the earl briskly again with her fan and dismissing him, "I am certain, after all this, I shall not hear of any untoward conduct on your part."

Changing the subject then, she turned to Lady Brentwood and demanded, "Alicia! James! What's this George tells me of your betrothal? And James! You scoundrel, why did you not tell me!"

Both offenders blushed rosily, and the earl bowed and made good his escape as Mr. Dickson glanced around, frowning, for George Dougherty.

Having heard what sounded very like a laugh from Cara and observing the amused sparkle in her eyes, the earl was at a loss to understand her polite, expressionless face. He still found it hard to credit that she could be pining for Mr. Dickson. Grinning to himself, he decided to go and find Miss Britmeyer and simply put Miss Brentwood to the test.

Half-listening to Lady Dougherty extract the story of her mother's engagement, Cara watched the earl move off and, feeling her spirits sink, couldn't help wondering where he was going. She would not have long to wait to find out.

He was soon to be seen talking and laughing with a flushed Miss Britmeyer at the edge of the cluster of guests in Cara's vicinity. Working his way round before Cara with Miss Britmeyer, the earl watched for her reaction to his blonde companion.

With satisfaction, he saw Cara draw in her breath sharply when she saw them and pivot, quickly turning her shoulder upon them and successfully appearing oblivious of their existence. He smiled. So! Perhaps Miss Cara Brentwood was not as indifferent to him as her face would lead him to believe! Mr. Dickson, suddenly, ceased to be a matter of concern to the earl.

He saw Cara lean toward Lady Brentwood, Lady Dougherty, and Mr. Dickson and speak briefly. A moment later the three of them moved off through the crowd in the direction, he guessed, of the card room. You won't escape me that easily! he addressed her silently and suggested to Miss Britmeyer that they go and speak with a friend of his he pretended to see over by the card room.

Arriving just outside the doorway, he assumed a perplexed tone and exclaimed, "Now where the devil did he go to?"

"Never mind," placated Miss Britmeyer, not anxious to share the earl with a male crony. "We will certainly see him again." And she swiftly changed the subject, as the earl had counted upon her to do.

The first time Cara looked up from her game of whist, she could not help but see the earl, who had carefully placed himself directly in her line of vision. And in the space of fifteen minutes, watching in horrified fascination, Cara was privileged to observe him back Miss Britmeyer up against the doorjamb and lean one arm against it, provocatively barring her way.

Miss Britmeyer, quite naturally loving every minute of his marked attention, responded as flirtatiously as the earl could have desired.

Despite herself, Cara could not restrain herself from following the earl's progress. His little scene quite broke her concentration, and, to Lady Dougherty's exasperation, Cara's loss of attention caused the two of them to lose the hand they had previously been winning to Lady Brentwood and Mr. Dickson.

"Cara Brentwood! Do you think you could confine your wandering attention to this card table?" asked Lady Doughety awfully, rapping her knuckles on the table in front of Cara. Swiveling her large body around in her chair, she looked in the direction Cara's eyes continually returned to and saw nothing but the earl innocently talking to Miss Britmeyer. Lady Dougherty harrumphed and turned back to glare at Cara.

"I am sorry, Lady Dougherty!" Cara apologized and seethed inwardly at the earl. She resolved to put an end to the problem. "Perhaps you would not mind exchanging places with me, ma'am?"

"If it will increase your concentration, I would not!" replied Lady Dougherty, heaving herself to her feet and walking round the small baize table.

Sighing gloomily, Cara sat down in the chair Lady Dougherty had vacated.

"Are we all ready to continue playing now?" asked Lady Dougherty with just the tiniest inflection of sarcasm in her voice.

Cara nodded, and Mr. Dickson dealt out another hand.

Looking up from her cards several minutes later, Cara was satisfied to see only the normal milling of guests as they watched over the shoulders of the players and waited their turns to sit in on a game with friends. She sighed again, relieved not to have to watch the earl positively make love to Miss Britmeyer before her very eyes.

Her relief, however, was short-lived. Expertly the earl began to maneuver Miss Britmeyer around the room until once again they stood directly in Cara's line of vision. I imagine, he thought cheerfully, we stand out nicely against this walnut paneling. He smiled.

Thinking his smile for her, Miss Britmeyer returned it. In spite of her mother's skeptical warnings, she was beginning to entertain the hope of eliciting a proposal from the earl.

Innocently considering which of two cards to throw down, Cara raised her eyes from her hand and received the shock of finding Miss Britmeyer and the earl once more before her gaze. She started, and her brows snapped together as she struggled to master her emotions. Quickly she lowered her eyes to the white faces of the cards in the middle of the table and kept them locked upon the upturned cards.

This cannot be happening! she groaned inwardly. Surely they are doing this purposely! But what conceivable reason Miss Britmeyer might have for deliberately flirting with the earl before her Cara could not fathom.

Rejecting that notion, she accused, Then *he* is doing it purposely! But even as Lady Dougherty had thought before her, Cara had to admit the earl did appear blamelessly unaware of her presence. He had not once, to her knowledge, glanced in her direction. And if he were doing this on purpose, she rationalized, assuredly — knowing him — he would have leered at me just so I should know he was doing it deliberately!

Utterly confused and unable to decide whether the earl was tormenting her deliberately or simply by unfortunate accident, Cara raised her eyes once more to regard the earl and try to discern if he were only acting unaware of her presence.

She saw Miss Britmeyer lean very close to him and brush against his leg with her dress. The earl raised his hand and appeared to play with a blond curl.

A moment later, he pulled something from it, for which Miss Britmeyer appeared to be very grateful, but Cara was no longer watching. Gritting her teeth, she swore not to look up again and threw down her

297

card.

Lady Dougherty's sharp intake of breath told her instantly she had discarded the wrong card.

A few minutes later, the game ended, and Lady Dougherty remarked dryly, "Well, we won that one, but by the barest squeak of a margin one could imagine."

"Play another game, Betsy," Lady Brentwood cajoled.

" 'Ndeed, must give us a chance to get our winnings back," agreed Mr. Dickson.

"No, I must go and do a little more visiting with some of my other guests. You three have monopolized me as much as I dare let you for this evening. I must go and check on George, too, you know. I vow he is just like a child, and he has been far too quiet. I haven't caught a glimpse of him recently—he is sure to be up to something! You will come and say good night before you leave?" she ended, patting Lady Brentwood's arm and rising from her chair.

"Of course," Lady Brentwood answered as her friend began to move off.

Lady Dougherty turned back and fixed Cara with a steely eye. "You could be a first-rate whist player, my dear, if you would only keep your attention on the game." She then moved off again and was seen chatting, making her way slowly among her guests.

Lady Brentwood laughed. "That was high praise from Betsy, Cara."

Cara smiled and, avoiding the direction of the earl and Miss Britmeyer, regarded her mother ruefully. "Don't I know it! I shall try to do better for her next time."

"May not be a next time," pointed out Mr. Dickson bluntly. "Betsy's partic'lar about who she sits lown with."

Cara shrugged. She really didn't care one whit what Lady Dougherty thought of her card playing. She could still see the earl laughing down at Miss Britmeyer out of the corner of her eye.

"Shall we play another game or follow Betsy's example and do a little more mingling?" asked Lady Brentwood.

Mr. Dickson was shuffling and reshuffling the deck of cards.

"It looks as if Mr. Dickson would like to play again," answered Cara. He smiled shyly and nodded. "Deal the cards then, sir, and I shall trounce you both," challenged Cara, trying to work up some enthusiasm. She kept her eyes carefully on the cards before her. He has probably found something on the front of her dress to finger by now! she thought indignantly.

After another half an hour of loo, Mr. Dickson announced, "Well. All for me. That's all m'money for tonight."

"Shall we visit a bit more and then go home?" asked Lady Brentwood. Neither the earl's companion nor his position had been lost on her. For the last half-hour Cara had played only halfheartedly, and Mr. Dickson was beginning to yawn.

Both her listeners readily agreed to her suggestion, and they all rose.

The earl, convinced now that Cara was not enamored of nor pining for Mr. Dickson, mercifully allowed her to leave unpursued. He remained where he was, flirting outrageously with Miss Britmeyer for another thirty minutes to assuage the twinge of guilt he felt for using her so shamefully and then politely took his leave of her.

He wasn't going to allow himself to feel too much guilt—she had proved herself quite a bit more of coquette than he had guessed.

Seeking Lady Dougherty out among her guests the earl took that lady by the shoulders and planted an affectionate kiss upon her plump cheek, leaving her gaping after him in surprise. But the earl, giving the devil her due, considered that if Lady Dougherty hadn't dragged him upon his arrival over to see Cara, he might still be laboring under the delusion that she was in love with Dickson.

At the door, he ran into George Dougherty seeing his guests off and keeping a watchful eye on both his footmen and the departing carriages to see that all went smoothly.

The earl slapped him heartily on the back, collected his ebony cane, and strolled off into the night twirling it and shouting behind him, "Send my carriage on without me, Dougherty, I'll walk!" Feeling more lighthearted than he had in days, he looked up and cheerfully warned the stars, "And the *next* time I see you, my fine red-headed "Gentleman Jack," you and I shall resolve a thing or two between us!"

Lord Dougherty put a hand to his chest, patting it to make certain it was still sound after the hearty slap on the back he had just borne. Raising one bushy white eyebrow, he wondered what had occurred to make the earl happy enough to want to walk home. It must've been something prodigious he thought, looking after the earl's retreating figure. But then, he continued to himself, it don't take much for the young'uns, and, reaching round to massage his lumbago, he went to see to the positioning of the next carriage.

Eighteen

Seated at the dining-room table, Cara read the invitation from Lord and Lady Moberly to one of the last balls to be given before the close of the Season. Stating that it was to be a masque that would not begin until ten o'clock the following Friday evening, it piqued her interest in spite of herself, and she felt her spirits rise in anticipation for the first time in weeks. She'd never been to a masque, but she felt certain it must be a formidable affair. *The ordinary outfits of the beau monde are outrageous,* she thought. *What must their costumes be like at a masque!* She smiled a little cynically but could not suppress a tremor of excitement in the bottom of her stomach.

In her anticipation, the three days until Friday seemed almost to creep by, they passed so slowly. But she was not the only one eager for Friday's arrival. The masque and the costume one had chosen to wear to it were the topics of every conversation at all the intervening parties.

Unlike all her friends, Cara refused to reveal what her costume would be, not even telling her mother. And when her admirers protested that they wouldn't be able to discover her, she retorted, "You will just have to search me out of the crowd then. 'Twill be a good test to see how well, in fact, you know me." When they returned doubtful faces in answer, she added tartly, "Come! It is the merest child's play for one who is truly in love to pick his beloved from the crowd—masked or not," for their exaggerated protestations had begun of late to pall on her.

Friday finally arrived. Cara sat on the settee with her mother's sewing basket beside her and a lapful of black net. As she painstakingly sewed tiny jet buttons onto the net, she tried to decide for the umpteenth time if the earl had been deliberately flirting with Miss Britmeyer in front of her at the Doughertys' rout.

Shaking her head dubiously as she bent over her work, she asked herself again, How could they have ended up so exactly in front of me—at least three different times!—by accident? I do not see how that could be possible.

Don't be nonsensical! she commanded herself a moment later, becoming vexed. Why should Lord Wrothby take pains to flirt before me? I want to think he was trying to make me jealous because it would show, at the very least, that he was not indifferent to me. But I am simply wishing my own feelings onto his behavior and reading more into it than is actually there, she resolved dolefully.

She had not seen the earl at any of the parties she had attended during the last few days, presumably because he had not been on the same guest lists as herself. She picked another jet button from the sewing basket and, turning it between her fingers, watched it glitter and wondered how the earl would have behaved toward her if she had.

The front door banging shut broke her reverie,

and she returned to her sewing with a start, concluding sharply, It doesn't signify in the least! I should have avoided him anyway.

Lady Brentwood entered the parlor, her cheeks pink from an afternoon drive with Mr. Dickson.

"What, back so soon?" Cara teased.

Her mother laughed. "I have been gone above two hours, and well you know it! Yes, I told James I wanted to try and get a little nap this afternoon so that I wouldn't disgrace you both by falling asleep in my chair tonight, and he thought that was such a good idea he has gone to do the same thing. I thought I would look in on you first, though." She eyed the black net curiously. "It looks interesting," she commented hopefully.

"Mmm, does it?"

"Well, a house doesn't have to fall on me. You aren't going to tell me yet, are you?" Cara gave a shake of her copper curls. "I'm going to have to wait until tonight?"

"Curiosity killed the cat," admonished Cara self-righteously.

"Stubborn child," pronounced Lady Brentwood and swung out of the parlor to take her nap.

"My own mother!" called Cara in a shocked tone, laughing after her. Moments later, she sewed the last jet button onto the black net and exclaimed, "Lord! Finally! The last one. Why I did not throw myself upon Ellen's mercy and beg her to do it, I do not know!" But, in fact, she had not liked to ask Ellen, for she had known the job was going to be excessively tedious.

Having finished her costume, she decided her mother's idea was not a bad one. She hadn't been sleeping well recently, and she also had no wish to feel tired even before they started out for the Moberlys'. "And there will probably be a sad crush to get in," she said aloud, thinking of having to stand in line outside waiting to enter and greet her hosts, as had happened at some of the more well-attended balls.

She gathered the black net, dotted now with tiny jet buttons, over her arm, returned the sewing basket to its place, and headed for her bedchamber to lie down.

Many hours later, both ladies were rested, bathed, and putting the final touches to their costumes in their rooms in preparation for the arrival of Mr. Dickson. The three of them were to eat a leisurely supper and then proceed together in Mr. Dickson's phaeton, hidden from the eyes of onlookers, to the Moberlys'.

"Has my mother gone down yet, Ellen?" asked Cara, meeting the maid servant outside Lady Brentwood's bedchamber.

Ellen stared. "N-No, miss. I'm to go back to her in a minute and help her to put on her mask without spoiling her hair."

Grinning at Ellen, Cara decided to surprise her mother and descended the stairs to lie in wait for her in the dining room. She knew her mother would first check on the table settings and fresh flower centerpiece before going into the parlor to await Mr. Dickson.

Several minutes later, Cara struck a pose as she heard the rustle of Lady Brentwood's skirts coming down the stairs.

Dressed charmingly as a shepherdess in a simple layered beige frock trimmed in blue and carrying a crooked staff, her mother entered the dining room.

She was brought up short by the sight of her daughter, standing at the end of the table, her green eyes glinting through the slits of her mask.

Lady Brentwood gasped, "Oh! Good heavens, Cara. You are magnificent!" She was silent a moment, taking in all of her daughter's appearance.

It was indeed an impressive one. She stood in a pearl-colored tiffany underdress, cut low with a scalloped edge across the bosom. In its simplicity of straight folds, it smoothly outlined the slimness of Cara's tall, graceful figure, and its soft nacreous color enhanced the creaminess of her skin. Over the tiffany, she wore the stiff black net, the tiny jet buttons glittering in the light with the gentle movement of her breathing. Her copper hair had been swept off her face and hidden in a striking black turban, patterned with small diamanté leaves. But the severity of the sparkling, black turban, which would have made another woman look plain and unprepossessing, only served to accent her large green eyes and point up the perfection of her other features. Long, black diamanté gloves, which covered her arms to well above the elbows, and a black diamanté half mask completed her costume to give her a mysterious, almost menacing appearance.

"You quite put me in the shade," commented Lady Brentwood when she had absorbed all of this. "Wh-what *are* you?"

"I am Black Nightshade, of course," Cara answered. "A white flower with dark berries. Poisonous, you know," she whispered and leered evilly at her mother. From the snuffbox in her hand, she took a pinch of snuff and blew it toward Lady Brentwood. "With my compliments — a little poison."

305

"Whatever you are, you're frightening," remarked Lady Brentwood, still staring.

"Thank you. I have been feeling positively *dire* of late, and I am giving my darker nature free license tonight," she intoned diabolically.

"Dire . . . ? Your darker nature?"

"Allow me to tell you that you look like just the kind of sweet innocent Black Nightshade loves to prey on most." She took a dramatic step closer to Lady Brentwood.

"Flowers — prey on things?" questioned her mother dubiously.

"These do." Cara took a second step.

"I think . . . I hear James at the door. I will just go and let him in." She retreated quickly into the hall.

"Coward," accused Cara and tested a maniacal chuckle. "Not bad." She heard her mother begin to laugh in the hallway. A moment later, she herself threw back her head in peal of laughter as Lady Brentwood returned leading a large, furry brown bear by the paw.

"James," crowed Cara, "I didn't know you had it in you!"

He gave a very unferocious roar. "Don't look s'bad y'rselves," he growled, addressing both women.

"How — how are you going to manage s-supper?" asked Lady Brentwood, choked with laughter.

He gave another roar which sounded suspiciously like a groan. "Shall have to take m'head off I s'pose," came his muffled voice through the bared teeth of the bear's head. This observation set both ladies to laughing again. "Think I may need some help," he remarked, struggling with both paws to undo the buttons that held the bear head on.

306

But it was several moments before the two ladies, wiping the tears of laughter from their eyes, were capable of assisting him. Finally, still chuckling while they unbuttoned buttons, they had him out of his paws and bear head, and all three sat down in a festive mood to eat a delicious supper of brisket of chicken with glazed vegetables removed by a dish of sweetmeats.

By the time they had lingered over another cup of hot tea for Mr. Dickson, a glass of claret for Cara—at which Mr. Dickson could not help raising his eyebrows—and a glass of ratafia for Lady Brentwood, it was time to leave for the masque. Merrily they buttoned Mr. Dickson back into his costume and, careful not to muss their hair, affixed their own masks again.

As Cara had foreseen, they found the Moberlys' driveway crowded with carriages waiting to unload their fantastically attired occupants before the grand stone staircase. In the end, tired of waiting in the phaeton, Cara suggested that they get down where they were and walk the remaining distance to the stairs. Her companions agreed, and they were soon standing on the steps greeting others and inching their way upward to be received by their host and hostess.

When the three reached the top, Lord and Lady Moberly, regal in dark purple and each with a crown of diamonds, greeted them gaily and tried vainly to guess their identities. Failing in this, they had to be told, at which they smiled good-naturedly and waved the three in.

Both Cara and Lady Brentwood stared in amazement at the incredible scene before them. The ballroom had been decorated lavishly with candles and fresh garlands of flowers of every conceivable hue. Large mirrors which had been set up along the walls reflected the riot of flowers, the yellow pinpoints of lights from the candles, and the extravagant costumes of the guests themselves. The center of the room was dominated by a large fountain, also decorated with an abundance of flowers and candles, and was irridescently sprinkling water. The ballroom itself opened along the length of one side into a courtyard of shrubs and trees, all threaded with strings of tiny white fairy lights. Indeed, the entire room looked as if it were the playground of fairies, and the fragrance of the flowers mixing with the strains of the orchestra floating to them over the heads of those who were already dancing did nothing to dispel that impression.

Cara and Lady Brentwood were entranced. Even Mr. Dickson, having been exposed to such lavish entertainment more often than the two Brentwood ladies, growled his approval through the teeth of his wooly bear head. Fascinated by the fantastic costumes, they began to drift away from the entrance and move slowly through the crowd trying to guess some of the identities that lay beneath the masks.

"There's Richard!" declared Cara, pointing and raising her voice in order to make herself heard over the growing noise of the crowd. "See? The white knight in that group of people over there—and Janie, too!" As Cara spoke, she lead her mother and Mr. Dickson through the crowd to join them.

Coming up behind Richard, she hissed in his ear, "What hath the White Knight to say to deadly Black Nightshade?"

Richard started and whirled to face her, a look of astonished admiration appearing on his face. "Cara?

Then this must be Lady Brentwood and Mr. Dickson," he stated logically, exchanging greetings with them. "Dash it, Cara, that's the best costume I've seen all night, er, outside Janie's, of course," he corrected loudly, catching Janie's attention. Smiles appeared all round their circle. "You must bear with me—oh, forgive me, Mr. Dickson!" He winked and elbowed his woolly friend in the side. "I have to say that, you know, or Janie'll get peeved and treat me to a fit of the vapors the next chance she gets," he continued in a mock whisper to Cara. The two Brentwoods and Mr. Dickson laughed.

Janie turned away from the couple she had been talking to and, joining their circle, admonished, "Richard! Stop whatever you're saying about me this minute! They might not understand you're just teasing." She gave them a long-suffering smile and declared, "He is forever making game of me," and put the back of her hand to her brow in an exaggerated gesture of martyrdom.

Observing their costumes, she exclaimed over them and then piped brightly, "I'm Richard's damsel in distress!" She threw him a sidelong glance under her lashes to see if he was watching and delivered her shot. "I wanted to be something more original, but *he,*" and she jerked her thumb in Richard's direction, "compelled me to wear this!" She smiled at Richard in gleeful revenge.

"Doing it up too brown, Janie," he laughed. "They don't believe a word of it!" He went to stand next to her and draped an arm about her shoulders.

"Yes, we do, Richard. We know you too well," Cara joined in, receiving a nod of approval from Janie.

"Oh ho! Ganging up on me, are you? Don't go too

309

far—Mr. Dickson and his sharp teeth will leap to my defense, won't you, Mr. Dickson?"

Mr. Dickson hesitated and then gave a shy roar in answer. The group burst out laughing, and he blushed rosily beneath the fur of his costume. As if she knew this, Lady Brentwood, still smiling, patted his woolly arm.

"Is that Lord Wrothby, Richard, coming this way behind that jester?" asked Janie. "Oh! His costume suits him perfectly!" she exclaimed.

Cara refused to turn and look in the earl's direction. Instead, she bent her attention on a satyr standing a short distance in front of her talking to a nymph.

The earl sauntered up with a wicked gleam in his eyes and greeted them. Choosing his costume deliberately, he had settled upon the masque as the most fitting of environs to broach the subject he wished to discuss with Cara. But he had not been able to resist the temptation to plague her one last time before he did so.

Miss Britmeyer, making an entrancing French aristocrat in a rose-colored empress gown, tripped smilingly after him.

Janie gasped and blurted in a shocked whisper to Richard, "I think she has *dampened* her skirts!"

But Richard, warily adding his greeting to those of the others saw only the gleam in the earl's dark eyes and fervently hoped that he was not going to be the object of the earl's pugnacity. Mentally he reviewed his recent activities, but he could think of nothing he might have unwittingly done that could have offended his friend.

"Ah, Miss Brentwood," boomed the earl, following the direction of her eyes.

Exonerated, Richard heaved a sigh of relief and settled back beside Janie.

"I perceive," the earl continued, "you have now developed a penchant for satyrs. Does your taste always run toward such, er, unsavory characters?"

Cara colored and turned to face the earl, her green eyes snapping. She had opened her mouth to deliver a stinging rejoinder, but her gaze fell upon his costume, and she gasped instead, stunned into momentary silence.

Lord Wrothby stood in black shirt and pants partially covered by a dark cloak, which was tied back to reveal a small, silver-handled pistol tucked into his red waistband. A dark hat, pulled rakishly over his eyes, and the bright red half mask he wore proclaimed him, undoubtedly, the highwayman!

As he, in turn, took in Cara's costume, his eyes widened in silent admiration, and he raised his eyebrows appreciatively. He allowed a slight smile, calculated to nettle her, to play around his mouth.

Miss Britmeyer did not like the look of that smile at all. And furthermore, she decided, she didn't like the tenor of this whole conversation, centering as it did on Cara instead of herself. It was a conversation that had gone on too long for her taste already—all the earl politely had to do was greet the chit! She determined to put an end to it.

Placing her soft, white hand on the earl's arm, she looked up at him enticingly and murmured, "Julius, they have struck up a waltz!" She turned and began to move off slowly, still with her white hand on his arm, drawing him prettily in the direction of the dancers.

The earl threw a smug smile at Cara, which she answered with a scowl, and bowed to the group, sweeping Miss Britmeyer into his arms and waltzing toward the orchestra.

Cara, he considered, grinning, had shown a most gratifying appreciation of his costume! When she had had time to cool down, he promised himself, he would single her out and, if he had to drag her off bodily, they should sit down privately and straighten a few matters out! Then his courtship might begin in earnest and adopt, er, more respectable practices.

He turned his head, as if he knew she was still watching him, and threw her another impertinent smile.

"Insufferable—!" ground Cara through clenched teeth, so incensed she could think of nothing rude enough to call him.

"—Puppy," finished Giles Denby helpfully, joining the group in time to witness the earl's theatrical departure. "No doubt about it. Do you know, he lured the Countess Hauterive, that little leading lady in *The Lady's Folly,* away from m—! Ahem! Er—." He stopped abruptly, his normally rosy cheeks flaming, acutely aware, after a dig in the ribs from Richard, that his subject was not fit for his present company.

"Ah, have you seen Lord and Lady Dougherty tonight, ma'am?" Richard addressed Lady Brentwood, trying to cover his friend's embarrassment.

"Why no, I haven't," she replied, her blue eyes twinkling merrily.

"Lady Dougherty makes a splendid Queen of Madagascar," he stated, winking at Cara, who was endeavoring with difficulty to regain her previous good humor. "I haven't yet seen Dougherty," Richard added, obviously relishing the sight.

That wretch had to have gone out of his way to choose *that* costume! Cara told herself angrily. And

he obviously came over here in it—with *that* woman
on his arm—just to vex me! she realized slowly, her
anger giving way to bewilderment. But why?

"Told me he'd only come as a ship's captain," offered Mr. Dickson, interrupting Cara's thoughts.
"Had Betsy sore as crosspatch over it—wanted him
t'be the King of Madagascar, y'know."

"Dougherty? The King of Madagascar!" exclaimed
Richard with a shout of laughter.

"Not Dougherty," stated Lord Denby, apparently
recovered from his embarrassment.

"Just so," agreed Mr. Dickson solemnly with a nod
of his bear's head.

"This deserves a little further delving into. Are you
with me, Denby?" chuckled Richard, starting to
move off in search of the unsuspecting Lord
Dougherty.

But Janie caught his arm quickly, piping, "Oh no
you don't, Richard! If you want to look for Lord
Dougherty, you can do it from the floor while we
dance. Come on," she coaxed, putting a hand on his
arm and employing Miss Britmeyer's tactics.

Richard gave in with a good grace, and together
they moved off, weaving their way through the crush
of people.

"Are you game, Miss Brentwood?" asked Lord
Denby.

"Lead on, Lord Denby," she accepted, relegating
the earl's behavior to the back of her mind. I will
puzzle it out later, she promised herself, determined
to enjoy her lavish surroundings. She smiled down at
Lord Denby, several inches shorter than she. "Let's
see if we can't collar George first!" And calling after
Richard and Janie to wait, they hurried after them.

Lady Brentwood and Mr. Dickson, not wishing

313

particularly to join in their search, were left quite happily to themselves.

Fortunately for the unsuspecting object of the two couples' search, he was soon forgotten in their delight in dancing. They traded partners and, as more and more of their friends began to join them on the floor also trading partners, Cara lost track of her original companions.

Since she had been unable to guess the identities of several of her partners, she didn't hesitate to accept the out-stretched hands of a gentleman in a black domino. But he drew her attention to himself by maintaining an unbroken silence, instead of making the usual polite small talk, and holding her a deal too close for her liking. She was unpleasantly reminded of Arthur Lyle, but the music ended before she could ascertain, by observing her partner from beneath her lashes, if that was indeed who he was.

When the dance ended, he released her and melted into the crowd, seeking another partner like any other dancer. And as she looked after him, another gentleman, dressed as a soldier, caught her up and swung her into the next dance.

The following hours, spent in a similar fashion, seemed to fly. Cara was enjoying herself as she had not done for several weeks. But when, from the dance floor, she thought she saw Lord Dougherty head toward the courtyard, she decided swiftly to follow him to escape the next dance and join him in seeking a much-needed breath of fresh night air.

The ballroom, filled to capacity now with people, had grown stiflingly hot. Or maybe, she realized as she dodged through the crowd, it is due to so much dancing. Noticing that Lord Dougherty was wearing the blue uniform of a ship's captain, she chuckled

314

softly to herself and thought, So Lady Dougherty lost that one! Then Lord Dougherty disappeared as several people cut before her.

When she arrived at the courtyard, he was nowhere to be seen. Feeling the cool night air on her flushed face, Cara assumed he had continued into the courtyard and was now hidden among the trees, and she walked on in the direction she had last seen him heading. But when, after several minutes' search, she still caught no sign of him, she gave up and slowed her pace, content to stroll for another few moments peacefully down the cool, quiet avenues of fairy-lit trees before she reentered once more the bright hubbub of the warm ballroom.

The earl's puzzling behavior came flooding back to her. Of a certainty he wore that highwayman costume for my benefit alone, she rationalized. No one else would understand the significance of it.

She hardly dared even think the next idea that presented itself to her. Could it be that he is not, after all, indifferent to me? she asked, unaware that she had spoken aloud. The stars twinkled brightly back at her from the black velvet of the sky but vouchsafed no answering signal.

It is time to go back, she chided herself. I am getting far too carried away out here! One does not fall in love with the man she has held up and put a bullet through and then marry him and live happily ever after! Her lips curved in a small cynical smile. You are a poor, silly fool, she addressed herself silently. That, indeed, would be a fairy tale!

She lingered, breathing in the sweet cedar and pine scents, wanting to believe a few moments longer in her dream and reluctant yet to leave the magical setting which made the earl seem a little less unattainable.

At last, she gave a deep sigh and, trying not to think of the dull pain in her heart, began to thread her way back. She came level with the border of courtyard trees and stopped, invisible in the line of dark green, to enjoy the scene of fantastic revelers that presented itself before her.

A cloaked figure, blending well in the night's darkness, stole noiselessly up behind her.

Giving another small sigh, she started forward to cross the remaining distance to the ballroom and felt, rather than saw, something dark snake out in front of her. Gasping in surprise, she raised one hand vainly to ward if off and felt a coarse cloth pressed roughly over her nose and mouth.

A heavy, sweet odor assailed her senses. The bodies of the revelers, already fantastic, began to distort themselves, waving and bulging before her until their vivid colors began to fade, and everything went black.

Cara's body slumped into the waiting arms behind her. The figure bent a moment to lift her limp body up in his arms, then wheeled and vanished into the darkness of the trees.

Nineteen

At three A.M., Lady Brentwood began to inquire discreetly of her friends if they had seen Cara in the last hour. It was very unlike her daughter not to check back with her at intervals to see how she did. Lady Brentwood had last seen Cara on the dance floor, but that had been several hours ago. A tiny frown appeared between her brows, and her blue eyes began to look troubled, but she held her peace, not wishing to discomfit her daughter if, youth being what it was, she had simply been enjoying herself and forgotten. But when another half-hour had passed with still no sight or word of her, Lady Brentwood confided her worry to Mr. Dickson, and he, gallantly, offered to search through the ballroom until he found her.

"Don't tell her I was worried, James," Lady Brentwood admonished, perturbed but expecting to find Cara had merely forgotten her in her own enjoyment.

Mr. Dickson then made an unsuccessful search of the ballroom and was heading back toward Lady Brentwood when he caught sight of George Dougherty and enlisted the aid of his friend.

Lord Dougherty had turned in the opposite direction from Cara and reentered the ballroom as she had continued on into the courtyard. He had seen her enter the rows of trees, not realizing that she was looking for him. Consequently he told Mr. Dickson he'd last seen her several hours back walking out for a breath of fresh air.

Mr. Dickson, delighted to have found someone who had seen Cara since she had been on the dance floor, promptly dragged Lord Dougherty back to Lady Brentwood to have him relate his information to her in person.

Far from relieving her mind, Lord Dougherty's news alarmed Lady Brentwood in earnest. "She cannot still be outside, James," she exclaimed anxiously when he didn't understand why she was still worried. "And you've just said she is not inside. Even if she had fallen and hurt herself, surely someone would have come across her out there by now. Oh, I don't understand this at all! Where can she be?" she asked, looking worriedly from Mr. Dickson to Lord Dougherty.

It was by this time nearing four A.M., and some of the guests were beginning to depart.

A footman liveried in the Moberlys' colors approached them. "You are Lady Brentwood?" Surprised, she nodded her assent, and he continued formally, "I was asked to deliver this note to you." He held out a silver salver.

"Thank you." Lady Brentwood lifted the note from the center of it.

The footman withdrew.

Fearing some calamity, Lady Brentwood unfolded the paper and read quickly. She looked up at Mr. Dickson in extreme perplexity when she had finished. "I don't understand," she repeated. "This doesn't make any more sense! The note says she has decided to marry Viscount Lyle after all, and . . . and she's eloping with him tonight!"

Mr. Dickson frowned back at her in disapproval of this shocking behavior. "Not th' thing, m'dear. Not the thing at all—should've waited and been married properly in a church."

Lord Dougherty clucked his agreement with Mr. Dickson.

"No, no, dear. You still don't understand. Cara has disliked Viscount Lyle enormously since he— since the Marstons' picnic. She would never have eloped with him."

A preposterous idea presented itself to Lord Dougherty. "You don't mean that he's *abducted* her, Lady Brentwood?!" he blurted.

"I'm not sure what I mean," she answered in confusion. "Oh, James! Surely he wouldn't—Where is Richard? He will know!"

"I'll find him. Don't worry, 'Licia, m'dear," replied Mr. Dickson, removing his bear head with some difficulty in order to have a clearer view. He then launched himself on his second search, leaving Lord Dougherty to stay with Lady Brentwood.

Intermittently he patted her shoulder awkwardly and said, "There, there. It'll all come right, you'll see." But he looked worried himself.

The earl, too, by now had been looking for Cara for some time. Becoming exasperated at her elusiveness, which was preventing the discussion he deemed crucial to the happiness of both of them, he had begun in the last hour a systematic search of the Moberlys' residence.

Concluding that she wasn't on the premises, he had just wondered with irritation if she had gone home when he saw a wild-eyed Mr. Dickson, carry-

319

ing his grinning bear head under his arm, rush past him. Assuming that if Dickson were still present both Lady Brentwood and Cara were in all likelihood also still present, the earl decided to follow Mr. Dickson in hopes of being lead to Cara.

But as the earl made his way through the crowd, the rather frantic expression Dickson had worn as he had passed impressed itself upon him, and he began to quicken his pace. His previous irritation gave way to a sense of uneasiness, which grew on him with every minute.

Thus it chanced that Mr. Dickson, as he retraced his steps, met the earl and, upon asking if the earl might know Richard's whereabouts, was provided with the information that Richard had left.

The earl, certain as he observed Mr. Dickson's face that something was amiss, politely offered his own services in Richard's stead.

Mr. Dickson, not knowing what else to do, promptly accepted them and came hurrying back to Lady Brentwood with the Earl of Malton in tow.

Lady Brentwood viewed him doubtfully, remembering his earlier behavior toward Cara.

Giving Mr. Dickson no chance to speak, the earl began calmly, "Richard, I'm afraid, Lady Brentwood, has already departed to deliver Miss De-Witt home." He smiled. "He may be occupied there for some time." Bowing, he repeated, "May I be of any service?" As she still hesitated, he added encouragingly, "If you wish, I can take a message to him."

Suddenly recalling that it was the earl who had helped Cara at the Marstons' picnic, Lady Brentwood took a deep breath and agreed. Quietly she explained the situation.

"I do not know what is the best course to take,

Lord Wrothby," she confessed, finishing. "I cannot believe even Viscount Lyle has abducted her."

The earl had listened to her, a frown growing more and more pronounced as she went on. He had no illusions about Lyle's morality. No act was beneath him. The black look the earl's friends so intensely disliked descended upon his brow.

Had the earl not already realized that he cared a great deal for Cara, he would certainly have known it at that moment. His heart constricted painfully at the thought of Cara at the mercy of a dissolute bounder like Arthur Lyle. Grimly he thought, If Lyle harms even one hair on her beautiful red head, I'll kill him! and then sensed for the first time in his life a small sample of the abyss that would engulf him if something should ever take Cara permanently from him.

Knowing Cara, the earl did not believe she would be easy to force into marriage, plainly the viscount's intent judging by the note. And if she refused, more than likely what the blackguard had in mind was — but that was *not* going to occur. The earl scowled murderously. "I can give you no assurance in that quarter, ma'am. There is no time to be lost," he stated brusquely.

Lady Brentwood looked stricken.

Lord Dougherty exclaimed, "The scoundrel! What's to be done?"

Mr. Dickson came out of his shocked silence and made a decision. Matter-of-factly, as if it were the most logical and simple thing to accomplish, he stated, "Not to worry, 'Licia, m'dear. I shall fetch her back for you." He caught her small hands in her large ones and, giving them a squeeze, marched off in the direction of the entrance before the astonished eyes of the three before him.

"James? Wait!" she cried, picking up her skirts and starting across the floor after him.

The earl laid a restraining hand on her arm. "I don't believe we need disturb Richard, ma'am. The fewer people know of this, the better. Lord Dougherty, if you will be good enough to convey Lady Brentwood home in your carriage, I shall follow Mr. Dickson's excellent example. As for what *you* can do," and the earl fixed him with a steely eye, "you may keep a still tongue in your head about this matter — or you will answer to me!" Leaving Lord Dougherty looking somewhat chagrined, the earl strode purposely off.

Lady Brentwood made a decision. "Come, George. I am going, too."

Lord Dougherty heard the determined note in her voice, so like that of his wife's, and knew it was no use arguing with her. In any case, he didn't wish to. He tucked his right arm under Lady Brentwood's and hurried with her to the Moberlys' entrance. He was feeling some of the same excitement of his war days and beginning to relish the thought of a wild midnight chase to rescue an innocent young girl.

At the door, he waited impatiently while Lady Brentwood went to retrieve her wrap and almost forgot to scrawl a note to his wife telling her, somewhat cryptically, that he was off on a mission of mercy and she should have to beg a ride home from Lady Beaufort or some other friend.

His carriage arrived at the bottom of the steps at the same moment Lady Brentwood returned with her own light shawl and Cara's. Lord Dougherty handed his note to a footman with a rushed command and clasped Lady Brentwood's arm, propelling her down the stone steps and into his carriage.

Giving his driver Mr. Dickson's address, he jumped in spryly after her, explaining, a trifle out of breath as he pulled the door to, "Dickson'll have to go home first to change his carriage and get his pistols. We'll join forces there!"

Surprised at his acquiescent behavior, Lady Brentwood could only feel relieved that she wouldn't have to argue with him to take her. And argue she would have, for she was determined to come.

Frowning with annoyance, the earl had gone to collect Miss Britmeyer, who had begged a ride home from him earlier on some pretext he could not now remember. While she went to get her wrap, he made a few discreet inquiries of the Moberlys' servants but was told by a stiff head footman that nothing untoward had occurred that evening. He was waiting restlessly for Miss Britmeyer when a hiss from the stairs drew his attention.

A grimy hand beckoned him outside the door, where the light dimly defined the figure of a young boy. He held out a dirty palm and asked softly, "Ye're wishing t'know of havey-cavey dealings tonight?"

The earl silently flipped several gold coins at him, which he neatly caught.

"Thanks, Guv." He grinned at the earl's generosity. "I seen two coves take sommat what looked like a dead body o'er th' wall back 'ere," he jerked a stubby thumb in the direction of the courtyard, "an' carry h'it off wit' 'em in a hack."

"When was this?" shot the earl.

"Two 'ours ago, easy," he replied.

"What direction did it take?"

"Oi'd say it were makin' for th' North bridge," he

said, scratching under his cap.

The earl flipped him another coin and went back inside.

Miss Britmeyer met him as he stepped through the doorway. "I'm ready. Was that your driver out there?"

Giving her his arm, he escorted her quickly down the stairs and helped her into his carriage. His informant had vanished.

Anxious to raise no suspicions, the earl allowed his man to drive them to Miss Britmeyer's residence, where she invited him to come in for a glass of Madeira. He declined politely, though somewhat shortly in his hurry to be gone, and she was left, a great deal piqued, to stand looking after him from her doorway.

He descended the stairs two at a time, climbed up to the coachman's perch and, taking the reins from a surprised Thomas, whipped up his own horses and drove them home at a spanking pace.

He leaped down, threw the reins back at his driver and curtly ordered his horse to be saddled and brought round immediately. "And Thomas! Send someone to check the North Bridge out of the city for a hack passing through some two hours ago!" he threw over his shoulder as he ran up his own steps and strode inside to the library.

Not bothering to change out of his costume, he snatched up his dueling case, trading one pistol for the decorative piece tucked into his waistband, priming it swiftly with a practiced hand. Then he concealed it under the folds of his cloak and retraced his steps.

Thomas held his black stallion, stepping restlessly at the ends of the reins.

"Well done of you, Thomas!" said the earl as he came down the stairs, threw a foot into the stirrup, and swung the other leg over the saddle.

Thomas answered him with the information, speedily ascertained for the earl, that a solitary hack, driving wrecklessly fast, had indeed passed out of the city over the North Bridge some twenty minutes after two o'clock.

The earl swore softly, letting go of his hold on the reins. His horse sprang forward, and Thomas was left to stand staring after his master and shaking his head, his lips moving inaudibly.

If Lyle had left by the North Bridge, he was indeed heading for Gretna Green. Knowing he would have to stop and change horses at the Red Boar in Sheffield and again at some later point, the earl set off grimly, keeping his eager horse on a tight rein until he, too, had passed over the North Bridge. Then he gave the horse its head, and they settled into a pace that made the dark shapes of the trees on either side of the road a blur.

At length, calculating he had gained at least half an hour on them, he rode into the Red Boar, halting only long enough to water his horse and make certain from the sleepy ostler that a hack had indeed stopped there.

Catching with pleasure the gold coins the earl tossed at him, the young ostler offered up an additional piece of information, "There was a gent waitin' 'ere with a coach to pick up th' lady they brung."

"Which direction did the coach take?" the earl shouted, starting off again.

"It were headin' north when it pulled out o' 'ere," called the boy. "An' th' hack went t'other way," he said to the empty night air.

Forty-five minutes later, the ostler had just dozed off in his bed again when the sound of wheels and then boots, crunching in the gravel of the drive woke him. Grumbling and pulling on his breeches hurriedly for the second time that night, he appeared to see to the newcomers' horses. They also seemed to have been driven hard, and their stocky owner, like the previous visitor, asked only to water them.

When the gentleman cleared his throat several times and hesitantly asked if a hack had stopped in earlier, the ostler raised his eyebrows but was not particularly surprised. Hoping to receive another boon similar to the one his first visitor had tossed at him, he gave out his additional information again.

"Oh no, then his horses will be fresh! We must go!" exclaimed the stocky gentleman excitedly and promptly forgot the ostler's existence altogether in his haste to get a white-haired gentleman back into the coach and get back on the road.

Just as the ostler was muttering, "Demmed aristos!" and mentally shaking his fist at the back of the coach, the side window was let down.

He glimpsed the pale hair of a woman and heard the clink of coins at his feet as the coach pulled off.

"Yer welcome, Oi'm sure," he said and grinned affably instead.

As light streamed through the coach windows, Cara woke to the sensation that she was moving and the realization that her body was crimped in an excessively uncomfortable position. Suddenly remembering her last distorted sight of the Moberlys' lighted ballroom, she opened her eyes and sat up.

The copper curls which had been neatly pinned under her black turban tumbled down her back.

"I would not advise such quick movements just yet, my dear," remarked Viscount Lyle solicitously.

"Viscount *Lyle?!*" Wincing at the violent pounding of her head, she silently acknowledged the wisdom of his advice. Painfully she opened her eyes again to find the viscount's over-bright hazel eyes taking in every detail of her disheveled appearance from his corner of the coach. Her turban was nowhere in evidence. Vainly, she tried to pin her hair back in place.

Putting a hand to her temple, she heard him say matter-of-factly, "Ether is inclined to make one rather ill, I'm afraid. I do so dislike the use of force. But, mayhap, at times, it is unavoidable. Forgive me, my dear. I fear you would not have accompanied me had I merely sent you my card." He gave her an ironic smile. "I should try to sleep if I were you. In a few hours we shall be in Newcastle where we shall stop and have a light meal, and you may freshen up. I have had the forethought to bring you a change of clothes." He paused and then answered the question she had not asked. "After that, we shall be only a scant hour from the Scottish border, where I intend to make you my wife."

She listened aghast, horror growing with the nausea she was beginning to suffer from the effects of the ether. "My mother—" she managed, her voice sounding weak even in her own ears.

"Would be too late—even should she not credit the note that was delivered to her from you telling her of your elopement with me."

"I sent no . . ." she began doggedly, feeling extremely unwell.

"I know," replied the viscount complacently and smiled at her.

"If I weren't so ill . . . I should . . . *kill* you . . .'' she said with effort. Fighting the nausea, she put her head back on the soft cushions of the coach and closed her eyes.

The viscount's only answer was a soft chuckle.

Silence pervaded the carriage.

Cara dozed intermittently and finally fell into a heavy sleep, lulled by the swaying of the carriage.

She woke again several hours later but kept her eyes closed to survey the viscount from beneath her lashes. Feeling much better now that the effects of the ether had begun to wear off, she pretended to continue to sleep as she reviewed what the viscount had said earlier, trying to think of a course of action against him.

Her mother, she felt certain, would not believe the viscount's note but would send someone after her. How fortunate that I told her of the Marstons incident! she thought thankfully. But I must devise a way to gain whoever she may send some time in which to overtake us! She remembered the viscount's saying they would stop at Newcastle, and her spirits rose at the opportunity it might afford her.

She peeped at the viscount through her lashes. He appeared to be sleeping. Thank goodness for that! she prayed silently, remembering with a shudder his actions at the picnic. It is out of all reason pointless to think of such things at this moment! she commanded herself sternly, and, putting such thoughts firmly away from her, she concentrated on thinking of ways to cost the viscount time in Newcastle.

She started, and her eyes fluttered open as the viscount seemed to voice her thoughts, saying, "Wake up, my dear. We are approaching Newcastle."

She stared out the window and watched with a sinking heart as they drove past the flourishing Crown Inn and pulled onto a smaller, less-traveled road. Moments later, after several turns, they pulled into the pot-holed dirt driveway of the Willow Tavern.

The viscount was not taking any chances. Anyone pursuing them, she knew, would stop at the larger Crown Inn. What would they think when they found no trace of her there? They will never be able to find this place! she thought dismally.

As if he had read her thoughts again, the viscount gave her a smug smile and said, "Off the beaten track, wouldn't you agree?"

Cara didn't reply as he helped her down onto the dusty drive. His coachman handed him a small valise, and he put his free hand under her arm and propelled her forward.

It was smoky and dark inside in spite of the sunshine outside. Cara wrinkled her nose against the stale smoke.

The viscount, appearing to know his way around, led her past a narrow flight of stairs into what seemed to be the tavern's only parlor and set the valise down.

"I will see to ordering our meal," he said conversationally. "You may freshen up in the room to your right abovestairs. Oh, ah, I have set my coachman to watch the door. Should you venture outside for any reason, he has instructions to escort you back inside immediately. A word of warning, my dear: I am afraid he is rather an uncivil fellow and would not handle you very gently." The viscount smiled pleasantly and left the room.

Cara moved to the window and looked out. She pushed the moth-eaten curtains aside and saw the profile of a large burly man sitting to one side of the door indolently watching a bowed, grizzled old man change the coach's horses. She didn't relish any kind of encounter with that gentleman.

Moving away from the window, she examined a chair for dust and seated herself in a position she hoped implied faintness. Please let this deceive him! she thought, ignoring the nervous fluttering of her stomach.

The viscount soon came back, carrying with him a bottle of wine and two glasses. Seeing her unchanged, he frowned and, putting the bottle and glasses down on the table that stood in the middle of the room, repeated, "My dear, I wished you to change. You are beginning to look sadly creased."

In what she hoped was a weak voice, she replied, "I am still a trifle faint, Arthur. I should like to wait until I have eaten."

"Very well." He looked at her white face closely. "It can wait." Shrugging, he went to pour out two glasses of wine. "Drink this. It should revive your . . . weakened spirits."

She doubted he believed her, but apparently he was going to humor her.

He came close to her chair and said softly, "I am an indulgent man, Cara." He touched her hair with one long finger. "Such beautiful, soft hair."

She sat very still.

But he only laughed and moved back to the table. Lifting his glass of wine, he toasted her, "Time enough for that later." He let his eyes sweep slowly over her figure.

She colored hotly, looking away in mortification.

A small woman with dark hair untidily caught at the back of her head entered the room with a large tray of food. She laid the cold collation of meats noisily out on the table and, finishing, looked up at the viscount in silent inquiry.

Curtly he said, "That will do. Shut the door behind you." He stood, gazing intently at Cara and holding a chair out at the table for her.

She rose and came slowly to seat herself in it.

Sipping at her wine, she forced herself to eat a thick slice of cold ham. The food dispersed the remaining effects of the ether, and leisurely she finished her glass of wine, beginning to feel somewhat restored.

"Arthur," she began in a low, urgent voice, "take me home. Take me back now, and no one need know but my mother and myself. I promise you we shall say nothing of this."

The viscount merely looked at her with his bright catlike eyes. "More wine, my dear?" he asked pleasantly as if he hadn't heard her.

"Please, Arthur!"

He leaned back in his chair. "Cara," he answered, enunciating her name with pleasure. "I have wanted you since the first moment I saw you." He stopped and said nothing for a moment, merely taking in the burnished copper curls, the dark green eyes which just now held a look of pleading, and the pale skin contrasted by the black net of her costume.

"I want you," he repeated huskily. "I was, perhaps, a trifle precipitate at the Marstons' picnic. But I have apologized for that, and you must not continue to be vexed with me—you are so beautiful. You don't realize the effect you have on men—on me." He paused. "I am wealthy, Cara. I can give you anything you could want. I ask little in return, and in time, you will—"

"No, Arthur! Take me back! You cannot force me to marry you! And nothing you do will make me say yes before a priest! Take me back now!" Cara cried passionately, losing her temper.

"You seem to have recovered from your faintness, my dear," he remarked mildly. "You will marry me," he stated. "One way or another you will become my wife—if not in your own eyes, at least in the eyes of the world after you have passed the night in my bed. It makes little difference to me. If you will not agree to let a priest marry us today, you will certainly agree tomorrow," he licked his lips, and his eyes smoldered, "if I still choose to make you my wife."

She continued to look rebellious, and he stood up and walked round her chair. Sliding a hand beneath the mass of copper curls, he rubbed the soft skin of her neck with his thumb. With his other hand, he fingered a copper tress. Musingly he remarked, "I do not like to mention it, my dear, but it should distress me immeasurably were certain, ah, transactions concerning a rather expensive, I should guess, emerald set come to light upon the desk of Chief Callahan."

Cara went white. A cold dread began to crawl up her spine.

"I think it is time you changed your dress." He moved both hands onto her shoulders and added, "And if it should take too long, my dear, I will come up and play lady's maid." His long fingers began to slide down the front of her dress.

"Don't!" Cara wrenched herself out of the chair. Retreating to where he'd set down the valise, she picked it up and, trying not to show her fear, walked with dignity out of the room.

Slowly, hearing them creak, she climbed the narrow flight of stairs. He is just trying to frighten me with his threats! she thought desperately. She gulped several deep breaths to calm her pounding heart and turned the corner, entering the small dingy room to the right of the stairs.

She put the valise down on the sagging bed. All I need do is keep my head! He is not going to inform Callahan of anything while he still holds me prisoner! It is only if—when I get away that that shall become a real threat, and I must deal with that then! Until then, I must take as much time as I dare in changing! Surely the woman who served us would not allow the viscount to—to—! She stopped, turning to regard the door of the small bedchamber and dubiously remembering the woman's silent attitude of acquiescence.

Fearfully, in case the viscount should change his mind and come up after all, she ran to shut the door and discovered that it had a small lock. She shot the bolt home and felt a little safer.

Moving as if she were in a trance, she pulled the black net slowly over her head, and, folding it carefully, laid it on the bed beside the valise. This she opened to find quite the most beautiful dress of cream-colored Brussels lace she had ever seen. But instead of winning her admiration, the dress forcefully brought home the reality of the viscount's intention and increased her anxiety a hundredfold.

She shook it out and spread it across the bed. I will not be afraid, I will not be afraid, she repeated to herself again and again. Even now, she told herself, trying hard to believe it, there is someone riding in pursuit of us, someone who shall catch up with us! And in her mind's eye, she could not keep herself

333

from seeing the tall, dark form of the earl on horse-back. The thought strengthened her courage.

I must simply take my time in changing, she told herself again, taking another deep breath and deliberately slowing her movements, which had quickened with fear at the sight of the beautiful dress.

Looking around the room, she saw a pitcher of water and went unhurriedly to pour it into a basin. Then, moving as methodically as if she had been at home in her own bedchamber, she removed the rest of her costume, folded it on top of the black net and put all of it back inside the valise, and washed, finished and ready all too soon to don the lacy dress.

She secured her hair, falling loose, behind her ears with her remaining pins and sat down on the edge of the bed to pass a few more precious moments.

A knock sounded on the door, and she started. A woman's voice, very likely that of the woman who had served them, said brusquely, "The gentleman says you are warned, Mistress. The next time, he comes."

Cara listened as the woman's step receded, breathlessly waited several minutes more, and then with a calmness she did not feel, slowly descended.

The viscount met her at the bottom of the stairs. "A few more minutes, and we should have had no need of a priest today," he said softly with a look in his eyes that made Cara hurry out of reach and precede him to the door.

She allowed the coachman to help her into the carriage to avoid the viscount's touch.

Viscount Lyle followed her swiftly, and they started off again, Cara's spirits sinking once more as the carriage swayed with the speed at which they were now traveling.

"May I say that you look exquisite in that dress, my dear?" He patted the cushions beside him. "Come and sit next to me."

"No!"

He lapsed into silence, apparently contenting himself for the moment with looking at her.

Cara ignored him and stared out the window at the late afternoon shadows. She strove to keep her panic from rising. Someone *is* coming after me. I have only to keep my wits about me and take up as much time as I can, she told herself over and over. It was a litany to the beat of the horses' hooves.

Some forty minutes later, the viscount broke the silence, saying quietly, "We shall cross the border soon. It is your decision — Gretna Green or The Royal?"

"I will never willingly marry you, Arthur," Cara answered equally, turning to look him steadily in the eyes.

In answer, the viscount thumped on the roof of the carriage with his cane. "You will be my wife. If not in your own eyes, in the eyes of the world," he repeated with awful certainty.

Cara turned back to the window and felt her stomach flip-flop nauseously.

If only I had a pistol! she thought despairingly and was struck by a sudden idea. Surely Arthur has one! If I could but find his and contrive to obtain it, it would more than even the odds between us!

Suppressing her excitement, she searched the inside of the carriage with her eyes, but no weapon was in evidence. Overwrought and exasperated with her own stupidity, she chastised herself, Fool! Of course he wouldn't keep it out in plain sight! It is very likely about him somewhere, and I cannot very well search him for it!

Her previous excitement drained away, and she tried to begin again. When we stop, I must look in the side pockets. If I cannot manage that, or if I manage it, and there is no pistol there, I shall simply have to make some kind of scene before the hotel proprietor or a servant. Surely they cannot all be as inhuman as that last woman!

Fervently she prayed that The Royal would not be as isolated and downtrodden as the Willow Tavern had been. And if it is? a small voice inside her asked. If it is, she thought, trying to plan for every circumstance, I shall just have to make a scene anyway and hope that all of the servants may not be indifferent to me.

Oh, if only the earl knew of this and cared enough to come after me! she thought wildly, unable to keep from pinning her hopes of rescue on the capable, self-assured figure of the earl.

But she had no further time to consider the earl. For, in what seemed to her to be only minutes after they had started out, the coach was pulling up to The Royal. Like the Willow Tavern, it was also off the main road, but it was larger and looked better kept than the previous inn.

The viscount left her in the carriage, locking the door from the outside, and went to arrange their accommodations.

Instantly Cara searched the side pockets on either door. "Nothing!" she exclaimed furiously as she pulled her hand from the second pocket.

She ran her hands along the backs and underneath the seat cushions hoping against hope that the viscount had secreted a pistol in those places. But again she found nothing and slapped the cushions in frustration.

Sliding hurriedly back into her previous position, she smoothed her skirts and looked up just as the handle on the door turned and it opened to reveal the viscount once again.

He helped her down and clamped his hand on her arm in a vise-like grip.

As they entered The Royal together, his grip tightened painfully. "One word . . ." he warned, and she gasped as his fingers dug into her flesh, and they passed in a matter of seconds the white-haired gentleman who might have aided her, standing behind the hotel desk.

The viscount steered her down a hall toward the back of the building and up a short flight of stairs. Opening the door to a large private apartment, he pushed her inside and disappeared, shutting the door behind him.

She heard the key turn in the lock and ran to the window to see if she might somehow contrive to escape through it. But looking down, she could see that the ground sloped off sharply to make the window at least three floors above ground level. If I tried to jump from this height, I should certainly break some bones, she thought, fighting to keep her anxiety at bay. And then how should I escape?

A soft knock came at the door, and the key turned to admit a young serving girl. She locked the door behind her, gave Cara a frightened look, and scurried to light a fire.

Crossing toward the girl, Cara began to explain her dilemma quickly and plead with the girl to help her. But the closer she came, the words tumbling out of her mouth, the more frightened the girl appeared until finally the maid threw up her hands with a cry of "Don't hurt me!" and ran to the door, unlocking it hastily and slamming it behind her.

"Wait—wait!" cried Cara in vexation.

The viscount entered on her heels and locked the door again with a smile. He explained matter-of-factly, "I have told them to disregard anything you might say because unfortunately your mind is unbalanced, and you are under the delusion, and have been for years, that I am holding you prisoner."

"How dare you!"

"However. If you should scream too much, my dear, I will gag you." He smiled smugly and put glasses and a bottle of brandy down on the table near the fire beginning to snap and crackle as the flames licked the wood. "I thought a drink might relax you. It has grown cool—come and sit down by the fire."

"No!"

He poured out two glasses and drank one off.

"Then I will come to you," he stated, and picking up the other glass, he advanced relentlessly, hastening to forestall each path of escape she tried.

At length, the apartment being only so large, he had her cornered.

She feinted toward him and then ran to his left between two armchairs.

Moving swifter than she would ever have imagined he could, he knocked over a chair and caught her by one arm, swinging her roughly backwards into his embrace.

He forced her head back and thrust the glass of brandy to her lips. Half of the fiery liquid burned down her throat, and the other half went spilling down the front of the creamy lace dress.

"Oh *dear,*" he said sardonically, his hazel eyes gleaming, "I fear you've spilled some. Come!" He dragged her ruthlessly over to the bottle of brandy. "I will get you a little more!" Catching her tightly once again to his broad chest, he forced the bottle to her lips.

Choking and spluttering for air, Cara again felt the liquid sear her throat and run down her chin onto her dress.

The viscount put the bottle down on the table. "Now," he breathed, "we will sit for a moment while you relax." Cursing, he dragged her, kicking and slapping at him, to the brown velvet couch against the wall. He pulled her onto his lap and endeavored to pin her arms behind her.

Cara began to grow hot and dizzy as the brandy took effect. The earl's black eyes floated mockingly before her, and she moaned. She could feel herself getting tired and, as she heard the viscount chuckle, knew her blows were becoming ineffectual.

Easily the viscount pinned her arms and then laughed exultantly as he held her, struggling helplessly. He seized the collar of the lacy dress and in one violent motion ripped the front of the gown open. His hot, wet lips came down on hers and, lingeringly, began to travel down the white column of her throat.

"No! Please, help me! *Julius!*" she screamed hopelessly, struggling drunkenly, determined to fight the viscount until she had no more strength left.

Twenty

Three splintering blows fell against the apartment door, the last of which left it hanging crazily on its hinges.

To the astonishment of both Cara and the viscount, the Earl of Malton burst through the doorway and had bounded across the room almost before the viscount had had time to look up in surprise. Seeing the earl nearly upon him, he jumped up, thrust Cara at him, and hurried for his cloak to obtain his pistol, hidden in the folds of dark cloth.

The earl caught Cara, steadied her, and followed swiftly on the heels of the viscount. As Lyle fumbled with his cloak, the earl grabbed him by the shoulder, wrenched him about, and hit him full in the face.

Reeling, the viscount desperately pulled the trigger of his gun through the folds of cloth.

Cara, dizzily holding onto the back of a chair, could not tell if the viscount's bullet had struck the earl or not.

With a murderous expression, the earl continued, unchecked, his onslaught on the viscount, and the viscount, having dropped both cloak and pistol now, began to strike viciously back.

The fighting went on interminably, it seemed to

ara, as she listened to the crash of furniture and the
ull thuds of flesh on flesh, giddily watching the two
en pummel each other and roll, locked furiously
ogether, around the floor. The sight, combined with
he brandy she had swallowed, began to nauseate
er, and she closed her eyes in an effort to keep her-
elf from being sick where she stood.

A moment later a deathly silence fell.

Afraid to open her eyes and see the earl's lifeless
orm, yet afraid, too, to keep them closed in the
vent the viscount was advancing on her once again,
Cara warred with herself and finally opened them as
he heard the sounds of someone moving about the
oom.

The earl, unhurt, wearing the most worried, anx-
ous expression she had ever seen upon his face,
tood in front of her with his cloak. Wordlessly he
laced it around her shoulders, drawing it together
n front to conceal the ragged opening in her gown,
nd tenderly put his arms around her. "He did not
urt you, my love?" he asked, his voice full of emo-
ion.

For answer, Cara burst into tears.

The earl let her cry, holding her tightly in his
trong arms until the sobs began to abate. Then he
eased gently, "Having endured far worse today than
little anxiety over your welfare, you are now damp-
ning my shirt because I offered you sympathy? If
hat isn't just like a woman!"

Cara gave a final sob that sounded suspiciously
ike a gurgle of laughter and, unrepentantly wiping
er eyes on the ruffles of his shirt front, raised her
ead. Belatedly his endearment registered, and she
tared. "Wh-what did you call me?" she asked. Her
houghts began to race and her heart to pound.

341

Could I have been right when I thought he was try
ing to make me jealous? When . . . when I wondere
if it might not show he cared just a little for me?

She stepped back suddenly, her large green eyes
still wet with the traces of tears, regarding him in
tently. "Why are you here?" she asked, her voice low
almost accusing. She had been so relieved to see him
she had not thought to question his appearance
There might be some bitterly innocent explanation!

"I should think that would be obvious," he an
swered huskily, with his crooked smile. But his black
eyes were equally intent.

"Ohh," Cara breathed and, with an expression o
blithe amazement, flowed liquidly back into his
arms.

The earl, unable to keep from thinking of what
she had narrowly escaped, folded her tightly once
again in his strong embrace.

Cara put her own arms around his neck and, hug
ging him fiercely to her, repeated wonderingly, "My
love." It was not immediately clear if she were refer
ring to the earl or simply unable as yet to believe that
he could ever have referred to herself using that par
ticular appellation.

The earl suggested, "Let us both sit down." He sa
wearily in the nearest armchair and pulled Cara onto
his lap.

She laid her head against his shoulder and asked
in a subdued voice, "How did you know where to
find me?"

"Because, my poor girl, I have been tracking you
since Sheffield. And a pretty chase you lead me,
too!" He threw a look of patent dislike in the direc
tion of the viscount's inert form. "He must know
every rathole in the country."

Briefly the earl explained Lady Brentwood's alarm and how, when Mr. Dickson had inquired—looking as he were all about in his upperworks, the earl noted rudely—of Richard's whereabouts, he had proffered his own services in Richard's stead. "I collected immediately you had gotten yourself into another scrape."

Cara choked and lifted her head from his shoulder to lean back and regard him with an eyebrow raised in tolerant disbelief.

Smiling at her, he pounded her back and went right on, "I knew, of course, that I couldn't leave you in the hands of that addlepate or—"

"Addlepate! You are a provoking creature, Lord Vrothby."

"Julius, please," he interrupted, pulling her back into his arms.

"Julius then," she agreed and continued, "—with a highly colored version of this adventure I am certain. And if I had any sense at all I should get up this minute and march out of here." Contradicting her words, she nestled back against his shoulder.

"I would imagine," the earl murmured into her jasmine-scented hair, "that your addlepate of a stepfather—"

"He's not my stepfather yet," Cara interrupted inconsequentially.

"—if he managed to follow your circuitous route at all, will be arriving any moment now. And I shall make him the happy announcement."

"What announcement?" Cara asked in a tone of contentment that belied any trace of curiosity.

"Our engagement, of course," he answered matter-of-factly, as if it were already agreed upon.

343

"I don't think I can marry someone who calls my stepfather a—"

"He's not your stepfather yet," broke in the earl irrelevantly.

"—an addlepate," she murmured.

"If you marry me," he coaxed, "your secret will be safe. I can't answer for it otherwise, 'Gentleman Jack'!"

"Blackmail, you wretch?" she asked, leaning back again to glare at him in mock anger.

"Julius, please," he corrected again. "It's the only way to deal with a notorious highwayman, you know," he answered and kissed her soundly.

Several moments later, Cara raised her head and remarked dreamily, "Of course you know I haven't a feather to fly with?"

"Of course," answered the earl, kissing her again. "Why else would you have been holding up innocent travelers when I met you?" he asked logically.

"Innocent?!" Cara spluttered, sitting up. She was really angry this time. "Those coxcombs I held up were just the sort that laughed and snickered while one of their friends robbed my father and caused his suicid—!"

Putting one large finger gently to her lips, the earl stopped her. "My beautiful darling," he began, looking at her so seriously that she became afraid of what he was going to say next. "Arthur Lyle is the one that, as you have quite rightly put it, robbed your father." Cara's eyes widened in disbelief. The earl went on, "I doubt if he ever made the connection between you and your father. His choice of you was probably the result of your own absurd beauty and a little bad luck on your part ever to have met him at all. But as you of all people know by now, better than anyone, Arthur Lyle is not and never has been considered a member of the *ton*. You cannot, my darling, hold them responsible for the actions of a bounder like Lyle."

Stupefied, Cara hid her face against the earl's shoulder. "Oh, Julius! If I'd known it was Arthur! If I'd known what kind of man he was! I loved my father so much — in spite of . . . of what he had become." The muffled tones stopped, and she was silent for several moments.

When she raised her head, her eyes were bright with unshed tears. "I thought I had to revenge his death, you see. I thought robbing the *ton* and using their money to buy a husband to support us was just punishment for the way they robbed my father of his life. If you could have seen him the day he died, Julius! But you are right. Arthur was not one of them. I cannot blame them for what Arthur did." She hid her face against his shoulder again. "I have been so wrong all this time!" She was silent again.

The earl had judged it wiser to let her talk. Now he soothed, "I know, my love. But let us put the matter in perspective. While the members of the *ton* do not normally go round killing one another, neither are they completely blameless," he concluded, smiling. "Let us forget the whole affair and put it behind us."

Cara was quiet, digesting this remark. At length, she realized the wisdom in what the earl had said and raised her head to say earnestly, "Agreed. Now let us forget the whole—" She stopped abruptly. "Oh Julius, Arthur knows I played the highwayman!"

"I don't believe you need worry over that, my love. I am certain he can be, er, persuaded to hold his peace!"

When Cara did not look convinced, the earl remarked testily, "Do not forget I am still in possession of his own ring!" He grinned roguishly. "That should very likely be distinctive evidence of any, er, villainy we choose to report!" The earl broke off, hearing voices and several pairs of boots coming noisily down the hall.

Mr. Dickson and Lord Dougherty, brandishing their pistols, and a third white-haired gentleman, vociferously trying to prevent them, burst through the doorway and halted. Assailed by the aroma of brandy, their mouths gaping, the same ludicrous face of bewilderment appeared on all three faces.

The white-haired gentleman recovered first, moaning and running his fingers through his hair as he surveyed his disordered apartment.

Mr. Dickson and Lord Dougherty looked from Cara and the earl to the viscount's crumpled form lying on the floor beside the table. They looked back to Cara, sitting with obvious safety and contentment on the earl's lap.

"Did you kill him?" asked Lord Dougherty finally, sounding disappointed.

As if to answer his question, the viscount stirred and groaned.

"I should have," growled the earl.

Lord Dougherty turned to the moaning innkeeper and barked, "Don't just stand there, man! Go and fetch your constable if you want your damages paid for!"

Silenced, the innkeeper blinked and then turned on his heel and hurried out of the room.

Lord Dougherty, flourishing his pistol, went to stand over the viscount as he got unsteadily to his feet.

"Don't understand," stated Mr. Dickson in confusion. "What happened?"

Just then, Lady Brentwood appeared in the doorway behind him and looked about her. "Why, that is easy, James," she replied calmly. "The earl has, er, apprehended Viscount Lyle before he could harm Cara?" Looking at the earl, she inclined her voice in a question and, receiving his nod, continued, "And, unless I'm much mistaken in my daughter's ridiculously happy countenance," she smiled, "asked her to marry him."

"Not the viscount, after all this —!" exclaimed Mr. Dickson, for the first time in anyone's acquaintance with him, about to become really angry.

Cara suppressed a laugh.

"No, no, James —"

"Astute as always, ma'am," approved the earl. "And having blackmailed an acceptance out of her, I think it is high time we all packed up and went home," he grinned.

The innkeeper returned with the constable.

"I believe Viscount Lyle here will be only too willing to settle with this fellow, Constable," the earl told the officer. "If there is any difficulty, you will let me know. Lord Dougherty has my direction. I take it we may leave things here in your capable hands, Dougherty?" asked the earl.

"'Ndeed you may!" he replied with relish, assuming an authoritarian tone of voice and turning toward the constable and the innkeeper.

"I will just send a note round to Lady Dougherty then to prevent her from worrying about you," suggested the earl.

"Damn decent of you, Wrothby," replied Lord Dougherty gratefully, a guilty look flitting across his features. Then he turned and began explaining matters to the two dubious gentlemen before him.

Everyone else filed out to enter Mr. Dickson's coach, setting off for home. When all the details of the night's events had been explained to everyone's satisfaction—which took some time on Mr. Dickson's part—they relapsed into a drowsy silence.

Lady Brentwood was thinking of her former life. Mr. Dickson reached over and patted her arm comfortingly. Putting that life behind her, she gave him a smile and pressed her hand over his.

Cara was feeling a small resurgence of faith in the aristocratic members of the *beau monde*. They were not saints, certainly, but at least they were not quite the black figures she had painted them, thinking they had abetted the robbing of her father. Sleepily she leaned her head against the earl's shoulder and felt him brush the top of her hair with a kiss.

Several hours later, Mr. Dickson's coachman tooled the carriage into London, and the gentlemen, promising to call the next day after a good night's rest, delivered the ladies home and drove off in the direction of the earl's residence.

The next morning, Cara and her mother rose none the worse for their harrowing night's adventure and had just finished a late breakfast when Mr. Dickson arrived, just as usual, to take Lady Brentwood out for a drive.

Cara was left to wander idly back and forth from the dining room to the parlor, waiting for the earl to call and growing more and more piqued as the morning wore on and he did not present himself.

Finally she heard the front door knocker bang and ran to seat herself and spread a periodical open upon her lap.

"The Earl of Malton," Bates announced unnecessarily, judiciously closing the parlor door after himself.

"And how do you feel today, my love?" began the earl solicitously.

"Wonderfully fine, thank you, Lord Wrothby," Cara replied without looking up from her periodical.

The earl blinked at her tone and frowned with irritation, at a loss to understand what he could have done to offend her since he had only that moment come in.

He went to stand by the window and look out. Not wishing to begin what he had come to say while she was in this mood, he remarked genially upon the weather.

Receiving a cold, monosyllabic answer, his patience snapped, and he strode back across to the settee, caught her by the wrists, and yanked her to her feet. "What the devil's the matter with you?" he demanded.

"Where have you been?" she snapped back, looking at him for the first time. She saw then the bruises beginning to appear on his face and instantly could have bitten her tongue off in contrition.

The earl blinked at her answer and then burst out laughing.

"Oh, Julius," Cara moaned, putting a gentle finger up to his cheek.

He drew her close. "I have been pointing out to Lyle the, er, advantages in keeping his knowledge about a certain red-haired highwayman to himself. And," he pulled a small black box out of his pocket, "while I was about it, I thought I should just as well fetch this."

Still chuckling, he opened the box. Inside, on the

349

dark velvet, lay a gold ring mounted with a single iridescent stone. He lifted the ring and caught her hand, slipping it onto her finger.

The blood stole into Cara's cheeks, and she bent her head to watch the firey play of colors as she turned her hand.

"Fire opal," said the earl in a low voice. "My mother's engagement ring from my father."

"I — I feel terrible," Cara murmured. "It is beautiful, Julius."

"You should," agreed the earl blithely. "I've no doubt I am committing a grave error in my choice of wife, but — "

"You are not! How dare you!" Cara interrupted crossly.

"But my fiesty love, if you will let me finish? *But,* I have also brought this with me to return to my headstrong bride-to-be as a reminder of her past escapades." From his other pocket, he produced her father's gold signet ring. "And," he continued with an all too serious gleam in his black eyes, "if you *ever* put it to the use you once did, I will have you know now, my fine red-haired highwayman, I will put you across my knee and soundly thrash you!"

Quite in contrast to his words, the earl folded her in his arms and began to kiss her ruthlessly.

"Never again," gurgled Cara, laughing and throwing her arms about his neck.

Just then the parlor door opened, and Lady Brentwood, followed by Mr. Dickson, stepped in. Startled for a moment to see her daughter wrapped in the earl's arms, Lady Brentwood smiled fondly at them and retreated, quietly pulling Mr. Dickson after her.

A Memorable Collection of Regency Romances

BY ANTHEA MALCOLM AND VALERIE KING

THE COUNTERFEIT HEART   (3425, $3.95/$4.95)
by Anthea Malcolm
Nicola Crawford was hardly surprised when her cousin's betrothed disappeared on some mysterious quest. Anyone engaged to such an unromantic, but handsome man was bound to run off sooner or later. Nicola could never entrust her heart to such a conventional, but so deucedly handsome man. . . .

THE COURTING OF PHILIPPA   (2714, $3.95/$4.95)
by Anthea Malcolm
Miss Philippa was a very successful author of romantic novels. Thus she was chagrined to be snubbed by the handsome writer Henry Ashton whose own books she admired. And when she learned he considered love stories completely beneath his notice, she vowed to teach him a thing or two about the subject of love. . . .

THE WIDOW'S GAMBIT   (2357, $3.50/$4.50)
by Anthea Malcolm
The eldest of the orphaned Neville sisters needed a chaperone for a London season. So the ever-resourceful Livia added several years to her age, invented a deceased husband, and became the respectable Widow Royce. She was certain she'd never regret abandoning her girlhood until she met dashing Nicholas Warwick. . . .

A DARING WAGER   (2558, $3.95/$4.95)
by Valerie King
Ellie Dearborne's penchant for gaming had finally led her to ruin. It seemed like such a lark, wagering her devious cousin George that she would obtain the snuffboxes of three of society's most dashing peers in one month's time. She could easily succeed, too, were it not for that exasperating Lord Ravenworth. . . .

THE WILLFUL WIDOW   (3323, $3.95/$4.95)
by Valerie King
The lovely young widow, Mrs. Henrietta Harte, was not all inclined to pursue the sort of romantic folly the persistent King Brandish had in mind. She had to concentrate on marrying off her penniless sisters and managing her spendthrift mama. Surely Mr. Brandish could fit in with her plans somehow . . .

Available wherever paperbacks are sold, or order direct from the Publisher. Send cover price plus 50¢ per copy for mailing and handling to Zebra Books, Dept. 4272, 475 Park Avenue South, New York, N.Y. 10016. Residents of New York and Tennessee must include sales tax. DO NOT SEND CASH. For a free Zebra/ Pinnacle catalog please write to the above address.